Praise for *Gan*

"This book has me completely gobsma
—*A Robertson, Amazon reviewer*

"I have enjoyed every book in the Alastair Stone series. I can hardly wait for the next book in the series when I finish one."
—*Nakita Thomas, Amazon reviewer*

"I've been hooked since book 1."
—*Penny B. McKay, Amazon reviewer*

Praise for *Necessary Sacrifices*

"R.L King has written another gripping, jaw-dropping, and yes, shocking installment to the Alastair Stone Chronicles."
—*clmoi*

"With
be at th
—*DE*

PLEASE RETURN TO LIBRARY REH

vn herself to

"It's g
descri
—*Ted Camer, Amazon reviewer*

reat to

Praise for *Path of Stone*

"Wow, this is one series that never lets you down."
—*Greenlite350, Amazon reviewer*

"You cannot go wrong with this series!"
—*Jim, Amazon reviewer*

"Wow! Just wow! I love this whole series and this installment does not disappoint!!!"
—*Amazon reviewer*

Praise for *The Other Side*

"Once again, R.L. King has delivered a masterfully constructed tale."
—*Jim, Amazon reviewer*

"This was the best Alastair Stone book yet!"
—*J. Michael Droke, Amazon reviewer*

"R. L. King does it again! Simply one of the best books I've read this year—and one of the best in an amazing series."
—*Greenlite350, Amazon reviewer*

"Warning—don't start reading this book if you have other things to do."
—*ARobertson, Amazon reviewer*

"What a ride!"
—*Wendy S, Amazon reviewer*

Praise for *The Infernal Heart*

"Another 'can't put it down' adventure in this series."
—*LC, Amazon reviewer*

"…The best book in the whole Alastair Stone Chronicles… this one really knocked it out of the park."
—*Christopher T, Amazon reviewer*

"Once you start, you need to get comfortable because you will stop reading all of a sudden and discover many hours have gone by."
—*John Scott, Amazon reviewer*

"…the best one yet! I couldn't put it down."
—*Kenneth B, Amazon reviewer*

Praise for *Blood and Stone*

"I have read every book in this series and loved them all…this one is no exception."
—*Soozers, Amazon reviewer*

"The writing is extremely good, and the plot and characters engaging. Closest author comparison probably Benedict Jacka and the Alex Verus series."
—*MB, Amazon reviewer*

"Have followed our expat mage from the beginning and this time around, it's a home run."
—*Amazon reviewer*

Praise for *Core of Stone*

"Once again R. L. King has come up with another great story for Alastair Stone. I enjoyed this as thoroughly as all the others and look forward to more."
—*Tahlia Newland, Amazon reviewer*

"I love it when a writer starts out strong in her career and just gets stronger. I have loved The Alastair Stone Chronicles from the beginning, but this one just blew me away."
—*Shawna Reppert, award-winning author of* the *Ravensblood* series

"I have loved the series as a whole but have to say this is a favorite just for the character growth."
—*Amazon reviewer*

"The Alastair Stone Chronicles is one of the best series I have read in years…"
—*Judith A. Slover, Amazon reviewer*

Praise for *The Source*

"Perhaps the best addition yet to an already amazing series."
—*Greenlite350, Amazon reviewer*

"A continued thrill to the urban fantasy reader..."
—*Dominic, Amazon reviewer*

"I consumed the four pack in less than a week. This a great series and one of the best ones I have had the pleasure to read in a long time."
—*Skywalker, Amazon reviewer*

"If you like Harry Dresden and The Dresden files, or Nate Garrett in the Hellequin series than this series is for you."
—*Amazon reviewer*

Praise for *The Threshold*

"Once you enter the world of Alastair Stone, you won't want to leave."
—*Awesome Indies*

"Excellent story as are all the others in this series."
—*Tahlia Newland, Amazon reviewer*

"I LOVE THIS BOOK!"
—*Claryn M. Heath, Amazon reviewer*

Praise for *The Forgotten*

"Alastair Stone is like Harry Potter meets Harry Dresden with a bit of Indiana Jones!"
—*Randler, Amazon reviewer*

"I loved the first book in the series, but this book is even better! … I didn't think I could be any more in love with the protagonist than I was in the first book …My only hesitation in giving it five stars is that, if

the next one is even better (as I suspect it may be) I won't have any-where to go with the rating."
—*Shawna Reppert, award-winning author of* The Stolen Luck, Ravensblood, *and* Raven's Wing

"This is actually an original idea - such a rare thing these days. Well written too."
—*Tahlia Newland, Amazon reviewer*

"From the first paragraph I knew I was in the hands of a competent writer, and from the second paragraph I was hooked to read on…a novel deserving of the full 5 star rating."
—*Awesome Indies*

Praise for *Stone and a Hard Place*

"The magic is believable, the characters could be people you know, and the twists, turns and mysteries to be solved glue your eyes to the page. You will never forget these characters or their world."
—*Jacqueline Lichtenberg, Hugo-nominated author of the* Sime~Gen *series and* Star Trek Lives!

"Somewhat reminiscent of the Dresden Files but with its own distinct style."
—*John W. Ranken, Amazon reviewer*

"I am reminded of Jim Butcher here…Darker than most Urban Fantasy, not quite horror, but with a touch of Lovecraftian."
—*Wulfstan, Amazon Top 500 reviewer*

"Dramatic protagonist sucked me right in…I instantly wanted to spend more time with Alastair Stone…I definitely want to see more from this author!"
—*Shawna Reppert, award-winning author of* The Stolen Luck, Ravensblood, *and* Raven's Wing

"Fast-moving fun!...[t]he book is full of the things I like in a book, and they are presented in a clean, brisk style. This is a book well worth checking out.."
—*Jason M. Hardy, author of* Hell on Water, Drops of Corruption, *and* The Last Prophecies

"Stone is a completely believable protagonist, and, frankly, damned likeable. We all wish we had college profs as engaging as he is!"
—*Silas Sparkhammer, Amazon reviewer*

ALSO BY R. L. KING

The Alastair Stone Chronicles

Shadowrun

(published by Catalyst Game Labs)

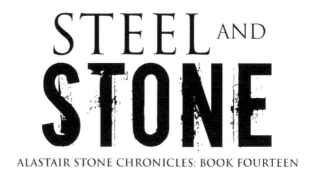

STEEL AND STONE

ALASTAIR STONE CHRONICLES: BOOK FOURTEEN

R.L. KING

MAGESPACE
PRESS

Part One

| CHAPTER ONE

I T TOOK ALASTAIR STONE three weeks to work out the ritual.

Part of that was because he wanted to make sure he got it right. This wasn't the kind of thing you wanted to cut corners on—if he allowed his mind to wander or got a variable wrong somewhere in the circle formula, he could end up sending himself off gods knew where. Quite possibly someplace where he wouldn't live long enough to figure out how to get back.

He spent every spare moment working on the project, checking and re-checking numbers, equations, and symbols. He'd figured out quite some time ago how to channel minuscule amounts of the strange magical power Trevor Harrison had taught him to access without burning himself out for indefinite periods; it wasn't enough to manage even the smallest of proper spells, but for his purposes this time, it was just what he needed.

A way to tap into the source of that energy so he could figure out how to reach it.

He still wasn't sure why he hadn't caught on to the idea ages ago: if he could identify the source of Harrison's magic power, he could design a ritual to travel there. If he could get there, maybe he could find Harrison himself, since his assistant Nakamura had all but admitted the man didn't spend much of his time on Earth. He had to go *somewhere,* and this seemed as logical a choice as any.

At least that was what Stone hoped. It might just be wishful thinking, and all of this effort would be for nothing. He might figure out how to reach the dimension only to discover that not only was Harrison *not* there, but the whole place was nothing but a raging cauldron of powerful energy that would consume him the moment he arrived.

When he was being honest with himself, that had definitely figured into why he'd taken so long to get the ritual worked out.

You don't have to do this, you know, he told himself one evening as he paced the circle he'd painstakingly drawn on the floor of his townhouse's attic. *You have other options.*

It was true: he *did* have other options. Jason, for a big one. His friend had literally come to blows with him a few weeks back, trying to convince him he was willing and able to supply the power Stone needed to use his magic. It didn't hurt Jason, caused him no distress, and the only inconvenience was that one of them would have to travel to the other's location for the next couple of months until Jason passed his private investigator's exam and moved back to the Bay Area. Putting aside Stone's reluctance to make himself dependent on Jason—or anyone—for his power, it was a no-lose situation.

Stone knew his reluctance was irrational: he would have done the same for Jason, or Verity, in a heartbeat if their situations had been reversed, and wouldn't have resented it in the slightest. But the situations *weren't* reversed, and the thought of such dependence went against wiring so deeply entrenched in Stone's psyche that it would probably take a whole fleet of therapists several years to unsnarl it.

And in any case, it wasn't just the reluctance. If it had been, Stone could probably have managed to suck it up and at least give it a try for a while. Perhaps it might even have worked out fine.

He stopped, throwing himself into a nearby chair and tossing back the last of the pint of Guinness he'd brought with him. Slumped, his elbows on his knees, he regarded the circle without truly seeing it. No, it wasn't just the reluctance.

It was his craving for the addictive rush of sensation he got when he took power from others. Jason, for whatever reason, couldn't provide that. Whatever had given him his unusual ability to provide power to mages—black *or* white—without experiencing fatigue or other negative effects had also arranged things so taking the power didn't come with any sensation for the recipient.

When Stone had been a white mage he hadn't minded that; he'd used Jason's power only when he'd needed a little extra punch for his spells, and hadn't known the difference. But once he'd gone black—once he'd ashed his own twin sister and claimed her massive well of power in order to prevent a series of horrific events—something had changed irrevocably. He didn't know if it was physical or psychological, but it didn't matter.

He *liked* the rush now. He *craved* it.

He could control himself—mostly. It wasn't as if he went around tapping random strangers for power, like some black mages did. But he'd already killed one person, and very nearly killed another. He couldn't even say he'd lost control, because he hadn't. He'd *wanted* to do it.

And that scared the hell out of him.

No, this was the only answer. He had to do this, as distasteful as the alternatives it presented him were: either risk sending himself into instant death if he'd guessed wrong about the dimension's purpose, or, if he did manage to find Harrison, begging the man to teach him what he needed to control the energy and use it as an alternate source of power.

He set the empty glass on the desk, got up, and took a final look at the circle.

Everything was ready. He'd tweaked and re-tweaked the symbols and sigils, checked and double-checked the ritual, examined and re-examined every potential pitfall he could think of. Several times over the past three weeks he'd awakened in the middle of the night with some new insight, leaping out of bed to rush up here and add it to his research notes. As far as he could tell, there wasn't anything left for him to do, except gather the courage he'd need.

He closed the attic door behind him and paused, leaning against it as he looked down the narrow stairway.

Getting up the courage to do the ritual was only part of what he'd need to do—and probably the easiest part.

| CHAPTER TWO

"**I** WAS WONDERING when I'd see you again," Verity said.

"Been—busy." Stone focused on unpacking one of the grocery bags she'd brought.

"You're always busy. But I didn't think ending my apprenticeship would mean we'd barely see each other anymore. If it had, I'd have argued for stretching it out a few more months." She was unloading the other bag, spreading out various items on the counter. Raider the cat leapt nimbly up to investigate the new additions; she scratched behind his ears and nudged him away. "I'm glad you invited me over. It's been like two weeks."

Nearly three, actually. She'd called him a couple times, but he'd made excuses, claiming to be too busy with work to get together. "I'm telling you, you didn't need to cook dinner. I could have picked something up on the way home."

"And I keep telling you: I *like* cooking for you. I really do. And this way I know you're eating something healthy instead of all that random takeout stuff you grab from God knows where." She grinned. "Win-win, right?"

"Yes, all right." Stone finished unpacking the bag and drifted over to examine the contents of the wine rack.

"Doc?"

"Yes?"

When she didn't reply, he turned back. She stood with her back to the counter, watching him with an odd look. "What is it?" he pressed.

"You doing okay?"

"Fine. Why?"

"I dunno. I'm getting the feeling you've been…avoiding me."

"I told you—I've been busy. That's all it is."

"And I told *you*—you're always busy, but you still don't avoid me like this. You used to find time for my magic lessons a few times a week, so I'd think you'd have more free time than ever now. Unless you've already got yourself another apprentice."

He chuckled, forcing a light tone. "Hardly. You were quite enough for me. I'm not ready to take on another beginner yet."

"What is it, then?"

Stone turned back to the wine rack. He crouched, studying the bottles a moment, and selected one. "What have you been doing with yourself lately? Still got the job at the coffee shop?"

There was a long pause, then a sigh. "Yeah. I'm working there during the day. They like me a lot. Even got a raise already."

"Brilliant. And you and Kyla are still getting on?" he asked, deceptively casual.

"Yeah."

She'd seen right through him, of course; he'd have been surprised if she hadn't. "Well, that's good."

"Yeah," she said again. "I helped out the Harpies the other night," she added, almost defiantly.

"Did you?" He set the bottle on the counter and paced at the edge of the kitchen, staying out of her way as she worked.

"Here," she said, levitating a knife toward him handle-first and nodding at the cutting board. "Cut that chicken into cubes, will you?"

He plucked the knife from the air, washed his hands, and set about the task without looking at her. "Helped them do what?"

"We caught this guy who's been preying on homeless women."

Stone didn't answer.

"He had some mental issues," she continued, putting a wok on the stove and firing up the burner. "We tied him up and made an anonymous call to the cops. They picked him up. Maybe he'll get the help he needs—or at least those women will be safer."

"That's quite admirable," he said.

"You don't approve, do you?"

"What makes you think so? You're not my apprentice anymore—I can't tell you what to do. I know you'll be careful."

"I will. They're not just a bunch of vigilantes. I've gotten to know them better—did you know one of them's a lawyer?"

"I suppose I didn't meet that one." He finished chopping up the chicken, put it on a plate, and set it on the sideboard next to the stove.

"No, I don't think so. And I've been teaching Hezzie a little bit, too."

"Thinking about taking an apprentice of your own already?"

"Yeah, no, that's not happening. But I figure if I can show her some things, I can help her be a better witch. Oh—and I forgot to tell you. I talked to Scuro again a couple weeks ago."

"Planning to get a magical tattoo?"

"Not yet. Maybe a normal one, but I'm still thinking about it. But no—I took him up on his offer."

"Which offer is that?"

"Remember when I was there with you?"

"Ah. Right." He touched his chest; the night he'd gotten the tattoo that helped him channel power more efficiently, Verity had accompanied him and healed the worst of the damage. Scuro had offered her a job doing the same thing for his other "special" clients. "I thought he was joking."

"Turns out he wasn't. He doesn't do that many of the magical tattoos—maybe one every couple weeks or so—but he was really impressed with how I handled yours, and how fast it healed up naturally after. So I've been playing freelance healer for him. He pays really well, too—if I keep it up, between that and the coffee-shop job I should be able to afford to pay for my place on my own."

Stone pondered that as he watched her stir-frying the chicken. He *had* been out of touch, if he had no idea about any of this. "That's—great news. I'm sure it's satisfying to earn money doing something you enjoy."

"It is. So far both the clients I've worked on have been really grateful—they even tipped me on top of what Scuro paid me."

"But I told you before—you needn't worry about your rent. It's certainly not a hardship for me to help you, and technically your apprenticeship was supposed to last a few more months."

"Yeah, but it's over now, and I'm sure you understand I don't want to take advantage of you."

Stone almost made a joke about how much he enjoyed it when she 'took advantage of him,' but something stopped him. They hadn't been together since the night he'd had the revelation about Harrison's magic. "It's no imposition, Verity. You know that."

"Speaking of housing," she said, deftly and obviously changing the subject, "When are you moving in to that new place of yours? It should be almost ready, right? Is working on it part of why you've been so busy?"

"No. I think my DIY days are at an end—I've already done everything I can safely do without buggering something up beyond repair. I've still got to have some professionals in to check it over and do the big jobs."

"What are you waiting for?"

He started to answer, then let his breath out. "Verity… I want to talk to you about something. But let's eat first, shall we?"

Her gaze flicked up to meet his. "Talk to me about what?"

"After dinner." He retrieved a pair of wineglasses from the cabinet and carried them to the table along with the bottle. Raider followed him and jumped onto the table.

"Uh…yeah, okay."

Despite both their attempts at light conversation, the meal crackled with a low undercurrent of tension. Stone picked at his food, his mind refusing to settle down despite the decisions he'd already made. This wasn't the way he normally did things, and the conversation he'd need to have with Verity wouldn't be easy—but that didn't matter. He had obligations now, and this, as painful as it would be, was the only honorable thing he could do.

That didn't mean he was looking forward to it, though.

He didn't miss Verity's nervous, suspicious glances at him throughout the meal, but he didn't acknowledge them, either. He wondered what she thought he planned to tell her. Finally, unable to eat anything else, he rose and took his plate back to the kitchen. Then he retrieved his wineglass. "Come out to the sitting room with me, will you?"

She'd already finished; wordlessly, she picked up her own glass and followed him out. When they'd settled into their familiar places—he in his ratty leather armchair, she with her legs curled beneath her on the sofa and Raider in her lap—she looked at him. "What's this about, Doc?"

He took a deep breath, forcing himself to meet her gaze. After all they'd been through together, he owed her this. "I…have a few things I need to tell you. I'd appreciate it if you'd listen to me, and save your comments or questions for the end. Can you do that?"

"I don't know," she said. "It depends on what you have to say."

"Well…" Why was this so difficult? Life had been a lot easier when he'd had fewer attachments. As it was, there were people he should be talking to that he *wouldn't* be talking to—he'd have to count on Verity to make sure word got around if something happened, because he didn't think he could have this conversation multiple times. "I've made a decision."

"What kind of decision?"

Her tension showed clearly in her aura; she'd never learned to hide it from Stone, even though she was normally quite good at concealing her feelings from others. "About something I need to do. And since it's going to affect you—and I need your help—I need to tell you about it."

"What are you talking about? You need my help? With what?"

As almost always happened when he was agitated about something, Stone found it impossible to remain still. He rose in an explosive motion and began pacing the room. "Remember the last time you—stayed over—and I mentioned that I was having a difficult time coping with being a black mage?"

"Yeah." Her expression stilled and grew fearful. "Doc, you're not thinking about—anything drastic, are you?"

"No. No, of course not," he said quickly, then amended: "Well…yes, actually. But not the way you think."

She got up, dumping Raider out of her lap, and came to him, gripping his arm. "What are you talking about? Tell me."

"I—" He pulled away from her, walked to the window, and pushed open the heavy drapes. The sun hadn't gone down yet; on the sidewalk in front of the townhouse two boys whizzed by on skateboards, followed a few moments later by a young couple deep in conversation. Stone watched them until they passed out of his field of view, marveling as he often did at how *normal* life could be just outside the window, oblivious to the turmoil behind it. He wondered how many of the other houses along his street concealed similar turmoil he'd never know anything about. "I've been thinking quite a lot about what Harrison said."

"You mean about having the means to find him?"

"Yes."

He heard her breath catch. "You figured it out? You know how to find him?"

"I think so, yes."

Footsteps, and then she was next to him. "Tell me. How?"

"I've got to go where he is. Or at least where I *think* he is. That's why I need your help."

"Wow. Uh…Yeah. Of course I'll help. I'll come with you. Just give me a day or so to talk to—"

"No, Verity." He gripped her arm with gentle pressure, touched in spite of himself by how quickly and readily she'd volunteered to accompany him on a dangerous and unknown errand. "No. I don't want you to go with me."

"Well…what, then? How are you going to find him? What did you figure out?"

"As I said, I thought again about what he said. '*If he ever truly wants to find me, he already possesses the means to do it.*' It's been driving me mad ever since you told me about it—I felt as if it should be obvious, but it wasn't. Until three weeks ago."

He turned to face her fully. "I know how to find him, because I'm already using the energy from where he is."

"Huh?"

"The way I use the magic he taught me—I open a conduit to another dimension and pull the power from it. I thought for the longest time that the place it came from was nothing more than a vast well of energy—that it would be insane and suicidal to ever attempt to travel there. I thought it would be like trying to teleport into the sun."

Stone released his grip and began pacing again. "I don't think so anymore, though. It's the only thing that makes sense, based on what he said—that wherever he's getting the power, that's where he *is*. And if I can get there, if I can find him, then I can convince him to teach me how to channel the energy properly." He flashed her a rather manic grin. "Don't you see? I won't have to take power from anyone else anymore, because I'll have all the power I could possibly want."

She stared at him. "So…you want to just…*go* to some other dimension, without having any idea what you'll find when you get there? Did you find it already? You know how to get there?"

"Yes. I've already worked out the ritual and set up the circle. I've double-checked it several times over the last couple of weeks. It's as solid as I know how to make it."

"How do you know? How did you find it?"

"That was what Harrison meant about already possessing the means to find him. I *already* access that dimension to pull power from it. If I can access it, I *already* know how to reach it. The only trick was figuring out how to reverse-engineer the process to get myself there, instead of pulling the power *from* there."

"So…" she said slowly, "if you don't want me to go with you, then what *do* you want me to do?"

And now came the hard part. No matter how he said it, how carefully he worded it, she wasn't going to react well. He knew that. Best to just have it out, then, he supposed. "I…need you to take care of things for me here, if…it doesn't go well."

Her eyes narrowed. "What do you mean, 'if it doesn't go well'?"

"Verity…" He let his breath out. "You know as well as I do that traveling between dimensions is never easy or without risk, and the outcome is never certain. Any number of things could go wrong. I could be wrong in my interpretation, and the place I go might end up being nothing more than a well of energy. I could end up in the wrong place, and not be able to get back. Hell, I might find Harrison and something could go pear-shaped while I try learning how to channel the power." He looked back out the window. "There are more ways this could go wrong than go right. And if they do…I've got a lot of obligations here. I can't simply disappear. I need someone who will tell the right people what happened, and see to—things."

"Things." She took his arm and turned him back around. Her eyes were hard. "You mean like telling people you're dead."

"Yes. Dead or…not coming back. And see to any—arrangements that need to be made. I've got my wills—magical and mundane—in order. If anything happens, go to England and find Ward and Eddie. The wills are with a man named Atthill—the contact info is in the desk in my study at the Surrey house. Aubrey can show you where. I've arranged with the University that I'm planning an extended research trip, in case I end up needing to be away for a long time. Even if I find Harrison and he agrees to teach me, I'm sure it will still take time. They didn't like it, but with the new endowment providing money for research, they can't exactly argue with me about it. And I'll need someone to look after Raider, of course; I assume I can count on you for that?"

Her face could have been carved from rock, for all the expression she showed.

"Verity?"

"Let me get this straight," she said in a low, even tone. "You're planning to go off and do something that will probably get you killed, and you want me to take care of your cat and let your friends know you're dead so they can go find your will?"

"Verity—"

"*Why*?" she demanded. "Why are you *doing* this?"

"I *told* you already. I've *got* to do it. I can't live this way any longer. Not without at least trying something else."

"So you're telling me you'd rather go off and try some crazy plan that will probably get you killed than to learn how to live with taking power from Jason?"

His heart pounded. His thoughts whirled. "I'm *telling* you," he said, in the same even tone she'd used, "that it's more than that. If that's all it was, I'd do it. I wouldn't like it, but we all have to deal with things we don't like. But Verity, I nearly *killed* someone. Even if Acantha was justifiable—and I don't regret what I did there, not at all—Tate wasn't. If Blum hadn't been there to stop me, I'd have killed him, and I didn't *have* to. I could have stopped him without killing him, but once I started, I couldn't stop. I didn't *want* to stop." He shook his head. "I won't risk that again. Not if I have an alternative."

She glared at him for several seconds without replying. "Okay, then," she said at last. "I want to come with you."

"No."

"Why not?"

"Because this isn't your problem. I'm not dragging someone else along with me in this. Either I'm right and I'll find him—either he'll agree to teach me or he won't—or I'm wrong, in which case, there's no way I'm risking your life, or anyone else's. That's not negotiable."

She whirled away from him. "Damn, but you can be maddening sometimes. You know that, right?"

"More than one person has told me that, yes," he said dryly.

"This isn't *funny*," she snapped, spinning back. Her voice shook and her aura erupted with billows of red agitation. Tears glittered in the corners of her eyes, though Stone couldn't tell whether they were tears of anger, frustration, sadness, or all three. "You don't have to do this. You don't have to take this kind of risk. I'll help you. Jason will. Ward and Eddie, and Aubrey—they all will. You can do this."

Stone took a deep breath and closed his eyes for a moment, then opened them and settled his gaze on her. When he spoke, his voice held no inflection. "Verity…you aren't my apprentice anymore. There's nothing I can say to force you to do anything. All I can do is ask. Can I count on you in this, or do I need to find someone else to do it?"

For a moment, he didn't think she'd answer. The way her aura looked, he wouldn't have been surprised if she simply walked out and slammed the door in his face. She held his gaze for several seconds, long enough to show him without any ambiguity that she wasn't in favor of this and she wasn't backing down. "Yeah," she finally said in a dead tone. "You can count on me."

"Thank you," he said softly. He pulled a card from his wallet and offered it to her. "I've set up a bank account and given you access to it, for any expenses that might come up. I've already made arrangements with my accountant to take care of the rent on the house, the bills, and all that sort of thing, so you shouldn't have much to do. I've no idea how long I'll be gone—even if this works, I doubt it will be quick. Thank you, Verity."

"Yeah." Once again, she looked as if she might simply leave, but instead she came over and put her arms around him. "Take care, Doc," she whispered. "Come back, okay?"

"That's the plan."

"Yeah, but you know your plans almost never work out like you want them to." She tightened the embrace, then stepped back to take him in. "When are you going to do it?"

"I thought tomorrow. No point in waiting."

"Can I watch the ritual?"

"Best if you don't, I think. There's nothing you can do to help."

"That doesn't matter. I'd just like to—see you off. That way at least I'll know nothing went wrong at the start."

He studied her a moment. "I suppose if you want to, then. If you'll give me your word you'll just watch."

"What, you mean instead of doing something to mess up the ritual so you won't be able to do this stupid thing?" She sighed. "Yeah, I promise."

"Right, then. Tomorrow night." He paused, and when he spoke again he heard a hesitation in his voice that hadn't been there before. "Would you like to…stay tonight?"

She, too paused. "I don't think so," she said softly. "I'll see you tomorrow, Doc."

| CHAPTER THREE

W HEN SHE ARRIVED the following evening, he half-expected her to have someone with her—most likely Jason, though he wouldn't have put it past her to take the portal to England and bring back Eddie Monkton or Arthur Ward in an attempt to talk some sense into him.

But no, she was alone. She didn't even have any grocery bags with her this time.

"Hi," he said, stepping aside to let her in.

"Hi."

Raider stopped threading himself around Stone's legs and looked hopefully up at Verity. She bent to pick him up, scratching his ears until he purred.

"He'll be in good hands, I see, until I get back," Stone said. "No secret he prefers you to me anyway. He'll probably consider it a holiday."

"So, you're still planning to do this."

"Are you surprised?"

"I was hoping you'd reconsider."

"I...can't, Verity. I know you don't understand that, but—I can't. I've got to do this."

She set Raider on a nearby chair. "Did you even try to call?"

"What?"

"Harrison. Did you even try to call the Obsidian first, to see if he might be there?"

Stone blinked. He *hadn't* tried that. "Er—"

"I'll take that as a no." She pointed at the phone. "At least humor me that much. Maybe you don't even *have* to go. That's what I'm talking about, Doc—why you need to not do this kind of thing on your own. You can't think of everything, and sometimes it's the obvious stuff you miss."

Sheepishly, heart thudding, Stone picked up the phone and pulled the Obsidian's number from his wallet. Was Verity right? *Had* he missed some other vital bit of his planning because he was too close to the situation, too emotionally involved? Could he avoid this entire process with a simple phone call?

The hotel's operator answered, and at his request connected him with Nakamura's office. Harrison's assistant answered quickly. "Yes, this is Nakamura."

"Mr. Nakamura. Alastair Stone."

"Ah. Good evening, Dr. Stone. How are you?"

"I'm looking for Mr. Harrison. He doesn't happen to be there, does he? Have you seen him recently?"

In the moment before Nakamura replied, Stone allowed himself hope. The man's next words quickly dashed it, though. "I'm sorry, Dr. Stone, but I'm afraid not. I haven't seen him for quite some time. Is something wrong?"

"No…nothing's wrong. I just wanted to discuss something with him. You don't expect him back anytime soon, do you?"

Nakamura made a sound that might have been a rueful chuckle. "You must know by now, Dr. Stone, that one doesn't *expect* Mr. Harrison. He shows up without warning, and leaves just as quickly. I wish I could be of more help. Do you want to leave a message for him, in case he does show up?"

"No…no, it's—nothing important. Thank you, Mr. Nakamura. Have a good evening."

As he hung up, he glanced at Verity. Her expression told him she'd gotten the message.

"Hey, it was worth a try," she said, looking disappointed.

"It was." He gripped her shoulder. "Don't look so upset. This might turn out to be far less complicated than I expect. If I can find him, perhaps I can convince him to come back here and teach me. I might not even be gone that long."

"If you get there at all." She bent to pet Raider, who was making circuits around her legs. "What if he won't teach you? Have you thought about that? What if he says, 'Sorry, but that stuff I sent you is all you're getting'?"

"I'll deal with that if it happens. I'm hoping we can make some kind of arrangement. He's a businessman—there's got to be something I can offer him." He nodded toward the stairs. "But come on—you're stalling, and I want to do this before I lose my nerve."

"Can't blame me for taking a shot, can you?"

Without replying, Stone picked up Raider, holding the cat up to stare into his big green eyes. "Now, listen, Raider: you're in charge while I'm gone. You take care of Auntie Verity, and I don't want to find out you've been throwing wild parties while I'm away. Got it?"

Raider's only answer was to tilt his head forward and lick Stone's nose.

Stone swallowed hard and pulled the cat in for a hug. Warm and purring, Raider settled into the crook of his arm.

"He doesn't want you to go either," Verity said.

No more stalling. Get on with it, or you never will. Gently, he set the tabby down on the nearest chair and headed for the stairs. "Come on, if you're coming."

He didn't turn back to see if she'd followed, but after a moment he heard her slow, reluctant footsteps behind him.

"Wow," she said, stopping just inside the doorway to the ritual room. "You *have* been busy."

He'd used nearly every inch of available floor space in the construction of the ritual; he'd even had to push some of the bookshelves to one end of the room. He stood next to her, trying to take it in with the fresh eyes of someone seeing it for the first time. One last check—he couldn't afford any complacency, or to take anything for granted.

The semi-permanent circle he'd created many years ago served as the basis for his work, but even that had been altered with additional chalk lines, arrangements of candles, braziers, crystals on stands, small mirrors, and carefully drawn sigils of sand and other powders. From that circle, he'd extended the design outward, augmenting the circle's original seven-foot diameter to nearly twelve feet. Most of the additional work had been done with chalk and various colors of sand and powdered minerals, but he heard Verity's gasp as she spotted some of the intricate work he'd done near the outer edges. "Is that...blood?"

"Yes. And before you ask, yes, it's my own, supplemented by a technique to extend it and keep it magically viable for a longer period. It would be easier if I had some of Harrison's blood too, but…that would rather defeat the whole purpose of the thing, wouldn't it?"

She pointed at the most unusual aspect of the circle. "What's with the doorway?"

Stone studied it. It was a simple, sturdy wooden door in a frame, which he'd purchased from Restoration Hardware last week. Both the heavy door and the frame were made of dark walnut; he had attached a stand that allowed it to remain upright without additional bracing. The door stood on the north side of the circle. Currently closed, it displayed additional sigils he had painted on it in white paint mixed with his blood. "You should be able to work that out on your own."

Her eyes narrowed. "You're making a portal."

"Of a sort, yes. It's not a true portal—that would have been far too complicated and expensive to do here. But when I activate the circle, if everything goes as planned, opening this door will open a way to Harrison's dimension."

"Why do you need it, though? I remember you told me about the time you went to fight that demon—what was his name again? Archie or something? I thought you just summoned a spirit to take you through."

"Yes, but this is different. This time, I need to do more than send my spirit through—my body has to go too. That's more difficult to manage."

She gripped his arm. "But…if you send your body through this doorway, how are you going to get back? I assume the portal doesn't just stay open the whole time, right?"

"Correct. Far too dangerous to leave an open portal to our world hanging about unattended, not to mention keeping it powered that long would require a lot more preparation and work than I have time for. When I finish what I've got to do there, I'll either have to build another portal to come home or, if I'm lucky, Harrison can just send me back."

"That's a lot of ifs."

"It is," he agreed. "But nobody ever made a useful magical discovery by sitting on his arse watching chat shows, did they?"

"I wouldn't know— I've never made one," Verity said dryly. She took his other arm and pulled him around to face her. "You're sure you have to do this? I know it's pointless to ask, but I have to take one last shot."

In answer, he leaned forward and kissed the top of her head. He felt her hands trembling, and shifting to magical sight revealed her unquiet aura. He nodded toward a chair on the far side of the room, pushed up against the wall next to the bookshelves. "Please sit over there, and no matter what happens, do not interfere with the circle. I'm not exactly sure how this is going to appear. Haven't had a chance to test it. And just to be safe, leave the circle standing afterward."

"Doc…" She let her hands drop from his arms, then pulled him into a hug. "You know all I want to do right now is go running through that circle, messing everything up and making it so you can't do this."

"I know that." In truth, part of *him* wanted to do that too—or wished she would. He nodded toward the chair again. "Off you go, then. There's a notepad on the desk if you want to take notes. Watch with magical sight—I think it will be quite a show, if nothing else."

With clear reluctance, she stepped back and carefully skirted the circle's edge. Despite her stated desire, she moved as gracefully as ever and never came close to smudging any of the edges.

After pausing to pick up the notepad and a pen from Stone's desk, she settled herself in the chair. "No luggage?" she asked with a shaky chuckle.

He didn't answer. Instead, he took several deep breaths and levitated into the center of the circle, where he stood facing the door. Glancing to his left and right, he saw his own reflection in two of the small mirrors he'd placed and wasn't surprised that he looked as if he'd seen a ghost—perhaps even his own. Clad in faded jeans and a black T-shirt featuring Pink Floyd's iconic "Dark Side of the Moon" rainbow prism, he looked more pale than usual, his dark hair tousled and his bright blue eyes shadowed with stress. He hadn't chosen the shirt on purpose, but now he thought with amusement that it was strangely apropos. For all he knew about his destination, he might as well be going to the dark side of the moon.

He checked the sigils one last time, verifying he'd built in the components he needed. The inner part represented this world, while the outer edges contained the essence of Harrison's magical source, gleaned from numerous tiny castings where he'd touched that source and done his best to understand it. Whether he'd been successful would remain to be seen, since like the portal itself there was no way to test it. No dry runs, no dress rehearsals. You only got one chance with this kind of magic, which is why the vast majority of modern-day mages possessed neither the knowledge nor the courage (or perhaps foolhardiness, depending on who you asked) to try it.

The last part of the circle, between the inner and outer sections, consisted of a narrow band of what looked like odd writing interspersed with more tiny sigils. Stone had produced this entire section using a quill pen and his own blood, painstakingly hunched over as he inscribed it. He had no idea if it would work, but if he'd done the job properly, it would add a sort of 'universal translator' component to the ritual, allowing him to communicate with any sentient denizens of Harrison's dimension and they with him. It wasn't a physical thing—he wouldn't instantly know whatever languages they spoke there, nor would they know his—but instead combined a highly limited form of telepathy with a specialized version of aura reading to convey meaning and even some nuance. While it was true that mages couldn't read minds, it was possible to get surface thoughts through careful preparation and a skill with auras. It might not be necessary at all—Harrison was a private man, and for all Stone knew he spent his time in some hidden pocket dimension with no other denizens— but it hadn't taken long to add the component.

By now, he'd forgotten Verity was even in the room with him. He turned slowly in place, using magic to light the individual candles and braziers. With a wave of his hand he brought over a bag from one of the bookshelves. After hanging its strap over his shoulder, he removed a small jar and opened it. Inside was a substance he'd prepared, containing more of his dried blood and a clipping of his hair. He took pinches of the substance and placed one in each of the three braziers: two on either side of the door and one behind him. All three flared different colors—the one to the left of the door the gold-tinged purple of his own aura; the one to the right the pulsing black and ultraviolet of Harrison's; the one behind him the silvery-gold of the energy from Harrison's dimension.

To his right and left, the mirrors now revealed shadowy, writhing figures behind his own reflection.

Under his breath, he murmured a protective invocation, designed to conceal him from anything that might develop an interest in the ritual. So far, the figures didn't appear to have noticed his activity, but he couldn't dawdle now. He couldn't keep this up forever, and if he lost his nerve at this point, the consequences could be devastating.

Last step, now.

Stone put the lid back on the jar, returned it to the bag, and withdrew a black-bladed knife. He floated the bag back to its original spot on the shelf, then gripped the knife in a shaking hand.

It all came down to this.

He glanced to the sides again, unable to resist another look at the figures in the mirror.

There were more of them now: two on one side, three on the other. They moved around as if walking through a room, but on each side, one appeared to have noticed his reflection. They moved toward it slowly, hesitantly, looking very much as he might if an unfamiliar entity had suddenly appeared in his midst. Studying. Hostile? Stone had no way to know. Best to hurry, in any case.

He stepped forward, still gripping the knife. He had prepared a path, lined on both sides with sigils and protective symbols, leading from the center of the circle to the door. He walked that path now—one step, two, three—until he stood in front of the closed portal.

From here, he could feel it thrumming with latent energy, even now when he hadn't made the final connection that would send power, from his own magic and from Harrison's energy source, coursing through it. Once the final conduit was in place, if he'd done this correctly, opening the door would reveal a portal that would take him directly to his destination. If fortune truly smiled upon his efforts, he might even get a brief second to evaluate what was on the other side, to prevent himself from stepping through into a conflagration of energy that would vaporize him instantly.

If he *wasn't* lucky, he'd simply have to take a leap of faith and hope for the best.

But he wouldn't know any of that until he made that final connection.

He tightened his grip on the knife handle, opened his other hand, and before he could lose his nerve, drew the blade across his palm. The blood for this final part of the ritual needed to be as fresh as possible.

Pain flared, and bright red blood welled up from the slash.

Holding his hand palm-up and cupping it so none of the blood would be lost, he lowered the knife to the floor. Then he stood again and faced the door. He dipped the index finger of his non-slashed hand in the blood, contemplated it a moment, and then began tracing additional figures on the portal's surface. Every few seconds he had to re-dip his finger, and everywhere he traced, the blood glowed a warm gold-red, illuminating his work. All the while he did this, he murmured an incantation under his breath. His hand shook, but he managed to hold it steady enough to complete the symbols he was inscribing.

After a few minutes, he finished his work. As he drew the last of the symbols and used one final stroke to link the final two together, the warm red-gold glow intensified, becoming less red and more gold. The images he'd drawn complemented the ones he'd added previously, tying them together into an intricate, roughly circular image about a foot in diameter.

"There we go…" he whispered, weaving a quick healing spell to seal the slash on his hand. Chancing a final glance to either side of him, he saw that there were now even more shadowy figures passing each other in the mirrors. So far, only the two—one on each side—seemed to be at all aware of him, though. They circled his reflection, occasionally reaching out with a tentative finger as if trying to touch him. Their postures radiated tension and confusion.

It was time to go.

Stone didn't look back at Verity—mostly because he feared if he did, he might lose his nerve and give up the whole mad plan. Instead, he straightened his shoulders and faced the door, which was still glowing with the pulsing golden light.

He extended his non-bloody hand, grasped the doorknob, and pulled the door open.

Inside, he saw nothing but more golden light and fog; no sign of the shadowy figures he'd seen in the mirrors. He thought for an instant that he might have seen the spires of faraway buildings, but the fog obscured them before he could be sure.

Clearly, there would be no hints.

Leap of faith it was, then.

"See you on the dark side of the moon…" he muttered, and stepped through the portal.

| CHAPTER FOUR

FOG SWIRLED ALL AROUND HIM, engulfing him. Some of it seemed to be physical, blocking any view of what might be surrounding him, but a different kind of fog rose in his brain. His vision swam, and suddenly he felt himself swaying. Instinctively he reached for the door frame, which should have been directly behind him, intending to steady himself against it until the feeling settled and he could move forward.

His groping hand touched nothing but air.

Heart pounding, he turned back to where the doorway should have been, and a chill gripped him.

The physical fog was already receding, but behind him he saw what looked like an expanse of pale street, and the tall forms of structures rising on the other side. Even though his vision was still blurry, and he couldn't clearly make out anything more than a few feet away from him in the dim glow of an elaborate streetlight, he knew one thing for certain: the doorway was gone.

He'd barely gone through, only moved a step away, but already it had vanished. That wasn't supposed to happen: portals, even temporary ones, usually remained for at least a few moments before fading, but this one had lasted only until he'd passed completely through it.

He blinked a couple times and staggered sideways as the swimmy feeling in his head intensified. Where was he? Had he made it to his destination, or was he somewhere else?

Got to find someplace to rest. It wasn't safe to be disoriented in an unfamiliar dimension—not when he had no idea if the residents were friendly. He'd just find a hiding place to lie low for a bit until he felt better, then venture out and try to locate someone he could question about where he was.

"You!" a sudden, sharp voice called from off to his left.

Stone froze, spinning toward the sound. His head swam again and he staggered once more, but the shot of adrenaline made a start at clearing his mind.

Three figures approached. All of them were tall and male; in the pale twilight he couldn't make out details, but the lines of their clothes looked unfamiliar.

"Yes, you," another of the three snapped. His voice sounded clipped, imperious—the kind that was used to being obeyed—but also relatively young. Perhaps early twenties, if that.

As the group drew closer, they stepped under the streetlight, giving Stone a better look at them. All three had shoulder-length hair and wore close-fitting pants, high boots, and sweeping, high-collared long coats that fluttered behind them like cloaks. Each coat had various pins and adornments attached to its collar and lapels, but Stone couldn't make out the details. He'd been correct about their ages: all of the men had young, unlined faces, and all featured the sneering, confident expressions of those who knew they had the upper hand.

Be calm, he told himself. Already the adrenaline had done its job; the swimmy vertigo had all but faded. He could deal with these young men if he needed to, but perhaps they could give him some information first.

"What can I do for you?" he asked. At least the translation component of the ritual seemed to be working.

"'*What can I do for you*?'" one of the men mocked. Pale and well-built, he had yellow-blond hair and the handsome, fleshy face of someone who habitually overindulged in many ways. He stepped forward, and his two friends joined him. "Listen to him."

They formed a ring around Stone, all three studying him as if he were something they'd just discovered on the bottom of their spotless boots.

"What are you doing here?" a second, with dark brown hair tied back in a ponytail, demanded. His tone was what one might use to address a dull-witted underling. "Are you lost?"

Now that they were closer to him, Stone could get a better look. Still doing his best to remain calm, he turned slowly and took them in one at a time. The third one, taller and thinner than his friends, had lighter brown hair. All three were clean-shaven, and carried themselves with the unmistakable air of wealth and privilege—Stone had seen enough of it growing up that he recognized it instantly. Their outfits were well made and similar: the same snug-fitting pants, boots, and sweeping, high-collared coats—but had enough stylistic variation that they didn't look like uniforms. Similar to a group of men on Earth wearing different suits, he decided. The only thing the coats had in common was that they were all some shade of blue.

"Darien asked you a question, dim pig," the blond man said. "You will answer."

Dim pig? That's an odd insult. Wondering if the translation spell had handled it properly, he turned pointedly back to the man who'd spoken. "Yes. I'm lost. Perhaps you might help me?"

The blond man stared at him in astonishment. "Show me your papers. Who do you work for?"

"Papers?"

Now all of them were looking at him as if he were slow of wit. "Your *papers,* fool. Where is your identification? Your work permit? Show us now!"

Stone patted his back pocket, but he hadn't brought his wallet with him. What good would his driver's license and green card have done him on some other dimension? "Listen," he said, trying to sound reasonable and not at all 'dim.' "I haven't got it with me. I've just arrived in town, and I'm looking for someone. I'm sure if I find him, he can straighten this all out. If you can just point me toward—"

The blond man smiled slyly at the dark-haired one, Darien. "This dim pig has no papers. No identification. No right to be in our city."

"Indeed," Darien said. He looked Stone up and down, taking in his faded jeans and black T-shirt, and wrinkled his nose in distaste. "Why are you dirtying our streets, scum? Who are you looking for?"

"A man named Harrison. Do you know him?" It was a long shot, especially given Harrison's previously demonstrated preference for privacy. But he had to try.

"Never heard of him."

"We should turn him over to the guard," the third man said.

The blond man's smile widened, and something unwholesome appeared in his eyes. "Oh, we'll do that. Can't have dim trash fouling our city. But not yet." He glanced around as if trying to spot anyone else who might be approaching, but the street around them appeared deserted. "I think we should have some fun with him first. It's not every day we find little lost pigs in Temolan. Usually I have to go down to Drendell and get my boots dirty to find them."

Stone took a step back. "Not a good idea," he said evenly. "If you won't help me, why don't you just go on your way and I'll find someone else who will."

"'Not a good idea,'" the third man repeated, laughing, doing a poor attempt at mimicking Stone's accent. He moved forward, positioning himself so he and his friends once again ringed Stone. "I think he's dim in more ways than one, don't you, Kethias?" He pointed at his own head and made a face suggesting mental deficiency.

"What's your name, pig?" the blond man, Kethias, asked.

Stone glared at him. "Well, it's bloody well not 'pig.' Get out of my way." He started forward. If they gave him any trouble, he'd show them why it wasn't a good idea to mess with strangers before you had any idea what they might be capable of.

Something picked him up and flung him out of the street. Before he could get his bearings and react, he slammed hard into a wall and crashed to the ground. Pain lit up his back as he struggled to rise; footsteps approached and then the three of them were there again, looming over him.

"You don't give orders to the Talented, pig. Not if you want to keep your filthy hide in one piece," Kethias said. He didn't look mocking now.

"This one doesn't know his place," Darien said. "We should teach him."

Enough of this. Stone didn't have time to deal with some other dimension's answer to a crowd of entitled rich kids out to cause a little trouble. Panting, he glared at the three of them and focused his will. He'd hit the blond one—he seemed to be the ringleader, and maybe taking him out would make the other two rethink their plans.

Without giving them time to react, he pointed his hand and lashed out with magical energy, intending to send the beefy blond man sailing back across the street with a powerful concussion blast.

At least that was what he planned to do.

In reality, nothing happened.

The three young men laughed as if they thought this was the funniest thing they'd seen all week. "Look at him!" Darien spluttered. "Is the dim pig trying to do *magic?*"

"I think he *is!*" The third man bent, his hands on his knees, his back shaking with his guffaws.

Stone struggled to his feet, heart pounding harder than ever.

This was not good.

This was not good at all.

How could his magic not work? He hadn't used Harrison's source in the ritual, so he shouldn't have burned himself out.

"Well, well," Kethias said. "Not only have we got a little lost dim pig without any identification, but we've got one who thinks he's one of us." He raised his hand and slammed Stone back into the wall. "What's your name, pig?"

Stone fought to free himself, but an unseen force had clamped around his neck, holding him against the unyielding surface. He closed his eyes and forced himself to concentrate—perhaps the magic hadn't worked before because he hadn't focused hard enough. Maybe wherever he was now, people accessed magic differently. All he had to do was find it, and—

The grip around his throat tightened, making it harder to breathe. "Your *name,* pig!" Kethias snapped again. "Don't make me crush your windpipe—you know no one will give a damn about scum like you. Just another piece of trash for the street sweepers to pick up in the morning."

Stone glared at him, but he couldn't break free of the grip. One look at Kethias's eyes told him the kid would have no compunctions about killing him. Best to play along for now. "Alastair…Stone," he got out through gritted teeth.

The grip vanished, dropping Stone to the hard ground.

Darien wasn't laughing now. "Nice try, pig. What's your *real* name?"

Stone decided against trying to get up. He didn't answer.

Kethias raised his hand again, this time picking Stone up by the front of his shirt and holding him suspended in the air in front of him. "You are quite the piece of work, aren't you? Now you're even brazen enough to claim a Talented name. You do know that's a crime, don't you? Do you want to re-think your answer? You can be executed for impersonating the Talented."

Panting, heart pounding, Stone stared at him. "What…are you…talking about…?" he got out between breaths. Kethias's magical grip wasn't obstructing his airway this time, but the sensation of dangling several feet off the ground suspended by the front of his T-shirt was nonetheless disconcerting. What the hell did he mean, 'impersonating the Talented'? Was Talented what they called mages? Was there already someone here named Alastair Stone?

"Come on," the third man said in disgust. "If we don't get moving, we'll be late for Nethria's party. Stop playing with this piece of trash and let's go."

For a moment, Stone thought they might tire of him and move on. But then Kethias flashed his wolfish smile. "Oh, I'll stop soon. But first our dim friend needs to learn his place. Come on—help me, and we'll finish faster."

He released his hold on Stone again, once more dropping him to the ground. Stone knew his only chance was to get away from these three before they killed him. Without magic that wouldn't be easy, but he had to try.

As soon as he hit the ground he launched himself forward, heading for an opening he'd spotted between two of the buildings. Perhaps he could lose himself in the darkness before they could catch him.

For a moment, he thought he'd made it. Despite the pain in his legs, his back, his neck, he ran as fast as he could. The narrow, darker space between the buildings could be an alley, a small street—he didn't know. All he knew was he had to get away. He reached the opening and forced a fresh burst of speed, not daring to cast a glance behind him.

Something slammed into the back of his legs at knee level, pitching him forward, and he crashed face-first to the ground, stunned. Before he could get back up an unseen force once again lifted him and tossed him back into the

50 |

R. L. KING

middle of the street. This time he landed hard on his arm; white-hot pain bloomed as he both felt and heard something crack.

The three laughing men moved in on him again.

He flung himself onto his back, his gaze flicking between them. Despite their laughing faces, their eyes looked deadly serious now. Focused. Intense.

No...no...It can't end like this...Not so soon...

A force like a fist made of rock slammed his shoulder.

A flurry of invisible knives flayed at him, opening bloody slashes, slicing at his shirt, his jeans, his unprotected skin.

Something that felt like white-hot fire erupted around him.

He screamed, rolling, trying to leap up and run, but once again the magical grip slammed him back down.

Their laughter rose louder. Never once did they touch him physically. Each time he caught a glance at one of them the expression was the same: they were *enjoying* this. This was the look of some slumming rich kid beating up homeless people for fun—and with no more regard for the humanity of their victim.

He tried magic again as the invisible force pulled him out of his fetal ball and something hit him hard in the stomach, but nothing happened. It wasn't as if the magic was there and he couldn't control it, but rather more that he had no sense of it at all. *This is how mundanes must feel...* he thought. *Except they don't know what they're missing...*

His entire body was slicked with blood now, his consciousness fading, a different kind of fog settling over his mind.

This is it, then...

This how it ends.

A little voice, the one that always seemed to have something snarky but ultimately true to say, spoke in the back of his mind: *You should have stuck with Jason. Always trying to do things the hard way so you don't have to depend on anyone...*

Look at where it got you.

Grayness crept up on him, growing darker...

"You there!" a sharp voice called. Or maybe it was just in Stone's head.

"It's the guard!" one of his attackers snapped. Stone couldn't tell which one anymore; their voices all blended together.

The rest of the conversation floated by, shifting between real and unreal, like a film running underwater. He picked up snippets of it as he passed in and out of consciousness.

—*What are you doing? Who is this?* —

—*Dim trash*—

—*in the street*—

—*teaching him his place*—

—*no papers*—

—*Off with you*—

Grumbles, followed by footsteps receding.

Now it was just the deeper, older voices...*the guard*?

—*Damn, now we have to*—

—*get it over with*—

—*take him back tonight*—

—*Probably die anyway*—

—*not our problem*—

He woke several times, only for a few seconds, each time to disorienting images he could barely make sense of.

Something picking him up.

Something carrying him, or perhaps bearing him along on some kind of stretcher.

Lying in what might be the back of a moving vehicle. The floor was hard and cold, and he both felt and smelled the sharp coppery tang of his own blood along with the fainter odor of harsh disinfectant.

Carried again, with no apparent regard for how much pain each jostling step shot through him. He felt cold, then hot. *Shock?*

In a room. Cream-colored walls. More people—men, women—dressed in shades of blue. Long coats, sigils. Expressions of distaste and disgust. *At me? Isn't anyone going to help? Am I dying?*

Do they care?

Glowing column. Unearthly glow.

Beautiful…beautiful…

Sort of like the portal back home.

Sense of wild disorientation.

Dark street.

Rain.

Smells of oil, of wet pavement, of rubber, of far-off burning wood.

Murmuring voices.

—leave him here? Shouldn't we—

—late already. Just—

—cares about dim trash? Should have—

Something dragged him by what was left of his shirt and dumped him to the ground. Rain pattered down, quickly soaking him. The shivering brought a bit more awareness; he cracked his eyes open long enough to see two broad-shouldered, long-coated figures striding off. They didn't look back at him.

Then a quick flash of the same otherworldly light he thought he'd seen before, and they were gone.

He was alone.

.

| CHAPTER FIVE

H E MUST HAVE PASSED OUT AGAIN. When he awoke he was still shivering; the rain still fell, soaking him to the skin and pattering down on the rough, cracked surface where he lay. *Sidewalk? Road?*

I've got to find shelter. And someone to help.

Shelter first. His brain moved sluggishly, barely able to hold a thought for more than a few seconds at a time, but his survival instincts told him trusting people on this world was something he'd need to be careful with. If he was going to survive this, he'd need to get someplace warm and dry. That was priority one.

He tried to push himself up on his arms, and twin sharp pains sent him slumping back down with a splash. *They broke my arm. And maybe my shoulder too.* Quick images of the rocklike magical fist pummeling him replayed in his mind.

He raised his head, blinking rain and blood out of his eyes, and tried to get a look around.

It was still dark; in fact, it seemed to be darker here than it had wherever he'd been before. Instead of pale streets and cream-colored buildings, the structures around him here appeared to be made of brick, blasted and abandoned. No lights shone in their windows, and the only two streetlamps he could see, one on his own side of the street and the other across from him, burned with faint flickers that barely reached far enough to illuminate the sidewalks.

Using his good arm, he tried to push himself up to a sitting position, and bit back a scream as more pain shot through his torso. *Broken ribs…possibly internal injuries too.* He slumped back to the ground, shivering harder and tasting blood. He couldn't get a proper breath.

It occurred to him that he might die here. In fact, that seemed the most likely outcome. If he didn't succumb to his injuries, the cold and rain would be just as deadly unless he could find warmth and shelter. And even then, without his magic he couldn't even begin to heal himself.

Desperate, he tried to concentrate, to focus—was there any chance his magic might have returned? Even though he hadn't used Harrison's power source as part of his ritual, maybe something about the nature of this place had the same temporary burnout effect. If he could get even a fraction of it to work, he might be able to heal the worst of the injuries and buy himself more time. If not, he didn't like his odds for lasting the night.

He closed his eyes, took a couple of hitching breaths, and tried to block out the pain long enough to focus his mental energy. On the positive side, it wasn't as hard as it might have been; on the negative side, he knew that was because he was settling deeper into shock. The pain might be fading, but his life force was fading along with it.

Nausea flared, along with the disorienting gray fog he recognized as the first sign he was about to pass out again. *No. Can't do that. If I do I'm dead…*

Deliberately, he moved his broken arm, then gritted his teeth against the white-hot lance of pain shooting through him. The pain did its job, though: the gray fog receded, creeping away like a reluctant scavenger. It still regarded him watchfully from the edges of his consciousness, though; it would be back, and soon. He knew he couldn't hold it off for long.

He had to get out of the rain. He couldn't even crawl, not with his broken arm and shoulder. His legs seemed better, relatively speaking: the slashing invisible knives had opened bloody cuts on them as they had on the rest of his body, but at least they didn't seem broken. If he could just find something to brace against so he could get up without using his bad arm, he might be able to—

He looked around, still blinking away the rain. Beneath him was something hard, uneven, and rough—cracked asphalt, perhaps. Had they dumped him in the street? All the more reason to move—if they had vehicles here and any came by, they'd hit him before they even spotted him.

And that assumed the drivers even cared whether they hit him.

He saw nothing he could use to pull himself up. On the far side of the street he spotted the dark forms of what might be parked vehicles, but they might as well have been on the other side of the world for all the help they'd provide.

You've got to get out of the street.

He listened a moment, trying to pick out the sounds of engines, but he heard nothing. No engines, no music, no conversations. This place seemed utterly deserted. Had the mysterious "guard" from the other place simply dropped him off in some abandoned wasteland, where they wouldn't have to deal with the consequences of his death?

Off to his left, a faint sound rose from the silence.

He tensed. Had that been a growl?

Remaining still and silent except for his harsh, ragged breathing, he listened again.

Definitely a growl. And it was getting closer.

Another joined it, from a different direction.

Dogs? Wolves?

Something worse?

I've got to get out of here.

If he could make it to the other side of the street, he might be able to drag himself into one of the parked vehicles. If they were abandoned, they might be unlocked. At least he'd be out of the rain, and it might afford some protection from the predators, especially if he could get there before they caught his scent. The rain might work in his favor, washing away the strongest of the blood-scent that would draw them toward him faster.

If he couldn't get up, then he'd have to find a way to crawl. He hitched a few more breaths, drove off the gray fog once more—he didn't know how many more times he'd be able to do that—and, using his unbroken arm and his legs, began to scrabble at the cracked road surface in an attempt to push himself toward the vehicles.

It was slow going, punctuated by many brief rest stops. His entire body was a solid wall of pain now; he couldn't even differentiate it any longer. His whole world became a series of inch-by-inch bits of forward progress, each one gained at the cost of increasing agony. The cracked, oil-soaked asphalt tore at his unprotected skin, the rain stung his bleeding cuts, and every time he moved he felt his broken ribs shift. His harsh, shallow breaths rattled in his throat.

More than once Stone was tempted to simply stop, to let himself slump onto the pavement and succumb to the gray fog, to cease caring whether someone ran him over or some hunting predator ripped him to pieces. At least then the pain would end, and it would be over.

He'd rolled the dice and lost the bet—Harrison wasn't here. This probably wasn't even the correct dimension. He'd made a mistake somewhere in the formula, and now he was desperately injured and stranded in a place where his magic didn't work and he had no hope of getting home.

He almost stopped. As his limbs grew colder and the gray fog crept in again, he almost convinced himself that giving in was his best option. It would be so easy to just—

No.

There was that voice again—the one that talked to him sometimes, when he was about to make a bad decision. Now, in addition to hearing it in his mind, he almost saw its source: a tall, thin figure standing over him. His own figure, whole and uninjured, its expression stern, implacable.

You're not giving up, it said. *It's your own bloody fault you're in this situation, and you're not checking out now.*

I...can't... he protested. He tried to say it aloud, but nothing came out. Blood bubbled at his lips.

The figure crouched next to him, the hem of its long black coat pooling around it, its black boots planted only inches from his head. How was the bottom of its coat not soaking up any water from the sodden street? *That's because he's not really there, you prat. You're hallucinating.*

Does it matter? the figure asked. *You can keep going, and you will. Get moving, damn you, before I kick your arse.*

Stone glared at it. *Bugger off. Let me die in peace.* But once again he felt the gray fog receding and clarity—such as it was, anyway—returning. *Damn you.* He spat blood, gritted his teeth, and gripped at the asphalt with bleeding fingers.

Another inch forward. Two. Three.

The growling he'd heard before sounded again. Closer this time. Behind him.

He scrabbled at the cracking surface with his feet, trying to propel himself faster. The uneven asphalt tore at his chest and abdomen through the shredded remains of his T-shirt. He glanced up; a faint tinge of light shone through the choking clouds above him. Was dawn coming? The dark forms of the vehicles still seemed miles away—how far had he managed to crawl? Had all that effort only gained him a foot or two of progress?

The growls—at least two of them—were closer now, almost as if they'd grown braver with the coming dawn. Stone paused a moment and raised his head, trying to spot their sources.

When he did see one of them, he froze.

The creature, whatever it was, stood perhaps twenty feet from him, on the same side of the street as the vehicle he was trying to reach. Between the rain, the scant light, and the fog in his brain, he couldn't make out details—but he didn't need details. What he could see was quite enough to send a cold shaft of dread through his body.

The thing was big. As big as a large wolf, at least. Though it did have canine characteristics—four legs, pointed ears, a thick tail that switched back and forth behind it—it was clear

R. L. KING

it wasn't a dog, or a wolf. At least not a normal one. Something about it suggested *wrongness,* though in the faded dawn light Stone couldn't put his finger on exactly why. It might have been the way it moved: shuffling and uncertain, instead of graceful. It might have been the shaggy patchiness of its rain-soaked, black-furred hide, or the way its gaze locked on Stone and then wandered away as if something had distracted it.

As he watched, heart pounding and the chill of renewed fear seeping through him to join the physical cold already there, the thing took a few steps forward. When it opened its jaws, Stone's breath caught.

Something in its mouth was glowing.

A sickly orange light shone around its large, pointed teeth, appearing to originate someplace at the back of the thing's throat.

It growled again, and as it did, the glow intensified. After a moment, an answering growl came from Stone's left.

Afraid to take his attention from the first one longer than a second or two, Stone quickly turned his head to look in that direction. As he suspected, a second creature had appeared. This one stood farther back, wary, almost as if waiting to see what its counterpart would do.

When Stone looked back at the first one, it was closer.

It stood only ten feet from him now, giving him an even closer look. Aside from the panting tongue lolling from its gaping jaws, it stood still as if carved from rock. Its eyes, fixed on him now, glowed a faint red.

Bloody hell…

A fresh jolt of adrenaline at the sight of the thing drove the encroaching gray fog back again. Stone stared at the creature in horror, unable to move.

Whatever this thing was—wolf, dog, or something else entirely—there was clearly something wrong with it.

Now that it was closer, more of its features came into focus: the scaly, bald patches where its fur had fallen out; the running sores on its legs; the bloated roundness of its belly; the runnels of drool suspended from both sides of its jaw. Though its eyes continued to glow a flickering red, they were only half-open. If Stone didn't know better—and he didn't— the thing looked to him like some kind of mutant creature suffering from radiation sickness.

None of that was the worst of it, though: that honor was claimed by the small, vestigial second head that hung at a crazy angle from the left side of the creature's neck. Only a quarter of the size of the thing's proper head, its jaws gaped to emit a thick, glutinous strand of shimmering drool. It had only one eye, non-glowing but open and staring off at nothing.

Stone's heart pounded faster. Whatever the hell this freakish thing was, he needed to get away from it. Perhaps if he moved slowly enough, he could—

He tried to fumble at the pavement again, to dig his fingers into the cracks, to propel himself away from the thing. If it attacked him in the middle of the street, he'd be defenseless. If he could just—

But he couldn't move.

He focused his will and tried to reach out with his unbroken arm, to grip the next handhold, to shove himself forward an inch or two with his feet as he'd been doing before, but his body simply refused to cooperate.

The thing lunged, leaping toward him with a loud howl, jaws stretched wide.

Almost as if it knew its prey wouldn't move.

Almost as if it had done something to immobilize him.

Stone, unable to do anything to defend himself no matter how hard he tried and left with no other choice, at last gave in to the inevitable. He closed his eyes and waited for the creature's teeth to sink into his flesh.

A loud *crack* split the air, followed by a yell, and then an animal yelp of pain.

Stone quickly opened his eyes to a shocking sight: the mutant wolf-creature was retreating, running far faster than he thought possible on its sore-crusted legs. The second one was nowhere to be seen.

He realized he could move again. Wildly, he looked around for the source of the *crack* and the yell—whatever had driven the creatures off might be as dangerous, if not more so.

A figure was approaching him from between two of the abandoned vehicles. As it entered the street it picked up speed, striding over to crouch next to him.

"Gods," it breathed. "What's happened to you?"

Stone blinked blood and rainwater from his eyes. The figure resolved into a dark-skinned man dressed in rough work clothes. He had short dark hair, a wide, unshaven face, and a crooked nose. His expression as he gaped down at Stone was full of horror and concern.

Stone tried to answer, but he couldn't make his voice work. The gray fog was coming back again, and this time he didn't think he'd be able to drive it off. "I—" he whispered, and tried to raise his hand. But then the pain rose again; his thoughts whirled, and his vision spiraled off into nothingness.

CHAPTER SIX

THE FIRST THING STONE NOTICED, even before he opened his eyes, was the sharp odor of antiseptic.

He didn't open them yet; his thoughts floated as if down a lazy river, but refused to settle on anything long enough to give him useful information. He was alive—maybe. He couldn't even be sure of that. Maybe this was some kind of weird afterlife where the air smelled like medicine and the backdrop consisted of a constant muddy hubbub of voices, too far away and indistinct to make out.

Oddly, there wasn't enough pain. Still some, certainly—an all-over ache that reached down into his bones and gripped hard—but nowhere near what he remembered feeling before. Had that all been a dream? Perhaps that was it. He'd dreamed those men had beaten him up, and those other men had dropped him like unwanted trash in a blasted-out wasteland populated by mutant two-headed wolf-things. This was one of those dreams he had sometimes when he was apprehensive about some magical technique, or reluctant to try it. The wolves were new, but the sense of powerlessness was not. Perhaps he'd never even stepped through that portal at all. Perhaps instead he'd gone out and gotten roaring drunk at some pub, and he'd now awakened in his own bed with a world-class hangover.

But if that were true, why did it smell like medicine? And what were the voices?

He cracked open his eyes as his heartbeat increased.

He didn't know much yet, but even the quick glance told him one thing for certain:

This was not his bedroom back in Palo Alto.

He blinked a few times, trying to clear his vision enough to get a good look around. Still he had trouble concentrating—the pulsing pain in his head felt like a giant's fist was in there, rhythmically squeezing his brain—but he forced himself to push past it. He had to know where he was.

He lay in a bed in what appeared to be a large, open room. The lights were dim enough that he couldn't make out any details, but as his vision came back into focus he saw another bed to his left, a third to his right, and two more across a wide aisle down the middle. The shades on the two windows opposite him were both pulled down, but enough light seeped in to reveal that it must be daytime. Everywhere he looked, the furnishings and décor were old-fashioned, utilitarian, basic: the chipped white metal frame at the foot of his own bed was the type you saw in old movies, the blanket thin and beige, the walls painted pale gray.

Was he in a hospital, or a prison?

He tried to push himself up before remembering that his arm was broken, and probably his shoulder too. He braced for the pain—but it didn't come. Certainly not as bad as before, at least.

He looked down at himself. Someone had tucked the thin blanket around him, leaving his arms and shoulders uncovered. His shirt was gone, and to his surprise he saw no sign of a cast or bandage on his injured arm and shoulder, though a few smaller bandages covered parts of his chest and arms. *What—?*

Tentatively he lifted his arm, once again preparing for a shot of pain, but once again nothing happened beyond the general achiness. That, and an all-over rush of fatigue that instantly dropped his shaking arm back to the bedcovers.

"How do you feel?" a female voice asked.

Footsteps approached, and a woman appeared in his field of vision. She looked to be in her thirties, tanned and solidly built, with pulled-back blonde hair. She wore a rumpled white coat.

"I—where is this?" His voice came out croaky, as if it hadn't been used in a while.

"You're in the hospital." She took something from her pocket, shook it, and briskly popped it into his mouth. After a few moments she removed it and examined it.

An old-style thermometer? Stone hadn't seen one like that in many years. "Er…" he tried again. "Hospital?"

"You're very lucky. You were badly hurt when you were brought in. If Rylan hadn't found you in the street when he did, you'd probably have died. Even so, we nearly lost you. It was a good thing Tanissa was making her rounds in the area." She moved to the foot of his bed and picked up a chart on a clipboard. "What's your name?"

Stone studied her for a moment before answering. Something about her question seemed wary. "How long have I been here?" With use his voice took on more strength, but he still sounded exhausted.

"Nearly five days. Can you tell me your name, please, so I can put it on your chart? They found no identification on you."

Five *days*? He'd been in this place nearly a full week? He struggled to remember anything about being here, but got nothing beyond the grotesque wolf-things stalking him as he lay bleeding in the dark, rainy street. "Alastair Stone."

There was no mistaking it this time: her gaze sharpened. When she spoke again, her tone hovered between tension and a kind of forced respect. "Are you one of the Talented?" she asked with care.

He blinked. "What?"

"It's a simple question."

"Er—" His memory went back to what the three young men who'd attacked him had said. They'd called themselves the same thing. *You could be executed for impersonating the Talented.* "I…don't think so."

"You don't *think* so?" Her expression changed again as she narrowed her eyes. "You either are or you aren't."

Stone wished the fuzzy fog in his brain would lift more; she was looking at him like she thought he was mentally slow, and right now she wasn't entirely wrong. "I'm sorry— I'm…unfamiliar with your customs. I'm not from this part of the world."

Another figure approached—a man this time. He had dark skin, dark hair, and wore a white coat similar to the woman's, though of a different style. "Is he awake? Did you get anything out of him?" he asked, glancing at Stone but not greeting him.

"He just woke up," she said. "Still under the pain medication and sedatives. I hope that's all it is—he might have hit his head."

"Could be all the worse." The man's expression was hard, resolute, and not at all kind. "We need to get him out of here before they send someone after him. He can't be found here."

"I told you, Milas—we're not releasing him until he's well enough to survive on his own."

"He's one of *them*," Milas protested, cutting a glare at Stone. "Do you honestly think he'd have done the same for one of us?"

"I honestly *think*," she said sharply, "that we're a hospital—such as we are—and he's an injured man. That means we're going to treat him. If they come after him, perhaps they'll be grateful that we saved him from being eaten by scavengers."

Milas snorted. "Sure they will. And I'll be moving into my mansion in the clouds next week." He glared at Stone again. "We'll be lucky if they don't take the place apart, just for spite. Just—patch him up and send him on his way before they find out he's been here." He spun and stalked off.

The woman watched him go, then sighed and turned back to Stone. "Sorry you had to hear that."

Stone tried to sit up, and to his surprise it didn't hurt nearly as much as he expected it to. "I'm sorry…" he said. "As I said, I'm not familiar with the way things work here. How did you—"

"How did we what?"

He indicated himself. "I don't remember anything about what happened after I passed out, but…I was dying. I know I was. If it's only been five days, how have you—"

"Ah." She nodded once, understanding. "We aren't without our resources, even here. I'm sure you're aware that some of your people live among us, and help us with their healing magic. As I said, you were lucky Tanissa was nearby when you were brought in. She's a gift from the gods. Even still, though, she couldn't heal everything. It will be a few days yet before you'll be ready to leave. Unless…"

"Unless…?" Stone's mind whirled. *Your people?* What was she talking about?

"Unless your people come after you and take you back to Temolan."

He closed his eyes, frustrated. "Listen," he said, trying to sound reasonable. "I haven't any idea what you're talking about. I don't have 'people.' I'm not from…this area. I was—visiting, and I guess I blundered into the wrong part of town."

"Can you tell me what happened to you? How were you injured?"

"Three men attacked me. And then someone else—I'm not sure who they were, but I heard the others call them 'the guard'—dropped me where you lot found me."

She tensed. "The Guard? *Dropped* you?"

"That's what I said." He pulled himself up a bit more. "Listen—I'm grateful for your help. More than grateful—as you said, if your people hadn't found me and sorted me out, I'd probably be dead. But I haven't got a bloody idea what's going on here. I came here looking for a man named Harrison, but I must have taken a wrong turn somewhere. Do you know him? Do you know how I could get in touch with him? I'm sure he can clear this all up." The effort of the long speech drained his meager reserves, and he sank back into his pillow, puffing.

She was staring at him. "Why would the Guard drop you here? Did you commit some kind of crime? But that doesn't make sense. The Talented handle their own affairs. They certainly don't involve *us* in them."

Stone let his breath out. "Can you explain this 'Talented' term you keep tossing around?" Once again, he remembered the three men who'd attacked him. "Are they the ones who can do magic?"

"Of course." She looked at him even more as if she thought him a slow child. "Aren't you one of them?"

That was an interesting question. Stone focused on her face, trying to summon a shred of magic power and examine her aura. If he'd been unconscious for five days and the process worked as it had when he'd used Harrison's magic, perhaps it had recharged by now.

But no—nothing happened. No bright aura shimmered around her, or around his own hand when he held it up. He changed his focus to the chart at the end of the bed, trying to levitate it. Nothing.

So, for whatever reason, temporarily or permanently, he was mundane here. He forced himself not to think about the implications of that—about how if he couldn't do magic and couldn't find Harrison, he'd never get home—and instead settled on his current reality.

"No," he said. "I'm not one of them. I'm not—Talented." *And if those three who beat me up are any example of what mages are like here, I'm not sure I'd want to be.* He entertained a brief but satisfying fantasy of showing the three entitled young bullies some *real* magic, but quickly dropped it. That wouldn't help him at all.

She gave him a sideways look. "I find that hard to believe."

"Why is that?"

"Because of your name, for one thing. If that *is* truly your name."

"You're the second person who's said that to me. One of the men who attacked me did, too. What's wrong with my name?"

"Are you sure you didn't hit your head?" She lowered herself into a metal chair next to the bed. "We didn't find any evidence of concussion or bleeding in your brain, but—"

"I didn't hit my bloody *head*," he said, impatient now. "Listen—why don't you just treat me like a foreigner on holiday who doesn't know the any of the customs here. It might make things easier."

She studied him for several seconds through narrowed eyes, as if trying to gauge ulterior motives. Finally she sighed. "I've got other patients to look after—I can't stay much longer. But I'll humor you for now, since you're still recovering from your injuries. The answer is, there's nothing wrong with your name—if you're one of the Talented. But you claim not to be."

"So the Talented have different types of names?"

"Of course. Our names are short and simple: a syllable or two. That's all we need. The Talented's names are more elaborate. Like everything else they do," she added. Contempt crept into her tone, but then she cast him a sharp, fearful glance.

R. L. KING

Stone blinked. She was acting as if she expected him to punish her for her words. "So 'Alastair' is a Talented name?" Again, his mind went back to the scene of his attack. He couldn't remember the names of all three of the young men, but one had been something like 'Kethias.'

"It's not one I've ever heard, but the style is correct."

"I suppose the customs are different where I'm from, then. Because I certainly don't have any magic talent." *Not now, anyway,* he thought. "If I did, do you think I'd have let myself be dumped half-dead in the street like last week's rubbish?"

She tilted her head. "You *didn't* have a house identifier on you, which is odd," she admitted. "And your clothes—what was left of them—were all wrong. But…"

"But—?"

"But none of us knew what to make of this." She reached out and pulled his blanket down, uncovering his chest.

For a moment he didn't know what she was talking about, but then it dawned. Back home, he'd gotten into the habit of magically concealing the small but elaborate tattoo on the left side, over his heart—the one that helped him channel magical energy more efficiently, so he wouldn't have to take it from others as often. But now, without powers, he couldn't hide it. And no doubt about it—the thing would look magical, or at least unusual, to even the most ignorant of mundanes.

"Ah," he said, thinking fast. "That doesn't have anything to do with magic. Not *real* magic, anyway." He smiled ruefully. "It has more to do with getting mind-numbingly drunk with some friends a few years back. When I woke up the next morning…there it was. They told me I'd done it on a dare. It's a bit embarrassing now, but I'm stuck with it."

She looked as if she wasn't sure whether to believe him, but finally stood. "Anyway, I need to get back to my other patients. Someone will be by with something to eat shortly, and I'll stop in to check on you later this evening. If you need help with anything, there's a bell next to your bed."

Stone glanced at it. Sure enough, an actual bell—not a buzzer or button—lay on the table along with a small water pitcher and a covered glass. "Thank you."

She nodded. "By the way—a piece of advice for you, whoever you are."

"Yes?"

"If you truly *aren't* Talented, I'd suggest choosing another name to go by. That one will get you in trouble everywhere you go—among the Talented *or* us."

"I'll—keep that in mind." As she turned away, he said, "Oh—Doctor?"

"What is it?"

"You didn't answer my other question. I'm looking for a man named Harrison. Trevor Harrison. Have you heard of him?"

"No, I don't think so. Who is he?"

Damn good question. Stone realized he had no idea who or what Harrison was here—what he did, how important he was, even what part of the world he lived in. And that was assuming the man was even here at all. "I'm not sure, exactly. I suppose he must be one of these 'Talented,' since I've seen him do magic."

"What does he look like?"

Another good question, given that the odds were strong that the man was certainly a good enough mage to hide his true appearance under an illusionary mask. "Tall chap, about my age. Pale, slim, fit, black hair, gray eyes—dangerous looking, I suppose you'd say."

"There are a lot of dangerous people among the Talented," she said. "Sorry—the name doesn't ring a bell. But if you're not Talented, let me offer one more bit of advice: stay away from them. With very few exceptions, we're better off staying out of their way and away from their attention."

| CHAPTER SEVEN

DESPITE HIS BEST EFFORTS to remain awake and study his surroundings, Stone drifted in and out of deep sleep several times throughout the day. Another woman, a few years younger than the doctor he'd been talking to, woke him at one point to offer him a bowl of something that tasted like oatmeal, along with some fruit juice. He hadn't thought he was hungry until he smelled it, but the woman had to warn him not to eat too fast as he began wolfing it down.

"Easy," she said with a pleasant smile. "You'll make yourself sick if you eat too fast."

The food was filling, but simple and bland—he supposed hospital food was hospital food, no matter what dimension you were on. As he ate, his mind spun with questions he wanted to ask the young woman, but by the time he finished the fog of fatigue had settled over his head once more. He didn't remember drifting off, but when he woke again she was gone and the lights were even dimmer than before.

He was about to try sitting up so he could get a better look at his surroundings when he heard low voices to his left. He caught the word *Talented* and tensed. Were they talking about him again, speculating about whether he was telling the truth? He closed his eyes and strained to listen. Normally he'd feel guilty about eavesdropping, but if they had something planned for him, he wanted to know what it was.

"—don't know if I believe him or not," a female voice said. It sounded like the doctor he'd talked to earlier. "He certainly doesn't *act* like one of them. And the Talented wouldn't be caught dead in those rags he was wearing."

"It could be a trick," a man said. Milas, the one who'd been suspicious of him before. "You know how they are, Byra. Some of them do it just for sadistic pleasure. If we trust him and he turns out to be one of those—"

"I don't think he is," Byra said. "You saw him when they brought him in. You heard Tanissa. Some of those injuries were magical."

"That just means he's got powerful enemies." Milas's tone was stubborn. "Do you really want them showing up here, looking for him? They'd destroy us without a second thought."

She snorted. "Come on, Milas, don't be stupid. Do you honestly think any of the ivory-tower Talented would dirty their spotless boots in our little corner of the slums? You heard him—the Guard dropped him here. They probably figured he'd die and they'd be rid of him."

"From where, though? Do you think he was in Temolan?"

"He didn't have any identification or work papers on him when he was found—I suppose they could have taken them before they dumped him. Maybe he saw something he wasn't supposed to see."

Milas sighed. "Still, I'm telling you: as soon as he's able to leave, we should get him out of here. He's a stranger, and you know as well as I do that strangers are trouble."

"He'll leave when he's well enough to get by on his own," she said firmly. Then her tone softened. "Have a little compassion—you know he's going to have trouble if he doesn't know anyone and he has no identification. Let's not make it worse for him."

"That's not our problem. I know you like to take in strays, Byra. Normally that's admirable, but we're all better off letting this one go."

The two of them drifted off in separate directions, Milas leaving the room and Byra bending over one of the beds on the other side of the ward.

Stone lay still, feigning sleep as he mulled over what the two of them had said. What was "Temolan"? Was that the city he'd appeared in, the one with the cream-colored buildings and pale streets? Was that where the Talented lived?

Byra, the female doctor, had mentioned "our little corner of the slums"—it certainly made sense that the Talented and the non-magical people lived in different areas, especially given the clear social stratification between the two. She'd also mentioned "work papers," so perhaps that meant at least some of the non-magical class worked among the Talented. Judging by the way Stone's small test sample of the Talented treated anyone without magic power, coupled with the way Byra and Milas had spoken of them, it probably meant that anyone without magic who was allowed in the Talented's cities fulfilled menial roles. Did the haughty mages clean their own toilets or collect their own rubbish? Probably not—unless they'd figured out a way to do it with magic.

He rolled over, trying to get comfortable against the low-grade aches that still plagued him. Their healer had done a good job, but she hadn't taken care of everything. He'd still have to heal some of this the old-fashioned way, and that would take time.

Another thought struck him: if he *was* in the right place, if he hadn't buggered up the ritual and sent himself off gods knew where, that meant Trevor Harrison was here somewhere. When Stone had met him, he'd certainly seemed to be powerful—probably the most powerful mage he'd ever encountered, even more than William Desmond or Madame Huan or Stefan Kolinsky. But how did he stack up against the others here? Were all the mages as potent as he was? More so, even?

That was a frightening thought: a whole world full of arrogant sadists who did what they pleased without consequences? Stone was suddenly reminded of an old *Twilight Zone* episode he'd watched as a child—he used to be quite a fan of the show during his boarding-school days—where the terrified residents of a small town were all at the mercy of a young boy with unimaginable powers. A boy whose every capricious whim had to be followed to keep him from growing angry and sending anyone who displeased him "to the cornfield."

Were they all like that here? Was Harrison? Stone remembered when he'd first met the man, back in Las Vegas—when he, Jason, Verity, and Harrison had traveled in the Obsidian's helicopter out to an abandoned military base where the Evil had holed up with a collection of schoolchildren they'd planned to sacrifice. Harrison had, without a second thought or any apparent remorse, waved his hand

and wiped out nearly a dozen Evil-possessed survivalists. What would he do here, where mages apparently had free rein to do what they liked without consequences? Had Stone misjudged him, thinking the man would be willing to help if only he could find him?

He rolled over again. It was possible, but he didn't think so. Why would Harrison send him the notebook containing the rudiments of his magical techniques if he didn't intend him to study them? Why would he tell Verity what he'd said, if he hadn't thought Stone might use that information to locate him?

No, Stone decided. Harrison was a lot of things, but he'd never given any indication of cruelty or sadism. He was arrogant, sure, but it wasn't the same kind of arrogance that the three young men in Temolan displayed. Stone had seen enough of both types to know the difference—one was the province of those who'd been born and raised in privilege, where every person and circumstance in their lives had convinced them they were better than the rest of the world. The other came from inner confidence, from the certainty that the person could handle anything life threw at them. Both could be dangerous—the second moreso than the first sometimes, and worse still when both appeared in the same person—but Stone respected the second while having nothing but contempt for the first.

None of that mattered, though, if he couldn't *find* Harrison. If he was here, did he live among the Talented? Was he perhaps even one of their leaders? Byra hadn't heard of him, or at least claimed not to—but how familiar were the non-magical with the doings of the Talented? Did Harrison even use the same name here? If the Talented took elaborate, multi-syllable names, was "Trevor Harrison" simply the name he went by when he was on Earth?

He sighed and settled into the pillow. This was pointless. He likely didn't know Harrison's name here, what he looked like, or where he spent his time. With none of that information, he had no hope of finding the man—and if he couldn't find him, then without his magic he had no way of getting home. Right now, if someone had offered him the chance to return home, return to his life of black magic and taking unsatisfying power from Jason, he'd have accepted in a heartbeat. He'd taken a big chance coming here. Usually his big chances worked, or at least he could *make* them work. This time, though, he'd failed.

"Are you all right?" a soft voice asked. "Did you need something? Some pain medication, or something to help you sleep?"

He opened his eyes to see the faintly backlit form of the young woman who'd brought his meal earlier that day. "Sorry. Didn't realize I was thrashing around quite so much."

She chuckled. "It's all right. I saw you when they brought you in. You were in bad shape. You've made a lot of progress, but you've got to still be in some pain."

"I suppose I am," he admitted. One of the things he'd noticed earlier in the day was that the hospital seemed to be operating at a technology level somewhere in the area of the nineteen-fifties or –sixties on Earth. Something had seemed off to him until he realized what it was: there were no beeping monitors, digital displays, or any of the other kinds of ubiquitous electronic background gadgets you came to expect in a modern medical facility.

She fluffed his pillow, then gripped his wrist to take his pulse. After noting down the result on the chart at the foot of his bed, she returned to his side. "Is there anything I can bring you?"

"No, thank you. But—"

"Yes?"

He glanced around. During one of his previous periods of wakefulness, he'd determined that aside from himself, two of the other beds in the six-bed ward were occupied. One of the patients appeared to be deeply unconscious, and the other was snoring. "Would you have time to sit with me for a few minutes? I've got some questions I'd like to have answered, and the doctors seem quite busy."

She, too, looked around the ward. "I could stay for a little while," she said. "We'll have to talk quietly, though, so we don't wake the other patients up. Let me check on them now, and I'll come back."

"Thank you."

He sensed she was as curious about him as he was about her and about this world—she did a thorough but quick job of looking in on the other two patients and returned a few minutes later with a chair. "There," she said, switching on a faint light next to his bed. "My name is Jena, by the way."

He shifted to his side, where he could get a better look at her. She appeared to be in her early twenties, with light brown skin, short dark hair in loose curls, and kind eyes. Instead of the white coats the doctors wore, she was clad in what resembled old-fashioned pale-blue scrubs. "It's a pleasure, Jena. They tell me my name isn't doing me any favors here, so I suppose I should find something else to go by."

"So you're really not Talented?"

He chuckled. "I've been told I am in some areas, but—no. Not the way you seem to use that term here. I don't have any magical abilities." He'd tested this again last time he'd awakened—still no sign of anything. "I suppose you can just call me Stone. Could that be a proper name around here?"

"It's unusual," she said, tilting her head. "But at least no one will accuse you of impersonating the Talented."

"Stone it is, then." He shifted again; his body still ached too much to remain in one position for too long. "Do you mind if I ask you a few questions that might sound very stupid? The sorts of things you'd think everyone would know?"

"I'll try to answer them. They did say your mind might be slow coming back after your injuries."

Stone didn't contradict her; if having her think he'd addled his brains was what it took to get his questions answered, then so be it. "Right, then. First one: I get the impression that these 'Talented' you speak of live somewhere else. Is that correct?"

"Yes. They live in the floating cities."

"Floating cities?" Stone couldn't keep the astonishment out of his voice. Did these people have enough magical punch to raise *cities?* He might be in more trouble than he thought.

"Of course. Temolan is the closest one to us here. That's where they think you might have been attacked."

"How many of these cities are there?"

"Five. I don't know much about how the Talented do things—it's really better not to—but there are five of them."

"So all the Talented live in five cities?"

"Most of them do, yes. Some split their time between the cities and living among us, supervising work operations. A few live here full-time and help out, like Tanissa does."

"She's the healer who worked on me? I'd like to thank her, if I could."

"You'll probably be out of here before she comes back," Jena said. "There aren't many like her, so she travels around a lot. You were lucky she was nearby when you were brought in, or you'd probably have died. Your injuries were beyond what we could treat here without magic."

"Yes, that was what I heard the doctors say earlier. So it's rare for the Talented to help out here?"

She looked at him like he'd gone crazy. "Oh, yes. They rarely want anything to do with us. The ones who come here to supervise usually have the lowest power, so they choose to work with us so they have someone to feel superior to." Bitterness crept into her voice, but then she cast Stone a fearful glance. "I shouldn't have said that. I'm sorry."

"Why not?" He narrowed his eyes. "You act as if you're afraid of me, Jena. Why is that?" He raised his hands, indicating his bandages and obvious condition. "It's not as if I could attack you if I wanted to."

She gave an uncomfortable chuckle. "I'm sorry. You learn not to speak against the Talented, even when they aren't around. You never know when they might be listening."

Once again, Stone thought of the little *Twilight Zone* boy sending people to the cornfield. "So I take it they aren't kind to you lot."

"Most of them aren't, no. Why should they be? They've got all that power, and we're nothing but the Dim." This time, the bitterness in her voice was obvious and undiluted.

Stone tensed. "The Dim?"

"That's what they call us. The people who don't have any magic."

He remembered one of the bullies referring to him as a "dim pig." "I see. Bit pretentious, aren't they?"

"That's an understatement. Mostly, we just avoid them. Except for the people who work where they supervise—on the big farms, the factories, that kind of thing—we usually don't even see them. The more powerful ones don't get their shoes dirty coming down here among us."

Stone pondered. Some of this didn't make sense. "Please bear with me—I know this is going to sound like a very stupid and insensitive question. But if they're so powerful and cruel, why don't they just kill you all?"

"They need us," she said. "They may not like it, but there are a lot more of us than there are of them. We do all the jobs they won't lower themselves to. We run the farms—well, except for their small luxury farms in their cities. We make a lot of the things they use and perform a lot of services they don't want to do. If they killed us, all that would go away, and they'd have to do it themselves."

"But if they can raise cities into the sky, aren't they powerful enough to use magic to do all these menial tasks?"

She snorted. "Maybe, if they wanted to make the effort." Glancing up at him, she added, "Besides, they're not all cruel. Most of them are like us—they just want to be left alone to do what they want. They don't want to be involved with us any more than we want to be with them."

"You could have fooled me," Stone said. "You didn't see the three who attacked me."

"The young can be the worst." Jena glanced around the ward. "All that power, and they haven't been given much responsibility yet. Most of them grow up eventually."

"And what about this Tanissa? Why did she decide to come here and heal people instead of living in one of these miraculous floating cities?"

Jena shrugged. "She doesn't talk about it much. I don't think she likes to discuss her past. But she seems to feel more at home among our people than among the Talented. We're grateful she does."

"All right, I won't ask." Already, Stone was growing tired again. "I don't want to keep you from your job too long. One more question?"

"Of course."

"When I was listening to the doctors talk earlier, one of them mentioned something about 'here in the slums.' Was she referring to the town in general, or something else? When I was dumped here, I didn't see any sign of people, vehicles, anything—and the buildings looked destroyed."

She picked up the water pitcher from the bedside table and filled Stone's glass. "It feels strange talking about things that everyone knows. I almost feel like you're playing some kind of joke on me."

"I promise you, I'm not," Stone said. "I hope all of this will come back to me—but it's very different where I'm from. I grew up in a—sheltered area. I really do appreciate your answering my questions, as daft as they may sound."

Silence filled several more seconds. Jena looked at her hands in her lap, then back at him. "The place where you were found—almost nobody goes there anymore. The town used to be much larger, back before the war."

"The war?" Stone sat up a bit more, surprised. "What war? When was it?"

She gave him another suspicious look. "How can you not know about the war? I don't care where you're from—*everybody* knows about the war." She stood, suddenly looking more nervous than before. As she snapped off the lamp, Stone saw a mask fall over her expression, too. "I'm sorry—I really do need to get back to work. I'll be around if you need anything."

Stone didn't try to convince her to stay. He recognized that look: it was the look of someone who'd let the conversation get away from her, and had now realized she'd said more than she intended to.

He sipped his water as he watched her depart, going over what she'd told him. So he'd been right about the Talented being the mages, and Temolan being the city where he was attacked.

But a floating city? Possibly more than one? That seemed too impossible to believe. Stone was a powerful mage—at least back on Earth he was—and on his best day, with a fresh infusion of power, he might be able to levitate a large car. Based on what he'd seen Harrison do, he thought the man might manage a bus, or even a train engine. But an entire *city*? Even with a whole fleet of mages at Harrison's power level working together in a ritual, the energy required would be astronomical. And that was just to get it up there—unless they lifted it into orbit, something had to *keep* it up there. In spite of himself, his magical curiosity couldn't help reasserting itself. Did magic work that differently here? Was the native power level that much higher than on Earth, that such things weren't just possible, but commonplace?

The speculation was pointless, though. Nobody was going to tell him, even if he found someone to ask. Here he wasn't a mage. He had no powers—he was nothing more than one of the "Dim."

Gods, what an insulting term. Back on Earth, mages referred to the nonmagical as "mundanes," which some of those in the know considered mildly demeaning, but it was nothing compared to this. The fact that magical people here called themselves the "Talented" and others the "Dim" told him quite a lot of what he needed to know about how society worked here.

So many questions. His conversation with Jena had left him with more than it had answered. Where was he now, and what was this "war" she'd mentioned? It sounded as if large portions of the population of this place had died in it, leaving the ground-level cities in ruin. What kind of war had it been? How long ago?

He thought of the area where he'd been dumped—of how deserted it had been, and of the strange two-headed wolf-things with the glowing jaws. Had the things been some kind of mutants? Had the war been nuclear? It didn't seem as if this world had that kind of technology, unless the mages were hoarding it.

But no—at that point, a much more likely answer came to him. He sat up straighter, wanted to call Jena back over and ask her, but he didn't. She was already suspicious enough of him without making things worse. For now, he'd have to make do with his speculation, but based on the bits and pieces of information he'd gleaned so far, it seemed like a fairly likely one: whatever and whenever this war had been, it hadn't been nuclear.

It had been magical.

| CHAPTER EIGHT

TWO MORE DAYS PASSED before Stone felt well enough to get out of bed for longer than quick trips to the bathroom or brief walks around the ward.

During that time, he didn't gain any other useful information, despite his attempts to question Jena and the female doctor, Byra, whenever they came by to check on him or bring him something. Both continued to treat him with brisk cheerfulness, but every time he asked any questions about the world or its workings, they either deftly changed the subject or suddenly remembered something else they needed to do. He didn't even bother trying to ask the other doctor, Milas, anything—the man never worked with him directly and seemed to be actively avoiding him.

He spent most of his time falling in and out of light dozes. Apparently television didn't exist in this world (or at least not here in the ward), and since the translation spell he'd cast didn't extend to printed matter, he couldn't read anything even if they gave it to him. That meant, without anyone to talk to, his restless mind decided its best course of action was to shut down and let him heal in peace.

When he was awake, he tried to listen as much as he could to the conversations around the ward, hoping to pick up useful information when they didn't think he was paying attention. This strategy worked to some extent: he found out that the unconscious man in the other bed had been unresponsive for weeks and they didn't think he'd ever wake up, and the woman who'd been snoring the night he'd talked with Jena had been the victim of some kind of work accident. The doctors discharged her the following day with her leg swathed in a bulky white cast.

Two more patients arrived the next day: an angry young man with a collection of bruises and bloody slashes, and a girl with a high fever. Jena and another similarly-dressed man— Stone figured they were probably this place's version of nurses—installed the two of them in beds at opposite ends of the ward, and the doctors worked over them. Pretending to be asleep, Stone found out that the young man had gotten into an altercation with someone else at a bar (*at least they have bars here,* he thought with some satisfaction) and the child's mother had brought her here as a last resort when her own attempts at care had failed. He dozed off at that point, and by the time he awakened again the young man was gone.

On the third morning, he awoke to someone gently shaking his shoulder. "Mm?"

Byra stood next to him. "Good morning. How do you feel?"

He did a quick evaluation. "Not bad, all things considered. Tired, but the pain's mostly gone."

"I'm glad to hear that." She checked his temperature and his pulse, noted something on his chart, and stood next to the bed. "You'll be happy to know that I think we've done everything we can for you here, so we'll be sending you on your way today."

"On my way?" Normally, getting discharged from a hospital would be good news. Now, though, it occurred to him for the first time that if he left here, he had nowhere else to go.

"You can't stay here forever," she said gently. "We've been unusually light on patients, and the weekend's coming up, which always means more. We don't have enough beds to keep you here once you're healthy."

He sat up. "I've nowhere to go." He looked down at the light pajama-style pants he wore as his only garment. "I don't even have any other clothes, unless mine survived."

"They didn't, unfortunately, except for your boots and belt. But I think we can find you something to wear."

He took a couple of deep breaths as he tried to get his thoughts in order. He must have been more out of it than he thought—he had spent literally no time thinking about what he'd do when he got out of here. He had no money—did they even use money here?—and no way to earn any. He didn't know the city, he couldn't read the signs, and aside from Byra and Jena, he knew no other people here.

"I—I'm not sure what to do," he admitted. "Do you have any suggestions? Do I owe you for the care here? I don't have any money."

"Patients here pay what they can," Byra said. "Don't worry about that. But you'll need to find a job and a place to stay. You can check the newspapers for job listings, or sometimes merchants will put signs in their windows."

Stone looked at his hands, feeling suddenly frustrated and ashamed. Here he was, a respected professor at one of the most prestigious universities on Earth, and he couldn't even read a fast-food menu in this world. "I—" he began, surprised at how difficult it was to make the admission. "As I told you before, I'm not from this area. I can speak your language, but…I can't read it."

Byra sighed. "All right. All right, you stay here for now and I'll ask around. A lot of people in the area owe us favors, so maybe I can find someone who can give you a job and a place to stay. Temporarily, anyway. Do you have any skills that might help you?"

"Unfortunately, nothing that doesn't involve reading." *Or magic,* he added to himself.

"Don't worry—I'll find you something." She pointed at his chest. "My advice, though, is to keep that tattoo covered, and don't say anything to make people suspicious. If they think you've got anything to do with the Talented, they won't want to take a risk with you. Just keep your head down and don't talk too much—at least until you get more familiar with the area. It's for your own good."

Stone wasn't sure how well he'd be able to do that—he had to get started looking for Harrison soon—but for now she was probably right. Best to get more familiar with the world outside this ward before he made any waves. "Thank you, Doctor. I appreciate the help."

"Of course. I can't just put you out on the street—I don't think you'd do very well, to be honest. You don't seem the type who's used to living rough. Jena will bring your breakfast soon, so stay here and I'll let you know what I find out."

She returned two hours later. Stone had finished a breakfast of oatmeal and eggs and was sitting up in bed, watching Jena and the other nurse as they made their rounds, when she came in carrying a bag. "Good news," she said when she reached Stone.

"You found me a job?"

"I did. Faran at the butcher shop needs someone to sweep up and make deliveries." She paused, watching him in expectation.

"Er—all right. Thank you."

"You don't have an objection to that?"

"Is there some reason I would?" He tilted his head, feeling he was missing something.

Her gaze lingered on him for several more seconds. "Most of the Talented find red meat distasteful." She shook her head as if clearing a thought. "Anyway, never mind. The job doesn't pay much, but Faran says you can use the spare room in back of his shop." She looked apologetic. "It's not much, but everyone's belt is tight around here. I was lucky to catch him—he was going to hire someone else, but he's taking you on as a favor to us since we patched him up last year when he slashed his arm."

Beggars couldn't be choosers, Stone supposed, and at least making deliveries would get him out in the world where he could start inquiring about Harrison once he got his feet under him. "Thank you. I appreciate it. I appreciate everything you've done for me. And please give Tanissa my thanks as well. I'd still like to tell her in person if I can." He had more than thanks in mind: as one of the Talented, even one who spent most of her time away from those like her, she might be his best chance of finding Harrison.

"I'll let her know. I'll give Faran a call if she stops in, and if he can spare you maybe you can come by."

"Thank you." Another piece of information gained: they had a way to make calls here. So they were *that* technologically advanced, at least.

Byra held up the bag. "I found you some clothes—they might not be a perfect fit, but I think they should be close. Go ahead and get dressed, and then we'll see how you're doing and get you out of here. Come out when you're ready." She pulled a curtain around the bed and departed.

Stone swung his legs out of the bed and experimentally stood. Traces of the old lightheadedness remained and he still felt weak, but given the shape he'd been in a week ago, he couldn't complain. He ran his hand through his tangled hair, then traced it along his jaw, feeling heavy stubble. More than just about anything right now he wanted a proper shower and a shave, but that could wait until he got where he was going.

He investigated the bag, spreading the clothes on the bed to examine them. They looked used but clean: two rough, long-sleeved shirts—one green plaid, one faded blue; a shapeless brown jacket; dark blue workman's trousers with a patch on the left knee; two pairs of basic white boxers and socks. The styles were similar to what he might see on Earth, but subtly different enough to remind him he was on another world: the shirt had no collar, for example, and fastened with hooks and loops instead of buttons, and the trousers buttoned rather than zipped. He couldn't read the words stitched on the tags inside them.

Moving as fast as he dared he donned the clothes, choosing the blue shirt. As Byra had thought, none of them fit him quite right: the shirt and jacket were little too large, and the trousers a little too short. At least he had his own boots, which was something. He didn't have access to a mirror, but that was probably just as well, since between the clothes, the scruffy week-old beard, and the wild hair, he was sure he looked like a badly-dressed scarecrow. *Good thing Byra already got you a job,* he thought wryly, wondering what kind of impression he'd make on a potential employer looking like this.

He put the remaining clothes in the bag, then pushed the curtain aside and looked around for the doctor. She wasn't there, but Jena was. "You're looking better," she said, smiling. "You've got some color in your cheeks."

"I'm feeling better, thanks to everyone here." Almost all of the bandages were gone and the bruises from his ordeal had faded by now, though he could tell he'd lost weight.

"Come on—I'll take you to the doctor. I hope everything goes well with you."

He followed her out, realizing this was the first time since he'd arrived here that he'd left the ward. Outside was an institutional-looking hallway lined with a few doors, most of them closed. The beige paint was peeling, the floor was cracked, and the ceiling tiles were stained, all reinforcing Stone's initial guess that this wasn't a high-end facility. As they passed an open doorway, he glanced through and spotted several people sitting or slumping in chairs, most of them looking injured or unwell.

Jena knocked on a half-open door farther down the hall. "Doctor, he's ready," she called, then pushed it open. She patted Stone's shoulder. "Good luck. It was a pleasure to meet you." And then she was gone, hurrying back toward the ward.

Byra sat at a desk amid stacks of folders, papers, and periodicals. She glanced up and looked Stone over. "Not a bad fit," she said. When he tried to offer her the bag containing the other clothes, she waved him off. "You keep them, so you'll have a change. Pull up a chair."

Stone lowered himself into the room's only other chair and waited.

"None of this is easy for you, is it?" she asked, studying him.

He saw no point in denying it. "Not really. I'm grateful for everything you've done for me—including the job—but I don't know how well suited I'll be for it, honestly."

"I know. It's obvious to me you're an educated man, wherever you come from. I'm still not convinced you don't have some connection with the Talented, but that's your business, not mine, as long as you don't cause trouble for us." She gave him a rueful smile. "But unfortunately, with no identification, no work papers—you don't have too many options. I've already explained your situation to Faran, and he's going to arrange to get you some forged papers in case you get stopped, but I won't lie to you: they won't stand up to much scrutiny, especially from the Talented. You won't be able to work in Temolan with them, even if you wanted to."

Stone thought he'd probably have to go to Temolan eventually on his search for Harrison, but he knew she was right. He'd bet money—if he had any—that the kind of identification required to work in the mages' city had some magical component to it, one the people down here couldn't duplicate. "I understand."

"And…even if the identification weren't a problem, the fact that you can't read our language will limit your options too. You're well-spoken, at least, so that will help." She patted his hand. "I know this is going to be hard for you, but as I said before, if you want my advice your best strategy is to keep your head down and your ears open. Don't get noticed by too many people. Pretend you're a bit slow-witted until you're more comfortable with the way things work around here. I can tell by just my short interaction with you that it will be tough. You don't strike me as the kind of man who likes anyone to think he's slow. But trust me, it's the safest way."

"I suppose it is." He indicated the papers, wanting nothing more now than to get out into the world, figure out what he was supposed to be doing, and get settled in so he could start looking for Harrison. "Is there anything I need to sign to get out of here?"

She pulled a clipboard from beneath a pile of papers, scribbled something on it, and slid it over to him. "Just this. I know you can't read it, but all it says is that both you as the patient and I as your doctor agree you're ready to be discharged. Sign on the bottom left."

Stone studied the page, trying to make sense of any of the strange printing that covered it. The language here didn't look like anything he'd seen on Earth; the alphabet looked vaguely runic, utilitarian and angular, though some of the characters had a tantalizing familiarity. Several of the blanks included typewritten words in the same script; he wondered which of them was supposed to be his name. He took the pen and scrawled his signature, glad it was illegible enough that no one would be able to read it.

She gave him a copy and unearthed a telephone. "I've got to get back to work, but I'll call Faran and have him pick you up. You can wait in the waiting room or outside, whichever you like. It's been good meeting you, Stone—whoever you are."

Byra didn't seem to be one for long goodbyes, so Stone rose, put the folded copy in his pocket, and left with his bag of spare clothes.

He opted not to wait in the waiting room. For one thing, there were no available places—every one of the mismatched chairs was occupied by either a sick or injured person or someone accompanying them. They all looked up and studied Stone with varying degrees of disinterest as he crossed the room and opened the door to the outside world, and before it swung closed he heard the unmistakable sound of a child retching. *Good choice,* he decided.

Outside, he stepped away from the door and paused for a look around. If he didn't know better, he'd have thought he was still on Earth, even despite the subtle but obvious differences. Those could be explained by a different location in the world, after all. He stood on what looked like a side street in a busy, older city. The buildings were mostly made of dark red brick; they looked weathered and poorly maintained. The sidewalk in front of him was cracked, as was the street—though neither were in as bad shape as the place where he'd been dropped. Across the street he saw a few buildings that looked like businesses, with more of the strange angular writing in their windows along with images that probably indicated their purpose.

None of the buildings were tall, with the tallest he could see only about five stories. Some looked as if they'd once been taller but their top floors had long ago crumbled or been broken off. From the war, perhaps? Stone decided he needed to find out more about this war, even though nobody seemed to want to talk about it. He looked further up, hoping to spot the floating city Jena had described, but the cloud-choked sky revealed nothing.

He noticed a few vehicles, but far fewer than he might have expected given his surroundings. All of them looked somewhat but not quite like Earth vehicles—older, battered, and functional as opposed to sleek or beautiful, with solid construction and dull paint jobs. Some were parked along the street, while a smaller number rolled slowly by. Occasionally people walked past in singles or pairs, glancing at Stone but paying him little attention. At least he mostly blended in now—the other people sported similar well-worn work clothes, though most of theirs fit better than Stone's did. Nowhere did he see the high-collared, sweeping long coats that seemed to mark the Talented.

He was looking around, noting the subtle differences in the design of the cars, the architecture of the buildings, even the light, when something that had been nagging at his subconscious finally bubbled to the surface: there wasn't any graffiti, nor any sign of litter blown against the nearby walls. He narrowed his eyes, focusing on the structures closest to him. Surely he must have missed it—with the rough, inner-city look of this place and what Byra had said about "everyone tightening their belts around here," it seemed unthinkable that some subset of unemployed young people wouldn't display their frustration by tagging up their territory.

But no—the structures, though dirty and weather-worn, were devoid of street art, and no food wrappers, drink cans, or wadded newspapers tumbled by in the faint breeze.

Interesting, Stone thought, wondering if there was a reason for it beyond an overly enthusiastic neighborhood litter-abatement program.

A horn honked, startling him. As he turned, a voice called, "You Stone?"

A boxy gray truck with a small pickup bed was pulling into an open space near him. Hand-painted on the truck's door was more of the angular script, along with the simple image of a creature that resembled a fat, short-legged red cow.

A man leaned out the vehicle's window, one muscular arm hanging over the doorframe. He looked to be in his fifties, with short, brush-cut hair, a neat mustache, and a square-jawed, heavy-browed face. He regarded Stone critically with small, dark eyes.

"Er—yes," Stone said. "You must be Faran."

"Yeah. Get in. I'm already late with a delivery for takin' the time to pick you up."

Stone hurried around the front of the truck and climbed in. Faran drove off before he'd even settled himself on the wide, stained bench seat. The truck's engine rumbled and wheezed, occasionally backfiring with a loud *pop,* as it jounced over the uneven pavement. The interior smelled like the aftermath of a roast-beef sandwich.

"So, Byra says you're not from around here." Faran kept his eyes on the road as he spoke, even though there was hardly any traffic.

"No."

"Got yourself beat up pretty good," he said. "Almost died, she told me."

"I'm much better now. Thanks to Byra and the others."

"Yeah. She said they had to get their pet Zap in to heal you up. I don't trust those bastards—not even the tame ones. Ain't no such thing as a tame Zap, not really."

Stone blinked. "Zap?"

"You know—the Talented." His sarcastic tone put finger quotes around the word. He glanced sideways in suspicion. "You ain't in with 'em, are you?"

"No. In fact, some of them were responsible for what happened to me."

Once again Faran glanced sharply sideways. "Byra said you were a little slow in the head. You don't sound it."

Stone was surprised at how much the words stung, but he supposed he shouldn't be. His magic might be gone, but his intellect was fine, and there was nothing wrong with his ego. "I'm still recovering. And I'm not familiar with the customs here. Byra thought it best if I didn't draw attention to myself."

"Well, you're messin' that up already. But hey, I don't care. You work hard and don't give me any trouble, we'll do fine. I don't give a damn about your history, as long as you're not a Zap or one o' their lapdogs."

"No need for concern."

"Good."

Faran subsided into silence. Stone leaned back in his seat, gazing out the window and watching the buildings go by. As they drove, he noticed the area grew marginally less blasted-looking: the buildings were cleaner and better maintained, the streets less cracked and potholed, and the people's clothes of better quality. Still, it was obvious to Stone that the area still suffered from poverty. He still didn't see nearly as many vehicles as he would in a similar Earth city. "Do most people not own vehicles here?" he asked.

"What?" Faran pulled the truck in next to what looked like a small market.

"Vehicles. Cars, trucks. I haven't seen many around."

"You *are* from somewhere else," the butcher said. He patted the truck's cracked dashboard. "Only reason I still have this is because I work on it myself to keep it running. Anyway, enough talk. You can start doing your job now. Get the order for the market out of the back and take it inside."

Stone got out of the truck and peered into the bed. A few boxes lay there, along with several packages wrapped in paper and string. Each had something scrawled on it in the familiar script. He almost told Faran he couldn't read, but then glanced at the painted sign on the market's window. One of the boxes had the same characters written on it. He checked to make sure it was the only one, then grabbed it and hurried toward the market's door. A quick look revealed Faran leaned back in his seat, picking at his fingernails with a pocketknife.

Aware of the butcher's impatience, he didn't waste time. He strode to the back of the small, dimly lit market and handed the box to a heavyset woman in an apron, getting only a brief impression of the mixed aromas of vegetables, breads, and meats as he passed the narrow, sparsely-stacked shelves.

"About time," the woman grumbled, eyeing him with suspicion. "Where's Faran?"

Stone wondered if he was supposed to collect payment, but decided Faran probably would have told him so if he was. "I'm—his new deliveryman. Thank you for your business," he said, and headed back out before she initiated further conversation.

There were no more deliveries after that. Faran drove the rest of the way in silence, pulling the wheezing truck into a narrow alley next to a small shop on a busy street. The same fat, red cow was painted on the front window. Stone couldn't be sure, but he estimated they were less than a mile or two from the hospital.

Faran got out and jerked his head toward the remaining packages in the truck's bed. "Bring those inside," he ordered. "Then I'll show you where you'll be sleeping." Without waiting for a reply, he disappeared into the shop. A bell on the door jangled as it slammed shut.

"Well. All right, then," Stone murmured. Clearly his new employer wouldn't win any personality contests. He wondered if the man had given him the job under protest, only because Byra had exercised some leverage over him. Was her hospital the only one in the area, or the only one that offered the services of a Talented healer? Faran might not approve of "Zaps," but it was hard to deny the advantage of having magical healing available for severe injuries.

It took him two trips to bring in all the packages. He stacked them in the storeroom where Faran indicated, trying hard not to show that even this slight effort had already tired him. Even if he was fully healed now, a week on his back in bed meant it would take time to recover his strength.

The butcher shop looked like something out of an old movie. Small and compact, it had the same look of being firmly settled in an Earth time period somewhere between the Forties and the Sixties. The front section contained a display case stocked with various cuts of meat, a counter, several hand-drawn signs, and not much else. The display case had refrigeration, but the unit providing it looked old and mechanical. The scales on top were mechanical too. A woman about the same age as Faran, wearing a white full-body apron streaked with blood and meat juice, watched Stone silently from behind the counter as he brought in the packages. Her eyes were narrow, her face set in an expression that wasn't quite a chilly frown, but it was on its way there.

"Come on," Faran ordered after Stone had brought in the last of the packages and retrieved his bag of spare clothes from the truck. "I'll show you where you'll stay, and then you can have lunch and get started. No slacking around here. I told Byra I'd give you a job, but that don't mean you're not gonna have to work hard."

"I have no problem with work," Stone assured him, hoping his endurance would hold out until he could get some rest.

"That's what I like to hear."

Faran led him through the shop, past the woman ("That's my wife, Runa," he said on the way by) down a narrow hallway in the back. He pushed open a door at the end of the hall and stood aside. "You can sleep here. Bath's next door down."

The room was barely large enough to accommodate a narrow bed and a wooden dresser not much bigger than a nightstand. A small lamp with a stained shade sat on top of the dresser next to a ticking mechanical clock with too many unfamiliar numbers. A tiny window with a skewed shade revealed a view of a dingy alleyway.

"It ain't much," Faran said, "but you won't be spendin' much time in it. Runa left you a few things in the bathroom, since Byra said you didn't have much."

"Thank you," Stone said, tossing his bag of clothes on the bed. "I appreciate your kindness."

"Oh, it ain't kindness. Pay for the job is forty bucks a week, but I'm keepin' twenty for your room and board, and another one this week for the stuff Runa got. No free rides around here."

Stone nodded, wondering if the currency here really was "bucks" or if the translation spell had rendered it into something he'd understand. "That's fine. Thank you."

"Yeah." Faran's voice held grudging approval, probably because Stone hadn't objected to the terms. "You'll eat good, though—you *do* eat meat, right?"

"Of course."

"Good. Makes me sick the way some people try to act like the damn Zaps and think they're too good for honest meat." He shook his head in disgust. "Can't even imagine why anybody'd want to imitate those bastards. Suck-ups. Anyway—" He glanced at his old watch. "Take a little time to get cleaned up, then come find Runa in the shop for your lunch and we'll talk about the job." He closed the door behind him, leaving Stone alone in the room.

He let his breath out slowly and gazed for a moment out the small window, wishing not for the first time that he'd never made the decision to come here. He'd already been here more than a week and wasn't a bit closer to finding Harrison, and now he was dependent on this job for food and a place to sleep. He doubted the gruff Faran would allow him much time off for his investigations—especially considering the man's opinion of the Talented—and until he got his endurance back, he probably wouldn't have much energy to do anything in whatever free time he was allowed. Right now more than anything he wanted to lie down on the narrow, uncomfortable-looking bed and sleep for two or three hours, but that wasn't an option. If he pissed Faran off enough to sack him already, he'd be on the street with nowhere to go.

Instead, he left the room and investigated the bathroom down the hall. It was barely large enough to turn around in, but it was clean and included a tiny shower cubicle. Laid out on the small sink were a wrapped toothbrush, toothpaste, a bar of soap, a comb, and an old-fashioned razor.

When he emerged from the bathroom twenty minutes later following a hot shower and a shave, he felt much more human, even despite the ill-fitting clothes. He headed back to the front of the shop and found Runa behind the counter, wrapping up an order for a young woman with a toddler boy. He waited until she finished and the customer left.

Runa looked him up and down and nodded unsmiling approval. "You look more respectable now, at least." She hooked a thumb toward a door. "Faran's in the back with your lunch."

Cheery couple, Stone thought. He wondered how much of it was due to their individual personalities, and how much to the hardship of living in this world without any magic talent.

The door led to a small room with a table and four wooden chairs, a refrigerator that looked even older than the unit out front, and two mismatched easy chairs. Faran sat at the table, halfway through a large sandwich. A closed envelope lay next to his plate, and another sandwich and a tall glass of water sat at the empty place across from him.

"Sit down," he said, waving Stone toward the chair. "You eat, I'll talk. We need to go over some things."

Stone, realizing how hungry he was at the sight of the food, immediately started on the sandwich. It was simple, made of only meat and bread, but delicious. The meat looked like beef, but didn't quite taste like anything Stone had ever eaten before.

Faran nodded once, apparently satisfied his new employee wasn't some kind of vegetarian Zap sympathizer. "Okay," he said. "First thing is, your ID. I want you to know I'm takin' a chance here, and I'm only doin' it as a favor to Byra. Understand?"

Stone nodded and swallowed his current mouthful of sandwich. "Of course. I appreciate this."

Faran grunted. He opened the envelope and pulled out a folded paper and a card. "She said you don't come from around here, and maybe things work different where you're from. That's strange, because I thought it was the same everywhere, but whatever. Anyway, here you have to carry your identification and your work papers with you all the time. Believe me, you don't want to get caught without 'em if one of those Zap bastards asks you for 'em." His voice dripped with contempt and bitterness.

"Yes—that's how I ended up in hospital in the first place. So you're telling me that these—er—Zaps can stop anyone they like, for whatever reason they like? Any of them can do this, not just the authorities?"

"They ain't s'posed to. But they do. And what are you gonna do about it? If you piss 'em off they can set you on fire, make your eyes pop out of your head, lift you fifty feet up in the air and drop you—and there ain't a damn thing you can do about it. That's why you stay away from 'em and don't get noticed. Just do your job and keep your head down, and you'll be fine. They hardly ever show up in our part of town unless they have some reason. One good thing about livin' in this hellhole, I guess."

"Understood." Stone wondered how such a society managed to keep running for as long as this one apparently had, but if the mage class was as powerful as it sounded like they were, the "Dim" had little recourse. How could you rise up against a group of people who could kill anyone they chose from a distance? It didn't appear that the tech level here was high enough to allow for things like large-scale mundane weapons of mass destruction, even if the mages didn't have ways to protect against them.

Faran pushed the paper and the card across the table. "Keep the card in your wallet, if you got one, and the papers on you whenever you're out on the streets. Like I said, though—they won't stand up to a lot of examination, so keep out of trouble."

Shame prickled at the back of Stone's neck again, but his next question couldn't be helped: "I'm not sure Byra told you—I obviously speak your language, but I haven't learned to read it yet. Can you tell me if there's anything on these documents I need to be aware of, in case someone asks me about it?"

The butcher stared at him in shocked frustration. "You can't read? How the hell are you gonna make deliveries if you can't read?"

"Don't worry," Stone said quickly. "I learn fast, and there's nothing wrong with my memory. If you mark on a map where the deliveries go, I'll get them there. I promise."

For several seconds Faran looked at him, as if trying to decide if he was worth taking a chance on. "Yeah, fine," he said at last. "We'll try it, anyway, but if you're too slow I'm gonna have to let you go. There's another kid who wants the job, and he *can* read."

He nodded at the card. "All that says is your name and that you live and work here. The papers say the same thing, with a little more detail about your job and that kind of stuff." His gaze flicked up. "What kind of name is 'Stone,' anyway?"

"It's…more common where I come from." Stone finished his sandwich. "Byra told me this ID card won't pass inspection in Temolan. Do some of the nonmagical people work there?"

Faran's eyes narrowed. "You're a strange guy, Stone. You sound smart, but you don't know things every five-year-old knows."

Stone didn't reply.

"Yeah. Some of 'em do," Faran said with a sigh, after waiting him out for a while. "You need special permission, and the Zaps watch the people up there a lot closer than they do here. Me, I don't know why anybody'd want to do it, but some people are willing to put up with more, I guess. Trust me—you don't wanna go there anyway. Stay down here and stay outta trouble." His expression hardened. "Favor or not, I get one complaint about you and you're out. You do what you're told, don't make trouble with the Zaps, and we'll be fine. Got it?"

Stone paused a moment to get his annoyance under control. This man acted like a job delivering meat and cleaning up the butcher shop was something worthy of high-level security clearance and fawning gratitude. Still, he needed money, and right now this was the only game in town. Maybe he could find something else later, but for now he'd have to put up with Faran's treatment. "I've got it, yes."

"Good." Faran drained the remainder of his water, finished his sandwich, and pushed his chair back. "Come on. I'll start you out on some close-by deliveries so you can get used to the area, and when you finish those you can clean up the shop after we close."

Stone followed him to the storeroom and listened as he pointed out a stack of wrapped packages in a large chest freezer and marked the location of each delivery on a hand-drawn map of the area. Naturally all the text on it was in the unfamiliar language, but a map was a map.

"These are all businesses you're deliverin' to," Faran told him. "Just match up the address on the package with what's on the windows, and you should be fine. You don't need to pick up any payment—it's already arranged. Just have 'em sign for the delivery. You can keep any tips they give you, but don't count on any, and don't ask for any. Do you understand?"

Again, Stone's annoyance rose. The man spoke slowly and distinctly to him as if he were dull-witted. "As I said, don't worry—I've got it." He took the map and put it in his coat pocket.

Faran eyed him sideways, but finally nodded. He pointed out the broom, rags, and other cleaning implements. "Make sure you scrub all the counters, pick up any scraps on the floor, mop, and sweep up the front. I want to see the place spotless. Once you finish the deliveries and cleaning, you're on your own until tomorrow. You can pick up your dinner from Runa after sundown. You'll start at sunrise tomorrow morning. Now go on—I'm already behind schedule today."

As he turned to depart, something occurred to Stone. "Wait—one more question."

"What is it?" Faran sounded impatient.

"How do I make the deliveries? Am I walking, or using your truck, or—"

"Nobody drives my truck but me. There's an old bicycle out back you can use. Now go on, before I change my mind about hirin' the other guy."

"Right…" Stone murmured. He pulled the map back out and spent the next few minutes comparing it to the packages in the freezer, then collected a few and headed out of the shop.

Faran hadn't been kidding about the "old bicycle." The thing that leaned against the wall behind the shop looked like something out of a museum, heavy and ungainly with a hard leather seat, chipped black paint, substantial fenders fore and aft, and big, well-worn balloon tires. A small, enclosed two-wheeled trailer cart attached to the back sported the shop's red-cow logo image and the same writing as on Faran's truck.

Stone eyed it dubiously—he hadn't ridden a bicycle since his University days, and never one with a trailer—but it was definitely better than walking, especially carrying the packages. He consulted the map one more time to fix his first couple delivery locations in his mind, loaded the packages in the trailer, then mounted the contraption and set off.

The city looked marginally less intimidating in the daylight, an odd combination of the familiar and the tantalizingly alien. Stone pedaled along the side of the street, splitting his attention between watching where he was going and taking in the area around the shop.

It wasn't too hot, fortunately. Patchy clouds dominated the sky, which was a little darker blue than Stone was used to; he took a few moments to once again try locating the floating city, and was disappointed when he found it: a small, dark spot hovering so high above them that he couldn't even be sure it was real. He'd need binoculars or a telescope to make out any detail, and since he hadn't seen any of those around here, he reluctantly decided it wasn't worth the effort.

The street, made of a substance similar to asphalt, still showed signs that it had rained recently. It bore no markings—no lines indicating traffic flow, crosswalks, or limit lines. Simple, utilitarian street lights hung from poles at regular intervals, and the only signs he spotted were on each corner, marking street names. The old, heavy bike with its trailer jounced and juddered over the frequent cracks in the street's surface, cushioned somewhat by the big tires.

He paused at each street corner, a couple times having to pull out his map and consult it before continuing straight or making a turn. He was glad there wasn't much vehicle traffic, though he did get passed by several other people on bicycles. Many of them flashed him odd, curious glances, but didn't stop or say anything to him as they went by.

He'd deliberately picked the closest building marked on the map for his first delivery, even though it would ultimately make more sense to head out to the farthest and work his way back. He'd do that once he got a better idea of the geography, but for now he wanted to get a success under his belt. Only a couple blocks from Faran's place, he pulled the bike to a stop in front of a small shop in the middle of a block.

Like most of the other buildings he'd seen, this one was made of dark red brick. It had two stories, and looked as if the proprietors might live above their business. He compared the writing on the window to the top package in the trailer, and was pleased to see they matched. The image above the writing, a flower with yellow petals, gave no indication of the business's purpose, but from the aromas wafting out from the open door, he guessed it was a restaurant. He grabbed the package and paused, wondering if it was safe to leave the bike with the other parcels while he went inside.

"You Faran's new delivery boy?" came a gruff voice from the restaurant's doorway.

Stone jerked his head up to see a small, beetle-browed man regarding him.

"Er—yes, I suppose I am."

"Deliveries around the back, fool," the man snapped. "You think the customers want to look at ya?"

"Right. Sorry. It's my first day."

"Yeah, fine." He shook his head in disgust. "I swear they get simpler every time. Go on—I'll meet you back there."

I guess I'm not getting a tip from this *one,* Stone thought wryly as he wheeled the bike down a narrow alley toward the rear of the building. He forced himself not to take the 'simpler every time' comment personally, though it wasn't easy. Once again, his frustration grew: he should be out looking for Harrison, not getting insulted by ill-tempered restauranteurs.

The man was waiting for him when he arrived at the back door, and stood aside to let him enter. "Take 'em in and stack 'em in the freezer there."

When Stone had finished carrying the packages inside and putting them in the freezer as indicated, the man muttered something that might have been a grudging thank-you, waiting for him to leave, then slammed the door behind him.

That went well. Stone studied the door for a moment, noticing a little bell next to it. Perhaps he was supposed to ring that to signal the owners of a delivery. Would have been nice for Faran to tell him that.

He continued making deliveries for the rest of the afternoon, heading back to the shop twice to pick up more packages. He was pleased to discover that his guess had been correct: every business location he visited had the same bell at the back door, and ringing it did summon someone to accept the delivery. By the time he rolled back in behind Faran's shop, tired but satisfied, he'd learned most of the streets in the area, memorized the delivery locations and many of the other nearby businesses, and even managed to collect a couple of tips—silver coins that jingled in his pocket. He had no idea how much they were worth, but at least he'd earned a bit of money. Maybe even enough for a drink. He'd noted the location of a bar a few streets away from the shop— whatever dimension you were on, a bar was a bar. Perhaps he could get some answers about Harrison there later along with his drink.

"About time," Faran said gruffly as he came in after parking the bike in the back where he'd gotten it. The butcher was behind the counter in the shop, wrapping up an order of something that looked like dark brown chicken. "How'd the deliveries go?"

"Fine." Stone paused a moment to catch his breath; normally, the distance he'd gone today wouldn't have tired him in the slightest, but after his week in the hospital his endurance hadn't returned yet.

"Okay, good. Didn't have anybody callin' to complain about you, so that's a good thing. I'm about to close up here. You can get started with the cleanin' as soon as I'm out."

Stone was more concerned about the cleaning than he was about the deliveries, since he wasn't sure what level of detail Faran wanted and in any case he had little experience with this kind of task. At least he didn't have many tools to work with: a broom, a mop, a bucket, a jug of cleaning fluid, a collection of rags, and something in a spray bottle that smelled like bleach. Also to his advantage, the shop wasn't large. He set to work, hoping his stamina would hold out long enough for him to complete the job.

It took him nearly two hours to finish cleaning up the scraps behind the counter, sweeping and mopping the floor, wiping down all the counters and the display cases, and putting all the implements back in the closet. By the time he was done, between all the deliveries and the cleaning he felt as if he'd worked harder than he had in years—which was probably true, given that the most strenuous thing he had to do at Stanford was walk from his office to his classes. He sat down, taking a moment to catch his breath. Hot and sweaty, he wanted nothing more than a shower before dinner.

The door to the back opened and Faran's wife Runa appeared, apron-clad and red-faced. "You want dinner?" she asked. She still sounded as if something about him rubbed her the wrong way.

"Er—yes, thank you. I'm sorry. Am I late?" He glanced around the shop, but it had no clock. "Lost track of time."

"Yeah, you're late. Don't let it happen again. Come on— I'm not runnin' a short-order kitchen here. You miss dinner-time, you're on your own from now on. Pick it up and take it back to your room. You can bring the dishes back in the morning."

He followed her to the back, where she handed him a covered plate along with utensils rolled into a paper napkin and an open brown bottle. "Thank you," he said, and got only a grunt in reply.

As unappealing as the company was, at least the food was good. After washing his hands in the bathroom (the shower would have to wait until after dinner at this point) he uncovered the plate to find several slices of hot roast meat, something pale green that otherwise looked and tasted like mashed potatoes, and a hunk of thick brown bread slathered in butter.

His room didn't have a table, so he sat on the bed with the plate balanced on his lap and his back against the wall. As he ate, his thoughts turned to what was going on back home. It had been a week now, assuming time worked the same here as it did on Earth. Had Verity told Jason about where he'd gone? At least he didn't have to worry about work for a while—he hadn't had much to do at the University this summer, and he'd arranged for a teaching assistant to take over with help from Mackenzie Hubbard, his fellow Occult Studies professor. Hubbard hadn't been happy about it, but Stone had covered for the man enough times over the last few years that he didn't think it would be a problem. That meant nobody expected him back until September.

Would he even *get* back by September? Idly he tried his magic again, trying first to view the aura around his out-stretched hand, and then to levitate the plate in his lap.

Nothing.

Not even a glimmer to encourage him that it might come back at some point, as it always had before.

A sudden thought struck him and he jerked up straight, nearly dislodging the plate: perhaps his magic wasn't back because the process of sending himself to this world had somehow drained his power. He was a black mage now— between everything else happening recently, he'd almost for-gotten about that! He needed power from an outside source to do magic. If the trip had siphoned off that power, he might just need a new infusion.

Of course, even without power he should be able to do simple things like read auras, but maybe things worked differently here.

That brought up new problems, though: was he willing to risk taking power from some stranger to test his theory? That was why he was here in the first place: because he didn't *want* to do that—in fact, didn't trust himself to do that.

He sighed, setting the plate and bottle aside on the tiny nightstand and swinging his legs around so he lay down on the narrow bed. He'd have to come up with an answer to that question, to decide whether he wanted to take the risk—but not tonight. Tonight, all he wanted was a shower and a good night's sleep. It felt good to rest, though. He'd just lie here for a few minutes, and then—

He didn't even realize he'd drifted off.

| CHAPTER NINE

S TONE WOKE ABRUPTLY to loud pounding on his door. "What—?" he mumbled, disoriented. Where was he? Who was shouting?

"Get out here, you lazy fool! Were you expecting breakfast in bed?"

The voice sounded angry, and it took him a second to identify it as Faran. He jerked upright, glancing at the window. The sun already shone in through the opening in the skewed shade.

Oh, bloody hell, I was supposed to start at sunrise!

"Just—just a moment," he called.

He'd fallen asleep in his clothes—he must have been even more exhausted than he thought following his first full day of activity after his stay in the hospital. He glanced down at himself in disgust: wearing the same clothes he'd worn yesterday and slept in ran counter to everything in his fastidious nature, but the way Faran sounded there was no chance the man would give him time to shower and change. Heart pounding, he swiped his hand quickly through his hair and flung open the door.

"Sorry," he said, breathless. "I must have overslept—guess I'm still recovering from my time in hospital. I promise, it won't happen again."

Faran looked him up and down, taking in his rumpled shirt, unshaven face, and disheveled hair with obvious distaste. "Look at you. I can't have you deliverin' my goods lookin' like that." His eyes narrowed. "Have you been out gettin' drunk?"

"No. Listen—as I said, I promise it won't happen again. I'm still adjusting to being here." He adopted his most persuasive tone, the one he used to get things through to his students. "You said yesterday you didn't get any complaints about me. I made the deliveries properly, right?"

"Well…yeah." Faran's tone was grudging.

"And was the cleaning to your satisfaction?"

"Runa said the place looked fine." Still grudging.

"There you go, then," Stone said. "I promise—I'll do a good job. Just give me a chance. Please."

Faran considered, then let out a loud sigh. "Fine. *One* more chance. You already missed breakfast—go make yourself presentable, and you can start in an hour. You'll have to move faster to make up the time, though, and I'm dockin' you a buck for startin' late. You mess up one more time, you're out. Take it or leave it."

"Thank you," Stone said. "You won't regret it."

By the time he finished all the deliveries for the day and cleaned up the shop, Stone felt tired but satisfied. It was a different kind of tired—not so much exhaustion from his injuries as a good, honest fatigue from a day's work. Runa even seemed to take a bit of pity on him, because she gave him two sandwiches for lunch and nearly twice as much for dinner as the previous day. He set his dinner plate aside and pulled on his jacket—no way was he going to waste another evening passed out in his room. He had people to talk to and questions to ask, and the bars were a good place to start.

He'd filled in more of the local geography today, which helped. Although he'd had to hustle to make all the deliveries in an hour less than Faran had originally allotted, he still had time to memorize a few more streets and add them to his mental map. Now he knew the locations of three bars of varying levels, along with the information he could glean by studying them from the outside. One was more of a restaurant that happened to include a sizable drinking establishment; one reminded him of the pubs back home in England, where the same group of people would gather in the evenings for ales and companionship; and the third, near where the inhabited part of the city met the blasted-out ruin where he'd been found, was clearly the type respectable people didn't go.

He hadn't asked anyone about Harrison on his deliveries, still not confident enough he could trust anyone to risk saying the wrong thing. Though this meant he didn't get any useful information on his route, he did get comfortable enough in his surroundings that his natural charm and charisma began to re-emerge while interacting with Faran's customers—and that meant he got more tips. At least now he could afford to buy a few drinks when he went out, and, when Faran paid him, perhaps even some new clothes so he didn't feel like a refugee from a rag-bag.

Faran had given him a key that would get him in the back door (though notably he hadn't trusted him yet with one to the shop itself). Despite the man's comment earlier about "going out and getting drunk," he *had* said Stone's time after work was his own. With his tip coins jingling in his pocket, he headed out.

At night, the city looked far more forbidding than it had during the day. Many of the streetlights either didn't work or flickered intermittently, and most of even the small number of vehicles Stone had seen were nowhere in evidence. The majority of the shops were closed this late, and the people he saw on the streets now—both men and women, he noticed—had a watchful quality to them, as if they half-expected someone to jump them. It wasn't obvious, but years of studying auras had given Stone a sort of sixth sense about it even without magical assistance.

Still, no one bothered him; in fact, no one even acknowledged him beyond quick grunts when they passed each other on the sidewalks. He wondered if there was anything to the apprehension he saw—*was* someone about to jump them? Were there dangers here beyond the appearance of the Talented, or the freakish scavengers poking around the edge of town? He'd certainly seen no sign of two-headed wolves or any other unnatural animals on his delivery rounds—was that because they didn't venture this far into civilized areas, or because they only came out at night? He glanced around nervously, but saw nothing.

Stop it. Just keep your wits about you and pay attention. Nothing's going to attack you.

He chose the disreputable bar as his first stop, partly because in his shabby, ill-fitting clothes, he'd probably fit in better there than in the more upscale versions. He wasn't sure whether it was his best choice, since the impeccably put-together Harrison didn't seem the type who would frequent such a place, but it couldn't be helped. As it was, he'd have to rely on charm and persuasion to get answers, since bribes were out of the question with his current financial situation.

As he approached the bar he could tell right away that, unlike the people on the streets near the butcher shop, this place's clientele had no issues with coming out at night. Even from a block away he heard the faint strains of music from inside, and as he paused to watch a moment, the doors opened several times and small groups of people headed in or out. Popular place, apparently.

Feigning a confidence he didn't entirely feel—he'd been in plenty of unfamiliar, disreputable bars in his time, but never with so little money and no magic—Stone strode across the street and opened the door.

Inside, the music got a lot louder, hitting him like a wall as the heavy door closed behind him. He stepped aside and looked around quickly to get impressions, pleased to see that the place didn't look so different from a dive bar on Earth: dark décor, tables and booths, and faded, old-fashioned-looking posters hanging on the walls. On the right side, the bar itself was lined with customers—mostly men, a few women, all wearing work clothes. Between the music and the loud chatter of the customers, Stone could barely hear himself think.

He walked in farther and selected a small table near the wall, where he could keep an eye on anyone approaching him. It was hard to see far due to the haze of smoke hanging in the air, but beyond the seating area he spotted what looked like a pair of shabby pool tables with more people clustered around them. Even from where he sat he could tell the layout was different enough that they probably weren't playing billiards.

For a while, he did nothing but lean back in his chair and surreptitiously watch the people at the nearby tables. They ignored him, but that was fine. All he was trying to determine was how much the drinks cost, so he wouldn't embarrass himself trying to order something if he didn't have enough money. He'd already learned the basics of this world's number system during his deliveries and recognized their equivalent of one through ten; to his relief, it looked like the silver-colored coins he'd been given as tips would buy him at least a few drinks—or some for him and some for whoever he plied for information.

A waitress came by shortly and paused at his table. "Can I get you something?"

He nodded toward the man at the next table, who was drinking what looked like a pint of ale. "I'll try one of what he's having."

"Right away." She hurried off and returned a few minutes later with a tall glass full of reddish-gold liquid. "That'll be twenty-five cents."

Again marveling at the way his translation spell handled monetary sums, he handed over one of the silver coins and she gave him a few smaller ones in change. "You're new around here," she said, looking him up and down. "Haven't seen you before."

He took an experimental sip. It didn't taste like anything he'd ever tried before, but it still fell neatly into the "beer" category, spicy and full-bodied. "This is good," he said.

"Thank you." He handed her one of the smaller coins as a tip and smiled. "You're right—I'm new in town. I wonder if you might be able to answer a question for me."

She glanced over her shoulder toward the room, but nobody appeared to need her at the moment. "I can try," she said with a mix of curiosity and suspicion.

"I'm looking for someone. A friend who was supposed to meet me in town, but I can't find him. I wondered if perhaps you might have heard of him." He watched her closely. "His name is—" he paused, catching himself before he revealed Harrison's full name and possibly his affiliation with the Talented. "—Trevor." He gave a brief description.

Either she was a much better actress than Stone would give her credit for, or she didn't know anything. Her expression went blank and she shook her head. "Sorry, friend. Never heard of him. Odd name—does he live here in town? What does he do for a living?"

"See, that's the thing—I don't know. I don't think he lives here, but we were going to meet here and…continue our travels…but I was delayed and missed our meeting."

"Got it. Well, I can ask around if you want, but not now. I have to get back to work."

"Of course. Don't let me keep you. I'd appreciate it, if you would. I expect I'll be in and out of here fairly frequently."

The waitress headed back into the crowd, and Stone sat sipping his drink and doing his best to watch the crowd without being obvious about it. He got the impression this was definitely a 'mind your own business' sort of place.

During the next hour of watching and nursing his ale to avoid having to buy another, he made several useful discoveries—though none of them got him any closer to finding

Harrison. For one, this place was clearly the place to go if you had illicit activities on your mind. He noticed one or more of the three scantily-dressed women who drank and chattered together at one of the back tables getting up several times and disappearing into the back with different men; once he spotted two furtive men exchanging a paper-wrapped parcel for an envelope and then quickly departing in different directions; and all around him, people sat tilted back in their chairs, smoking something that probably wasn't tobacco. Stone had smelled a similar aroma a couple times on his deliveries, wafting down from upper windows. Given the constant state of stress most of these people seemed to live under, it didn't surprise him at all that some turned to drugs to make their days and nights more bearable.

Unfortunately, this was getting him nowhere. He finished his drink and got up, giving a rueful smile and a head-shake to one of the ladies at the back table, who'd been giving him the eye for the last twenty minutes, and left the bar. Clearly, if he was going to find Harrison, he'd have to ask more questions—or try another location.

He tried not to get discouraged by thinking about how many ways things could go wrong. He still wasn't certain he'd even traveled to the correct dimension, but even if he had, this world could be as large as—or even larger than—his own. He could have landed thousands of miles from Harrison's location—the equivalent of dropping down in London while his quarry was in Los Angeles. If that were true, the technology level here meant it was unlikely he'd ever find Harrison.

He'd have to get bolder, and more creative.

As he left the bar, something flashed in the corner of his eye. He turned quickly and thought he spotted a pair of glowing eyes watching him from a dark alley. Even though they disappeared instantly, and he wasn't sure he'd even seen them, his heartbeat increased. He sped up his stride and glanced back over his shoulder several times on his way back to the butcher shop.

| CHAPTER TEN

S TONE GREW INCREASINGLY FRUSTRATED over the following week as his careful inquiries continued to provide no useful information.

Every day was the same: get up at dawn (that was hard enough, as back home he routinely stayed up late and slept well into the morning), make his deliveries, and clean up the shop when he returned. He figured out how to use the alarm clock so he didn't oversleep again, and Faran seemed satisfied with his work, so that was something, at least. That, and the butcher trusted him with more wide-reaching deliveries, allowing him to see more of the town and add to his mental map.

The town, he discovered, had clearly been much larger in the past. Several times as he pedaled the old bike through the streets on his way to his destinations, he drew near areas that appeared abandoned or occupied only by squatters. In those areas, the buildings looked like they'd weathered a long-ago bombing and never been rebuilt. The electricity was spotty or nonexistent, nobody seemed to be maintaining the streets or the structures, and the few people he saw were dressed even more shabbily than he was. Though he didn't venture far into

R. L. KING

these blighted areas, he could see that the further out they stretched, the worse they fared.

He wondered if the ruins had anything to do with the war. He still hadn't asked anyone about it, and during his evening wanderings—split between the dive bar, the local pub, and another working-class bar he found closer to the center of town—no one ever mentioned it. He wasn't sure if that was because everyone knew about it and accepted it—people didn't sit around regularly talking about Vietnam or Iraq, after all—or because they were afraid to bring it up. Either way, Jena's reaction at the hospital told him he'd best be careful about raising the subject himself.

One good thing later that week was that Faran paid him. "Good job," the butcher said gruffly one evening, handing him an envelope after he'd returned from his delivery rounds. "I decided not to dock you the buck for bein' late that first day. Shop's closed tomorrow, so no deliveries. Go get yerself some decent clothes so you look respectable. There's a shop on Green Street that's cheap." He paused. "Oh—one more thing."

"Yes?"

"I got word from a couple customers that you been askin' around about some guy you're lookin' for."

"Yes. Is that a problem?" He'd briefly questioned two or three of the shopkeepers on his regular delivery route a couple days ago, the ones he'd developed a good relationship with as indicated by his tips. Of course they'd known nothing, but hadn't seemed suspicious and promised to keep their ears open.

"You shouldn't be gettin' chummy with the customers. Just make your deliveries and get out." He narrowed his eyes. "Who's this guy you're lookin' for, anyway?"

"A—friend. I was supposed to meet him when I arrived in town, but I got attacked before I could find him."

"He live here?"

"I don't think so. We were going to do some traveling." That was the cover story he'd been using—best to stay consistent, in case anybody compared notes.

"Yeah, whatever." Faran waved him off. "Not my problem what you do on your own time, as long as it don't reflect on me. Go on—and don't get yourself drunk and show up late for work tomorrow."

"I wouldn't think of it," Stone murmured.

Determined not to waste a free day, he set off before Faran could find something else for him to do. He was on foot this time, since the bike was only for deliveries, but by now his endurance had returned to the point where walking around all day wasn't an issue.

He had four chunky bronze-colored coins in his pay envelope and the tips he'd received for his deliveries, so his first stop was the clothing shop Faran had recommended. It was two blocks away on a busy street, and by the time he reached it a good number of people were out walking along, chatting and looking in shop windows. He pushed open the door and headed inside.

Half an hour later he emerged with two parcels containing three shirts, another pair of trousers, and a few sets of boxers and socks. All of them were simple and cheaply made, but at least they fit him better than the ones he had, and he could afford them. He'd spent most of his weekly pay on them, glad he'd collected enough tips to supplement it. He didn't bother asking the shop's proprietor about Harrison— he couldn't imagine the elegant mage frequenting a shabby, cut-rate clothing store.

After returning to the shop to change into one of the new outfits and drop the rest in his room, he set off again. His plan today was to try identifying places where people might know Harrison—perhaps a bookstore, more upscale bars, or even a gambling establishment if he could find one. He realized as he walked, feeling much better in clothes that actually fit him, that he knew next to nothing about the man. Aside from his being a mage, wealthy, and connected somehow to the Obsidian in Las Vegas—all things Stone had learned by observation—Harrison had revealed little about himself. He was clearly an extremely private person; it wasn't as if Stone could simply look him up in the phone book.

He stopped for a moment, amused by the thought. He'd seen a few public telephones on his wanderings. What if he *could* look Harrison up in the phone book? Wouldn't it be perversely funny if he'd spent all this time asking people when all he'd needed to do was check this dimension's equivalent of the White Pages? Only two problems with that, however: although he'd seen public phones, he hadn't seen any phone books, and he didn't know what Harrison's name looked like in the world's angular script. Ah, well.

After two more hours of walking, his discouragement grew. He hadn't spotted anything that resembled a bookstore, or even a newsstand. Did people not read here? Despite Faran's annoyance that Stone couldn't, it didn't seem to bother anyone else. Sure, he'd seen plenty of written communication: his own work papers, signs and posters, and writing in shop windows, for example. But it occurred to him that he'd seen no books, no magazines aside from the periodicals in Byra's office at the hospital, and only a few newspapers. Odd. He wondered if the Talented read, or if they somehow developed their powers organically. There was, after all, no guarantee that people learned magic here the same way they did on Earth.

Stone's stomach rumbled, and he realized it was past lunchtime. He should probably go back to the shop, where presumably he could get lunch from Runa as part of his weekly board, but he estimated he was at least two miles away. He still had enough money to buy something, and he'd doubtless pick up more tips when he went back to work tomorrow.

He sniffed the air. Something smelled good, like spicy, roasting meat. A quick look around revealed a medium-sized eatery with a red-painted façade, clearly the source of the enticing aromas. As he watched, several people entered and others left, many of the latter carrying grease-stained paper bags. Anyplace that popular had to be good, Stone decided, and headed for it.

Inside, the warm shop smelled even better, the roast meat mingling with spicy vegetables and a hint of fish. It included only three tiny tables, all of them occupied, with the rest of the floor space taken up by a line of people waiting to order. The customers chatted amiably as they waited, and Stone noticed they appeared to come from all walks of life, from a few well-dressed businesspeople to parents clutching children's hands to several clad in simple work clothes like his own. He took his place in line and smiled at the middle-aged man who'd turned toward him. "Popular place, this."

"Oh, yes." The man returned his smile. "I come here at least once every week—their fish sandwiches are delicious. The wait is worth it."

"Good to know." Stone studied the board above the counter. For the first time, he consciously noticed that the items listed included hand-drawn images to indicate what they were, along with the usual angular writing. There were sections with a fish, one of the fat cow-like creatures on Faran's butcher-shop window, and something that looked like a long-legged chicken. Below them, another section included two types of drink containers: a mug with steam coming out of it, and a tall cup or glass. Perhaps he'd been more correct than he thought about the general population's ability to read—or lack of it. "Which one do you recommend?" The line moved forward a bit, and Stone followed.

"Oh, you can't go wrong with any of them. The tarlfish is especially good."

Apparently the translation spell couldn't come up with anything to substitute for *tarlfish,* so it rendered it as is. "I'll try that, then. Thank you. I—"

A sudden hush fell over the restaurant's interior. It started behind Stone, which was why he hadn't noticed it initially, but quickly rippled forward as the other people in line all turned around to face the door.

For a moment, Stone had the wild fear that they were all looking at *him*—had he done something wrong?—but it quickly became clear that wasn't the case. Every person in the place was looking at something *behind* him, their eyes wide with carefully controlled fright.

Slowly, Stone turned too, and a bolt of ice shot up his spine.

Two more people had entered the shop, but only an instant's glance told him they didn't fit in with the regular customers. A man and a woman, both stood tall and straight; the woman had dark skin and long, flowing white hair, while the man was red-haired and ruddy-cheeked. Both wore the high-collared, sweeping long coats Stone instantly recognized from his ordeal in Temolan—the woman's in bright blue, the man's in a rich chocolate brown with blue highlights. A series of pins and amulets decorated their lapels, and the woman wore a glittering golden necklace with a blue-gem pendant.

Behind him, Stone became aware that the other customers were shuffling backward, stepping out of line and pressing themselves against the wall. Nobody, not even the ones closest to the door, attempted to leave the shop. Stone, moving slowly so as not to attract attention, shifted back along with the rest.

No one spoke, and all eyes remained on the newcomers.

"Welcome!" one of the servers behind the counter called. His voice shook a little and he looked terrified, but he nonetheless pasted a wide smile on his face. "You honor us with your presence. What can we get you today?"

The dark-skinned woman offered a cold smile. "My companion wishes to go slumming. Apparently he has heard good things about your little…shop here."

"Er—of course, of course. We're honored. Please tell us what you'd like and we'll get it for you right away."

The red-haired man studied the menu as if examining bugs under a microscope, while his female companion swept her gaze over the crowd without acknowledging or even appearing to see any individual people.

Stone recognized the look of magical sight. He thought about attempting to calm his aura—his experience in Las Vegas when he'd burned out his powers previously had shown him he could still do this even without magic—but then stopped. Everyone in this room looked like they were about to wet themselves in fear, so calm would stand out more than terror. He glanced at the others near him; they'd all cast their gazes downward, looking at the floor and shifting nervously from foot to foot. It didn't take aura-reading ability to pick up the tightly wired tension in the room. Near him a woman, her face dead pale, clamped her hand over a toddler boy's mouth and held him close.

"What do you recommend?" the red-haired man asked. He sounded bored, as if speaking to an underling or a household pet.

"Uh—well, the tarlfish sandwich is our most popular, sir."

The man considered. "All right. I'll have that. Merinda?"

"Please," she drawled with contempt. "I can wait until we return home. Just…get me a cold tea, I suppose."

"You heard the lady," the man said to the server. "And make it quick. We haven't got all day to stand around in here."

"Yes, sir. Of course. Right away." The server gestured at his fellow workers, who immediately began scurrying around to assemble the order.

Pressed against the wall with the other customers, Stone took that opportunity to surreptitiously examine the two Talented. The first and most obvious thing he noticed was that their clothes and boots were spotlessly, unnaturally clean. Even the ground-skimming hems of their coats showed no hint of dampness or grime. *Magic,* he thought. It had to be. Not even that difficult, either—back home when he'd still been a white mage, he'd put a permanent enchantment on his black wool overcoat that allowed him to wear it in warmer weather without discomfort.

Compared to the other customers, all of whom were dressed in drab, faded colors, the Talented pair's outfits stood out for their bright, vibrant hues as well. Like the three men who'd attacked him in Temolan, these two wore shades of blue. Stone wondered if the color had some significance—did it indicate a social station, a role, or did people from Temolan simply have an unnatural affinity for blue?

He dropped his gaze again as Merinda, bored, wandered over to the group of terrified customers. She examined them with the disinterested attention of an anthropologist observing a collection of zoo animals, then made a face suggesting she couldn't imagine how anyone could live like these poor, backward savages. With a sweep of her coat, she turned back toward her red-haired companion. Stone forced himself to remain still and keep his aura steady.

The servers had finished putting together their order. The man who'd waited on them hitched up his manic smile and slid a plate across the counter, along with two tall paper cups of tea. "There you are, sir. It's an honor to serve you. Will you be dining here, or shall I package it up for you?"

Stone didn't miss the desperate undercurrent of his tone: *please don't stay please don't stay...* He also noticed he didn't mention a charge for the food.

At the words 'dining here,' the customers who had been sitting at the tiny tables all hastily got up and backed away, leaving all three empty.

The red-haired man flicked his gaze toward the tables, and his lip curled in distaste. "No, we'll take it with us." He flipped a silver coin onto the counter. "That should suffice."

"Yes, sir. Thank you, sir. Enjoy your meal." Moving fast but taking utmost care, he wrapped the sandwich, put it in a bag, and added lids to the cups of tea. He offered the bag to him with shaking hands, glancing up at him and then back down at the counter.

The man regarded the bag, then made a casual gesture and it lifted off the counter along with both cups. One of the cups floated to Merinda, who plucked it out of the air with her thumb and forefinger, and he took the other and the bag. The two of them started for the door.

Stone could almost feel everyone holding their breath. The ordeal was almost over—all they had to do was hold it together for a few more seconds.

The two Talented reached the door. The red-haired man raised his hand to open it, then stopped. Slowly, he opened the bag, looked in it, and turned back to the counter. "I ordered dipping sauce with this. Are you trying to cheat me, pig?"

Terror flooded across the server's face. Of course the man *hadn't* ordered sauce—every silent, frightened person in the shop had heard every word of his order—but he couldn't say that. "Sir. I—"

The man strode with deliberate calm back into the shop. "You *are* trying to cheat me. You thought I wouldn't notice until I was home. That I wouldn't be bothered to return."

"Sir—please. I'm sorry. Let me—"

From the doorway, Merinda watched with amusement.

Stone risked a glance between the two of them, anger growing, forcing himself not to let it show in his aura or his body. These two had *intended* to do this. They'd meant to as soon as they'd entered the shop. He didn't need aura reading to be sure of it.

"So…" the man said. "What should I do with a worthless, dishonest pig?" He set the bag and cup on the counter, then put a finger to his chin and regarded the server's fellow trembling workers. "What do you think I should do with him? He makes you all look bad, after all."

None of them answered. They all stared down at the floor as if they knew exactly what was coming.

"I could burn down your entire pathetic shop," the man mused. "What do you think, Merinda? Are you in the mood for some roasted pig?"

"Please…" the server whispered. "Please don't…I'm sorry…"

The man's gaze settled back on him. "Do you take responsibility for your mistake, then?"

"Yes…yes, sir. I do. I'm sorry." His voice shook so hard his words were barely intelligible.

Keep it together, Stone told himself, struggling to call up his meditation technique, to calm his mind just enough so he didn't spring at these two arrogant wastes of space. Nothing could come of that but his own death and probably those of everyone present.

The man appeared to consider again. "All right, then. I'm feeling generous today, so I won't make your entire misbegotten lot suffer for your stupidity." With no change of expression, he jerked a hand upward.

The server didn't even have time to scream. His body lifted off the floor, his hands flying to his neck as he struggled and gasped for a breath. The red-haired man allowed him to hang there for a few seconds, then made a sharp gesture to the side.

Everyone in the shop saw the flash of purple light, and they all heard the sickening *snap* as the man's neck broke. Audible gasps, quickly stifled, went up from several people.

The Talented man held the body suspended for only a moment, then let it drop in a heap behind the counter. "There," he said, with no more inflection in his voice than if he'd just asked for a cup of coffee. He addressed the other servers. "Let that be a lesson to you. You won't ever try to cheat one of your betters again, will you?"

"N-no, sir. No. Never," one of them stammered.

"Good. That's what I want to hear." Using magic, he picked up the bag and the cup. He scanned the crowd, none of whom dared to look at him. Then, without another word, the two of them swept from the shop. The bell on the door tinkled as it shut behind them, jarringly loud against the unnatural quiet.

For several seconds, silence hung in the air as everyone turned toward the window and watched the two Talented leaving. Then, as the pair disappeared around a corner, a loud collective sigh of relief sounded from all sides of the room. Stone might have thought it callous, but he understood it and didn't hold it against them: it could easily have been all of them, instead of one. Behind the counter, one of the man's fellow servers bent to move him aside and lay him out on the floor, while the other moved to a nearby telephone. Some of the customers quickly left without ordering, while others returned to their places in line. All of them looked frazzled and shell-shocked.

Stone did his best to calm his rage and his jangling nerves. "Does that happen often?" he asked the man he'd been talking to before.

The man looked startled. "The Talented showing up? No. I've never seen it happen at this place, anyway. But I've heard a lot of stories. You've never seen them?"

"No. Not…here." Stone let his breath out, reminded once again of that old *Twilight Zone* episode. Apparently, the Talented were capricious and cruel enough that even visiting a takeaway restaurant was enough to cause the nonmagical people to hyperventilate in terror, even before they got away with murder. He glanced at the counter, where the other server had joined the first to tend to their fallen coworker. "That's…barbaric. I felt so helpless…so angry. It's—"

"We got off easily." The woman behind Stone glanced back toward the door, then lowered her voice. "One of my friends told me one time three of them went to a restaurant downtown, and when their order wasn't cooked the way they liked, they lit the waiter on fire, then went back to the kitchen and torched the chefs. The whole place nearly burned down. My friend said they thought it was funny."

"And they get away with this?" Stone's outrage rose, despite his attempt to blend in. As a mage himself—at least back on Earth—he had the power to do the things these so-called "Talented" did, but the thought of these people not only doing them but getting away with them angered him. "People just—put up with it?"

Both the woman and middle-aged man gave him odd, fearful looks. "What can we do?" the man asked. "We have no powers. The Talented do what they like, and all we can do is stay out of their way and hope we don't set them off."

Stone thought about the looks on the group's faces—on the doomed server's face—and clenched his fist in his pocket. Nobody should have to live like that. Once again, he wondered if Harrison was one of these "Talented," and if he condoned—or even participated in—this kind of reprehensible behavior. If he did, would Stone even *want* to learn magic from him?

The man and woman were still flashing him nervous looks, so he forced himself to calm down and nodded. "Of course," he said. "I hope it doesn't happen again anytime soon."

"You and me both," the woman said fervently. "I thought I was going to faint. If I had, they'd probably have killed me too."

Amazingly, it appeared the remaining servers intended to go back to business as usual, but Stone was no longer hungry. He left the line and headed out. As he walked down the street and looked for a place to sit so he could calm down, his heart continued to race, adrenaline coursing through him. *Give it up,* he told himself in disgust. *You can't change this world. If you try, they'll kill you.*

You might if you got your magic back, his interior voice pointed out. *At least you might show a few of these entitled bastards what happens when their prey fights back.*

But that wasn't happening yet—it might never happen. He tried not to think that he might be stuck in this world as one of the "Dim" forever, at the mercy of these monstrous mages, if he couldn't find a way home. A stray thought struck him suddenly from nowhere: a memory of the atrocities he'd recently found out his own ancestors had committed—acts every bit as horrible as those of the Talented. *You don't get a pass. You could easily have been one of those monsters if you'd been born here. Don't think for a moment you're immune.*

Still seething but now with a side of guilt, he watched people drift past. They talked among themselves, unaware of what had just happened so close by—or perhaps they had seen it so many times they'd grown indifferent to it. He wasn't sure, and didn't want to know. He'd intended to do more exploring, perhaps looking for a gambling hall where he could question people about Harrison, but his encounter with the Talented redirected his plans.

If he wanted to find out about the Talented, he'd need to talk to one of them. And he only knew one who wasn't likely to kill him for the attempt.

CHAPTER ELEVEN

THOUGH NONE OF HIS DELIVERIES had been near it, Stone had no trouble finding the hospital/clinic building where he'd recovered from his injuries. He pushed open the door and stepped inside, glancing around.

The waiting room wasn't as full as it had been when he'd left, probably because it was later in the day. About half the chairs were occupied by what looked like a mix of sick and injured individuals; nobody's problems looked life-threatening. *That's good—perhaps that means they'll have time to talk to me today.*

He walked up to the desk, where a woman he didn't recognize was writing something in a book. "Excuse me…"

She glanced up, then back down. "Sign in and take a seat," she said in a rote voice. "We'll call you when it's your turn."

"I'm…not here for treatment," he said. "I was hoping to talk with someone here."

The woman frowned, looking up again. "Talk with someone? Who?"

"Well…Tanissa, if she's here. Or if she's not, Byra."

"About what?" Suspicious, narrowed eyes joined the frown.

"Well—I was a patient here recently. I had some questions. Is Tanissa here?"

"Yes, but she doesn't have time to—"

"Please." Stone put on his best persuasive tone. "I promise I won't take up much of her time—I know how busy she is. But it's terribly important."

She bit her lip, considered, then sighed. "I'll see if she wants to talk to you," she said at last, grudgingly. "What's your name?"

"Stone. Tell her she worked on me a couple of weeks ago. Saved my life. I want to thank her for that, too."

"Take a seat."

Stone didn't take a seat—he figured if he hadn't managed to pick up any exotic illnesses from this dimension yet, he probably wouldn't do it from casual contact, but there was no point in taking chances. He leaned against the wall and wondered how long he'd have to wait. The room contained no magazines or other diversions; nobody else seemed to mind this. They talked quietly or remained silent, staring straight ahead.

Nearly half an hour passed before anything happened. In the meantime, the woman continued calling out names, and one or more of the other patients got up and shuffled to the back. Occasionally, the door to the back would open and someone would come out, or someone new would come in from outside.

Stone had decided he'd give it another ten minutes before saying something, when the woman looked his way. "Stone?"

He hurried over. "Yes?"

"Tanissa says she'll talk to you, but only for a few minutes. She's very busy, and has other cases she needs to attend to."

"Thank you so much. I promise, I'll make it quick."

She nodded toward the door. "Through there, first door on the right. Wait for her there."

The door opened on a small, windowless room that looked like a combination between a storeroom and an office, with a tiny desk and single guest chair wedged between metal shelves stacked with cardboard boxes. Stone took a seat in the guest chair and amused himself by scanning the papers on the desk. After two weeks he could now recognize some of the simple words, though not many.

After a while, the door opened again and a woman appeared. "Stone?"

Stone leapt to his feet. "Tanissa, I presume."

She chuckled. "That's me. Sit down—we're not formal here."

He resumed his seat, looking her over. She appeared to be in her middle twenties, sturdily built without quite reaching plump, her brown hair cut in a no-nonsense bob. Her simple but well-made outfit was topped with a white coat. *No blue,* Stone noticed immediately. None of the pins or amulets he'd seen on the Talented, either. She didn't look any different from the other doctors he'd seen.

Tanissa returned his scrutiny. "You're looking a lot better than last time I saw you."

"I should hope so," he said dryly. "Thank you for that, by the way. I understand I was in rather bad shape when I was brought in."

"That's an understatement. The man who brought you said he found you out in the Barrens, in the middle of the street." Her curiosity showed clearly on her face, but she didn't ask.

"Yes." He took a deep breath. "Tanissa, I wonder if I might ask you a few questions."

Her expression grew guarded. "Maybe. It depends on what they are. I don't have a lot of time—"

"I promise, I'll make it quick." He leaned forward and met her gaze. "I don't know if Byra told you, but I'm—new to this area. Unfamiliar with the customs. I come from quite some distance away, where we do things much differently."

"She mentioned that you were an odd man," she said. "I can see what she means, just by listening to you."

"How is that?"

She tilted her head. "You're well spoken, but Byra says you can't read. You have a tattoo on your chest that looks magical, but no sign of magical abilities. You have the manners of someone who was raised in wealth, but when you were brought in you were wearing strange rags. And according to your records you claim your name is Alastair—a name I've never heard, but that marks you as one of the Talented. You're a contradiction, is what you are. And that makes everybody around here nervous. Me included."

Instead of answering, Stone merely nodded. "You're not like the other Talented I've seen, Tanissa. Not at all."

"No." The single word was clipped, remote.

"Byra said you don't like to talk about your past. But you grew up with them, didn't you?"

"I don't want to talk about—"

Even without aura-reading ability, Stone couldn't miss her sudden tension. "I know," he said. "I don't want to pry, but—I'm getting a bit desperate, to be honest. I came here looking for someone, and I've had no luck tracking him down. Since you're the only one of your kind I have a reasonable chance of talking to without being incinerated, I've got to take a chance." He lowered his voice. "Please, Tanissa—just a few questions. I give you my word I won't reveal anything you tell me."

She made a bitter sound, halfway between a chuckle and a snort. "You haven't been here very long at all, if you think you can make that promise."

"What do you mean?"

"If you know something the Talented want to know, they'll get it out of you, and there's no way you can stop them."

"They read minds?" Stone asked quickly, glancing up. If they did, that would make them different from Earth mages—and a lot more potentially dangerous.

"No. They can't read minds. At least, I've never heard of any who can. But they're…adept at torture. Some of them enjoy it. I'm sure you're aware of that."

Stone thought about the three young men who'd nearly killed him. "Oh, yes. Quite so."

She shuffled some of the papers on the desk. "Listen—I've got a good thing here. I can use my abilities to help people, instead of lounging around in luxury, being waited on. The powers that be in Temolan don't like it—they don't approve, and think I might not be in my right mind—but they look the other way. I have as little contact with them as I possibly can, and I want to keep it that way. I'd like to help you, but I've already helped you in the only way I can—by saving your life. I don't want to know anything else about you."

This time, she did stand. "I'm sorry, Stone, or Alastair, or whatever your name is. Please don't come here again."

He didn't mean to do it—certainly hadn't intended to when he came here, but at the sight of his last and best lead preparing to leave the room, he took a chance. If she killed him, or turned him in to the authorities in Temolan, at least he wouldn't die as a mundane making meat deliveries in some blighted town on a foreign dimension.

"I'm from another world," he said quickly, under his breath.

She'd been reaching for the door, her back to him. At his words, she stopped. "What?"

"You heard me."

Slowly, she turned back. "What are you talking about?"

Stone lowered his voice further. "I'm not from your world. I've come here looking for someone I need to find, but I—took a bit of a wrong turn on the way."

Still moving slowly, never taking her eyes off him, she moved back around the desk and sat down. "Just a minute." Her expression went fuzzy for a few seconds, then she switched back on. "Okay. Nobody can listen in on us now. What do you mean, you're from another world? There aren't any other worlds."

"There are," he said gently. "I can't give you details, but it's true. It's why I seem well educated, even though I can't read your language—because I *am* well educated. Just…somewhere else. It's why I can speak and understand your language: it was part of the magic that brought me here."

Looking at him as if trying to decide if he was mad, she said, "If that's true—how did you get here?"

"That's—hard to explain. But where I come from, I'm…Talented as well. We don't call it that, but it's the same thing." He touched his chest. "My tattoo *is* magical, but my magic doesn't work here."

"It doesn't work."

"No. I haven't figured out why yet. That was one of the things I thought I might discuss with you."

She looked at the papers on the desk again, and swallowed. When her gaze came up again, it had hardened. "I'm sorry. I was worried your brain was damaged when you were injured, and now I'm sure of it. I think you should go now."

Stone didn't miss the undercurrent of fear in her tone. Something was scaring the hell out of her, that was obvious. Was she afraid of the other Talented finding out about him—or more specifically, finding out that she had some connection to him? "I don't want to cause you any trouble. I promise, if you'll just answer my questions, I'll leave and you won't see me again. But—"

"I'm sorry," she said again. "I can't help you. You really need to go now. I've got patients to look after."

Stone stood, sighing. He couldn't force her to talk to him—in fact, she could force him to leave if she wanted to. She could even kill him, if he scared her enough. Perhaps her fear was justified, and he was putting her in danger merely by being here. Still, he didn't want to leave without *something.*

He took one last, desperate chance: "All right, then. I'll go. But I don't know if they told you—I'm looking for someone here. One of the Talented, though I don't know what connection he has with the others, if any. His name is

Harrison. Trevor Harrison. Have you heard of him? Can you give me any leads on where I might look for him, without getting myself blown up or killed by the Talented for my impertinence?"

Tanissa swallowed hard, and once again Stone didn't miss the fact that she paled at the mention of the name. "No, they didn't tell me that. Where did you hear that name?" She glanced at the door.

A little flutter of excitement rose in Stone. She'd heard of Harrison—he was sure of it. Even if she didn't know him or know where to find him, it was Stone's first piece of concrete evidence that he hadn't landed on the wrong dimension. "I told you—I'm trying to find him. I knew him—several years ago. I think he might be able to help me."

"Help you how?" Again, her gaze flicked toward the door, almost as if expecting someone to burst in on them.

"Long story. Short answer: he might be able to help me get home. And…to get my magic working again."

Silence hung in the air. Tanissa didn't meet his gaze; she straightened the papers on the desk again, adjusted a framed print on the wall, and looked at her feet. "That's a dangerous name, if you're talking about the man I think you are. I wouldn't go throwing it around indiscriminately if I were you."

Stone frowned, glad that he'd had the sense not to use Harrison's last name during his inquiries. "Dangerous? Why?"

"Look—" Even her voice shook now. "You need to go. This is all I'm going to tell you. If you come back, I'll have you removed, and I'll tell everyone you're not right in the head. You could get locked up for that, or worse. That's how serious I am. Understand?"

"I…do," Stone said slowly. "I promise—I won't come back. Just tell me *something*. Who is Harrison here?"

Another long silence stretched out, even longer than the last one. "He's a ghost. A legend. I'm honestly not sure he even really exists—or if he ever did."

Stone gaped at her. "I—don't understand. What do you mean, doesn't exist?"

Her nervousness was clearly growing. "I haven't heard anything about him in years—not since I was a teenager, still living in Temolan. Nobody's seen him. Nobody ever sees him. He's wanted by all the mage houses, but they can't catch him—and that shouldn't be possible. Honestly, I think he's just a kind of bogeyman—something the Talented's leaders made up so they can have an enemy, since they can't fight each other anymore."

"Why…can't they fight each other?" Stone narrowed his eyes, convinced if he played this carefully he might get more information than he'd hoped.

No such luck, though. Tanissa's mask settled back over her face and she shook her head. "No. I told you—that's all I'm going to say." She moved toward the door again. "You need to go now. And remember, you promised not to come back."

"Wait," Stone said, holding up a hand. "You didn't tell me anything useful. All you said is that he's a ghost—but he's *not* a ghost. I've met the man in person, back where I come from, only a few years ago, and someone I know spoke with him just a couple of months ago. I know he exists. You said he was a bogeyman—what is it he's supposed to be doing that's so terrible?"

She gave a harsh laugh. "Nothing. That's what's so insane about the whole thing."

"What do you mean?"

"Look—I don't know anything about what's going on with the Talented leadership. Maybe if he exists, he *is* doing something, and even most of the Talented don't know about it. I don't want to get involved." She paused, studying him, then lowered her voice to a whisper. "The only rumor I've ever heard is that he's growing some kind of rebellion among some of the people here."

"Rebellion? You mean among the non-magical people?"

"Yes, but that's even crazier than the other stuff. It would never work—there are too many of the Talented, and you've seen how cruel and vengeful they can be. Most of the people here have never heard anything about it, or him. They wouldn't want to even if they could. They're content to live their lives and stay completely away from the Talented— which is what you should do, if you're smart. Now, go on. I have work to do."

Stone stopped in front of the door. "One more thing— have you heard any rumors—any at all—about where the people involved in this kind of rebellion might go? *If* it were really a thing, anyway." He met her gaze with a pleading one of his own. "I won't get you involved. I won't mention your name at all, I promise. And I'll be careful. But I've got to do something."

She dropped her gaze and didn't answer.

Stone sighed. He'd tried, and at least she'd given him more than he had before. Given her obvious fear, it was more than he had the right to expect.

"All right," he said softly. "Thank you, Tanissa. You won't see me again." He reached for the doorknob.

"Wait."

He stopped but didn't say anything, afraid he might startle her if he did.

"I truly don't know anything about what you're looking for. I wasn't lying when I said I thought it was all just rumors—stories people tell each other to help them get through the day. But you might try the Fisherman's Rest. It's a bar down by the docks. Go after dark, and be careful—it's a dangerous place." She glared at him. "But watch who you talk to. And if you mention my name, I *will* tell people you're not right in the head. And my word carries a lot of weight around here."

Stone merely nodded and slipped out of the office.

She closed the door behind him, and he heard the *snick* of a lock engaging.

CHAPTER TWELVE

S TONE DIDN'T SLEEP MUCH that night. Dusk was falling as he got back to the butcher shop in time for dinner, served by a dour-looking Runa. She did seem to approve of his new clothes, however.

He sat on his bed, barely thinking about eating as he went over what Tanissa had told him. So Harrison *was* here somewhere, and if she could be believed, he was some kind of legendary, mysterious figure that the mages were trying to find. The "mage houses," she'd mentioned—he was an enemy of all of them. Stone wondered how many of them there were, and what Harrison had done to become such an enemy. Before, Jena had said there were five of the floating cities—did each one have its own house, or were there multiple houses per city?

Then there were the rumors of a rebellion. In all the time he'd spent sitting in bars, nursing drinks and keeping his ears open, he'd never heard of any such thing. All the mundanes he'd encountered—he refused to call them the "Dim," even in his own mind—had seemed terrified of the Talented, and certainly hadn't given any indication that they'd want to rise against them even if offered the chance. Even those like

Faran, who made bitter remarks about the mages, seemed to do so out of fear rather than any sense of rebellion.

How could they do it? Mundanes wouldn't stand a chance against mages, especially not at this world's technology level. If any sort of movement existed at all, it would have to be deep underground and probably cell-based to avoid any of the Talented finding out about it; based on what he'd seen of the mages so far, Stone had no reason to believe they wouldn't cut a swath of destruction across dozens, hundreds, or even thousands of innocent mundanes if they heard even a rumor of such an organization.

If the rumors were true, could it be possible that some of the Talented were cooperating with Harrison? That was the only thing that made sense, the only way such a rebellion would have even a prayer of succeeding. Surely *some* of them had to be decent—even in a society where an entire class of people was raised with an unassailable sense of their own inherent superiority, there had to be at least a few of them opposed to treating the nonmagical populace with contempt and cruelty. Hell, Harrison himself, as cold and driven as he might be when focused on a goal, hardly seemed the type to torment innocent people for entertainment.

Stone set his plate aside and ran his hand through his hair. None of this mattered, not really. As much sympathy and outrage as he felt for the mundanes here and the capricious brutality they lived under, he was hardly in a position to bring about society-wide social change. Ultimately, all he wanted to do was find Harrison and see if the man could teach him to wield his power source without burnout. If he could, great. If he couldn't, then he wanted to go home, resume his life, and accept that he was a black mage now.

❖

The next day he barely managed to get out of bed on time to bolt down a quick breakfast and start his delivery rounds. It was a good thing he'd memorized the stops on his route, as very little of his mind was present as he pedaled around and carried packages into the back rooms of shops. Even his tips suffered, due to the lack of the usual charm he deployed with his customers. By the time he hurried back to the shop at the end of the day, did his cleaning (he'd gotten it down from nearly two hours to less than one by now), took a shower and finished dinner, it was fully dark.

Time to go to the Fisherman's Rest.

Faran was outside, smoking a cigarette and tinkering under the hood of his old truck, as he headed out the back door. "Goin' out again?" the butcher asked. His brow furrowed in obvious disapproval; he'd made no secret that he wasn't pleased his deliveryman spent so much of his off-work time going out at night and returning so late—apparently respectable people remained home during the hours when they should be sleeping.

"I am, yes." Stone didn't try to argue with him—he knew the butcher didn't have any problems with his work, and as far as he was concerned, it was none of the man's business what he did on his own time. Faran had said as much, though it was clear he hadn't exactly meant it.

"Lurby said he sees you down't Bella's Tavern two-three times a week."

"Is that a problem?" Bella's Tavern was the disreputable bar where he spent much of his time trying to pick up rumors.

"You tell me," Faran said, shrugging. "Ain't a nice place, Bella's. They got cheap women there, and bad sorts. Even criminals, I hear." He removed the cigarette from his mouth, spat, and replaced it.

"I'm not looking for cheap women—I couldn't afford them if I were." He jingled the meager remains of his tip money in his pocket. "Spent most of my pay on new clothes, so all I can afford is a drink or two until next week."

Faran grunted. "Just don't let me hear nothin' about you gettin' up to trouble. Remember, folks know you work for me. Can't have you reflectin' badly on the business. I hear tell you doin' that and I'll cut you loose."

"I understand." Stone tried not to sound annoyed—Faran gave him some variation of the same lecture at least once a day. He waved before the man could get up a head of steam. "See you tomorrow. Have a good evening." He almost added, *Don't wait up,* but decided it was best not to push it.

He wasn't completely sure where the Fisherman's Rest was, but he did know where the docks were. So far he'd avoided them, based on some of the conversation snippets he'd overheard at Bella's Tavern—he'd never been much of a fighter, and without his magic it hadn't seemed wise to go where he stood a decent chance of getting jumped again. Now, though, he'd have to take the chance. He buttoned up his coat against the damp, chilly air and set off walking.

As he walked, his thoughts turned once again to Harrison. The man was indeed a mystery—even more so than he'd thought before. Before his chat with Tanissa, he'd thought Harrison was just another mage in this world, but now it appeared he had a more substantial reputation here. When had he come to this world, and why? Had he been seeking a quiet place to get away from Earth? Was he a dimensional explorer who, for some reason, had decided to establish a more permanent base here?

And then there was the big question: how was he able to use magic when Stone couldn't? Despite his best efforts and many attempts, Stone had still been unable to use Harrison's magical source here, which seemed strange to him. He'd even, in a moment of desperation earlier in the week while pushing through a crowd on his way back from his deliveries, tried to drain a bit of power from a guy wouldn't stop trying to jostle past him. He'd deliberately moved into the man's path, allowing a collision and making his attempt as the two of them muttered hasty apologies.

Nothing.

So he couldn't do Harrison's magic, he couldn't do white magic (no surprise there), and he couldn't do black magic. But magic clearly *existed* on this dimension—in fact, it seemed to be much stronger than it was back on Earth—and just as clearly Harrison must be able to do it if he could get back and forth between here and Earth. So what was the difference?

He'd have to continue that line of thought later. He was approaching the dock area now, and once again the buildings grew more shabby and blasted-looking with each block he covered. An odd odor—almost but not quite the same as it smelled near the sea back on Earth—gradually began to permeate the air, and a light mist covered the cracked streets. Remaining watchful but keeping his posture and stride confident and purposeful, he continued on as if he knew exactly where he was going.

He didn't pass many people on his way. Once, a group of three men on a street corner looked him over as he went by; a block down, a wheezing vehicle that looked like it had been cobbled together from scrap iron and spare parts slowed as it crawled past him, but then resumed its normal speed and turned left at the next corner. Other than that, the street remained deserted.

Another block and a right turn toward the water revealed a glow through the fog. As Stone approached it, it resolved into a low, squat building. Though it had no windows, the series of flickering, multicolored lights shining along its roof-line and the large sign in the window featuring two words in blood-red paint with a twisting fish between them— surprisingly artistically rendered, compared to some of the other signs Stone had seen—suggested he'd found his destination.

As soon as he pushed open the door and entered, he could tell this wasn't the same kind of place as even the sketchy Bella's Tavern. While Bella's featured loud, jangly music, games, and working-class camaraderie, the Fisher-man's Rest had a darker ambiance. Even with his current inability to see auras, Stone could almost read this place's anyway: Purpose. Desperation. A place for people with nothing to lose.

A few customers shot him narrow-eyed, suspicious glances as he entered, but then quickly returned to their business. He couldn't get a good look at any of them even if he wanted to, since except for a few signs behind the bar and weak little lights on the tables, the place was so dark he couldn't even see his feet clearly as they crunched over something on the floor.

He went to the bar and waited for a break in the shoulder-to-shoulder crowd pressed against it. Both men and women, he noticed, the women every bit as hard-eyed and purposeful as the men. No giggling good-time girls here. Watching for a few moments revealed that the only way to get a drink was to shove in. Stone didn't like it, but the last thing he wanted to do was stand out, so he picked a spot between two smaller men and pushed his way through. They moved aside as little as possible, but they let him in.

He'd learned a few beer brands during his time at Bella's, so he got a pint of the spicy ale he'd picked up a taste for and stepped back, looking for a table. It took him several minutes of scanning the room, but eventually he found one near a wall and settled down to watch, trying to determine his next step. Without his magic, without the ability to read auras, he felt like he was missing one of his primary senses. Did he dare start making discreet inquiries? He glanced at two large, rough-looking men hunched over a nearby table, but looked away when one of them turned his way.

"I seen you before. At Bella's."

Stone started, twisting back around.

A man had dropped into the chair across from him and set a pint glass of something almost black on the table. Small, wiry, and unshaven, he wore an oversized dark coat and a cap pulled low over his eyes. Stone thought he might recognize him from the tavern, but couldn't be certain.

"Er—I've been there, yes," he said.

"What're you doin' here, then?"

Stone shrugged. "Looking for a change of scenery."

"Nobody comes to the Rest for a change o' scenery," the main said with a derisive snort. "Not unless ye like the stink o' fish and dopeweed. So what're ye *really* here for?"

Stone studied the man, wishing once again for the ability to size up his aura. His eyes, small and glittering under his cap, settled steadily on Stone, and his expression was somewhere between suspicion and anticipation. "I'm—looking for a friend. Someone told me he might come here."

"That right?"

"That's right."

The man pulled a small knife from his pocket and began picking his fingernails with studious care. He finished three of them before flicking his gaze back up. "So who's this friend?" His tone was deceptively casual.

Stone tensed. Something about the man's body language seemed subtly off to him, though he couldn't identify why. "Nobody important," he said, shaking his head. "I think he's moved on, actually."

"Tell me," the man insisted. "I'm a social guy. I know everybody 'round here. If he's been here, I'll know it—or know somebody who does."

As he struggled with how to answer without increasing the little man's suspicions, Stone noticed two other men disappearing down a hallway at the back of the bar. He realized he'd seen several similar instances—sometimes singles, sometimes groups of two or three—going down the same hallway. He'd thought they were heading to the bathrooms, but none of them ever came back out. "What's over there?" he asked, cocking his head toward the hall.

"Over where?"

"I keep seeing people going down that hallway, but nobody comes back out. Where are they going?"

The man narrowed his eyes. "What do you want?" he asked, his voice growing cold. He leaned in a little closer. "Just so ya know, I got three guys watchin' ya, where you'll never see 'em until they're on ya. I been watchin' ya since ya turned up here. Unless you give me the answers I want, you ain't gettin' outta here. We don't like strangers—especially not ones askin' too many questions. Okay?"

Stone studied him more closely. Was it possible that what he'd taken for mere suspicion might be laced with a healthy dose of fear? In a society like this, where the people were in constant danger from a threat they couldn't hope to counter, it made sense for strangers to be monitored. Still, it wouldn't be wise to show fear of his own. "Why do you care?" he asked.

"Like I said—we don't like strangers. Strangers are trouble."

"So I'll go, then." Perhaps if he could get out of here, he could risk coming back some other night.

The man shook his head. "You ain't goin' nowhere. Not yet. Now, who's this friend yer lookin' for? And I'll warn you—I'm real good at spottin' lies, and you won't like what happens if you lie to me."

Stone met his gaze and nearly jerked in surprise. The guy was watching him with the unmistakable fuzzed-out look of someone using magical sight. It was subtle, and he'd probably have missed it if he hadn't been so close, but this near he had no doubt. "Good at spotting lies, are you?" he asked casually. "Tell me—do any of the rest of these people know?"

"Know what?"

R. L. KING

Stone dropped his voice to a near-whisper and leaned forward. "That they've got a…what do they call it?…a 'Zap' in their midst?"

The man's reaction wasn't obvious. He didn't jerk in his seat, or glare, or splutter out a denial—but he didn't have to. The subtle twitch of his jaw and sharpening of his gaze was enough.

Stone allowed himself the tiniest of cold smiles. "It seems we all have secrets, don't we?"

The man relaxed again, and his own smile was wider and more confident. When he spoke again, he'd dropped most of the street-tough affectation. "Not sure how you figured it out, but if you think getting up and announcing it to the room will get you anywhere, go ahead and try it. I'll wait." He leaned back, picked up his pint, and took a long drink.

Stone didn't do that. He continued watching the man and said nothing.

"Good choice," the man said, looking satisfied. Then his expression once again grew hard. "Now, what do you want?"

"I told you, I'm looking for someone I know. I don't see him here, though." Stone knew he was repeating himself—he did it to give him time to consider the new information he'd just received. If it was true this man was Talented, what was he doing in the middle of a mundane dive bar? Spying? Perhaps his challenge for Stone to reveal him to the crowd had been a bluff, but he didn't think so. And if it wasn't, that meant the people here *already* knew he was a mage. Did that in turn mean he might be part of the underground movement Tanissa had mentioned? Was Stone right about the possibility that some of the mages were cooperating with the mundanes?

That was a lot of unanswered questions, and dangerous ones to bring up with as little knowledge as he had.

"And I asked you before—who is this friend? What makes you think he might be here at all?"

Stone decided to take a small chance. "His name is Trevor. Tall, black hair, gray eyes, about my age. I heard he might know some people who frequent this place." He met the man's gaze as he spoke, hoping if the man could read auras, he might pick up that he meant more than he was saying.

The man showed no recognition at the mention of the name, but he did tilt his head and regard Stone with curiosity at his last words. "Really? Interesting. That's an odd name— like I said, I know most of the people who come here, and I've never heard that one. I think you might be making this story up to save your own neck."

Stone was trying to decide how to answer when a woman dressed in rough, baggy work clothes hurried up to the table. She leaned down and whispered something in the man's ear, and he tensed.

"Well," he said. "Looks like it's your lucky day, friend, even if it's not mine. I have to go deal with some urgent business, so you're off the hook. My advice is to get out of here and not come back. If I see you around here, our chat won't be as pleasant. Got it?"

Stone gritted his teeth. *Damn* not being able to use magic! How did mundanes ever get anything done? "Fine," he said, glaring. "I'll go. But I'm not going to stop looking for my friend."

"Do what you like. Just not here. Don't try to follow me—my guys are still here, and if they see you do anything but finish your drink and walk out that door, it won't go well for you."

The man got up and headed away after the woman. Stone watched them until they disappeared into the crowd—and realized that was exactly what they *had* done: disappeared. One moment they'd stepped behind a group of men, but after a second the men parted to reveal an empty space.

Curiouser and curiouser, Stone thought as he too got up. But how the hell was he going to find out anything else if he couldn't even come back here without risking another beating—or worse?

He glanced around, looking for the "guys" the man had mentioned, but saw no sign of anyone watching him. Perhaps the man had been bluffing—or perhaps they were mages too, using some version of the disregarding spell he himself used frequently back on Earth. Clearly, if this place was indeed one of the meeting spots for an underground rebellion, they were highly suspicious of strangers. It certainly made sense given the stakes, but it meant any chance Stone had of connecting with them would require care and ingenuity.

After a brief thought of trying to sneak away under cover of stopping by the bathroom and perhaps taking a peek at what was going on down that hallway, Stone instead made a show of leaving through the front door. Perhaps he'd try again in a few days, when they weren't expecting him.

For now, he couldn't shake the crawling feeling on the back of his neck that warned him he was being watched.

CHAPTER THIRTEEN

S TONE RETURNED TO HIS ROUTINE for the next two days, focusing on making his deliveries and cleaning up the shop. He did go out in the evenings, but only back to Bella's and only for a couple of hours. He tried to tell himself it was because he was giving the situation at the Fisherman's Rest time to settle back down, but that wasn't all of it.

In truth, his frustration had grown to the point where it was affecting his confidence in his next course of action. *Stop it,* he told himself angrily one late afternoon, as he pedaled back toward the shop after his last delivery. He'd decided once again to avoid the dockside bar that night. *You're acting like one of* them.

You are *one of them,* his traitorous little voice pointed out. *Those mages can kill you as easily as they can the rest of the mundanes, and there's not a damned thing you can do to stop it.*

That was true enough—but they weren't lurking around every corner, especially not in Drendell. Aside from Tanissa, the pair at the eatery, and the man at the Fisherman's Rest (assuming Stone's assessment of him had been correct), he hadn't seen any other Talented in town. So far, the two who'd seemed friendly toward the mundanes had dressed like them, and the dangerous ones were easy to notice in their spotless peacock finery. "Subtle" didn't seem like a quality the Temolan Talented valued highly.

Damn it, he was tired of being a mouse. If something was going to happen, he'd have to *make* it happen—otherwise, it would be all too easy to get complacent, to put off action until settling in and making a home on this world seemed a viable option.

That was *not* a viable option.

Barely conscious of what he was doing, he pedaled faster as his anger grew; the empty trailer bounced and rattled behind him. He knew what he was going to do now: take the bike to the shop, finish cleaning up, and then head back over to the Fisherman's Rest. If the man was there, he'd take him aside and tell him exactly who he was looking for. If it got him killed, so be it—but if the man was part of the underground rebellion and Harrison was connected with it as well, it might finally get him some answers.

He spotted the glow up ahead when he turned the corner onto the shop's block. He slowed the bike, noticing that none of the people he usually saw moving up and down the busy street were around. In fact, the whole street seemed strangely deserted.

Suddenly conscious that he was very much alone out here, he pulled the bike into a nearby alley and left it there. It would be safe enough for a few minutes, but riding down the middle of the road with the clattering bike-and-trailer rig would make him too conspicuous. Buttoning his dark coat, he slipped back out onto the street and moved toward the glow, keeping to the shadows.

As he drew closer, he spotted a plume of smoke against the night sky, and the unmistakable acrid odor of burning wood filled the air. *Something's on fire.* Odd that he heard no sirens. Was it possible no one had reported it? It looked fairly close to Faran's shop—surely the law-abiding butcher would have—

Stone's heartbeat increased as a bright lance of terror pierced him. *No—it can't be—*

Still remaining close against the buildings and hidden in shadow, he rushed toward the fire.

In another half-block, his fears were confirmed.

Faran's formerly neat little butcher shop stood at the center of a conflagration, the bright orange flames licking upward nearly twice the height of the two-story building and the billowing smoke rising even higher. The space where the front display window had been yawned like an open, jagged-toothed mouth; more flames reached outward toward a sidewalk littered with glittering shards of broken glass.

A pair of fire trucks, painted dull white and in only marginally better condition than Faran's old pickup, were parked askew across the street in front of the shop, blocking traffic as several firemen tried to stanch the blaze with two hoses. Even from where Stone stood, he could see it was futile: the flames were too bright, too intense to be dissuaded by the firefighters' ineffectual efforts.

What could burn like that? The shop itself, like most of the other buildings in Drendell, was made of brick, and as far as Stone knew, Faran wasn't storing natural gas or piles of kindling or anything else highly combustible inside the shop.

Heart still pounding, he crept further forward when he spotted three people standing in a darkened shop across the street, huddled together and observing the firefighters' struggle through the window. Could they be Faran and his wife, watching their livelihood burn to the ground while consoled by one of their merchant neighbors?

But no, as he drew closer, the silhouettes resolved themselves into a taller, thinner man and two women, neither of whom had Runa's short, stout shape. He recognized the shop as a bakery, and the man as its proprietor. He hurried down the street and ducked into the shop. "What's happened?"

The three jumped, startled, so focused on the fire that they hadn't heard him come in. "It's terrible," one of the women said. She ran a shaking hand across her blotchy, tearstained face and braced herself against the window with her other hand. "So horrible…"

"What happened?" Stone asked again. "Was there some kind of accident, or—"

For the first time, the man seemed to recognize him. "You're Faran's deliveryman, aren't you?" He glanced toward the fire and then back at Stone, the fear on his face evident.

"Yes. I was just returning from my rounds. Are Faran and Runa all right? Did they get out?"

The younger woman burst into renewed tears, and her older female companion joined her. "Oh, dear gods, it was terrible," the older woman said. She had strong, plain features, and didn't look like the type who wept often. "I saw them leaving—"

"You saw *who* leaving?" Stone demanded. "Faran and Runa? They got out?"

"No, no…" She dissolved into sobs again.

A hand touched Stone's arm. When he glanced up, the male baker pointed silently at something in the street, just beyond the fire trucks.

Stone looked where he pointed, and something inside him clenched when he saw the stout, sheet-covered figure lying there. "No…" he whispered. "Is that—"

"It's Runa," the younger woman said. She'd gotten her tears under tentative control, but her voice still shook and her breath still hitched. "T-they haven't found Faran yet. They think h-he was…inside…when it—when they—"

Stone gripped her arms. "Tell me what happened. Who are you talking about?"

"The—the T-Talented," she said. "I saw them leave. Two of them. The place was already burning…and then Runa…she—she—" The woman buried her face in the man's chest.

"She ran out into the street, screaming," the man said, meeting Stone's gaze over top of her. "She was on fire—it was too late for anyone to do anything to help her. Before we could get there, she collapsed in the street. They think Faran is still inside."

Stone stared at him, feeling suddenly as if he might be sick. Nobody could survive those wild flames. "No…" he whispered.

"I saw them leaving too," the older woman said, bitterly. She nodded toward the street. "Two men. They just walked out of the shop, protected by a bubble. They walked away like they didn't even care. Like they hadn't just—"

Stone clenched his fists, his thoughts whirling. He wanted to act, to run after the murdering mages, to do *something*—but even as the thought came, he knew it would be pointless. Even if they were still in the vicinity, he had no hope of—

A figure came hurtling up the street and slipped into the shop, where it paused, panting. The older woman hurried to him and pulled him into their little group. "Kuri, thank the gods. We thought you'd—"

The young man rose from his crouch, still panting as if he'd run a great distance. Stone recognized him as the baker's teenage son, who helped out in the shop. The two often passed each other on their delivery routes. Now, though, when his gaze fell on Stone, his eyes widened in terror.

"You have to go!" he gasped out, pointing toward the rear of the shop. "Now. Right now. Go!"

His father looked him sternly. "Kuri, what are you—"

Stone glanced out the window, but saw nobody else approaching. "Why? What's going on?"

"They're coming back!" His voice shook, and tears sprang to his eyes. "You have to go. Please—they found the bike. They're looking for you. That's why they came to Faran's shop in the first place. They were waiting there for you, but one of them got impatient when you didn't show. Please—go before you're seen." His gaze darted to the firestorm across the street and the covered figure of Runa, and the wild horror in his eyes was unmistakable: *go before you get my family killed too.*

As often happened when he was under major stress, Stone's confusion burned off and his mental gears clicked into place. He'd have time to process all this later—for now, he had to act.

"Yes," he said quickly. "I'm going."

The baker and his wife had caught on now as well, and couldn't hide their relief. "You can go out through the back," the man said, pointing. "The alley's dark—keep your head down and run as far away from here as you can get."

Stone nodded, not missing the look of desperation that had crept into the older woman's expression as well. They wanted him gone, and he didn't blame them. "Thank you," he said, and took off for the back of the shop. As he slipped out the back door, he thought he smelled the cloying, sweet stench of burning human flesh on the smoke choking the air, but perhaps it was only his imagination.

| CHAPTER FOURTEEN

S TONE DIDN'T DO what the baker said after he left the shop; not exactly, anyway.

He didn't run. Unlike the mundanes, who likely knew little of the ways magic operated and were probably kept in the dark by the Talented, he was certain running would be a bad decision if the mages were looking for him. They were probably scanning for auras, and even if they didn't know what his looked like, the sight of someone running headlong away from the fire would no doubt raise their suspicion.

Instead, he set off at a brisk walk directly away from the bakery—away from where Faran's butcher shop was even now burning to the ground.

Away from where two people had died because they'd helped him, and where the deaths might not yet be over for the night.

He kept to dark alleys and shadowy streets, doing his best to stay hidden without appearing to move suspiciously. At first, he didn't pay attention to where he was going, except *away*—if the mages were looking for him, he wanted either to escape them or lure them as far from Faran's street as he could. At least that way they might leave the others alone.

He didn't stop walking for nearly an hour, taking circuitous routes through bad neighborhoods, pausing only long enough to get his bearings. He didn't look closely at his surroundings until his legs grew so heavy from fatigue that he had to stop before he fell over.

One look at the blasted-out buildings, heavily cracked streets, and flickering lights told him he was on the edge of the Barrens. He glanced back over his shoulder, checking to see if anyone had followed him, but the road behind him appeared deserted. He had no idea what time it was; it couldn't be too late, though, since he'd arrived back at the shop shortly after sunset. His stomach rumbled—he hadn't eaten anything since a sandwich at lunchtime. A sandwich made by Runa, he remembered—Runa, who'd never make another sandwich because of him.

Stop it. Time for that later.

He dared not venture out looking for food. If the mages were searching for him, he had no idea how long they'd persist, or whether they'd put out the magical equivalent of an APB on him. Could they track him using the clothes they'd found in his room, or had they thought to collect them before burning the place down? No point worrying about that—if they could track him, he couldn't stop them. If not, his best bet was to stay under cover and lie low for a while. Perhaps they'd think he'd fled the town when he found out they were looking for him.

The buildings here were all abandoned, their windows broken, their upper levels toppled, their doors missing or hanging askew on rusted hinges. With one more quick look around to make sure nobody had seen him, Stone entered the nearest one, a squat structure with a sheared-off roof over its second story.

Inside, it was dark. The air smelled of dust, rot, and dried urine. His feet crunched over old bits of wood and crumbling bricks. "Anyone in here?" he called.

Farther into the building, something skittered. Stone froze, trying to identify the source, but he couldn't. It sounded small, though—probably rats or cats or something. Certainly not large enough to be one of those mutant wolf-things.

Most of the building's interior structure was gone now; the knocked-down or crumbled walls left a dim, open space. The only exception was the remains of a room on the far side. Mostly intact, it was still missing the top part of two of its walls, and the door was gone. Still, it seemed to be the most defensible part of the building, assuming some other squatter hadn't already claimed it.

"Anyone here?" he called again as he approached it. When no reply came, he picked his way across the floor and peered with caution through the doorway.

It was too dark to see much, but his eyes had adjusted enough by now to reveal he was alone. More bits of wood and brick littered the floor; on the far side was what looked like the remains of a nest where someone had slept. Further investigation revealed its occupant was long gone, though—the food remnants in the empty cans had dried, and a thin layer of dust covered the ripped, jumbled bedroll.

Heart still pounding, Stone looked around for ways to make the little room defensible. He doubted he'd sleep much tonight, but he dared not venture out, even to try going back to the Fisherman's Rest. With the mages looking for him, he didn't know who he could trust, and even if he did, he wouldn't risk getting anyone else killed for helping him. Not until things had settled down.

After investigating the ground floor of the small building, he found a stout piece of wood that might be useful as a club. He carried it back to the bedroll and added it to a small pile of bricks he'd already gathered there. They weren't good weapons and certainly wouldn't give him much chance against mages, but at least he might have a chance of dissuading any scavengers that might come by.

He collected the empty food cans—there were five in all, marked with the angular writing and images of beans and soup—and spread three of them across the open doorway. The other two he balanced precariously on the sill of the broken window. If he *did* nod off and anything tried to enter the room without expecting his little traps, the sound might give him enough time to react.

Finally, as secure as he could manage, he picked up the bedroll and shook it, raising a cloud of dust and barely avoiding a coughing fit. It reeked of funk and old body odor, but at least it would help him keep warm as the night's temperature dropped. He settled himself into the room's back corner where he could see both the window and the door and gathered it around him.

He couldn't sleep even if he'd wanted to. The combination of the air's chill and the growl of hunger was bad enough, but those he could ignore if necessary using his meditation techniques. What he *couldn't* ignore were the images of Faran's and Runa's faces, and the thoughts of how they must have suffered under the cruel mages' torture. He could almost hear their screams in his mind as they burned, and it was all because of him. Because Faran had taken a chance on the odd stranger Byra had asked him to help.

In an attempt to drive the horrifying, guilt-ridden visions away, he clasped his hands around his drawn-up knees and took stock of his situation. Things weren't looking good all around. Most of his meager possessions had been destroyed in the fire—he assumed the mages hadn't thought to take them, or they'd have used them to find him by now. He never thought he'd be relieved at the Talented's impatience, but in this case it might have saved his life. All he had left were the clothes on his back and the few coins he'd gotten as tips on his delivery rounds today, which wouldn't be enough to buy more than one or two cheap meals.

With a sense of grim amusement, he thought about his current situation versus what he'd left behind on Earth. *Good one, Stone,* he told himself bitterly. *Back home you'd be warm and snug in your bed right about now after a good meal and a drink.* He never thought much about how, following William Desmond's and Adelaide Bonham's bequests, he was now a multimillionaire—wealth was something he'd grown up accustomed to and it didn't dazzle him—but right now he couldn't help seeing the irony as he sat here huddled under a stinking blanket, poorer than the most downtrodden of homeless people on Earth.

All because you couldn't accept your lot, his unwelcome little voice told him. *All because you were too proud to let Jason help you. You're doing just brilliantly, aren't you?*

Shut up, he told the voice, but with no conviction behind it. *This isn't helping.*

He wondered what Verity was doing now. He'd been gone nearly two weeks—would she think he wasn't coming back? How long would she wait before she brought others in on what he'd done? Would she hunt down Arthur and Eddie for help, or try to find Madame Huan?

For a brief moment, hope flared at that thought—Madame Huan was one of the few people on Earth who *might* have a chance of tracking him down. But then the hope died as he remembered that she was once again out of the country on one of her artifact hunts, and Verity wouldn't have any way to contact her.

He sighed and lowered his head to his hands. Hell, he even missed Raider. Right now, a warm, furry cat curled up next to him, loud purr rumbling in the silence, would be welcome and appreciated. He'd seen a few catlike creatures in this world, but never up close and always skulking down darkened alleys. Perhaps people didn't keep pets here, at least not the mundanes. Maybe the constant uncertainty and fear they lived with made them unwilling to risk it.

Something skittered. Stone stiffened, jerking his head back up. A flash of pain shot through him as the vision of the two-headed mutant wolf thing rose in his mind—he *was* close to the abandoned Barrens area, after all. Did the scavengers come in this far if they smelled fresh prey? He snatched up his wooden club and flicked his gaze back and forth between the window and the door, ready to leap up if anything came in.

The skittering faded as whatever caused it moved off, but Stone didn't let himself relax until several minutes passed without its return. He let his breath out and settled back, leaving the club close by.

It was going to be a long night, and he didn't think he would sleep for any of it.

❖

He awoke to the sound of voices.

For a moment, he thought they were in his dreams. Despite his cold and hunger he'd managed to nod off, dreaming that Faran and Runa were shouting at him for getting back late from his delivery rounds, only to have their heads erupt in flame as two menacing, long-coated figures rose up behind them. One figure had his face, and the other one had Harrison's.

Stone snapped awake, heart thudding. He closed his eyes and listened. Surely the voices must have been in his mind. Nobody could—

But no—there they were again. A man and a woman, both speaking in tones so low Stone couldn't make out what they were saying. More squatters? A drunken couple on their way home from one of the bars? He had no idea what time it was, or how long he'd been asleep.

Moving with care, he pushed the bedroll aside and crept across the floor, keeping below the level of the window. Careful not to dislodge the cans he'd set as a trap, he rose until he could barely see over the sill—and froze.

The two figures weren't close—at least half a block separated them from the building where Stone hid. But even from here in the faint moonlight and the flickering illumination of a dying streetlight, the sweeping silhouettes of their long coats marked them as Talented. Stone's breath caught in his throat. Were they looking for him? Why else would they be out here this time of night? As he watched, the two figures turned and began heading in his direction. Quickly, he dropped down so even the top of his head wasn't visible from the outside.

Think, Stone, he ordered himself as he crouched there, his heartbeat increasing and his breathing quickening. *You can't do magic, but you* know *magic. Don't lose your head now.*

Assuming magic here worked similarly to Earth's, if they were searching for him they'd be looking for his aura. They might have other kinds of detection spells, but if they did he was lost anyway—there was no way he could outrun their magic, and if he tried they'd spot his aura instantly. Especially out here in the dark, where it would blaze like a beacon. His only hope was to hide it. Since he didn't think he could do that with magic, he'd have to use the mundane method: cover it up.

He snatched up the bedroll, lowered himself back down into the room's corner, and pulled it over himself, making sure to draw his legs up and cover his body completely. It wouldn't fool them for a moment if they actually entered the room, especially if they had light spells, but if luck was with him they'd pass by if they didn't spot the telltale glow of an aura through the open window. The hard part was that he couldn't risk peering out to check—if he uncovered even the top of his head, his powerful aura would instantly reveal his location any magical searchers. He'd have to be patient and wait.

The voices grew closer—close enough that he could hear them even through the heavy cloth over his head.

"He's not here," the woman said, sounding bored and annoyed. "Why are we even wasting our time out here? Who is he, anyway? Nothing but a Dim nobody. Let's go back. All we'll find out here is stinking squatters and scavengers from the Wastes."

"Just a little while longer," the man replied. "If we find him, Garionus will be pleased enough that I finally might get free of Temolan."

The woman snorted. "In your dreams, my friend. You'll need to do more than track down a runaway Dim pig for that to happen."

Stone remained still, holding his breath, terrified that his stomach would growl or the dusty air would cause him to cough and give away his position. As he lay there he realized—though he didn't know *how* he knew it—that the two Talented weren't speaking the same language as the mundanes he'd been interacting with the last two weeks. Did the mages have their own language? It made sense—as proud and arrogant as they were, they'd be unlikely to speak the same tongue as the common "Dim" among themselves—but the translation spell seemed to be handling it effectively. Did that mean he could speak it as well? Had he spoken it, unwittingly, when he'd first arrived here and the Talented thugs had hassled him? That knowledge might come in handy if he managed to evade capture.

The voices came closer. Now they were talking about a party they planned to attend after they finished here. To Stone's horror, it sounded as if they'd paused only a few feet from his window. Thoughts rose unbidden: had they spotted him? Were they toying with him like cats with a bedraggled mouse, waiting to see how long he could remain still before he had to move or cough? If he poked his head out of the bedroll, would he see them standing outside the open window, smiling with malevolent amusement as they waited to immobilize him with a spell, or even kill him?

The temptation to peer out, to check, became nearly overpowering. *No,* he told himself. *They haven't seen you. Just stay still and they'll move on. Don't bugger it all up now.* Joining the temptation was the equally compelling fantasy of leaping up, club in hand, and trying to take them down before they could get their spells off. If they weren't expecting him, if he caught them by surprise, he might be able to manage it. The satisfaction of bashing one of these conceited bastards' heads in would be pleasant, no doubt. He wondered if these were the two who'd killed Faran and Runa. If there had only been one of them, he might even have tried it.

He gripped the club tighter. Remaining still was the more intelligent decision, but he still felt shame and anger at his mouse-like behavior. Jason would have attacked them. Hell, *Verity* probably would have attacked them.

And gotten themselves killed. Use your brain—it's your best hope now. Live to fight another day. Live to find Harrison. Then you can fight back.

As Stone wrestled with his own inner struggle, the voices outside continued murmuring to each other. They stayed there, not more than ten feet from Stone's hiding spot, for what seemed an eternity but what in reality must not have been more than a minute or two. Then they moved off again and eventually faded to silence.

Stone held his breath for a full thirty seconds before letting it out, and waited five more minutes before venturing from his hiding place to peek out the window.

The two Talented were gone, as far as he could tell. The only moving form he saw was some small creature darting across the street and passing under the flickering streetlight.

Exhaustion and renewed hunger gripped him as his heartbeat slowed and the adrenaline of the terrifying previous minutes faded. Despite his near-overwhelming urge to get up, to run, to find a new hiding place now that this one might have been compromised, he remained where he was. He had no idea which direction the two searchers were heading, or how much longer the planned to keep up the hunt. If they'd checked this area they might not check it again, but fleeing in some random direction might put him directly in their path again—and he might not be so lucky a second time. No, best to just stay here and remain vigilant. He'd head out when the sun was up, and his aura wouldn't give him so readily away. *They probably don't know what it looks like,* he reminded himself. *Don't act like a fugitive, and they won't treat you like one.*

He hoped, anyway. Either way, it promised to be a long, tense night.

| CHAPTER FIFTEEN

S TONE DUG HIMSELF OUT from his bedroll when the sun's light peeked in through his broken window. He blinked blearily and ran his hand back through his tangled hair as the reality of his situation once again settled over him.

Despite his fear that someone would discover him, he'd managed to sleep fitfully for a brief time, but it had done nothing to alleviate his growing hunger and exhaustion. He'd have to get something to eat, or at least to drink, soon—he couldn't afford to grow weak from hunger and thirst or he might as well turn himself in to the nearest long-coated figure he spotted.

It was a testament to how far he'd fallen that he suffered a brief regret at leaving the stinking bedroll behind. He wouldn't be coming back here, and taking it with him would mark him as odd—something he couldn't afford. Besides, he knew he couldn't stay out on the streets for long. For one thing, without anyone to help him, he had little experience with living rough—and that was on Earth. Add in a society he was barely familiar with, and he didn't like his odds.

The vision of the fire at Faran's shop steeled his resolve once again: he'd have to do something, find someone to talk to, progress further on his search for Harrison—even if it put him at risk. At least two innocent people had suffered excruciating deaths because of him, and he owed it to them not to simply roll over and give up.

No, he had places to go. He'd decided on his next actions during one of his wakeful periods last night—there was only one logical choice.

The time for polite inquiries was past. Promise be damned, this time he wasn't going to take no for an answer.

As he hoped, the hospital/clinic was open even at this early hour. He stopped on his way only long enough to use one of his five remaining coins to buy a pastry and beg a cup of water from a bakery, then hurried toward his destination with the purposeful walk of someone who knew where he was going. The best way not to draw attention to oneself, he'd learned many years ago, was to look as if you belonged where you were. It must have worked, because he passed several people walking by on their way to work and all they did was glance disapprovingly at him before moving past. That much, he couldn't help—he'd done his best to make himself presentable, but after his night wrapped in the old bedroll, he knew how he must smell.

He paused outside, gathering his thoughts and coming to terms with the fact that he could be making a decision that would get him killed, then pushed open the door and strode inside.

This early, only a few people sat in the waiting room: a pale, coughing child with his worried father, an old man who stared straight ahead at the opposite wall, and a pregnant young woman. The woman was the only one who even glanced at Stone; the others seemed to be in their own worlds of misery.

He didn't recognize the woman at the counter—she wasn't the same one he'd talked to on his last visit. He marched up to her and said in a soft but insistent tone, "I want to talk to Tanissa."

A brief look of something—alarm?—passed across the woman's face, and her gaze sharpened. "She isn't here."

Was she lying? She was definitely scared about something, but Stone couldn't tell what. "Can you contact her? Does she have a phone? It's vitally important I talk to her, and I'm not leaving until I do."

Her expression grew stubborn, but there was no mistaking the fear beneath it. "Sir, you can't—"

"I can and I will. I'm sorry—I don't want to cause trouble, but I've had a very bad night and I've no more patience for waiting. Please call her and tell her there's someone here who needs to talk to her."

"You can't talk to her," said another voice.

Stone glanced up quickly and was surprised to see Byra, the blonde doctor who'd arranged his job with Faran, standing in the doorway.

"Why can't I?" he demanded. "I know you people have phones. Why can't you—"

By now, all the patients in the waiting room had looked up and taken an interest in the conversation. Byra's gaze, nearly as fearful as the front desk woman's, shifted to them, then back to Stone. "Come with me," she said, with a head jerk toward the rear of the clinic.

With a final glance at the desk woman, Stone followed her through the door. She didn't speak again until they were in her office, the one where Stone had signed his discharge papers.

"Tell me what's going on," he insisted without sitting down. "As I told the woman out front I've had a very unpleasant night, and I'm done being polite. I want to talk to Tanissa, and I'm not leaving here until I get some answers."

"You can't talk to her," Byra said, looking suddenly weary. "She's gone."

A chill sliced through Stone. "What do you mean, she's gone?"

"They took her away last night. You shouldn't be here."

The chill spread, and he stopped pacing. "Took her away? Who did?" He ran a hand over his face. *Gods, what have I started?* "You—know about Faran and Runa, right?"

She nodded without looking at him. She appeared to have aged ten years since he had last seen her; strands of her neat hair hung over her eyes, her white coat appeared even more rumpled than usual, and she looked as if she'd tried using makeup to cover the fact that she'd been crying. "A friend called here last night to tell us. They didn't mention you, so I wasn't sure whether you'd gotten away."

"You said they took Tanissa." He leaned forward to grip the edges of Byra's desk. "Who did? The Talented?"

"Who else?" A hint of bitterness touched her tone. "I don't know how they found out you were here, but I shouldn't be surprised—they have ways of finding out all kinds of things. Maybe they got it out of Faran or Runa, before they—" She paused to get herself under control, then met his gaze. "Either way, they showed up last night and told Tanissa she'd been called back to Temolan."

"Called back—?"

"They've never approved of what she did here—they thought it was a waste of her time and talents, healing the Dim." Now there was no mistaking her bitterness. "They're all the same up there—they don't care whether we live or die, as long as we do our work and remember our place." She let out a loud sigh. "Anyway, they took her. I'm not sure if she was under arrest or not, but I doubt she'll be coming back. So no, you can't talk to her. And I suggest you get out of here if you know what's good for you—and for us."

She didn't say it, but she didn't have to—Stone heard it in his mind as if she had: *for the gods' sake, get out of here before you bring down the same thing on us that you did on Faran and Runa.*

"All right," he said softly. "I'll go. I don't want to cause trouble for you here. But I can't run from them forever—I've got to get some answers."

"I'm sorry. I can't help you anymore," Byra said. She looked miserable. "I honestly wish I could—but I have the people here to think about. If the Talented came for us, the people in this area wouldn't have anywhere to go." Her gaze came up. "Without Tanissa, people are already going to die. *You'd* have died, if she hadn't been here to help you. I can't take any more risks."

Stone looked at his hands, still gripping the desk. She was right, of course—it was clear that associating with him was the equivalent of walking around town carrying a bomb with an unknown timer: it wasn't a question of *if* the thing would go off, but *when.*

"You're right, of course," he muttered. "I'll clear out before anyone else sees me. Perhaps I'll leave town—go somewhere else, where they don't know me."

She gave him an odd look. "I keep forgetting how much you don't know. You can't leave town—not easily, anyway. You'll never be allowed on the train without proper papers, and certainly not looking like that." She opened her desk drawer and removed a leather purse, from which she plucked a small quantity of coins. "Take these. It's not much, and it won't help for long, but—" Her expression softened, though the fear never left it. "I'm sorry. I truly am. I'd help you more if I could, but I've got a young daughter at home, and—"

"I understand. And thank you." Stone took the coins and put them in his pocket. "Is there a back door I can leave through, so I won't be seen?"

"Yes, I'll show you." She looked relieved. "Come on. And good luck to you." She opened the office door and glanced back and forth, then waved him out.

He followed her down a hallway, past the clinic ward where he'd recuperated; as he glanced through, he spotted Milas, the other doctor who hadn't wanted to allow him here in the first place, standing next to a bed. His back was to Stone, though, so he slipped past. From the other side of the ward, Jena the nurse happened to look up and notice him. Their gazes met for a moment, then she smiled sadly at him and turned away.

Byra opened a door onto an alley. "This should be safe," she said, looking left and right.

"Thank you. I appreciate your help—again."

"Please—don't come back here anymore. I know that sounds cruel, but—"

"I know. I understand. And…" he added, gripping her arm briefly, "I'm so sorry about Faran and Runa."

She nodded, looking at her feet. "Me too. They were good people." Without another word, she slipped back inside and the door clicked shut behind her, leaving Stone standing alone in the narrow alley.

Alone, with the best of his remaining options now gone.

As far as he could see he had only one more left—the Fisherman's Rest.

| CHAPTER SIXTEEN

STONE MANAGED TO AVOID CAPTURE for the remainder of the day, but he wasn't sure whether that was because the Talented weren't searching as diligently for him as he feared, or because his efforts at lying low and not raising anyone's suspicions were working.

He kept moving but didn't skulk around, grateful that his brief period as Faran's deliveryman had given him a good idea of where things were in this part of the city. It was difficult not to look over his shoulder, convinced several times during the day that someone was following him, but he managed it. Now more than ever, fitting in and not doing anything to attract anyone's attention was vitally important. If he looked like he had something to hide, someone would start thinking he did. And he had no idea if any of the mundanes here were in collusion with the Talented.

He used a couple of his small stash of coins to buy another cheap shirt, and cleaned up as best he could—which wasn't very well—in the store's bathroom. He couldn't do anything about shaving, or about the fact that his coat still smelled like the old bedroll, but he didn't plan to get close to anyone until tonight anyway.

As he sat in a park eating a sandwich he'd bought from a street vendor, he thought about what Byra had told him that morning. So the Talented had "taken" Tanissa. What did that mean? Had they killed her? Did they kill their own with as much callous disregard as they did the mundanes? Had they put her in jail for daring to help a stranger? Forbidden her to return to the cities of the "Dim"? He had no idea. Just another thing to feel guilty about, even though he knew intellectually that it wasn't, unless the mere fact that he'd come here at all was cause for guilt. It wasn't his fault these people had such a buggered-up society that the magically talented could screw up the lives of the mundanes with impunity.

It wasn't his fault, but Faran and Runa were still dead because they'd helped him. And even if Tanissa had only been forced to return to Temolan, a lot more people would die because the hospital didn't have its magical healer anymore.

He sighed, wadding up the paper from his sandwich while he watched a group of children running around, shouting and tossing a ball back and forth between them. They looked as carefree as any group of Earth children, which seemed incongruous to Stone after everything that had happened over the last day or two.

He quickly got up and left, driven by some deep fear that even being near him might bring harm to them.

He waited until full dark before heading to the Fisherman's Rest. Before he went there, he used another of his coins—the supply was getting quite low already—to buy a knit cap to pull down low over his eyes. If he was right and the Talented didn't know what his aura looked like, everything he could do to make himself blend in with the faceless crowds would help.

The place was packed tonight, the air full of dopeweed smoke and jangly music and conversation. Nobody paid him more than cursory attention as he entered and pushed his way through the crush of bodies, looking for a place to sit where he could keep an eye on the door. This time he didn't find one: all the small tables were occupied, with more customers standing shoulder to shoulder at the bar. It was hard to see in here, probably on purpose, but he did his best to scan the faces around him in search of the man he'd talked with the other night. This time, he was planning to take the man aside and ask him point-blank about Harrison. Assuming he could even find him, of course. He didn't even know his name, and nothing about him had looked sufficiently different from many other men in here to use as an effective description.

He shoved past more tables—three burly workmen drinking and laughing, a pair of oddly hunched, hooded figures, a tiny, dark-haired woman sitting across from a hulking pale man—to the front of the bar and ordered an ale, then carried it to a spot next to a bulky jukebox. It occurred to him that he still had no idea what he was going to do. He'd seen no sign of the man he'd talked to the other night, nor even the woman who'd called him away. Should he just pick someone at random and ask? That was dangerous, but he didn't have many other options, nor anything to lose at this point. He couldn't sneak around, doing his best to dodge the Talented, forever. If they decided they wanted to put sufficient effort into tracking him down, he couldn't stop them. His best bet was to find Harrison before that happened.

As he considered these thoughts, his gaze fell on the hallway he'd spotted the other night—the one people had been walking down in occasional singles and small groups but never coming back from. Perhaps the answers he sought were there. If he could get somewhere before anyone realized he didn't belong here—hell, if he could get himself grabbed by somebody for trespassing—at least then he'd have a better chance of finding the people who knew what was going on around here.

Here goes, he thought. He took a long drink of ale, then headed with purpose toward the hallway, doing his mundane best to keep his aura under control in case any of the Talented were in here watching.

When two men moved to block his way, they did it so subtly that at first he didn't realize that was their intent. To anyone else who might be watching, they simply appeared to be two·tipsy workmen pausing to have a conversation in an open doorway.

"Excuse me," Stone said. "Could I get by, please?"

"Sorry," said one of them, without moving. "Private hallway."

Stone tilted his head. "Aren't the bathrooms down there?"

"Closed for cleaning," the other one said.

"Come back later," said the first.

"Closed for cleaning?" Stone didn't try to hide his disbelief and astonishment—in fact, he exaggerated them. "This place is packed full, and the bathrooms are closed?" He craned his neck trying to see past them, but it was too dark to make out much beyond an empty hallway.

"Sorry," the second man said. "You can go piss off the dock out back if you want."

"Look," Stone said, exasperated. "This is absurd." He leaned in closer to the first man. "I'm looking for someone, actually. I was talking with him the other night when I was here, but our conversation was interrupted. Skinny chap, dark coat, short."

"He got a name?" the man asked.

"I didn't get it. We were interrupted before we got very far. He was going to help me look for another friend. Man named Trevor." He watched the man's face carefully for any sign of recognition.

There was none. "Sorry, friend. Nobody here by that name—and the other guy sounds like half the guys in here." He waved a hand, indicating the crowd, and made a derisive chuckle. "And a few o' the women. Now go on—like I said, the can's closed. Come back later if you can hold it, or go to Benbo's up the street if you can't."

For a moment, Stone considered trying to push past them and make a run for it down the hall—they probably wouldn't expect it, and he might get to see something before they caught him—but he didn't. Getting himself beaten up again wouldn't help his cause, and this time there wouldn't even be a magical healer to patch him up. He took a deep breath. "Listen," he said, leaning in even closer. "This man I was talking to the other night—he was…special."

The second man snorted, and oddly appeared to relax. "Give it up, man. Whoever he is, he probably found somebody else. He ain't worth it. Now get outta here."

Stone sighed. "Fine. I'm going." He took his glass and headed back to his vantage point at the jukebox. This was getting him nowhere fast. Would he have to resort to questioning random customers after all? He didn't want to, but—

Wait.

He replayed the conversation again: "*...or go to Benbo's up the street.*"

It was probably an offhand statement—he didn't know what "Benbo's" was, but suspected down here it had to be another bar—but what if it wasn't?

What if the man *had* recognized Harrison's name, or knew who he'd been talking to the other night, and was giving him a clue about where to go next? It made sense—an underground organization working against a powerful enemy like the Talented would need to be absolutely sure any new recruits weren't spies before allowing them access to their secrets.

You're being absurd, Stone told himself. *Grasping at straws now.*

But what other choices did he have?

He glanced back toward the hallway; the two men were still there, appearing to have an animated conversation over their beers, but once he caught them flashing quick glances in his direction. At the tables, the three workmen he'd noticed were still there, but the hooded figures and the mismatched couple were gone, replaced with another couple and four more workmen.

He finished his ale, left the glass on top of the jukebox, and headed for the door. On his way, he asked a random customer which way Benbo's was.

The swaying young man hooked a thumb over his shoulder. "Oh, yeah—go outside and turn left. It's two blocks or so down." He raised a rolled dopeweed joint the size of his index finger, took a long pull, and offered it to Stone with a goofy grin.

"Thank you," he said hastily, waving off the joint and hurrying out.

Outside, the crisp sea air was a welcome change from the Rest's smoke-filled interior. A light, cold breeze blew off the water; Stone couldn't see the docks from where he stood, but he could hear the water lapping against them. He paused a moment to take a few deep breaths and clear his head, looking around for anyone who might be watching him.

Nobody was, as far as he could tell. A few people lingered in front of the bar, but all of them appeared to be occupied with their own conversations. After a moment, a group of them bid each other goodbye and took off in two different directions, neither of them in the direction of Benbo's.

Stone glanced left, the way the weedhead inside had told him to go. The street was mostly deserted at this time of night, the crumbling brick buildings bleak against the cloudy night sky, but far off in the distance he saw lights through the mist: blues, yellows, greens. *That must be the place*, he decided, since he spotted no other lights in that direction. He buttoned his coat against the air's damp chill and set off at a fast walk.

He quickly realized his destination was farther away than he'd thought. From where he'd stood in front of the Fisherman's Rest, the lights looked only a block or two away, but as he walked, a long time passed before they seemed to get any closer. The weedhead had said "two blocks"—apparently they had long blocks down here, or else the man's perception of distance was less than reliable. Stone glanced back over his shoulder toward the Rest; it wasn't as brightly lit as Benbo's, and had already receded so far into the mist that he could barely pick it out.

When he turned back toward his destination, someone was standing in front of him.

| CHAPTER SEVENTEEN

STONE STOPPED, eyeing the man with wary caution. He looked like many of the others he'd seen back at the Fisherman's Rest: pale, scruffy, unshaven, dressed in dark work clothes and sturdy boots. "Yes, can I help you?" He shifted his gaze to the sides, wondering if more of them lurked in the mist.

"Want to talk to you," the man said. He indicated a narrow alley between two darkened buildings. "Let's go where nobody can see us."

"Do you think I'm an idiot?" Stone asked, narrowing his eyes. "Listen—I barely have enough money to buy a sandwich and a pint of ale. So if you're planning to mug me—"

"I hear you're lookin' for somebody." The man appeared unruffled by Stone's words. His posture remained casual, his arms hanging loosely at his sides, and he displayed no obvious weapon. "If you're not interested, then—"

Stone tensed, suddenly even more on guard. "I might be," he said with care. "Do you know where to find him?"

"Come over here." The man looked around as if he expected someone to jump them. "It's not safe to talk about this kind of thing out in the open."

Considering for only a moment, Stone nodded and followed the man into the alley. If this was a mugging, he'd hand over his meager store of coins and do his best to escape, but after all this time he couldn't risk passing up an opportunity to get closer to Harrison.

"All right," he said when they had moved back into the alley's shadows. "Now tell me—do you know where the man I'm looking for is?"

"No." A light flared as the man lit a cigarette—a regular one, not dopeweed this time. He held out the pack. When Stone shook his head, he said, "I don't know where he is. Nobody at my level knows where he is. But I know the right people to talk to if you want to find him."

Stone leaned against the wall so at least one direction was defensible. The alley was so dimly lit that all he could see was the man's shadowy figure and the tiny orange pinpoint of his cigarette. He lowered his voice to a near-whisper. "Let's just be clear before I trust you—tell me something to prove you know who I'm looking for."

The man chuckled in the darkness. "It ain't you who needs to trust me—it's *me* who needs to trust *you*. I'm guessin' you know how dangerous it is to talk to the wrong people. Just ask Faran and Runa about that, yeah? The Zaps are everywhere—you could be a Zap spy, for all I know."

"How do you know I'm not?" Stone asked. "How do I know *you're* not?"

"You don't. And neither do I. But I don't think you are. We've had eyes on you ever since you started droppin' dangerous names. Wanted to make sure you wouldn't bring the Zaps down on us if we talked to you."

Stone shook his head. "At this point, all I want is to find him. I need to talk to him about something important."

"Important?"

"Nothing that affects you lot," he added hastily. "Something I need to find out from him. Now—can you help me find him, or should I go on my way? I won't tell anyone we spoke, but if you know what happened at Faran's shop, you know I haven't time to waste."

The man appeared to consider his words; it was hard to tell when Stone couldn't see his face clearly. "Yeah, okay," he said at last. "I told you—I don't know where he is. It's dangerous for anybody on the streets to know things like that. But I do know people you can talk to."

That made sense—he'd speculated before that if some kind of rebellion was growing among the mundanes, it would have to be cell-based to keep the mages from ripping through the organization every time they caught one of its members. "All right," he said. "Take me to these people. I'll do what I can to help you—though I warn you, it probably won't be much. I'm not exactly at my best at present."

"That's all right. A lot of us aren't. Come on—and keep up. It's never smart to stay in one place for too long."

"How far are we going?"

"Not too far. Just follow." Without waiting to see if Stone complied, he headed further into the alley.

Stone quickly caught up with him, his longer stride easily keeping pace with the shorter man.

The man didn't seem inclined to talk as he stopped at the other end of the alley, looked both ways, then darted across the street into another narrow space between two more buildings. Stone tried to keep track of where they were going, but it wasn't long before they'd passed into an unfamiliar area dominated by more crumbling brick buildings. Here, whoever took care of the town's infrastructure didn't even bother keeping the streetlights lit—by the time they'd gone what Stone estimated to be a quarter-mile, he'd seen only one faintly flickering light. He wondered if they were heading into the Barrens, and kept a cautious eye out for any of the mutant wolf-things or other hostile wildlife.

"How much longer?" he asked at one point, barely loud enough to be heard.

"Shh!" the man cautioned. He held up a hand, looked around him, and his posture tensed. "Quick—in here!" He ducked into another alley and crouched behind a pile of wooden boxes.

Stone hurried to follow, glancing back over his shoulder. At the far end of the street, he spotted two figures. Were they wearing long coats? He couldn't tell, but better to be safe. Complying with the man's frantic gestures, he moved behind the boxes and crouched behind them, out of sight of the street.

"Shh…" the man whispered again. His posture remained stiff and fearful as he peered with caution around the corner of one of the boxes.

Stone, afraid if he tried to look too and those *were* a pair of Talented out there, remained ducked securely behind the boxes. He waited what seemed like several minutes before his companion relaxed.

"Okay," the man said, rising. "They're gone. Damn slumming Zaps are always a problem."

"Slumming?" Stone stood up behind him, checking the end of the alley for any other signs of movement.

"Yeah. Some of 'em like coming down here so they can feel good about themselves for how much better they have it. Sick bastards, if y'ask me. Anyway, we're almost there. Let's keep moving before they decide to come back."

Stone followed him down two more streets and three more alleys before they finally stopped. At this point, he was sure the man was leading him on a circuitous route, trying to disorient him so he wouldn't be able to find his way back to wherever they were taking him. That was fine with him—it was better than being herded along blindfolded. If this went well, he'd meet up with whoever the man's secret contact was and find out how to approach Harrison, and he wouldn't *have* to come back here.

Halfway up another alley, the man stopped in front of a closed door. He knocked—twice, then three times—and then stepped aside, glancing up and down the alley. Less than a minute later, Stone heard a *click* on the other side.

The man opened the door and waved Stone in, then followed him and closed the door behind them. They now stood in a narrow hallway that smelled of dust and spicy food. "Just through here," the man said, pointing at another door ahead of them. "Sorry about all the running around, but we had to make sure nobody was following you."

Stone opened the door and stepped through into a small room with no windows. An uncovered, overhead light illuminated what looked like a temporary crash space: mattresses on the floor, a pair of old couches, a table with two chairs. The room was currently empty, but there was another door on the other side. He turned back to the man, who'd come in behind him. "When are they going to—"

He stopped.

Something—he couldn't identify exactly what—had changed in the man's expression. Tensing, he felt his heartbeat increase. *Stop it,* he told himself angrily. *Nothing's wrong. You're jumping at shadows again.*

But the man was standing in front of the door they'd just come in, and he was eyeing Stone under the brighter light as if examining something on a laboratory slide.

Stone narrowed his eyes. "What's going on?" he demanded. "Where are the people you were taking me to?"

"We're right here," came a smooth voice from behind him.

| CHAPTER EIGHTEEN

S TONE WHIRLED—AND FROZE.

He hadn't heard the two people standing behind him enter the room. They were there now, though, in front of the other door, looking smug and unruffled—a man and a woman. He didn't recognize either of them: the man had dark skin and swept-back blond hair, and the woman was pale with long, dark auburn tresses. What he *did* recognize, though, all too quickly, were their long, high-collared coats.

Oh, bloody hell, no…

He didn't hesitate—he knew if he did, he was lost. Instead, he spun again and threw himself toward the smaller man who'd brought him here, intending to shove him aside and escape through the door he blocked. If he could get back out to the street, he might be able to run fast enough to evade them long enough to find a hiding place.

He didn't even make it to the man before his feet lifted off the floor and his hands locked at his sides.

"Now, why are you running away?" the man asked with a deceptively amused smile. "We have a lot to talk about."

"You've been giving us quite a lot of trouble for the past few days," the woman said. She stepped forward and paced around Stone, examining him from every angle. "You don't look like much—not bad looking for a pig, but ultimately just another one of the faceless Dim." She came back around in front of him so he could see her, looking thoughtful. "But you're *not* one of the faceless Dim, are you?" She glanced past him to something past him. "You may go," she said curtly.

Stone heard the door close behind him—the one he'd come in. "So he was on your payroll, was he?" he asked.

The man chuckled. "Oh, no. We don't *pay* them. We…make them offers it would be in their best interests to accept." His gaze flicked to their surroundings, and his lip curled in distaste. "But we can talk later. I can't stand to be in this disgusting place a moment longer."

Stone struggled against the magic holding him suspended in midair, but he might as well have tried to escape from a block of ice. He could move his head, but that was all. "What do you want?" he demanded. "Or is this just another example of tormenting people who can't fight back because it gets you off?"

A quick flash of anger crossed the woman's face. "I wouldn't," she warned. "You're not exactly in a position to ask questions, and if you annoy us, we could make life unpleasant for you."

"You're already doing that," Stone pointed out. "You aren't going to kill me—if you wanted to do that, you wouldn't have set up this ruse to lure me here. Obviously you lot can get away with killing whoever you like—they're nothing but the 'Dim,' right? So clearly you want something from me."

"Oh, we do," the man said. "We definitely do. But you need to remember, before you get too cocky—there's more than one way to extract information. If you play nicely, we'll use the ones that don't have…permanent side effects. Otherwise…"

In spite of himself, Stone tensed, his heart beating faster. He wasn't getting out of here, that was obvious—best to play along for a while until he had a better chance to escape. "What do you want, then?"

"That's for later, after we get out of this hellhole," the woman said. "No more talking now." She twitched a hand.

Stone tried to reply, but discovered to his horror that he couldn't. His mouth moved, but no sound came out. He glared at the pair and tried to fight past the magical block, but couldn't even manage a feeble moan.

"Let's go." The man made a gesture, and Stone began floating along between them as they left the room through the far-side door. He could do nothing but watch helplessly as they traversed another hallway and exited through a door into another alley, where a boxy, beat-up van waited.

Stone only had time to speculate about why these two haughty Talented would drive such a scruffy-looking vehicle before they opened the back door and pushed him inside, then slammed it shut behind him and climbed into the front. The full-body lock broke, dropping him with a crash to the floor. He quickly scrambled up and lunged forward, but an invisible barrier stopped him. Stepping back, panting, he looked around him as the van began to move.

Inside, the space looked nothing like its exterior might suggest. Instead, the front seats were made of pale tan leather, there was no steering wheel or gauges, and the cracked windshield was replaced by a wide-open expanse of sparkling glass. The back portion that held Stone was a featureless space with white walls, a hard metal floor, and no view of the outside. When he tried to open the side door, he discovered that no seam was visible from in here. As far as Stone could tell, the small cubicle had no exits.

The van was moving now, but the only way he could tell was by looking out the front window and seeing the buildings moving past. Otherwise, he experienced no sensation of movement: no tires bouncing over uneven streets, no bumps and jounces as they hit one of the innumerable potholes, not even slowing or stopping for the occasional pedestrian or other vehicles. He heard no telltale engine rumble—was his cubicle soundproofed, or were they floating? Was this some kind of magically-powered van disguised to look like one of the mundanes' ramshackle vehicles?

He moved up to the invisible barrier separating him from the two Talented in the front seats. "Hey!" he called. "Where are we going? Where are you taking me?" Already, the view out the front window looked unfamiliar; he didn't recognize the streets they were passing, but the dark brick buildings looked in better repair and the streetlights were actually doing their job.

They didn't answer; they didn't even act like they'd heard him. He watched as they chatted between themselves, no more mindful of his presence than a pair of dogcatchers would be of a barking stray they'd picked up. "Oi!" he called again, louder. "I asked you a question!" He pounded on the invisible barrier, but his efforts had no effect except to make his hand tingle where he'd contacted it.

The van drove for a few more minutes, now in territory Stone was sure he'd never seen before. It pulled up to what looked like a warehouse, where a roll-up door opened to admit them. The two Talented got out, and a moment later the van's side door slid open as well.

Any thoughts Stone might have had of escape departed. The two of them were standing there, and two more long-coated figures stood behind them. All of them were watching him closely.

"Don't try anything," the woman who'd caught him said calmly. "If you do, we'll be forced to knock you out."

"Just come along like a good little Dim boy, and everything will be fine," said the man. The tone he used was the same one someone might have used on a child or an animal back on Earth.

"Let's get a couple of things straight first," Stone growled. "I'm not 'Dim,' and I'm not a 'boy'. Or perhaps all that magic has done something to bugger up your eyesight." He knew he had no chance of escaping, so he didn't waste the energy to try, but that didn't mean he planned to let these conceited bastards get away with treating him like rubbish.

The woman glared at him, and once again his arms locked at his sides. "Watch yourself, pig," she warned. "We're supposed to deliver you relatively unharmed, but…accidents happen." She made a gesture.

Instantly, Stone's body felt as if they had hooked him up to an electrical current. He went rigid, gritting his teeth as sharp, jagged pain shot through him. It lasted only a few seconds; when it ceased, he slumped as much as he could in the magical grip, panting.

"That was just a small taste," the man said. "Best to just keep your mouth shut. You'll have plenty of time to talk later, trust me. Now, are you going to walk with us, or do we need to bring you along?"

"I'll walk," Stone said.

"Good," the woman said, smiling in satisfaction. "See, Yarian? Even the Dim can see reason when…properly incentivized." She jerked her head forward. "Come on," she told Stone. "Walk, then. Through the doorway over there."

The two of them took up positions on either side of him as the spell holding his legs immobile lifted. His arms still remained rigidly stuck to his sides. He glanced pointedly at each of them, paused just long enough to let them know it was his idea and not their order that moved him forward, then began walking in a purposeful manner—not too slow, not too fast—toward the indicated doorway. "Where are you taking me, anyway?"

"Just keep moving."

When they passed through the opening, everything changed. Instead of a dingy warehouse, they now stood in a hallway carpeted in medium blue. The walls, not brick but some smooth material, were painted a pleasant cream color, and sconces along the walls provided bright but indirect light. The two mages who'd met them in the warehouse hadn't followed them through, but two more, both women this time, swept past them and disappeared through another doorway. They nodded and murmured polite greetings to Stone's captors, but didn't acknowledge his presence except to eye him in the same way one might examine a piece of furniture.

"She said keep moving," the man said. "Through the door there." At the end of the hall, a blue door swung open.

Something prodded Stone from behind, but it didn't feel like the man's hand. It occurred to him that during all of his encounters with the Talented, from his initial one with the bullies in Temolan to this one, not once had any of them ever physically touched him.

The room beyond the door was large and airy, and didn't look at all as if it belonged in the dark, dingy warehouse they'd entered. It had the same cream-colored walls as the hallway, but instead of carpeting, some pale granite-like substance shot through with metallic blue veins covered the floor. Stone glanced upward and was surprised to see a large skylight letting in a velvety-black night sky.

On the far side of the room was a glowing disc on the floor. It was perhaps six feet in diameter, protruded above the floor for about six inches, and was surrounded by a waist-high railing. Its main structure was made of the same pale stone as the floor, and the inner diameter glowed with shifting lights: red, blue, green, yellow, purple. It looked somehow familiar, though Stone was sure he hadn't seen anything like it since his arrival here. Beyond the disc, two more Talented sat at a table playing a game where they moved the pieces around using magic.

They glanced up as Stone and his captors entered. One immediately went back to examining the game board; the other one looked Stone up and down as if annoyed that he was sullying their pristine floor. "Who's the Dim?" he asked.

"Just somebody the Council wants to talk to," Stone's male captor said.

The Council. That sounded important, Stone supposed. Had his questions caught the attention of the higher-ups in Temolan?

"The Council wants to talk to a Dim?" Bored contempt laced the man's tone. "What are we coming to?" He waved them off and returned his attention to the game, where his opponent had just levitated four different-colored pieces, spun them in an intricate dance, and set them down in different places.

Something prodded Stone again. "Move," the woman said. "Onto the disc."

With sudden clarity, he remembered why the disc had seemed familiar before. "That's a teleportation portal," he said with a challenging glance toward her.

"Well," said the man, speculatively. He sounded surprised. "Seems there might be more to our Dim friend than we thought. Perhaps that's why the Council wants to talk to him. Now enough talk, pig. I won't warn you again. Step onto the disc."

Stone had never seen a teleportation portal that looked like that before—all the ones he'd seen on Earth had been vertically oriented, like doorways, but the shifting pastel colors were the same. Could the mages here have perfected some other kind of teleportation? He remembered odd flashes of light from the night he'd arrived here, when the Guard had taken him down to Drendell. Maybe this was how they got back and forth between Temolan and Drendell.

He stepped forward and mounted the disc, stopping in the center. Nothing happened, beyond a faint buzz he could feel through his boots.

The two Talented took positions next to him, one on either side. It was a tight fit, but they still stood as far away from him as they could, their noses wrinkling.

"Sorry," Stone said with obvious insincerity. "Trying to keep away from you lot means having to sleep in some unpleasant places. Do you think I could have a shower and some fresh clothes before I talk to your Council?"

"Quiet," the man snapped. His expression changed to one of concentration, as did the woman's on Stone's other side.

The world shifted.

It was over before Stone had a chance to think about it. Sudden disorientation gripped him, and he staggered forward, blinking. Something took hold of him and righted him before he could pitch forward.

"Let go, I'm all right," he snapped, blinking.

This room looked similar to the one they'd just left, except it was larger, included two additional teleportation pads, and had no skylight. Stone didn't get a chance to see anything else before they hustled him out of the room, down another hallway lined with shifting abstract prints, and through another door. At the end of the hallway, a large window looked out on a series of tall spires dotted with twinkling lights.

One thing Stone noticed immediately was that everything here was clean. More than clean—utterly pristine. Everywhere he looked—the walls, the floors, the doors, the artwork—looked perfectly, glowingly *new,* with no wear, no fading, not even any stains on the blue carpet where someone might have spilled coffee or tracked in a bit of dirt from outside. The effect was disconcerting—though the place's appearance had nothing in common with it, it reminded Stone of old-style science fiction television shows before they'd caught on that things people actually *used* would be more worn and dingy.

So they've got magic enough to waste on keeping things spotless, he mused as they entered another small cubicle. The door slid shut and the cubicle began to move, even though neither of his captors had given it an obvious command. In fact, if this was an elevator, it didn't even have any buttons or floor indicators.

"Nice trick," he commented. "Magical elevator. You lot do like to show off, don't you?"

The man flashed him a warning glare, and a faint hint of the electric jolt from before shot through him again.

When the door opened, it wasn't on a pleasant cream-colored hallway with blue carpeting, but on a dark gray passage with a gray stone floor. No natural illumination showed here; Stone wondered if they were underground, if such a concept even made any sense in a floating city.

Another door opened, and a woman came out to meet them. "Caught him, did you?" she asked. She was taller than either of Stone's captors, with broad shoulders, a prominent jawline, and a shorter, less elaborate haircut than any of the female Talented Stone had seen around. She wasn't wearing the typical long coat, but her spotless dark-blue shirt and light jacket sported pins and amulets bearing the same symbols as the others wore.

"It wasn't difficult," his female captor drawled. "They're picking up a few of the others at the Fisherman's Rest too. They're scheduled for execution in a few days, I hear, or possibly exile. Some of them might have gotten away, but they won't elude us for long."

Stone tensed. Execution? Exile—to where? Had the Talented raided the Fisherman's Rest, looking for members of the underground rebellion? Was that because of him and his questions? He bowed his head—if so, it meant more death or torment on his conscience, and not a damned thing he could do about it. Would they execute him too, when they found out he couldn't give them the information they sought?

"Good, good," the new woman said. "I'll take charge of this one and get him ready for questioning. Anything I should know?"

"He's got a mouth on him," the man said. "Disrespectful. But…what does it matter? He's Dim. He won't give you any trouble, and you can always shut him up if he annoys you."

"True enough."

His lip curled. "Oh, and he stinks. I think he's been sleeping in a garbage pile somewhere."

The woman glanced at Stone, then back at the pair, levitating a clipboard and stylus to them. "That's the Dim for you. But then, the whole town down there is a garbage pile, isn't it? It's not like any of them can help it. Sign here, and then you can go collect your fee."

Fee? *Bounty hunters, then,* Stone thought. It made sense—it meant the real Talented authorities wouldn't have to dirty their feet on Dim territory.

"Thank you. Now off to something much more pleasant." Without another glance at Stone, the two bid the other woman good night and departed.

The woman turned back to him. "*You're* what they were after?" she asked with contempt, obviously not expecting an answer. "Hard to believe, but I don't ask questions." She gestured, and Stone's legs locked again along with his arms, then he lifted off the floor and floated forward in front of the woman.

"I can walk," he snapped.

"Eh, this is easier. Shut up."

She floated Stone into a more brightly lit room with tile walls. On one side was a large open shower cubicle with three nozzles; the other side included a bank of lockers behind a long metal bench attached to the floor. A chill, several degrees colder than the outside hallway, hung in the air here.

"Strip down and get into the shower," the woman commanded. "They're right—you *do* stink. You've probably got lice, too—half the Dim prisoners I get in here do."

The lock on Stone's body vanished, staggering him forward again before he caught himself. "Am I a prisoner, then? What's the charge? I haven't done a bloody thing to set you lot on me."

"I said shut up and strip down. You can do it yourself, or I can help you." She raised a menacing hand, indicating that her "help" probably wouldn't be his more pleasant option.

"Fine." He slipped out of his jacket and tossed it on the bench. At least he'd get a shower out of the situation, if nothing else.

"Hurry up. I don't have all night to stand here and watch you."

For a second, he thought about trying to catch her by surprise—he doubted any of the mundanes these people captured had ever done that, so he might get the first shot in—but quickly decided against it. It wasn't the time yet. Clearly they didn't want him dead, at least not yet, so he could bide his time and hope for an opportunity later.

With a sidelong glance toward the woman, he slipped out of the rest of his clothes and, making a show of not being the least bit self-conscious about being stark naked in front of a strange, hostile woman in a chilly room, he strode into the shower cubicle and waited under one of the nozzles. "No knobs," he observed. "I guess you'll have to—"

The nozzle roared to life, hitting him with a high-pressure jet of cold water. Spluttering and shivering, he stepped out of the stream and found a bar of soap on a small shelf behind the nozzle. He scrubbed down as fast as he could, then rinsed off; when he glanced up, he saw the woman watching him with no expression, beyond perhaps faint impatience.

As soon as he finished the nozzle cut off and the deluge stopped, leaving him standing there, dripping and shivering even harder than before. "G-got a towel?" he asked through chattering teeth.

A gray towel levitated in his direction, but stopped several feet short of reaching him. "Come out here," the woman ordered, pulling it back. Her expression was sharper than before as she stared hard at him.

"Give me the towel," Stone protested. "It's bloody cold in here. If you see anything you like, you can look your fill after I dry off."

The electric jolt rocked him again, dropping him to his knees with a yelp of pain. "One more comment like that and I might just start picking more…specific targets. Am I clear?"

"Crystal," Stone bit out through gritted teeth.

"Good. Now get up."

He slowly got to his feet and stood, still shivering. He glared at her, making his silence every bit the act of defiance that his comments had been.

She moved in closer, looking him up and down like she owned him. She raised her hand and a faint buzzing sensation passed over his body. "There. That should take care of any lice." Her gaze settled on his chest. "What is that?" she asked, pointing.

He looked down, as if he didn't know exactly what she was referring to. "What?"

"On your chest. Where did you get that tattoo?"

"Don't remember. Got drunk with some mates one night and next morning, there it was." He did his best to keep his aura steady, even though he knew it probably wouldn't do him any good. At least the tattoo wasn't glowing here— probably for the same reason his magic wasn't functioning.

"Those look like magical sigils."

Stone shrugged. "How should I know? I'm nothing but a Dim pig, remember? How would I know anything about magic?"

Her gaze sharpened further, and for a moment, he thought she might follow through with her threat. Instead, she examined the tattoo for a moment longer, then stepped back and used magic to throw the towel at him. "The Council's interrogators will find out what they need to know. No point in my wasting my time with you. Dry off."

As he caught the towel and began to dry himself, she turned toward his pile of clothes. With a grimace of disgust, she first used magic to remove his ID card and papers from his pocket, then gathered the clothes into a stack on the floor and ignited them in a flare of bright-red magical fire. Then she used another spell to move the ashes into the shower cubicle and rinse them down the drain. "You'll find clothes that don't reek in the locker."

One of the locker doors swung open, revealing a neatly folded set of tan clothing. "Hurry up," the woman ordered.

Stone did as he was told. The clothing was ill-fitting and even more poorly made than the stuff he'd bought back in Drendell. It consisted of loose pull-on pants, a short-sleeved shirt similar to a scrub top, and thin slippers. The shirt had something across the back in stark black script, but Stone couldn't read it. Temolan's answer to a prison jumpsuit, apparently.

The woman examined his papers and work card while he dressed. When he finished, she tucked them into her pocket and once again used magic to lock Stone's arms to his sides. "Walk ahead of me," she said. "Out the door and turn right."

He didn't have a lot of choice, so still shivering from the cold shower, he complied.

She directed him down one hall, then through a heavy door and into another one. "In here," she said, opening a second door with magic and motioning him inside.

He paused a moment to examine the room she was directing him to. It was, as he'd expected, a prison cell, and it had none of the comforting cream-and-blue elegance of the building's other floors. Instead, it resembled what he might have expected a cell from sometime in the previous century on Earth to look like: metal walls and floor, heavy steel door with a small barred window set into the top and a slot at the bottom, and a steel sink bolted to the wall with a toilet next to it. A metal shelf with a thin mattress extended from one of the long walls, and a bright, bare light bulb protected by a metal cage hung down from the ceiling.

"Nice place," Stone commented, striding into the tiny cell as if it were the penthouse suite at the Waldorf. "I'd give it five stars for comfort, but I'm afraid I'll have to knock one or two off for ambiance."

"Silence," the woman said.

"So how long will I get to enjoy your hospitality before this Council of yours turns up to talk to me?" He paused to inspect the sink, ignoring her. "Can't imagine they'll fancy being rousted out of their beds this late at night just to question some poor Dim sod, will they?"

"I said *silence!*" the woman snapped. With a wave of her hand, she picked him up and flung him into the wall above the bed. "They will come when they choose to, and no sooner."

Before Stone could struggle back up, she had backed out into the hall. The door slammed shut with a loud *clang* followed by the *snik* of a lock engaging. Another panel snapped closed over the barred window in the door.

"That went well…" he muttered, swinging around to sit on the bed. He leaned back against the wall and examined his surroundings in more detail, but nothing new presented itself. Instead, he took stock of his situation.

Overall, things weren't looking good. He was locked in a featureless cell deep in the heart of the Talented's floating city. He was surrounded by hostile mages, many of whom seemed to have a deep hatred of the "Dim" and either sadistic streaks or total disregard that allowed them to treat the non-magical denizens of this world with callous cruelty. He was no closer to finding Harrison, and indeed, aside from Tanissa's comments about his being a "ghost" and a "legend," he still had no way to know if the man even existed here. Had the skinny little man he'd initially talked to at the Fisherman's Rest been nothing more than another Talented plant, placed there to intercept potential recruits to the rebellion?

Hell, *was* there even a rebellion, or had that all been an elaborate ruse on the part of the Talented to weed out the subversive elements among the Dim?

Had even Tanissa been part of it, working from deep cover?

He let his breath out slowly, trying not to shiver. *You've done it now, Stone,* he told himself. When would they come to question him? What would they question him *about?* It seemed fairly clear that they didn't want to kill him—not yet—or he wouldn't have gotten away with making those flippant comments to the bounty hunters or his female jailer. But why not? Clearly they had no problem with it, judging by what some of their number had done to the server at the sandwich shop, and to Faran and Runa for no other crime than helping him. Just as clearly, the Talented's society didn't have many strictures against injuring or killing the Dim. Was it even considered a crime, or did they have free rein to take their teleporters from their shining cities in the sky down to the slums of Drendell and use the inhabitants for target practice?

Even though he knew it wouldn't do any good, he held up his hand and tried to shift to magical sight. At this point, he wasn't sure he'd be able to escape even if his magic had returned, but at least he'd have an ace in the hole. Tentatively, with nothing to lose, he even tried Harrison's magic. If it burned him out, he'd be no worse off than he already was.

Nothing happened. He slumped, disappointed even though he'd expected nothing else. Perhaps his magic simply didn't function in this world.

"Fine, then," he muttered, lying down on the thin, hard mattress. "Your move, I guess."

He didn't think he'd fall asleep, not with the harsh overhead light and the uncomfortable surface and the lingering chill from the cold shower, but he must have been more tired and drained than he thought. He wasn't sure how long he lay there, drawn up and staring at the metal wall, but his last thoughts as he dropped off were of home: wondering what Verity was up to, wondering what was going on at the University, and wishing he had warm, purring Raider curled up on his chest.

| CHAPTER NINETEEN

THE LOUD, METALLIC *CLANG* of the door opening woke Stone from his uncomfortable half-sleep. He quickly sat up, pushing his hand back through his hair, and blinked blearily at the figure standing in the doorway. "What—?"

"On your feet." The voice was male, sharp and implacable. "Now."

"Oh, am I finally going to get to talk to someone?"

"Up," the man snapped.

Stone couldn't see him very well since he was backlit in the doorway, but he recognized the familiar long-coated silhouette. "Fine, fine," he said, standing. "Do I get breakfast? Or at least a moment or two to clean up?"

Instead of answering, the man raised a hand.

Stone's arms wrenched behind his back and locked there. Something that looked like a green blob floated over to him, and a moment later he felt ropelike tendrils lashing his wrists together.

"Move," the man said, "Or I'll cuff your feet together too and drag you."

Stone didn't think he was kidding. "Fine, fine," he said. "I'm coming. As it happens, I *want* to talk to your bosses. Perhaps we can clear some things up."

"Quiet." The man jerked his head toward the door; when Stone walked through it, he slammed it shut behind them.

Stone didn't see much point in trying to antagonize the man further, so instead he concentrated on his surroundings, taking in and doing his best to memorize every turn in the route they took, the location of every door, and any land-marks that might help him get out of here if the chance presented itself.

They didn't leave the lower levels, Stone noticed. The scenery remained uniformly depressing, utilitarian, and gray. He wondered if they ever held Talented prisoners here, or if those—assuming there were any—were deemed worthy of more pleasant décor. He also wondered if they were holding any other nonmagical prisoners, since he hadn't seen any sign of anyone other than his captors and a few other mages since they'd arrived in Temolan.

Before long the man opened a door at the end of a hall. "In here."

Stone entered the room and looked around. It looked similar to the cell he'd been taken from, except larger: gray walls, metal floor with a drain in it, no windows. The air in here was as chilly as it had been in the shower room. A single, hard metal chair was bolted to the floor in the middle of the room, and several other chairs—more comfortable ones, Stone noticed—faced it a few feet away. All of them were empty. The room was otherwise featureless.

"Sit," his jailer said, pointing at the metal chair.

Stone sat in the chair. As soon as he was settled, he felt the substance holding his hands behind his back morph, and then something forced his arms around behind the chair back and the stuff locked them together again.

"Hey!" he protested. "No need for that. It's not like I'm going anywhere." The position wrenched his shoulders back, creating a constant discomfort that didn't quite reach pain. He shifted, trying to get more comfortable, but quickly discovered it wasn't possible. Probably on purpose. He shivered, glaring at the man. "We *are* getting on with this soon, right?"

In answer, the man merely turned and exited the room without another word. The door clicked shut behind him, leaving Stone once again alone.

He glared around at the walls. "This is getting bloody old, you know," he called. "I'd have expected better of a bunch of mages."

His voice echoed around the metal walls, but nobody answered.

"Come on," he called. "*Somebody* come and talk to me. I'm beginning to think you lot have something against me."

Still no answer.

Stone slumped back in his seat and sighed. This was their show, and apparently they'd move it along on their own schedule.

He had no idea how long it was before anyone showed up, but the knots in his shoulders told him it was at least an hour. When the door opened—a different one, this time, on the other side of the room where no door had been before— Stone jerked his head up from the meditation technique he'd been using to remain as comfortable as he could manage.

"About time," he snapped. "Your interrogation techniques leave a lot to be desired."

Suddenly, he couldn't breathe.

It was as if something had blocked his throat, preventing him from drawing in air. He tried to relax, to hold his breath and wait out his unseen tormentors, but the sensation didn't lift. Instinctive panic kicked in; he thrashed in the chair, bright pain wrenching his shoulders, but the chair didn't move and whatever held his arms immobile didn't budge.

Spots rose in front of his vision, then grayness, then black.

When he raised his head again, blinking, his head pounding, one of the chairs in front of him was occupied.

He hadn't seen anyone come in—the man must have done it while he'd been blacked out. He swallowed hard, drew in several deep, refreshing breaths of the chilly air, and examined the silent figure sitting in front of him.

He didn't know how he knew it, but he was fairly sure this man was someone important. Perhaps it was the fact that he was older than the other Talented he'd seen, tall and distinguished-looking with light brown skin, intense green eyes, and short-cut, bright white hair overlaid with a faint blue tone. He wore the same type of outfit the other Talented had worn, but the cut of his high-collared long coat suggested an almost military precision. Several small pins or amulets aligned in neat rows on his lapels.

"So," Stone said, his voice sounding ragged. "Are you finally going to talk to me?"

The man appeared unruffled. He rose from his chair and began pacing languidly around the area in front of Stone, as calm as a well-fed panther.

"Let's set some ground rules," he said. His voice was soft but carried the unmistakable tone of someone used to having his orders obeyed. "The first one is that I will ask the questions, and you will answer them. Is that clear?"

"If you get on with asking them," Stone muttered. "This charade is getting old."

The blocked-airway sensation returned, but only for a few seconds—long enough to show that the man could use it again whenever he liked. The guy didn't even change position. "The second is that you will respond only to my questions. Any disrespectful outbursts will be punished."

"Respect is earned," Stone said. "So far, you lot are nothing but a bunch of overpowered bullies. And we both know you don't want me dead—if you did, you've had plenty of chances to kill me already."

Pain—intense, agonizing pain, like someone had lit his every nerve ending on fire—sliced through Stone. He went stiff, clamping his teeth down against the scream he refused to give voice to and tried desperately to reach the meditation techniques he'd been using before.

The pain stopped an instant before he lost the battle. He sagged in the chair, his shoulders screaming in protest, and closed his eyes, panting. Sweat beaded on his face and ran down his back, making him shiver even more in the cold air.

"Respect is commanded," the man observed, his tone still never rising above its previous calm. "And I command it. Do you understand? Because while that didn't cause any physical damage—the next time, it will."

"Ask your questions," Stone said through gritted teeth, without looking up.

"I will ask them when I'm ready." More sound of slow pacing. "You aren't like any of the other Dim I've seen come through here. Why is that, I wonder."

Stone didn't reply. He sat back, trying to take some of the pressure off his shoulders, and waited.

"Not like any of them. Not even the Outcasts, though they are what you most remind me of. Have you been speaking with any of them?"

Stone remained silent just long enough to let the man know that he, too, could speak on his own timetable. "I have no idea what you're talking about," he finally rasped.

"Indeed." The man moved until he was standing in front of Stone. He pulled something from his pocket and consulted it. "This says your name is 'Stone.' That's an odd name. I've never heard it among the Dim."

"I'm not from around here." Stone flicked his gaze up, and wasn't surprised to see that the man held the work card and papers he'd gotten from Faran.

"Where *are* you from, then?" He shook out the paper and studied it. "These are, of course, forgeries. It's a shame about what happened to that Dim butcher and his wife. They should never have gotten themselves involved in such things. Dangerous, wouldn't you say?"

Stone glared at him. "You didn't have to kill them. They didn't do anything wrong."

"Ah ah," the man said, holding up a finger. "Remember what I told you about speaking out of turn. I'll give you one more chance. You *are* Dim, after all, and the Dim are known for their...mental deficiencies, in general. Now—I asked you a question. Where are you from?"

"You wouldn't have heard of it."

"Oh, I don't know. I'm fairly well traveled. Try me."

Stone couldn't tell if the man was watching him with magical sight, looking for changes in his aura—if he was, he was hiding it very well, but there were people who could do that even on Earth. "Palo Alto," he said.

The man considered. "And where is that?"

"Just north of Mountain View, and south of Redwood City."

The pain returned, but only for a second. "It wouldn't do well for you to lie to me."

"I'm not lying. It's the absolute truth."

Oddly, the man didn't push it. Instead, he began pacing again. "You were found on the streets of Temolan by the Guard."

"Found after having the stuffing beaten out of me by three of your upright citizens," Stone snapped.

"What were you doing in Temolan? How did you get there? I checked—you aren't listed among the Dim who have permission to work here, so you wouldn't have been allowed to use the teleporters."

"I don't know how I got there," Stone said, deciding that as long as the man was going to ask him questions he could answer without giving away anything about his true reasons for being here, he might as well appear to cooperate. And in any case, the answer was true, at least to a point. He had no idea what had directed him to Temolan, unless that was where Harrison was.

"Careful…" The man raised his hand, and his eyes narrowed.

"It's true," Stone said quickly. "I *don't* know how I got there. Something—or someone—must have dropped me there. I was trying to find my way out when I was attacked."

"I see. And why do you suppose someone would drop you in Temolan? The Dim aren't welcome there, unless they have legitimate work reasons. For any of the Talented to bring a Dim there unauthorized would be a serious crime."

Stone shrugged. "Don't ask me. I don't know how your society works—except that it's seriously buggered up. Why don't you go looking for whoever brought me here? Or the ones who nearly killed me? Or is that not a crime?"

Either the man was saving up his punishments for later, or he'd decided not to make good on his threat. Instead of zapping Stone again, he merely fixed him with a stern expression. "It isn't for you to question, especially if you were where you had no permission to be." Once again, he began pacing. "What is your real name?"

"That *is* my real name."

"I don't believe you. I was told you used another."

"I used the rest of my name, from where I come from. I was told that was—problematic."

"Problematic? Why was that?"

"Because apparently you lot are overly sensitive about substituting syllables for prestige, and I had too many for a mere Dim."

"Your *name*," the man said.

Stone's airway blocked again, remaining that way for a few more seconds than the previous time. He glared again until it cleared, then said firmly, "Alastair Stone."

The man nodded, as if that was what he'd expected. "Yes. That's what I was told. You do know that impersonating the Talented can carry a sentence of death, or exile."

"Exile? To where? Out where the two-headed mutant wolves run free?"

"Don't play stupid, Dim. I know that's your natural state, but you aren't doing yourself any good by emphasizing it." He paused and consulted another paper from his pocket. "What is your connection with the Talented?"

"You mean aside from being hunted down by them for something I didn't even do?"

"Answer the question."

"I don't have one. I'm not sure why you think I do. Obviously I don't have any magical abilities, or I wouldn't be sitting here now."

The man stopped in front of him again. He raised his hand and pulled back sharply, and the front of Stone's thin shirt ripped open. He pointed at the tattoo on his chest. "What is that, then? And please, don't waste my time giving me the story about your drunken evening with your friends. We both know that isn't the truth."

Stone didn't answer.

"Are you one of the Outcasts? From another city, perhaps?"

"I don't know what you're talking about. What are the Outcasts?" When the man's gaze sharpened, he quickly added, "Listen—if you have a way of telling if I'm lying to you, use it! I come from a place where things are very different. It's the truth."

The man studied him for almost a minute, pacing back and forth. "I don't think you're an Outcast," he mused. "But we'll put that aside for the moment. After all, we've got all the time we need to get your secrets out of you."

"Why don't you just read my mind, then?" Stone demanded. He watched the man closely for a reaction. "You can do that, right?"

"Of course we can. But that will be a last resort, since it leaves the mind in a...less than pleasant state. It's better if you answer my questions voluntarily."

Stone didn't let his reaction reach his face, but inwardly he smiled. Apparently he hadn't lost his ability to spot lies, even without magic. He decided to let his interrogator think his bluff had worked—it might prove useful for later. "You don't need to read my mind. I've got nothing to hide. I told you—I don't even know why you're so interested in me. I've done nothing wrong. I was delivering orders for the butcher shop and spending my evenings having a few drinks at the bars. Are those crimes?"

"No."

"Well, then, what's the problem?"

"For one thing, you were in possession of forged work papers. That *is* a crime, and you'll be punished for it. Likewise, it is a crime for any of the Dim to be in Temolan without authorization. But neither of those is why you're here."

He walked to the centermost of the three chairs and sat down, leaning forward with his elbows resting on his knees. "What do you know of a man named Harrison?"

Ah, here we go. Stone had wondered if he would get to that eventually. "Who?"

This time, the man used the electric current instead of trying to suffocate him. He jerked and bucked in his chair until it stopped, clamping his mouth shut against a scream.

After a few seconds, the man waved a languid hand and the pain stopped, leaving Stone panting and shaking.

"Would you like to try a different answer?" He turned and bent until his face was level with Stone's. "Let me explain something to you, Dim, just in case you haven't caught on to it yet. You are in a bad situation here. I can do whatever I like with you—I can even kill you, if I determine you aren't cooperating fully. Oh, the Council might be displeased, since they want the information you can provide, but they trust my judgment. It will be a mere slap on the wrist for me.

"But I don't need to kill you," he added. "Not yet, anyway. That would be...wasteful. So far the methods I've used on you have been fairly gentle, with no permanent effects. That could change. Or I can give my healer colleague a call, which will allow me to do truly horrific things to you. My colleague will then heal you after you've had a chance to experience them for a while, and then we'll start all over again until you talk. I don't *want* to do that—it's messy, and I honestly don't enjoy that kind of thing, even against the Dim. But the Council wants answers, and it's my job to get them. Do I make myself clear?"

Stone, his heart still pounding hard from the latest jolt, could only stare at him. "You people are monsters..." he whispered. "All of you." He braced for another attack.

It didn't come. "We aren't," the man said instead, rising to stand. "You may think so, in your limited way, but everything I'm doing here is for the greater good."

"*Your* greater good," Stone muttered.

"I'm not going to debate philosophy with a Dim," the man said dismissively. His expression hardened again. "Now—my patience is growing thin. You will answer my questions."

Stone bowed his head. He had no doubt the man was telling the truth, and that he was willing to resort to full-blown torture to get the information he sought. He also knew without his magic he had little chance of withstanding such treatment. His best bet was to keep his aura under control and tell as much of the truth as he could, especially since he realized he didn't know much that could get anyone, including himself, in trouble. "Fine," he said. "I'll answer your questions. What will happen to me if I do? Are you planning to kill me?"

"Of course not. You'll be put in prison, where you'll be given work suited to your…limited abilities. We always have need of those to perform the most menial and unpleasant tasks here in Temolan. I won't lie to you—it won't be enjoyable, but you'll be safe as long as you behave yourself. And it's better than execution, or exile."

Bloody brilliant. What a thing to look forward to. And there was that mention of "exile" again. He decided not to ask about it now. "Fine," he repeated, shoulders slumping. They still hurt from pulling against his bonds. "What do you want to know?"

"As I asked before—what do you know about a man named Harrison?"

"Not much. That's the truth," he added quickly. "I only ever met him once."

"You met him?" That seemed to surprise the man. "When?"

"Years ago."

"Where?"

"In a place you've never heard of." At the man's warning glare, he added, "A place called Las Vegas." Once again, he watched for any reaction that revealed his interrogator might have heard of it, but there was none. He glanced up, taking a chance. "May I ask *you* a question?"

"You may ask. Whether I answer—or punish you for your insolence—will be up to me."

"No insolence," Stone said. "Just genuine curiosity. Who *is* Harrison here? What is he?"

The man seemed honestly taken aback by the question. "What do you mean by that?"

"Just what I said. I only met him briefly, a long time ago, and it was a long way from here. Why do you care about him? Is he somebody important? Is he wanted?"

"He is a traitor," the man said, his expression darkening. "And that is all you need to know. Why were you seeking him now?"

"Because I wanted his help with something."

The man looked at him with disdain. "What could he possibly help *you* with? Did anyone contact you about him? Did you talk to anyone in Drendell?"

"Yes. But they turned out to be working for you lot—or those bounty hunters you hired to find me." He didn't say anything about the man he'd initially talked to at the Fisherman's Rest, and took care to control his aura—as best he could manage, anyway, since he still couldn't see if his efforts were doing any good.

"Yes, we've heard the Rest is one of the places they look for recruits. It won't be any longer," he added with satisfaction.

"Did you burn it down like you did Faran's shop?" Stone asked before he could stop himself. Once again, he braced for attack.

And once again, the man didn't take the bait. "No," he said calmly. "But we did arrest its owners, workers, and several of the customers. Depending on what we get out of them, they'll be subject to exile or execution. The Fisherman's Rest will need to be under…new management." He focused on Stone again. "Now…answer this next question carefully, because if you lie to me, I promise things won't go well for you. Did you find any leads to locate Harrison?"

"No," Stone said. "Other than to ask at the Fisherman's Rest, which was why I was there. Do you honestly think that if I knew how to find him, I'd have spent my time delivering meat and hanging about at dodgy bars looking for information?" He wondered if they'd captured the mage he'd talked to, or if the man had actually been in league with them, scouting out potential rebels.

"Who told you to ask at the Fisherman's Rest?"

Stone met his gaze, hoping hard that his aura control was still working. "Someone sent me a note. It came to the shop one day."

The man's expression grew dangerous. "You can't read, Dim. I know this. How did you read a note?"

"I didn't," he said, keeping his voice even and injecting just enough of a tremble into it to feign fear. "They'd drawn a picture of the sign. I remembered passing it on my rounds."

"What did you do with the note?" Either the man believed him, or he was stringing him along hoping for more.

"I destroyed it. Burned it. I already had the feeling that letting on I knew anything about Harrison was a bad decision." He met the interrogator's gaze. "I was right about that, apparently, wasn't I?"

The man stared at him for several seconds, then turned away. "That will be all for today. We will review what you've told us, and if we have any further need for you, we'll resume later at a time of our choosing."

"What will become of me now?" Stone asked.

"That will be up to the Council." Without another word, he turned and left the room, closing the door behind him.

Stone slumped in his chair, letting his breath out and wondering how long they'd leave him here before someone came after him. Right now, even the hard bed in his cell seemed preferable to sitting here in this chair with his shoulders forced back and his hands immobilized. He shivered against the room's chill air and tried to find some motivation to keep fighting. Sudden despair gripped him—what was the point anymore? He was stuck here, he wasn't getting out, and the best he could hope for at this point was some job cleaning toilets instead of death or being sent out to become a meal for the mutant scavengers.

Not for the first time—or the twentieth—he cursed himself for his pathological inability to leave well enough alone.

The door opened again and a woman came in. She wore an outfit similar to the female jailer who'd taken him to the showers last night. "Come on," she snapped. She gestured, and the bindings holding Stone to the chair released him.

He slumped forward, barely catching himself before he fell, then stood. She locked his arms to his sides again and directed him back to his cell. This time, he didn't even bother trying to memorize the route.

| CHAPTER TWENTY

THE NEXT SEVERAL DAYS passed in a blur.

Every one progressed in the same way: A harsh blare awoke Stone early each morning. Following a cold shower and a tasteless but filling meal eaten under a minder's stern scrutiny, he was taken to the interrogation chamber for more questioning. Apparently the Council had decided it wasn't done with him after all.

It wasn't always the same interrogator—the imposing man alternated with a slender, dark-haired woman and an older man with a chubby face and small, mean eyes—but the questions didn't change much. They all wanted to know what he knew about Harrison, and he couldn't tell them anything he hadn't already told them, no matter how many different ways they asked. Despite the initial interrogator's warning about physical torture, they never used any on him beyond the electrical jolts; in fact, never once did they touch him at all. He began to get the impression that the lofty Talented would rather dive naked into a vat of raw sewage than lower themselves to touch a Dim.

For his part, he answered their questions and did his best to cooperate with them; the exception was that he never revealed that he'd once had magical powers. That wasn't difficult, since they never asked him about it. Of course not: it wouldn't occur to the Talented that some lowly Dim pig would ever have wielded magic. They never mentioned Tanissa at the clinic—he was fairly sure they hadn't questioned her extensively, because they didn't bring up either what she'd told him about Harrison or what he'd told her about being from another world. Apparently her recall back to Temolan had been for associating with him at all, not for revealing forbidden information to him. That also probably meant she wasn't some deep-cover agent for the Talented. That, at least, was a relief.

Following the interrogation sessions, he was taken to another part of the complex and put to work. The tasks were simple, physically demanding, and mind-numbing: scrubbing floors, cleaning bathrooms, carrying heavy loads of the prison's laundry. Based on what he'd seen of the way things ran around here, Stone was certain his captors, if they'd wanted to, could easily have automated all of these tasks using magic, but instead they left them to the Dim. It was another data point in his increasingly negative view of these people.

He wasn't the only one performing these tasks—he often saw other prisoners, clad in the same shapeless tan garments he wore, toiling away under the watchful eye of Talented guards. Sometimes these others would glance at him in curiosity, or he at them, but they were never permitted to speak to each other beyond what was needed to do their jobs.

One day, as he stood in the sweltering hot laundry room tossing stacks of dirty prison uniforms into a surprisingly mundane and old-fashioned-looking industrial washing machine, he noticed a pair of prisoners on the other side of the room briefly whispering to each other while they folded clothes from the dryer. The Talented guard wrenched them away from each other and hit them with some spell until they both collapsed, twitching, to the floor. Stone didn't know if they were unconscious or dead, but he didn't see either of them again after that.

He'd noticed quickly after he started working here that the guards appeared to be both more brutal and less skilled as mages than the other Talented he'd met; their uniforms were simpler than their superiors' (though still far more elaborate than necessary for their prison-guard roles), and the higher-ups, on the rare occasions they came down here, treated them with brisk courtesy rather than overt respect. Stone wondered if there were stratifications even among Talented society, based on different levels of magical power. It made sense—on Earth there were varying degrees of magic from minor talents all the way up to truly potent practitioners like Madame Huan and William Desmond. For the most part, the higher-ups didn't deign to interact with Stone and the other Dim prisoners, but on the rare occasions they did they maintained a haughty distance; the guards, on the other hand, seemed to revel in snapping orders at the prisoners or punishing them for minor transgressions. Almost as if they were lording it over the only people they could legitimately consider themselves superior to. Stone filed that away as another data point.

He tried his best to keep his spirits up and his mind occupied as he worked. Since the tasks didn't require any thought or initiative—the Talented guards often mocked the prisoners for their cognitive limitations—it meant he could check out mentally while performing them. Mostly, he kept his brain exercised by going over various magical formulae and rituals; he'd tried thinking about his life back home, but that did nothing but add to his growing despair and sense of hopelessness. Why think about what it was looking more and more like he'd never see again?

The day's work was long and unrelenting—the prisoners were allowed only brief breaks to use the bathroom or bolt down their bland, meatless meals—and by the time Stone was taken back to his cell at the end of each session, he was exhausted. He never saw a clock, nor did he ever see any outside lights; he wondered if they even *had* windows down here, and wondered also if the average citizen of Temolan had any idea what life was like for these unfortunate Dim prisoners.

Or if they even cared.

| CHAPTER TWENTY-ONE

THE FIRST MORNING they didn't take him for questioning, Stone grew concerned. Instead of escorting him down the familiar hallway to the interrogation room after he'd had his usual cold shower and bland morning meal, they took him a different way, down a corridor he'd never seen before.

"No questions this morning?" he asked his guards, even though he wasn't supposed to address them unless spoken to.

"Quiet," the guard said, using magic to shove him along. They didn't bother immobilizing his arms anymore, and he didn't try to escape—where would he go? If he was ever going to get out of here he'd need a plan, and so far none had presented itself.

Their destination was a large, industrial-style kitchen. As the guard pushed open the double doors (again using magic), a solid wall of heat hit Stone, along with a strong odor of scorched oil and a concentrated overlay of the tasteless porridge the prisoners were fed. Several tan-clad prisoners moved around the various stations and counters, but they weren't cooking; instead, Stone spotted some cleaning counters, some scrubbing floors, and others carrying large cans of rubbish. Three more guards, two at the near end and one at the far, kept a vigilant eye over the proceedings.

"You're working in here today," one of Stone's guards said.

"Enjoy," the other one said, with a nasty laugh. Both departed as one of the two kitchen guards approached him.

An hour into the job, Stone had already determined this was the worst one yet—even worse than cleaning the bathrooms. At least the air had been chilly there, which made the hard physical work bearable. The kitchen, on the other hand, was swelteringly hot courtesy of two massive ovens on the far side. Stone was put to work scrubbing the cracked tile floor near one of these ovens, and by the time half an hour had passed he was drenched in sweat.

"Keep scrubbing," one of the guards ordered when he stopped to wipe his brow and catch his breath. "When you finish that section of floor you can have some water. Not before."

Stone returned to his task without a word, once again trying to check out mentally and perform the task by rote. "That section" was the entire side of the room—it would doubtless take him at least another two hours to finish it, probably longer. If his previous assignments had been any indication, the guards took sadistic pleasure in identifying any missed spots and forcing the prisoners to do them over.

As he worked, he wondered why they hadn't taken him for questioning again. Did they finally believe him that he knew nothing more than he'd already told them? They hadn't asked him anything else about his tattoo or magic in general, focusing mostly on his relationship with Harrison. Had they finally accepted that he didn't *have* a relationship with

Harrison? And if so, what then? Would he become just another forgotten member of the Dim prison workforce, destined to be driven until he died, like the poor sod a few days ago who'd collapsed in the laundry?

There was only one small advantage to working in the kitchen, Stone discovered on his third day there: the guards didn't seem to mind as much if the prisoners talked among themselves, as long as they kept it to a minimum and got their work done. They barely paid attention to the prisoners at all unless they weren't doing their jobs, preferring to lean back in their chairs and chat with each other.

Most of the time this didn't matter, because each prisoner had his or her own work area and they didn't get close enough to each other to talk. But Stone quickly realized that if he started scrubbing at one end of his section of the floor and finished at the opposite end, he'd end up only a few feet away from the prisoner assigned to the next section, a pale young man with scraggly blond hair and a perpetually hopeless expression.

"How long have you been in here?" he asked the man when he got close enough that he could speak quietly.

The man looked up, startled, and then returned to his scrubbing. "Huh?"

"How long?" Stone repeated. "How long have you been here?"

"I dunno. Long time."

"What's your name?"

"Tomba." The young man's suspicious gaze flicked toward the guard, then to Stone's face, then back to his work.

"I'm Stone. What did you do?"

"Huh?"

Stone wondered if his workmate truly *was* one of the Dim—and not in the magical sense—or if he'd simply been ground down by too much of the mind-numbing work and demoralizing conditions. "What did you do to get arrested?" he asked patiently.

"Oh. They said I was stealin' from the factory where I worked."

"Were you?"

"Was I what?"

"Stealing from the factory."

"Oh." The man focused on a small area of the floor, scrubbing vigorously to get a stain out. "Yeah, I guess I was."

"Quiet over there!" snapped one of the guards, who'd come patrolling around the corner. "If you've got energy to talk, I'll find you more work!"

Stone returned to his work with a sigh. It was good to hear another voice that wasn't his captors, but his own company seemed more intellectually stimulating than Tomba's. The young man, eyes fearful, turned his back on Stone and concentrated on a different part of the floor.

After Stone finished his own section of floor, the guard ordered him to carry cans of rubbish to an incinerator in an adjacent room. Two more guards were stationed in there, keeping careful watch on the proceedings—*they probably don't want to give the prisoners unfettered access to fire,* Stone thought sourly. *Afraid they might toss themselves in instead of the rubbish.*

He gripped the heavy can and tried not to drop it while he waited in line behind two other prisoners. He was keeping himself occupied by going over a spell formula in his mind when he thought he heard the word "Stone." He stiffened, forced himself to relax so his reaction didn't reach his aura, and focused on the guards' conversation. It was hard to hear clearly over the sound of the other prisoners dumping the garbage in the incinerator.

"—that one's trouble, I hear," one was saying to her partner.

"—won't be here much longer," the other one said. "I hear he's being sent to the Arena tonight."

"—too bad, he's a good worker."

"—lazy, like most of them—don't question the word from on high—"

Stone shifted his gaze sideways just enough to get a brief glance at the guards in his peripheral vision. This didn't sound good. What was the "Arena"? Were they talking about him? Had he been mistaken thinking he'd heard his name? What—

He tensed.

The two guards were looking directly at him.

Quickly, he jerked his head back and focused, heart pounding, on hustling the can forward. When it was his turn, he tossed the rubbish in the incinerator's yawning, fiery mouth and then hurried out with the empty can. He didn't look at the guards as he did, but wondered if they were still watching him, or if they'd realized—or cared—that he'd overheard them.

The Arena? What could that be? A different work assignment, somewhere else? Some kind of punishment? As far as he knew he hadn't done anything wrong—he'd done what they'd ordered him to do and hadn't made any trouble as he continued his futile attempts at working out an escape attempt.

As he put down the empty can and waited to pick up another one, he noticed Tomba shuffling nervously behind him. He'd apparently finished his floor section and been given garbage-can duty too. Stone glanced forward; there were two other prisoners ahead of him picking up cans. Quickly, he turned half-sideways, looking back over the kitchen, and muttered, "What's the Arena?"

"Huh?" Tomba looked startled and nervous to be spoken to again.

"The Arena. What is it?" He cast a quick look in the man's direction.

Tomba eyes got wide. "The Arena? You don't wanna know about that."

"Tell me."

He shook his head several times, his gaze cutting toward the guard who, so far, was ignoring them. "L-leave me alone. Stop asking me stuff."

"Just tell me what it is, and I'll stop."

"Nobody comes back from it. Not ever. It's where they—" He yelped as the guard hit him with a crackling bolt of energy.

"Keep moving! No talking!" the guard snapped. "If I have to say it again you'll regret it!"

Stone stumbled forward and picked up another can. When he risked a look behind him, he saw that one of the guards had taken Tomba out of line and was hustling him over to another section of the floor, far away from where he and Stone had worked before.

Barely noticing the weight of the smelly garbage can as he carried it to the incinerator room, Stone kept returning to "the Arena." They were sending him there? *Nobody ever comes back from it, ever,* Tomba had said. Was it some kind of execution method? Was he being exiled, as they'd threatened? If so, would there be any way he could escape, or would he be torn apart by the freakish scavengers? Why had they suddenly decided to do this? Was it because he couldn't provide any other useful information to his captors, so they had no further use for him?

For the rest of his work shift, he had trouble keeping his mind on what he was doing as it refused to stop speculating about this new development. Twice, the guards zapped him with painful jolts when he worked too slowly, and by the time the shift was over and he was back in his cell with another bowl of tasteless porridge, he'd come no closer to any reasonable conclusion. When the remainder of the evening passed without incident, he began to wonder if he'd misheard the guards—whatever the Arena was, perhaps they were talking about someone else. He'd have to look around tomorrow and see if any of the usual prisoners in his work group were missing.

He lay down on his thin mattress and turned toward the wall. They did turn the overhead light off eventually, but it was never at the same time and he always found it hard to get to sleep until it was dark. Tonight, he doubted he'd sleep much even if they did turn it off.

The door clanged open, startling him out of a half-doze. "Up," ordered a sharp voice.

"What—?" He scrambled to his feet, blinking. Was it morning already? Had he managed to sleep through the blaring alarm?

The tall, broad-shouldered woman who'd processed him the night he'd arrived stood in the doorway, looking impatient. She gestured, locking his arms to his sides. "Come on."

Stone didn't move. His heart pounded; was this what the guards had been talking about earlier? "Where are we going?"

"Quiet. Walk." She used magic to nudge him along.

With no other options available, he walked. "Where are you taking me?"

She didn't answer. Instead, she directed him down several hallways and into the magical elevator that had delivered him into the bowels of Temolan. As they rode upward, the woman pulled something from her pocket. She settled a dark hood over Stone's head.

This was new. "Don't want me to know where I'm going?"

A painful current jolted him, and he sagged against the elevator wall. "Shut up, or you'll have an unfortunate accident before you even get where you're going. Nobody will care, trust me."

So they *were* taking him somewhere. To this mysterious "Arena," perhaps? He remained silent, not doubting the woman's words. At least he wanted to see where he was to end up.

After walking for a short distance, the woman directed Stone to take a step up, then lowered him to a bench. A door slammed shut, and then a faint jerk indicated they were moving again. Another elevator? One of the floating vehicles he'd been delivered in? He couldn't sense the woman near him, so he ventured, "Is anyone else here?"

"Yeah," said a voice from the other side.

"I'm here," said a third voice, female this time, to his left.

Stone braced himself for another zap from the guards for talking, but it didn't come. Nobody else yelped, either. "Are you prisoners too?"

"I am," said the man.

"Yes," said the woman.

"Do you know where they're taking us?"

"To the Arena," the man said, bitterly.

"They didn't tell you?" the woman asked.

"They don't tell me much," Stone said. "What's the Arena?"

The two other prisoners were silent for a long time. "You don't know?" the man finally asked.

"No. I'm—not from this area. I was arrested for…having forged work papers."

A long sigh; Stone wasn't sure which of the two it came from. "It means we're dead," the woman said.

Stone tensed. "Execution?"

"They don't call it that," the man said. "This way they can get away with saying we have a chance."

"Explain," Stone said. "I'm Stone, by the way. I assume there aren't any guards in here with us."

"They don't need to be. It's not like we're getting out of here. I'm Geral," the man said.

"Petra," the woman said.

"So what's the Arena?" Stone asked again. "Why does it mean we're dead?"

"You really don't know?" Petra asked.

"I haven't been a prisoner very long."

"It's something *they* do to entertain themselves," Geral said. "We've just heard rumors—it's not official, but everybody knows about it."

"They take some of the prisoners and make them fight," Petra said. "They watch, and bet on the fights."

Stone tensed. "So they're running some kind of prisoner fight club?" He almost added, "and they're *allowed* to do that?" but he didn't. Apparently the Talented—especially the upper echelons—were allowed to do whatever the hell they wanted to do.

"Like I said, it's not official. Nobody admits to it on record. But it's been going on for a long time. They can only keep so many prisoners in Temolan, so they use the Arena to get rid of some when they start getting overcrowded."

"They don't like having too many Dim in their beautiful city." Petra sounded every bit as bitter as Geral.

"So—how does it work?" Stone asked. "Do you know?"

"Not for sure," Geral said. "Nobody ever comes back when they get sent to the Arena. But the rumors say that they make the prisoners keep fighting each other until they get killed. One on one. The winner goes on to the next round, and they keep doing that until only one's left."

A chill ran down Stone's spine. "That's...barbaric."

"Yeah," Petra said, in a *that's obvious* tone.

"What happens to the one that's left at the end?"

"Nobody knows," Geral said. "Maybe they heal 'em up and it starts all over the next night." He snorted. "Not that it matters to me—it won't be me."

"Me neither," Petra said. "I don't even know *how* to fight."

Stone sighed. It disturbed him, how resigned these two sounded to their fate. So that was how his Talented captors planned to get rid of him, without offending whatever vestigial, husklike consciences they might have left. They wouldn't even have the decency to give him a proper execution.

"Bloody hell…" he murmured. He was no fighter—without his magic, he probably wouldn't last through a single bout.

"Sorry," Petra said, and now she sounded sympathetic. "That you had to find out like this, I mean."

"Maybe it'll be quick, at least." Geral said. "Sometimes it is."

Stone was spared answering by the sound of the door opening. "Out, all of you," a voice ordered.

"Nice knowing you," Geral muttered.

CHAPTER TWENTY-TWO

THEY KEPT STONE'S BLACK HOOD ON until they'd herded him into another room with the locker-room reek of sweat and funk and old wood. Far away, he heard the faint sounds of what might have been cheers. He didn't know how long they kept him waiting there, his arms locked to his sides, but it was quite some time before something whipped the hood off, revealing a rough, dimly lit room with a tile floor and scarred wooden benches lining the walls. The room had two doors, both closed, a bank of lockers, and no windows.

A man stood on the other side of the room, eyeing him with distaste. "You won't last long," he said. He was young, not much older than the bullies who'd attacked him when he'd first arrived in Temolan, and had the same kind of conceited, entitled expression. He had dark, shoulder-length hair and wore a version of the now-familiar high-collared long coat, this one black with blue accents. Like all the other Talented Stone had seen, his hair and clothes were spotless.

"Where am I?" Stone demanded. "What's going on?" From outside, the cheers rose louder, then receded.

"You're at the Arena," the man said. "You'll be fighting soon."

"Fighting? With who?" *They expect me to be stupid—maybe acting like it will get me some information I can use.*

"Shut up. Get changed, and don't take all day about it. Maybe if you die fast, they'll give me somebody who might last a while next time." He waved his hand and one of the lockers opened.

"Wait—you're telling me I'm to fight to the death? Why? What did I do?" He looked in the locker; it contained only a pair of drab, gray athletic shorts with a green stripe down each side.

"Stop asking questions, pig," the man growled. "Get changed, or I'll kill you myself before you get a chance to fight."

Stone slipped out of his tan prison uniform and donned the shorts. The man eyed his tattoo in suspicion, but then shook his head. From another locker, he pulled an armband with a couple of figures written on it—they were in a different script Stone recognized as the Talented's, but he couldn't read them—and used magic to attach it snugly around Stone's upper right arm. "You won't be much entertainment, that's damned sure, but maybe some of the other fights will be better. Come on—you can watch the next few from the waiting area, so maybe you'll get some idea what to expect. Through that door. Don't embarrass me, all right?"

He gestured, and the door on the far side of the room opened. The cheering was louder now. "Go on," he said, giving Stone a hard magical shove toward it.

Stumbling, he went through, and it slammed shut behind him. When he spun to try it, it was locked.

He stood now in a small cubicle, perhaps four feet square. The door was on the back wall; the two side ones were made of wood, high and solid, and the front wall was barred, like a cage. The floor under his bare feet was rough concrete.

Outside the cage stretched a large, circular space with a dirt floor. The walls ringing it, painted blue, rose about ten feet high; interspersed at regular intervals around them were more barred cages like the one that held Stone. He could see other shadowy figures moving behind some of the bars— other prisoners? He couldn't see well enough to tell in the lowered lights. In the middle of the dirt area was something that looked like a large, dark stain. Blood? Again, he couldn't be sure.

He looked up, following the hubbub of voices. As he suspected, a number of long-coated figures, both men and women, sat around the perimeter of the dirt arena, leaning over for better views. Most had drinks in front of them, and the ones closest to him looked carefree, smiling, chattering among themselves.

Rage and disgust filled him—clearly, they didn't give a damn that their entertainment involved watching human beings kill each other. Again, he wondered where Harrison was, and if he had any connection to these barbaric practices.

A loud bell drove off further speculations. A moment later, bright lights switched on over the arena, illuminating the dirt floor. Now, Stone could see that the stains he'd spotted previously *were* blood, and some of them looked fresh. He tried to get a better look at the prisoners directly across the circle from him, but he still couldn't make out any specific detail.

An amused, drawling voice boomed over unseen speakers—or perhaps they used magic to amplify their voices, too.

256 |

"Welcome to any newcomers. We'll be getting the next match started in just a moment. Before that, let's meet our next two competitors, shall we?"

Two loud *clangs* sounded on the left side of the circle and the right, as the barred doors on two of the cubicles slid upward.

"Come on out," the amused voice called. "Don't be shy. Let's have a look at you."

For a moment, nothing happened. Then, as Stone gripped the bars of his cell and watched, two figures stumbled into the dirt ring. It appeared that something had pushed them out: one barely got his feet under him to avoid falling, while the other went sprawling and quickly scrambled back up.

The two were both men, one tall and dark-skinned, the other shorter and pale. Both were clad only in the same drab gray shorts Stone now wore—the dark man's had a red stripe, the pale man's a yellow one—and both had the same cloth wraps around their upper right arms. They looked warily around and the pale one tried to dart back into his cell, but the barred doors had already clanged shut again.

"Excellent, excellent," said the voice. "In the red-striped shorts, we have Holan. He's been a longtime 'guest' in Temolan, arrested last year for disrespecting lawful authority. He'll be fighting for Elithria tonight." Up above, a woman stood and raised her hands, to more cheers. "I'm sure he won't disappoint her! Isn't that right, Holan?"

From around the arena came laughter. Holan, for his part, looked scared and miserable and didn't acknowledge the announcer's words.

The announcer didn't seem to mind. "On the other side, in the yellow stripes, we have Geral. He's a relative newcomer to our system, and he's here because he disobeyed a direct order."

Stone stiffened. Geral—the same man who'd been in the transport with him.

"She was dying!" Geral yelled, shaking his fist at the unseen speaker. "I was just trying to help her!"

"Look at that fire!" The announcer's voice dripped with contemptuous amusement. "If he fights as well as he talks, we should be in for a good bout! Geral will be fighting for Donastian."

The crowd erupted in cheers when a man stood in the stands, then quieted.

"Before we get started," the announcer continued, "just in case some of you haven't noticed, we have not one but *two* distinguished guests tonight. Everyone, please welcome Chanandra and Olystriar, from the Temolan High Council!"

The spotlight fell on two figures sitting in an elevated box. Neither rose, but both acknowledged the swelling cheers that rose from the group with languid waves.

Stone examined them until the spotlight winked out—so *these* were two of the Talented's leaders, architects of this insane system. Chanandra, a small, slim woman, had dark hair pulled back from a sly, narrow-eyed face, and an equally sly smile. Her expression was one of anticipation. Olystriar had broad shoulders, dark brown skin, and bright blond hair. His face revealed nothing of his thoughts. Stone memorized both faces, in case he should ever encounter them again.

Not bloody likely. I'll be dead before the night's over.

"And…begin!" the announcer called.

In the dirt circle, Geral and Holan didn't move. They eyed each other warily, as if each one expected the other to make the first move, but neither did.

The crowd booed.

"Now, now," the announcer said. "You know the rules. Whoever wins at the end of the evening gets his freedom. But if you *refuse* to fight—"

Suddenly, both fighters went rigid. Holan jerked and shuddered, while Geral clawed at his throat. Stone gripped the bars tighter, heart pounding.

Whatever had taken hold of them vanished as abruptly as it had come, and both men dropped to their knees in the dirt, gasping.

"That will be your last warning," the announcer said. "Put on a good show, or you'll be slaughtered like the pigs you are!"

That, apparently, was enough for Holan. With a roar of rage, he leaped up and flung himself forward toward Geral, arms outstretched. The crowd cheered once again.

Geral didn't get out of the way in time. He barely managed to throw himself sideways and avoid the worst of Holan's attack, but the other man was larger and taller. Both of them crashed into the wall and went down, each trying to get a good shot at the other.

Stone glanced up in time to see Geral's "sponsor," Donastian, stand up and lean a little over the partition. He fixed his gaze on Geral and made a gesture.

Suddenly, Geral found new motivation. He yelled something unintelligible, flung Holan off him, and threw himself on top of the other man, flailing his fists and raining blows down on his opponent's face. Holan fought back, kneeing

Geral in the gut to knock him off, then leaping at him to renew his own attack. All around, the crowd continued to cheer.

"That's the way to do it!" the announcer called. "Looks like Donastian is using a little inducement to light a fire under Geral. What do you all say—shall we liven things up?"

The cheers grew to roars of approval.

From somewhere high above the arena, two small objects dropped down and landed in the center of the dirt ring, several feet apart. From Stone's vantage point it was hard to tell what they were, but it soon became obvious: both Geral and Holan hurried forward to snatch them up, and they glinted in the overhead light: crude, long-bladed daggers.

The two men began circling each other with wary caution again. Both were puffing with exertion and drenched in sweat. Blood poured from Holan's nose and ran down his face, and Geral was clearly favoring his right leg.

Suddenly, Holan spun toward the stands. With a shout of rage, he flung his knife directly at Elithria.

It bounced off an unseen shield and dropped back to the dirt.

The crowd erupted in laughter.

"Oh, that's a good one!" the announcer crowed. "How many times have we seen them try that? It never gets old, does it?"

"Fight, you cowardly pig!" yelled a man from the stands, as Holan's knife levitated back to him.

The two combatants stumbled toward each other again, and Stone noticed with horror that they didn't seem to be moving entirely under their own power. Something was nudging them into action—more magic, no doubt. He wondered if anyone in the audience was allowed to affect the fighters, or only their "sponsors."

As the crowd continued to laugh and jeer, Holan and Geral seemed to give up their resolve not to fight. They circled, slicing at each other with the knives, their faces set in growing anger. Each time one of them drew blood—first Holan on Geral's arm, then Geral across Holan's broad chest—the crowd's cheers rose until they echoed off the arena's unseen ceiling. Blood pattered to the dirt floor; whenever one of the fighters was knocked down or fell to his knees, the mixture of blood and dirt coated his body with a grimy film.

Stone didn't want to look. He didn't want to watch one of these men kill the other one. But he couldn't look away. This was destined to be his fate sometime tonight, so if he were to have any chance of surviving it, he'd need all the data he could gather.

When the end came, it came fast—and not even deliberately. Geral and Holan were circling each other again, their knives held out in front of them, their gazes locked on each other, looking for an opening to slash. Suddenly Geral, now caked with bloody mud, dashed forward, ducked under Holan's longer reach, and flailed his blade madly toward the taller man's stomach.

Holan jumped back, barely avoiding the attack, but in the process, he tripped. In a wild attempt to catch himself before he fell over and put himself at Geral's mercy, he pitched forward. His knife swung wildly.

Geral screamed, a loud shriek that was almost instantly cut off. His hands flew to his neck.

The crowd exploded in cheers, many of them craning forward for a better look.

Stone, gripping his bars, stared at the scene in horror. Somehow, without meaning to do it, Holan's strike had slashed across the side of Geral's neck. He must have hit the man's jugular vein, because bright red blood bubbled and spurted from beneath the terrified man's hands. Geral scrabbled at the wound, trying to stanch it, to hold the blood in, but it was already too late. He went white and collapsed to the dirt. He twitched twice, and then his hands fell away and he lay still. A red puddle appeared beneath his neck and grew rapidly larger, soaking into the dry dirt.

Amid the deafening applause, laughs, and jeers from the crowd, Holan appeared to be in shock. His eyes were so wide Stone could see the whites all around them, and he stared down at Geral's body with a kind of disassociated disbelief. His hold on the knife began to loosen.

Then, suddenly, it tightened again. Tears streaming down his face, he yelled something Stone's magical translator couldn't handle, and then plunged the blade into his own chest. A moment later he, too, had fallen to the dirt next to his dead opponent.

If Stone had thought this crowd possessed even a shred of humanity, enough to be shocked by what had just occurred, he was mistaken. If anything, the cheers grew *louder*.

"Well!" called the announcer in glee. "Seems we've got a double casualty this time! Too bad, Elithria—your man's the winner, but I don't think he's going to last long enough to manage his next fight!"

The spotlight fell on Elithria, who smiled ruefully and shrugged. "Such is the way," she said, her voice amplifying as well. "Perhaps I'll have better luck next time!"

"There's the right attitude!" the announcer crowed, chuckling. "All right—just a brief break while we take out the trash, and we'll get to our next match. You're going to like this one, I promise!"

Stone slumped, gripping the bars in impotent rage. In desperation, he checked once again to see if his own—or Harrison's—magic had returned. If it had, he planned to cause as much mayhem as he could manage, starting with that contemptible announcer and working his way as far as he could get through the Council members, the two "sponsors," and the crowd members before they took him down. He knew he wouldn't get far, but if he could manage to take out even one of these sadistic bastards, it would be worth it.

But his magic hadn't returned. Of course it hadn't. It wasn't going to, and soon he'd be out there in the dirt and the blood and the muck, trying to stay alive without killing some other poor sod as unfortunate as he was.

He didn't like his odds.

He watched as two more fights passed, his despair growing with each. The second consisted of a pair of women— Petra wasn't one of them—clad in the gray shorts and matching gray tank tops. Once again they clearly didn't want to fight each other, and once again the crowd used magic to "encourage" them. This time they didn't get daggers, but long, thin-bladed swords. The fight lasted longer than Geral and Holan's had, but ended when one of the women, spurred to near-madness by her sponsor's incessant poking, drove her blade through her opponent's eye. The victor was herded back to her cage amid loud cheers; before she made it, she dropped to her knees and vomited on the ground. The crowd laughed, and someone magically tossed her back into the cage. It slammed shut behind her.

The third fight was different. Two men again, one with a purple stripe on his shorts, the other with white. Both looked in better shape than Geral and Holan had, their muscles rippling.

"This should be entertaining," the announcer called. "Their sponsors, Millia and Vestereth—who, as most of you know, have been bonded to each other for years—have been experimenting with some alchemical mixtures that should ensure these two fighters will put on a good show for us. Elar, in the purple, is a murderer. Utha, in white, was caught committing atrocities on at least three children. Let's watch them, friends!"

Stone had no idea what was in the "alchemical mixtures"—or, for that matter, if the loathsome announcer was telling the truth about Elar's and Utha's crimes—but the instant they were ordered to, both men roared and lunged at each other. They fought like mad things, punching, kicking, grappling—even biting bloody chunks from each other's skin. Once, when they turned for a second in Stone's direction, he got a look at their eyes and flinched back. Both men had the crazed, unhinged expressions demonstrating that they had little control over their actions.

The crowd was eating it up, cheering and pounding their mugs on the arms of their chairs. This time, the fighters weren't given weapons—they obviously could do a fine job of killing each other with their bare hands, feet, and teeth. Stone, from his cage, felt ill watching them. These men weren't even human anymore—and it wasn't their fault. When the spotlights briefly picked out their sponsors in the audience, a man and a woman sitting next to each other, their faces showed excited anticipation and, to Stone's disgust, sharp curiosity. This was an experiment for them, to see how their concoctions would perform under real-world conditions. He mentally added them to his target list should his magic suddenly return.

The fight lasted nearly twenty minutes before one of the men got a good hold on the other's neck—Stone couldn't even tell which was which anymore, since both were crusted head to toe in the bloody mud—and snapped it with a *crack* that echoed so loudly above the cheers that he was sure it must be magically amplified.

"What a fight!" the announcer yelled. "Oh, my, that was *amazing!* Let's give some applause to Millia and Vestereth, for making such a show possible! Perhaps some of you might speak to them about getting hold of their latest brew—this one's a winner, don't you agree?"

The crowd enthusiastically agreed.

Meanwhile, the winner of the bout—Stone still couldn't identify him—appeared not to be coming down from his chemically-induced rage. In fact, he seemed to be in the grip of some kind of fit. He roared, charged around the dirt arena, and tore at his own skin with his hands almost as if he were overheated. His wild gaze darted around the crowd, and then he dived toward his dead opponent and began clawing at the man.

"Oh, dear," the announcer said, not sounding the least bit distressed. "Seems our friends haven't *quite* worked all the bugs out of their elixir yet. Might want to wait a bit with those orders! Meanwhile, let's get these two out so we can prepare for our final first-round fight of the evening!"

Instantly, magical grips took hold of both the live man and the dead one, separating them and shoving them through two different openings—the live one into his cage, and the dead one out through a door that only appeared at the end of each bout.

Stone was so caught up in his disgust in the whole proceeding that it took him a moment to process the announcer's words.

Final first-round fight of the evening.

That's me, then. No more time.

In a few minutes, he'd have no choice but to try to kill, or at least incapacitate, an unknown opponent. Would he face another one punched up on Millia and Vestereth's vile alchemical brew? Or worse, would they force *him* to drink it?

It didn't matter, though—brew or no brew, he knew how it would end. He was no fighter. Unless they put him up against someone as unskilled at it as he was, it was only a matter of time.

"All right!" The announcer was speaking again. "All right, friends, are you ready for our last fresh pair of the night? The winner of this match will go on to face Elar, since I'm afraid Holan has succumbed to his self-inflicted injuries." Once again, he didn't sound the least bit sad or regretful about this.

"For this last match," he continued, "we have a special combatant, and he'll go against someone I'm sure will be a crowd favorite. First, let me introduce you to Karol. He's only been a guest of our system for a few weeks—a fine worker, slower of wit than even the typical Dim, but big and ready to prove himself!"

A cage on the other side of the dirt circle opened, and a man entered, looking around nervously. He was about Stone's height but had at least fifty pounds on him, with broad shoulders and powerful legs. He wore shorts with an orange stripe, and his expression seemed almost bewildered, like he didn't know where he was. Blinking against the bright lights, he swiped a hand across his face and stood waiting in the center. The crowd jeered and laughed; somebody tossed a hunk of bread at him, and it bounced off his chest. He looked down at it, then back up.

"His opponent," the announcer called, "is also a new-comer—both to our system and, to hear him tell it, to our very way of life here in Temolan. He claims to be from somewhere far away, and doesn't know our customs. I guess this is where he learns, right? Say hello to Stone."

Stone's cage bars shot upward, forcing him to let go. The crowd cheered, and he could see the anticipation on their faces. They'd been waiting for him—the upstart newcomer who'd been asking too many questions.

When he didn't move out of the cage, something shoved him in the back, hard. He stumbled out, caught himself before he went face-first into the bloody dirt, and stopped, regarding Karol from several feet away. He shivered; the air was cold out here, colder than it had been inside the cages. The damp soil squelched under his bare feet.

"Look at him," the announcer said. "Quite a specimen, wouldn't you say? You wouldn't think a skinny wretch like him would have a chance against the likes of Karol, but—" he dropped his voice to a conspiratorial murmur that still came through clearly to the room "—there are rumors that he thinks he's one of us! Look at that tattoo on his chest—it looks magical, does it not? And I'm told he even had the nerve to use a name that would mark him as one of the Talented."

The crowd erupted in laughter, boos, and jeers.

"Watch carefully—perhaps we'll see some magic tonight, friends! Perhaps this newcomer will surprise us all!"

"Karol will rip his guts out!" cried a man from the stands. Another hunk of bread, along with some kind of wadded-up food wrapper, sailed down and hit Stone.

"Start the fight! We want blood!" shouted another.

The announcer laughed. "I see you're popular tonight, Stone—or whatever your name is. Show us some of that magic, won't you? Begin!"

Heart pounding hard, Stone didn't move. He kept his gaze fixed on Karol, watching as the other man took a tentative step in his direction. He knew his only hope, if his opponent was indeed slow-witted, was to anticipate his attacks and avoid them, then do something to incapacitate him—kick out one of his knees, perhaps. He wasn't strong, but he was fast. If he could make it so Karol couldn't catch him, maybe they'd call the fight a draw. He doubted it—the crowd was already calling for blood and wouldn't be satisfied with less—but if he could do something decisive while he was still fresh, he might get out of this alive.

Karol, however, had no such plans. As the spectators continued to yell mocking encouragement to both him and Stone ("Kill the skinny pig!" and "Show us some magic!" being the most common respective cries), his brows knit and his face set in a frown of angry resolve. With a shout, he spread his arms wide and leaped at Stone.

Stone dived out of the way, landing hard and rolling up. *Bloody hell, he's fast!* He stood, panting, feeling but not daring to look down at the grit and blood now coating his body.

"Hit him!" a male voice shouted. "Fight, you coward!"

Karol went after him again, and this time he managed to duck sideways, lashing out with a kick toward his opponent's knee. It didn't connect solidly, but the man's pained *oof!* told him he hadn't missed. He backed away in triumph.

"Use some magic!" the same male voice called, laughing.

Stone flashed him a quick glare, then focused back on Karol. He wondered if the organizers of this fiasco would give them weapons, or be satisfied with Karol ripping him apart with his bare hands, as Elar had done in the previous bout. *Even if I win this one, I'll still have to face* him, he reminded himself.

"Stop runnin' away!" Karol yelled, and made another lunge at Stone. "I'll kill ya fast!" He didn't look bewildered anymore—he looked determined, like a bull who'd finally figured out that the only way out of the ring was to trample the bullfighter.

Stone was pleased to see his opponent was limping a little, at least. He waited until the last moment, then made another dive to the side—but this time Karol was ready for him. Instead of plowing through as he'd done before, he mirrored Stone's movement and threw himself in the same direction, his heavy, muscular arms wrapping around Stone's upper body and driving him with a crash into the wooden wall.

The crowd went wild. "That's it!" a man shouted.

"Kill him!" a woman added.

"Show us some magic, pig!" another man yelled.

Stone barely avoided hitting his head on the wall, but the rest of him wasn't so lucky. He jerked and writhed, trying to wrest himself from Karol's grasp, but he didn't have the strength to do it. Instead, he brought his foot up and tried to kick his opponent again. Unfortunately for him, the way Karol was holding him meant he couldn't see where he was aiming this time, so the blow went wide and only glanced off the other man's tree-trunk leg.

Karol slammed him into the wall again, and then once more. All around them the crowd cheered, anticipatory sharks circling wounded prey.

Stone, acting with an animal's desperation now, renewed his attempts to extricate himself from Karol's grip, but even madman's strength wasn't enough. Karol threw him to the bloody dirt and dropped on top of him, straddling his abdomen and raining blows down on his upper body.

"I got you now!" he yelled, triumphant.

Stone spat blood and tried to buck upward to throw the man off, but any minimal combat skills he might possess didn't extend to wrestling.

He might as well have been stuck under a car, for all Karol moved. Stone's opponent seemed to ignore his efforts, as a grown man might ignore the ineffectual struggles of a boy. With a wild yell, he raised his hands, brought them down around Stone's neck, and began to squeeze. He leaned down until his wide, grinning face was only inches from Stone's.

This is it. I'm dead.

And then something unexpected happened.

The grip didn't tighten. Karol appeared to be bearing down with all his strength, his hands wrapped around Stone's neck shaking with his effort—but Stone felt only minimal pressure. *What—?*

"Play along," Karol hissed, barely moving his lips around his bared teeth. "Grab my armband and hold on tight. Make it look good." His voice didn't sound dull or feeble-minded now.

"What—?" Stone whispered, staring at Karol as if he'd suddenly sprouted wings.

"Do it!" he insisted. "We don't have much time."

Stone thought about it for only a second. He had no idea what was going on, but if Karol was the real deal he was already dead, so he had nothing to lose. Pretending to be choking under Karol's onslaught, he flailed one arm at his throat, trying to rip the man's hands free, and the other landed on his opponent's armband. He gripped it and held on tight.

Instantly, he began to feel woozy. His body, already slicked with sweat and grime and blood, felt like it was cooking from the inside. His limbs didn't work anymore. *What did you do to me*? he tried to protest, but the words got lost from his brain to his mouth.

Karol's hands tightened around his neck, and black bubbles billowed in front of his eyes. He didn't even feel it when his head fell back and hit the dirt.

Part Two

| CHAPTER TWENTY-THREE

W HEN STONE'S CONSCIOUSNESS RETURNED, he didn't smell dirt, or blood, or sweat. He didn't hurt, or even feel disoriented. He wasn't lying on a thin, hard mattress; in fact, the surface under him felt soft, and he was covered with a blanket.

He opened his eyes. The room was dark; all he could see were shadowy shapes.

Am I back in the hospital? But no, that didn't make sense. He didn't smell medicine, and anyway why would the Talented bother putting a fallen Dim fighter in the hospital?

Why aren't I dead? He sat up as it came back to him: Karol had done something to him. But what—?

A faint, soothing light came on. "Ah, you're awake. How do you feel?" A female voice, one he didn't recognize.

He twisted around to look. A young woman sat next to the bed, watching him. When she caught him looking at her, she smiled.

How *did* he feel? He glanced around the room—it was a bedroom, simple but well-appointed, with heavy drapes on the window blocking any outside light, a tall wooden armoire, and a small table with two chairs. The bed he lay in was soft, with a substantial quilted comforter covering him. "I—"

She chuckled. "I know—this has got to all be fairly confusing for you. Would you like anything? Something to eat? Or should I clear out so you can take a proper shower? We cleaned you up when you got here, but I'm sure a nice hot shower would be welcome."

Stone looked down at himself, pushing the covers away. They had indeed cleaned him up; there was no sign of the blood, grime, or sweat from the arena, and he was now dressed in fine pajama bottoms—not the thin things he'd worn at the prison, or the gray shorts. His armband was gone too.

"What I want," he said slowly, "is to know where the hell I am. What happened to me? How did I—"

She held a hand up. "Believe me, you'll find out everything. But not from me. Trust me—get yourself cleaned up and dressed, and then I'll take you where you can eat something and ask all your questions. There's a selection of clothes in the armoire—I'm sure you'll find something you like." She patted his shoulder. "Don't worry—I promise, you're safe now and you'll get answers to whatever you want to know." She indicated something on the nightstand next to the bed. "Just use the intercom there to call me when you're ready, and I'll take you there."

He looked, startled. Intercom? Sure enough, the thing on the stand looked like a modern-day intercom button and speaker, something that wouldn't look out of place back home on Earth. *Was* he on Earth? Had they somehow sent him home when he was unconscious? Questions bubbled and jostled in his mind, demanding answers. "Listen, I—"

She gripped his shoulder, and there was nothing deceptive or concealing in her expression. "Trust me," she said. "I know you've got to be pretty confused right now. Just bear with us, all right?"

His mind locked on a question. "Just tell me one thing before you go. Where's Karol?"

"He's fine," she assured him. "You can talk to him later." Without waiting for him to ask anything else, she waved and disappeared through the door, which she closed behind her. He noticed there was no *snick* of a lock engaging.

Tentatively, he swung his legs around and stood up, ready to slump back if he felt dizzy—but he didn't. Whatever vestiges of what Karol had done to him in the Arena had passed. He wondered how long he'd been unconscious. Were they still in Temolan? Back in Drendell?

No point in wasting time on speculation. You aren't going to figure it out on your own. Instead, he crossed to the door and tried it.

It opened readily, revealing a carpeted hallway lined with a few other doors. *So I'm not a prisoner. That's something, anyway.*

Deciding that since these people had obviously rescued him from certain death, it was rude to go wandering around in their house without permission, he stepped back into the room and closed the door.

Next, he opened the armoire. Hanging inside were several shirts of various colors, several pairs of dark trousers, and a couple of dark jackets. A shelf below held a few pairs of shoes and boots, and drawers along one side contained shorts and socks.

He pulled one of the shirts out and examined it. Simply but exquisitely made of fine fabric and stitching, it mirrored the style he'd seen wealthier men wearing in Drendell. He quickly assembled an outfit and laid it out on the bed, then went into the bathroom.

Like the bedroom it was simple but luxurious, complete with a spacious, glass-walled shower cubicle etched with an abstract, geometric pattern and a selection of toiletries and fluffy white towels on a shelf nearby.

It had been a long time since a shower felt this good, especially after all the cold ones back at the Talented's prison. He took longer than he needed to, luxuriating in the sensation of the hot water stinging his back, then dried off and found a fresh razor near the sink. By the time he emerged back into the bedroom, he felt more human than he had since he'd arrived on this world. Even better, all the clothes fit him as if they'd been made for him. Whoever these mysterious rescuers were, he owed them a debt of gratitude.

Right, then—let's see if they're telling the truth about getting some answers. He hit the button on the intercom. "Hello?"

The woman answered with refreshing swiftness. "Ah, there you are. Feeling better?" Her voice held the hint of a warm chuckle.

"Much better, thank you. And I'll feel better still if I can get some answers."

"You will. I'll be right there."

She arrived only a couple minutes later, knocking on the door and then pushing it open. She looked him up and down. "You look a *lot* better," she said, approvingly. "I'm Vynna, by the way."

One of the mundanes, then, by her name. "Couldn't have been much worse," he said with a wry smile. He could see her better now—a slim, blonde young woman in her early twenties dressed in slacks and a green blouse, her plain face made more attractive by her sparkling green eyes and cheerful expression. "I'm—"

"Alastair Stone. I know." She motioned for him to follow her.

He tensed. She knew who he was? What the hell was going on here?

Instead of asking more questions this woman obviously wasn't going to answer, he followed her, examining his surroundings as he went.

They appeared to be in a large, upscale house. The place's décor matched his room: simple, elegant, purposeful, with very little ornamentation. He hadn't seen anything like it back in Drendell. They passed an open doorway and he got a brief look out a window before they moved on: outside were tall trees and rolling hills, and he spotted the shadowy forms of more buildings. From the light, it looked like morning.

"Here we are," Vynna said. She waved him through another doorway into a sitting room furnished with comfortable-looking sofas. A floor-to-ceiling picture window looked out on a walled garden awash with brilliant color.

The room had a single occupant. She'd been sitting on one of the sofas looking out the window, but rose as they arrived. "Well," she said. "So you're Alastair Stone. I've heard a lot about you. Nice to finally get to meet you."

Stone eyed her with suspicion. Why did everyone here know who he was, and not seem bothered by it? "I'm afraid you have me at a disadvantage," he said. *That's a bloody understatement.*

The woman smiled. Of medium height and slim, she had an athletic build and wore a no-nonsense shirt, trousers, and boots. Shoulder-length dark brown hair framed an intelligent, purposeful face. "This must all be fairly confusing for you. We're sorry about that—and about how we had to get you out of there. We couldn't take any chances that they'd catch on. That would have meant certain death for everyone involved, and not a quick one, either. Please, sit down. I'm Errin, by the way."

"Pleasure to meet you." Stone took a seat on the sofa opposite her. "You *are* going to tell me what's going on, right?"

"We'll answer all your questions," she said. "I'm sure you're hungry, though—I know what they feed the prisoners in that hellhole in Temolan."

As if on cue, Vynna, who'd disappeared back through the doorway during the introductions, returned carrying a tray. She set it on the table between Stone and Errin. "Enjoy," she said. "Let me know if you need anything else." Then she left again.

Stone couldn't help it—after several days of nothing but tasteless porridge, the heaping plate of eggs, bacon, and something that looked mostly but not quite like pancakes set his mouth watering. A sparkling glass of fruit juice and another of ice water completed the spread.

"Go on," Errin said, chuckling.

He didn't need a second invitation. "Thank you," he said, and immediately set about devouring the meal. Questions could wait a little longer. The food was delicious, though he supposed he would have thought the same of anything with flavor at this point.

Errin, for her part, didn't speak while he ate. Instead, she looked out the window and waited patiently for him to finish.

At last, he pushed the empty plate away. For the first time since the fire at Faran's shop, he felt full. "Thank you," he said again. "That was brilliant. Now—questions? I've got quite a lot of them. Were you serious about answering them all?"

"Very serious."

He eyed her with sudden suspicion. "You seem very accommodating—that's something I haven't encountered much of here. How do I know you're not another one of *them*, trying to lure me into revealing something? They've already tried intimidation and torture—perhaps they've decided to try the carrot this time instead of the stick."

"I can set your mind at ease about that, Dr. Stone," came another, familiar voice.

Stone jerked his head up. "Bloody hell…" he whispered.

Standing framed in the doorway, watching him with an expression of veiled amusement, was Trevor Harrison.

CHAPTER TWENTY-FOUR

"**I**T'S...*YOU.*" Stone didn't even care how dumbfounded he must sound. "You're—here."

"He's a sharp one, isn't he?" Errin commented with a grin.

"He has his moments," Harrison said drily.

Stone continued to stare at him. He looked much the same as he remembered from the last time they'd encountered each other: tall, slim, imperious, his blue-black hair a stark contrast to his pale complexion and winter-gray eyes. Instead of a fine suit, he wore a simple white shirt and black trousers, but as before everything about him seemed unnaturally put together. The effect was similar to, but not quite the same as, the Talented's preternatural spotlessness. "How—did you—"

"How did I find you?" Harrison didn't move from his spot in the doorway. "It wasn't difficult, once I received word you were here. I apologize for the delay—I only recently found out." He glanced at Errin, then back at Stone. "I also must apologize that I'll be unable to remain here at the moment. I've some urgent matters I must attend to, but I hope you'll join me later tonight. I'm quite interested to find out why you're here."

"Wait," Stone protested, leaping up. "You've only just got here and you're leaving again?"

"Only until this evening, but I wanted to assure you that you are safe here. I understand you've been through some difficult experiences."

"That's a bloody understatement," he said, unconsciously echoing his earlier thought. He suspected he'd be getting quite a lot of mileage out of it over the foreseeable future.

"Errin can answer many of your questions. She is not a mage, but she should be able to satisfy most of your curiosity. Anything else, I can answer tonight." He made a slight bow. "Until then, Dr. Stone—I am pleased to see you, and I look forward to our conversation later."

Before Stone could protest again, he departed.

Stone let his breath out. "Well. All right, then."

Errin chuckled. "He's like that. You get used to him eventually. Now—about those questions. We can stay here and talk, or we can take a walk. I'd imagine you might like to stretch your legs a bit, and get out in the sun."

"Yes. Let's walk." He *did* want to stretch his legs, but he also wanted to get a better look around wherever this was.

"Good. I'll show you around," she said, as if anticipating his thought.

The moment they stepped outside, Stone knew they were neither in Drendell nor in Temolan. Gone were the mage city's tall, pale spires, or Drendell's gritty urban brick structures and grimy abandoned vehicles. Instead he saw neat, meandering streets dotted at wide intervals with buildings. Some were obviously homes, while a cluster of them appeared to be a small business district. Beyond them, Stone spotted rolling hills and what looked like large swaths of orchards, farms, and ranchland. Past those, things faded to a haze he couldn't see past. "What is this?" he asked. "Some kind of rural community?"

"Not exactly. Welcome to New Argana."

"What is New Argana? Another town, like Drendell?" Clearly they weren't floating, so this couldn't be another of the mages' cities unless somebody around here had truly world-class illusionary skills.

"Not exactly." As they drew away from the house and into the street, Errin gently gripped Stone's shoulders and turned him around to face behind him.

Once again, he gaped. He couldn't help it.

Rising up out of a craggy hill some distance away was an enormous black tower, stretching up so high that its upper floors were lost among swirling clouds. From this far away he couldn't see any features on it aside from a few faint blue flickers that danced around it like tiny lightning strikes, but even in his mundane state he had no doubt this thing had to be deeply, profoundly magical. "What the hell—?"

"That's the Nexus," Errin said. "The center of our little settlement here."

"The…Nexus?"

"Trevor's tower. He'll explain more to you about it tonight—that's the magic stuff I don't get involved in, and he explains it better than I do anyway, trust me. Come on—let's keep going."

Stone could barely tear his gaze away from the black tower, which bore more than a passing resemblance to a rougher, more organic version of the Obsidian back on Earth—but after a few seconds he hurried to catch up to her. She wasn't answering questions—she was adding more! He supposed he should start somewhere before things got out of hand. "Where is this place? New Argana, you called it?"

"In the middle of the Wastes—far enough in that none of the Talented would ever dare try to find it, even if we weren't fully protected."

"The Wastes?"

She glanced at him. "I guess you're going to need to tell me what you already know."

As they walked down the pleasant street—*no cracks or potholes,* Stone thought idly—two more people passed them. The middle-aged man and woman were both dressed in the same simple, well-made style of clothing Stone wore.

"Hello," the woman called, waving. "Beautiful day."

"It is," Errin agreed. To Stone, she said, "These are Lanytha and Balen." She nodded toward Stone. "And this is…Alastair. He just arrived last night."

"Pleasure," Stone said. He'd noticed long ago that nobody shook hands on this world, so he didn't offer his.

"Indeed," Lanytha agreed. "Welcome."

The two moved on, and Stone and Errin did likewise. "Lanytha and Balen," Stone mused. "If you have the same naming styles here, then—"

Errin smiled. "—then Balen is non-magical, and Lanytha is a mage. That's exactly right. And yes, they are a couple. They've been bonded for several years. That's why they're here, as it happens."

"I don't understand."

"They'd kept their relationship secret for a long time. She was a wealthy member of the Talented in Sholandre, with him posing as her 'Dim' servant. She was exiled, and she managed to pull enough strings to get him exiled with her.

Normally the Dim are killed, or sent to things like the Arena."

Stone didn't miss the disgust that seeped into her tone each time she used the term "Dim." "Wait," he said, remembering the talk of exile he'd heard back in Drendell. "Exile to where?" He let his breath out in a loud, frustrated sigh. "There's so damned much I don't know, I don't even know where to start!" He wondered if any of it would even matter—if things went the way he hoped, he'd convince Harrison to teach him magic and then he'd be on his way home before he'd need to learn anything about this world's bizarre history.

But still…his curiosity, as always, reared its head. Staying or not, this was fascinating stuff.

"It's all right," Errin assured him. "It's a lot to take in. Tell me what you know, and I'll try to fill in the rest. You'll have plenty of time to learn it all if you're joining us here."

"I—" Stone began, uncomfortably. "I don't know that I am. That's what I need to discuss with Mr. Harrison tonight. But—I don't know much. I know the mages live in floating cities and don't like the mun—the non-magical people very much. I know there are a lot more non-magical people than mages, and they live on the surface in towns that look like they used to be a lot larger. And something about a war. Can you tell me about that?"

"Hold on, hold on." Errin said, holding up her hands to stop him. "I'll give you the short version, and you can fill in the details later."

"Fair enough. Anything will be more than I have now." He tilted his head. "What do you do here, by the way? You seem to know Mr. Harrison fairly well. You two aren't—?"

"Bonded? A couple?" She laughed. "Hardly. No, I'm kind of his—right-hand woman and chief mechanic around here."

"Mechanic?" That seemed an odd combination of roles.

"Sure. I build things." She nodded down the street ahead of them, where some kind of vehicle was approaching. As it drove by, Stone noticed it had little in common with the rusting, broken-down things he'd seen in Drendell. Instead, it looked like someone had started out with a modern Earth car but gone in a completely foreign direction—more mechanical, less electronic, but it moved silently and without any sign of exhaust.

"You built that?"

"Not that one specifically, but I helped with the design. We use a combination of magic and mechanical design to make them work. You'll see later."

Stone realized he'd gotten sidetracked again, and had to grin. "Okay, you're right. No more new questions until you've answered the old ones."

"You want to know about the war."

"Yes. Who fought it? How long ago was it? What happened to the cities?"

Errin walked on for a few more moments before answering. "The war was the reason the mages live in the floating cities."

"There are five of them, right?"

"Five, yes—one for each of the five major factions. Used to be six, but the sixth is gone. Anyway, as you might have figured out, many of the mages are a contentious, arrogant bunch."

"Hadn't noticed," Stone said wryly.

"They used to live on the surface, with the non-magical people. They still treated us like dirt, mind you, but they had their own towns, and their own districts in the major cities that were a lot nicer than the rest. And they used to be all over Calanar." She pulled a notebook and pen from her shoulder bag and paused to make a sketch.

Stone studied it; it looked like an irregular mass, but without any reference points, he couldn't tell what it was supposed to be. "Calanar?"

"That's the continent," she said, tapping the drawing with her pen-tip. "Close enough, anyway. And there used to be cities all over it. But as often happens when you get people with too much power who were all raised to believe they were the center of the universe, they started to divide up into factions. And each faction started having its best magical minds switch focus from working on things to make their lives better to things that would make the others' lives worse."

"Magical weapons," Stone said.

"Yes, that's putting it mildly. Magical war machines. Horrible spells designed to kill by the thousands—all of them tried to outdo the others, and of course they spied on each other to try to steal the best of them for their own faction."

"And they *used* these weapons?"

"It started out as an accident—one house got scared after they heard rumors another one was going to attack first, so they struck pre-emptively. And then of course all the other ones responded in kind." She shuddered.

"You...don't remember this, do you? Was this in your lifetime?"

She shook her head. "No, no. It was many years ago, long before any of us were born. But the result of it was, most of the cities were destroyed, and most of the population—magical and non-magical—died. And," she added with a look of disgust, "most of the land mass became unlivable."

"Unlivable? Are you talking something like—magical radiation? Fallout?" Even on Earth, large concentrations of powerful magic could have that effect; he remembered the location of Burning Man out in the middle of the Nevada desert, where ten ley lines converged to form an area of immense power, but one where mages couldn't remain for more than a few weeks without ill effects.

"That's exactly what I'm talking about. The physical damage was bad enough—it destroyed large sections of most of the cities—but the magical damage was worse. The coastal cities were the least affected and recovered fastest—nobody's sure why—but the interior of the continent is full of…well, not many people know for sure, except the Travelers, and they're not telling."

"Travelers?"

"They live in the Wastes—they're nomads, and they're…odd. The magic changed them. They keep to themselves. Anyway," she continued, "before I get sidetracked, let me finish this. So after the war, which only lasted a short time as you might have guessed, the surviving mages realized they'd have to do something. So they got together and hammered out some agreements. That's when the mage houses were created. They agreed to make the war magic—the big spells, the war machines, all of that—illegal. And since they didn't want to live on the ground anymore and deal with the consequences of what they did, they all got together and figured out how to build cities they could raise up above the land."

"How did they do it?"

"Nobody remembers anymore. The records were lost years ago, and the new generations have gotten lazy. Something to do with ley lines, is all I know. You can ask Trevor when you talk to him—I'm sure he knows more about it, if you want details."

He most certainly *did* want the details. He made a mental note to ask Harrison about it later. "So…they've all been living in peace and harmony ever since?" He remembered what Tanissa had said, back in Drendell, about how the Talented presented Harrison as a bogeyman so they'd have someone to unite against since they "couldn't fight each other anymore."

Errin snorted. "Not even close. They're still as arrogant and power-hungry as they ever were, and they're always looking for ways to increase their own house's power and prestige. But the Grand Council—that's where each city sends representatives from their own Councils so they can hash things out—has mostly kept everything civil. The truth is everybody's scared witless of another war, so that keeps them under control."

"I see." Stone walked along next to her in silence, hands in his pockets, and studied the rolling landscape. All around, the area looked peaceful, well-tended, and untroubled. "You said this place was in the middle of the Wastes. But didn't you say that was the area the magic made unlivable?"

"Yes. That's why nobody comes out here—because they can't. They'd be killed before they made it more than a few miles in."

"By magic?"

"By…any number of things. Things don't work in the Wastes the way they do in the rest of the world. Magic often doesn't work right, or at all—or else it drives people mad. There are pockets where the magic is more powerful and twisted than it should be, and parts where it doesn't function at all. And to make things even worse, some of those pockets move around, so you can never be sure exactly where they are. There are still remnants of some of the old weapons out there—some of them possibly still functional—and a lot of the wildlife has been…changed." She shuddered. "That's why exile is almost worse than execution. It's not like you have a chance, if they mark you and send you out with nothing but the clothes on your back. Nobody ever comes back."

Stone thought about the two-headed wolf things in the Barrens outside Drendell. "Then—how are you lot here? How do you survive?"

"Because of the Nexus." She pointed back toward the black tower. "Remember I told you there used to be six major factions?"

"Yes…"

"Argana was the sixth. It was the most powerful and prestigious of all of them—which meant when the attacks came, they hit Argana the hardest. When they tried to raise their own city after the war, there weren't enough of their people left to do it, or else something went wrong. Nobody knows for sure anymore. It crashed back to the ground, killing more of them. The rest got absorbed into the other houses—the ones who didn't disappear, anyway. This settlement is built on the ruins of the original Argana."

"But wait—I thought you said this *was* Argana."

"That's Trevor's doing. He calls this place New Argana. Nobody asks him why." She shrugged. "He can call it whatever he likes, since he's in charge of the settlement here. And if you know him at all, you know he isn't the type to answer too many questions."

Interesting, and even more confusing. If Harrison was a dimension-hopping mage from Earth, why was he leading a settlement on another plane? Did he have more connection with this place than Stone initially thought? Perhaps even some connection with the original Argana? He made yet another mental note; if this kept up, he'd need to start writing them down. "So how does the Nexus keep you from the harmful effects?"

"Like I told you before, it has to do with ley lines. It stabilizes the area, and keeps the harmful magic out. I can't explain it—that kind of knowledge is something we can only superficially understand, since we're not mages."

Stone didn't correct her. Right now, he *wasn't* a mage, and if Harrison couldn't help him, that wouldn't change here. He added another mental note to ask about it later.

"All I know is that the area is naturally a lot more resistant to harmful magic because of where it is—that's probably why they picked it in the first place, even before the Nexus was built. But the tower concentrates the ley line energy and provides a lot of power that we can use for all sorts of things: defense, building, making the place livable. And so far, we don't even think anybody who isn't one of us knows about this place's existence, let alone has any way to get here."

This was all a lot to take in, and Stone was sure he hadn't even scratched the surface of everything to learn here. He decided to change gears to something more personal. "This is all fascinating. I guess I'll have plenty of time to ask about it, and I plan to. But right now, I'd like to know how the hell you people got me out of the Arena, under the noses of all those Talented bigwigs. Obviously Karol was in on it. So he's one of you?"

"He is, yes." They'd reached the edge of a meandering river; Errin changed direction to a path alongside it. "He's been undercover inside the Temolan prison for a while now. When Trevor got word you were here and had been captured, we worked out a plan to get both of you out. You're dead, by the way."

Stone blinked. "I am? I'm feeling better than I have in quite some time."

She chuckled. "You aren't as far as the people in Temolan are concerned. Karol strangled you to death inside the Arena. Your body was taken out like so much trash and tossed in the incinerator."

"I…see." That seemed odd, but then he caught on. "Ah. So no one will be looking for me anymore."

"And no one else will be killed on suspicion of helping you."

Stone thought of Faran and Runa, and hoped the baker and his family hadn't suffered a similar fate. He bowed his head. "Are they all like that?"

"Are who all like what?"

"The Talented. Almost without exception, every one of them I encountered was some kind of sadistic monster. Are they raised like that, to treat the non-magical people so dreadfully?"

She looked troubled as she walked along. "That's a hard question to answer. The short version is that no, they're not. You saw some of the worst of them—the leaders, the aristocrats, the ones who go down to the towns on purpose because they know there aren't any consequences for what they do. And the ones who are lowest in the mage hierarchy, so they look for situations where they can feel superior to somebody. They can be the worst of all, honestly. But…a lot of them, the ones who stay in the cities, just want to live their lives. Even most of those regard the 'Dim' as inferiors—they can't help it, that's the way they're raised from the time they're born—but they don't wish us specific harm."

"And what about the other ones? The ones like Lanytha?"

"There are more of those than anyone suspects, I think, quietly doing what they do behind closed doors, terrified of being discovered. We try to find them when we can, but it's difficult. The consequences of defying the Talented leadership are too high—most of them are afraid to take the chance."

Stone, remembering the way it was in Drendell when he was trying to find Harrison, nodded. "Karol told me to play along in the Arena, to grab his armband. Was there some kind of contact chemical on it to knock me out?"

"Exactly. It's something one of our alchemists whipped up—it simulates death and conceals itself from magical scans once it's applied. It put you into a state of suspended animation for a while, long enough for our people to get you out. We had to make it look completely believable."

An ingenious idea, but it raised more questions. "How did he get it, though? How did he find out what he was supposed to do? Do you have other spies in the prison? Spies among the Talented?"

She flashed a wicked grin. "We have a lot of spies—including some in very high places. I'm safe in saying that we know a lot more about them than they do about us."

Stone felt suddenly overwhelmed by all this new information. Even though he felt better than he had since he'd arrived here, his several days of hard labor and inadequate food inside the prison were catching up with him. "This is all…amazing," he said, stopping to look out over the sparkling river. "Every time you answer one of my questions, it raises more."

"It's all right," she said. "Like I told you before, you're safe here. Take your time." She eyed him critically. "You look tired. Did I push you too hard?"

"No, no. It feels good to be outside. I thought I'd never see the sun again. I want to keep asking you more questions—I want to find out *everything* about this place—but I think it might have to wait a bit. Can you just—show me around for a while?"

"Of course. Come on—if you can walk long enough to get back to my place, you can sit down for the rest of the tour."

By the time they reached Errin's large, neat home, Stone was glad he didn't have to walk anymore. She opened a garage to reveal one of the sleek vehicles he'd seen cruising around Argana's streets. This one, painted a shining silver, had the swoopy, streamlined look reminiscent of cars from the middle part of Earth's twentieth century.

"Very nice," he said, looking it over before climbing in. "And it runs on magic?"

"Well, magic powers it. But like I said, most of it is mechanical. Now, sit back and relax."

For the next couple hours, Errin drove Stone around Argana. It was a small settlement—he estimated perhaps a few hundred people, assuming Harrison wasn't hiding a lot more in the Nexus tower. Except for the tower, most of the buildings were low-slung, rising only one or two stories, and spread out. It was nothing like the packed Drendell or even what he'd seen of Temolan, where he supposed they had to build up rather than out by necessity. She drove him past farmland dotted with crops, and grassy, rolling pastures with herds of animals—he recognized some of the fat cow-things pictured in Faran's butcher-shop window. The business district was small but well stocked: Stone spotted what looked like several different kinds of food shops, restaurants, clothing stores, a bar, and even a library. "People read here?" he asked, surprised.

"Of course." She seemed surprised by the question. "The mages arrive well educated, naturally. The non-magical people back in the cities aren't educated past basic levels they need to do their jobs, but most of them learn fast once they get here."

Ah, so that was it. He should have guessed: of course the ruling Talented would want to keep the mundanes ignorant and fearful. He wondered if a concentrated uprising among the larger mundane population would have any chance of overwhelming the mages. "Do you produce everything you need here? That seems like it would be difficult, with such a small population."

"Not even close. We grow and raise most of our own basic food, but we import a lot of what we need, mostly from the cities down here. We even get some goods from the Talented's cities." She grinned. "I told you we have friends in high places. The mages produce some of what we use, and we have quite a number of craftspeople, both magical and non-magical. Oh, and Trevor has sources for some amazing things—I have no idea where he gets them and I don't ask, but so far he's never failed to come up with anything I need for my work. And some of what he's got in the Tower is—" She shook her head in wonder. "—I couldn't even begin to explain how it works, but he seems to understand it."

Hmm. Stone suspected he knew *exactly* where Harrison was getting hold of these exotic items.

"Anyway," she said, pulling back into the garage at her house, "that's about it for the overview tour. If you stay with us, you can see things in more detail later. I'm afraid I'm going to have to leave you for a while, though—I've got some work I need to finish. But make yourself at home. Vynna will get you something to eat. After that, I'd suggest you might want to rest before you talk to Trevor tonight. I suspect you two will have a lot to discuss, and I'm not sure the man ever sleeps."

| CHAPTER TWENTY-FIVE

ANOTHER OF THE SLEEK CARS showed up at Errin's house later that evening. It was already dark by then, and Errin was just pulling up when Vynna came to let Stone know the driver had come to take him to his meeting with Harrison.

"We won't wait up," Errin told him with a smile. "I hope you get the rest of your questions answered."

So do I, Stone thought.

He'd spent most of the rest of the afternoon sleeping, following a delicious lunch. He hadn't *meant* to sleep the day away, but he must have been more tired than he'd thought. He'd only awakened when Vynna knocked on his door to give him time to clean up, change clothes, and eat a light meal before Harrison's driver showed up.

"He didn't really need to send you to collect me," Stone told the driver as he climbed in to the black vehicle. "I think I can walk that far."

"It's no trouble," the driver assured him.

The Nexus tower turned out to be farther away than Stone had thought. He wasn't sure if magic or some kind of optical illusion was in effect, but it took them ten minutes to get there after leaving Argana behind and heading out along a narrow road that meandered up the rocky hill on which the tower perched.

Stone studied the featureless black wall as they drew closer. He didn't see anything resembling an entrance, but wasn't surprised when the driver kept going as if he planned to run into the tower's side. As he suspected, the car hit the wall and continued through in to a large, open area. "Nice," he said. "That's some fancy illusion work."

"You haven't seen the half of it," the man said, chuckling. He pointed toward a door. "Just through there. You're expected, so just stand on the teleportation pad and it'll take you where you're going."

"Teleportation pad?" *Bloody hell. He's got them here too?* "Er—right, then. Thank you."

The car sped off as soon as he exited. His heart pounded with excitement—even if Harrison couldn't help him get his magic working here, he no doubt could send him home, and if he could get home with some knowledge about how teleportation worked…

Stop it, he told himself. *You're getting ahead of yourself.*

As soon as he stepped through the door, it was as if he had returned to Earth. The hallway was like any other in an upscale modern-day commercial building back home: soft, dark gray carpeting, lighter gray walls, indirect lighting. He could have walked into any office building in the business district of any large city.

Except for the glowing disc on the floor at the other end.

Stone hurried to it and then stopped to examine it. It looked similar to the ones he'd seen when they'd taken him to Temolan after he was captured: about four feet in diameter, encircled by a sleek, brushed-metal railing with a single entrance point.

He experienced a brief moment of panic: *What if Harrison doesn't know my magic's gone? How am I supposed to operate this thing?* He had an amusing mental picture of getting stranded down here, having to pace around waiting for Harrison to wonder what had become of him and come looking. *Great way to make an impression.*

But then again, Harrison also knew that, even *with* his magic, he didn't have any experience with teleportation beyond the Earth portals which obviously worked quite differently. Ah, well—he wouldn't know if he didn't try.

He took a decisive step onto the pad, centered himself on it, and stood still, waiting for something to happen.

For a second, he didn't think anything *had* happened—at least until he saw that the scenery had changed. "Bloody hell…" he whispered, impressed in spite of himself.

Instead of the gray-carpeted hallway, he now stood in a small room. The floor here was rich, dark wood, the walls painted slate gray. There had been no sense of jarring disorientation, no lurch or buzz or indeed any other sensation of movement or magic.

"Good evening, Dr. Stone," said a voice. "If you'll come with me, I'll take you to Mr. Harrison."

Stone stared. Standing in the doorway was a…*what the hell* is *that thing*?

The best way he could describe it was to call it some kind of mechanical robot. Standing about shoulder-height on him, it had a pleasant, neutral humanoid face with glowing gold eyes, a broad-shouldered body that tapered down to a single wheel, and arms made of metal pieces held together by cables and conduits. It didn't have a working mouth, but its voice sounded clear, undistorted, and just a bit otherworldly.

"Er—Right. Lead on, then."

"This way, please." The thing spun on its wheel and rolled off at a leisurely pace.

Stone hastened to follow it, wondering how many more astonishing shocks he was in for this evening. He studied the thing from the back as it led him down another hallway; even though it was clearly some kind of robot, it didn't have a high-tech, science-fiction feel to it. Rather, it looked like something that had been cobbled together from high-end spare parts by someone who was a master at matching components. The effect worked, giving the thing a soothing, efficient feel. Had Harrison built this? He remembered Errin talking about being the "chief mechanic"—maybe this was another of her inventions.

The robot-thing stopped in front of a pair of dark-wood double doors. "Just inside," it said, as the doors swung silently open. "Have a pleasant evening." Before Stone could say anything else, it rolled off.

Stone watched it go before stepping through the door.

His first impression was that the room he was standing in reminded him of something, but it took him a few seconds to realize what it was. Then it came to him: the place looked similar in design and layout to Harrison's penthouse back at the Obsidian in Vegas, where they'd first met. The same dark wood floors, the same kinds of sparse but exquisite furnishings, the same style of angular, minimalist art pieces. It even had the same sweeping, floor-to-ceiling windows, though these looked out not over the blazing Las Vegas strip but rather a velvety black sky dotted with thousands of stars. The effect was eerie, but nonetheless breathtakingly beautiful.

Trevor Harrison stood, as he had when Stone had first met him, framed against the window. He turned when Stone appeared.

"Good evening, Dr. Stone. I apologize for my absence earlier today." He wore the same black trousers and crisp white shirt he'd worn earlier that day, now with the sleeves turned up. He held a glass in one hand.

"Er—that's…all right," Stone said, feeling suddenly at a loss for words. "Your friend Errin gave me the tour, and I slept for half the afternoon. Must have been more tired than I thought."

"I am not surprised. Would you care for a drink?"

It suddenly struck Stone how long it had been since he'd had a decent drink. "I would love one. Thank you. This has all been—quite a lot to take in."

"Indeed." He crossed to a small bar, then gave Stone a questioning glance.

"Whatever you've got—aside from the spiced ale, I haven't tried any of the liquor here."

Harrison offered a slight smile. "We're not limited to Calanarian spirits here, Dr. Stone."

"Oh, really? Well, surprise me, then. Believe me, I'm not picky at present."

Harrison studied him a moment, then selected a bottle, poured a generous shot, and floated the glass over to Stone. "Please—sit down. Make yourself comfortable. I suspect you have a great deal you wish to discuss."

"You people truly are masters of understatement." Stone took an experimental sip and grinned. "Oh, that's brilliant.

Haven't had a decent scotch—or *any* scotch—since I got here."

He took the indicated chair, which faced the magnificent view out the window. "I don't even know where to begin, to be honest. I suppose I should start by thanking you for getting me out of that hellhole in Temolan. I thought I was dead for sure."

"I apologize that it took as long as it did." Harrison sat opposite Stone. "I had no idea you were here until I got word that someone named Stone was looking for me."

"Yes, well, I did try to be discreet about it—especially after I found out you were some kind of legendary wanted figure most people don't even believe exists." Unable to contain his curiosity any longer, Stone leaned forward. "If you don't mind, Mr. Harrison, could I just start with some questions? As I said, I don't even know where to begin, but shall I just jump in somewhere?"

Harrison inclined his head. "I will do my best to answer. And then perhaps you will answer a few of my own questions."

"Of course. If I can, anyway. The one thing I'm learning painfully around here is how much I *don't* know." He took a couple of breaths, trying to calm his whirling thoughts; right now, his head felt like one of those old-fashioned spinning cages full of ping-pong balls they used to pick lottery numbers out of. For lack of a better strategy, he decided on a chronological approach. "To start with—how the *hell* did you get out of that portal? How are you even alive?"

"As you might have guessed, I have access to techniques you weren't aware of."

"You mean teleportation."

"Yes."

"So you—what—just popped over to the Evil's dimension, set that crystal, then popped back here?"

"Yes."

"But—how did you even survive? You'd taken a point-blank shot to the chest, and you went to a place where you should have died nearly instantly even if you were at full capacity."

"I am…difficult to kill, Dr. Stone."

Stone got it loud and clear: Harrison didn't plan to elaborate on that. "Okay, then—you're telling me you can do interdimensional teleportation without a gateway?"

"Yes. With some limitations, of course. But essentially, yes."

"Bloody hell, that's *amazing*. Can others here do it as well? I know the mages in Temolan have teleport pads they use to get to the surface, but…" He trailed off, inviting Harrison to answer.

Harrison's unsettling gaze never strayed from Stone. "No," he said at last. "They have access to teleportation techniques, obviously, but they are limited to this dimension."

Stone mulled that over. "I…see," he said. Another deep breath. At any other time, he would be peppering Harrison with questions about the techniques and how they worked, but right now he had more pressing matters on his mind. "Listen—Mr. Harrison—I would love to chat with you about this. Believe me, I would love nothing *more* than to chat with you about this for as long as you're willing. But before I can do that…well, I've got a problem. And it's the reason I've come here in the first place."

"I had wondered why you were here. And how you managed to discover my location."

"That was your doing," Stone said. "You gave my apprentice the key when you spoke to her a while back."

"Ah." A brief look of approval, and then the impassive mask was back.

"You said I already had the means to find you. That stumped me for quite some time, but then something happened to make me more…motivated. I worked out that if I already had the means, it must have something to do with tracing the power source you tap for your magic."

"Excellent, Dr. Stone. I am impressed by your ingenuity. In truth, I didn't expect you to discover the answer." He set his glass down. "Although I suppose I should have, given the progress you made with the rudimentary notes I sent you."

"Yes, well—that's part of what I want to talk to you about. But first—right now asking you about anything to do with magic would be pointless…since I don't have any at present."

Harrison raised an eyebrow. "I had heard you were without your magical abilities, but I thought my reports were mistaken—or that you were feigning your power loss."

Stone snorted. "Feigning? Do you think I'd have let those arrogant bastards treat me like rubbish—nearly kill me several times—if I'd had a choice about it? No, Mr. Harrison—I'm currently as mundane as your sofa. Possibly more so, given how magical this world seems to be. I'd suspected it had something to do with the typical burnout, but that doesn't seem to be the case."

"Burnout?"

"You don't know?" That was news. Stone had begun to suspect there wasn't much Harrison *didn't* know, especially when it came to magic.

"I'm afraid you have me at a loss, Dr. Stone."

Well. That was somewhat comforting, at least: Harrison hadn't revealed his methods to Stone without warning him that using the power source would burn out his own magical abilities for anywhere from a few hours to a few weeks, depending on how much he tapped it. "Nakamura didn't tell you? Surely you've spoken to him since the last time we talked."

"I have. He mentioned that you had an issue with your magic shortly after the situation at Burning Man—he said you believed accessing my techniques had affected your ability to use magic. But I directed him to do a bit of discreet checking and he discovered you seemed to have recovered. At least you never attempted to contact him about it again."

"I did recover—at least to the extent that my magic returned. It was never that bad after that, mostly because I never risked using as much of your energy source again."

"Indeed." Harrison's eyebrow rose again. "I was not aware of that—certainly not when I provided you with the information I sent. Forgive me, Dr. Stone, if it caused you inconvenience."

That's putting it mildly, Stone thought, remembering how close he'd come to committing suicide when he thought he'd permanently lost his magical abilities. But that was in the past, and there was no point bringing it up now. "I've learned to…deal with it," he said. "I only use it in emergencies now—truthfully, it's saved my arse on more than one occasion, so I suppose it's a fair trade-off. But that's not why I'm here."

Harrison waited silently, picking up his drink again.

"I know your magic is on a completely different wavelength than anything most of us use back home, but you're certainly familiar with the contrast between black and white magic?"

"Of course."

"Well—the short version is, something happened recently that forced me to switch teams."

"Switch…teams?" His eyes narrowed. "You have become a black mage."

"Yes. Exactly. I didn't have a lot of choice—if I hadn't done it, people I cared about would have died. But now I'm having—issues with coping with it."

"Issues." Harrison leaned back in his chair. "What sort of issues?"

"I went black because I had to ash someone—a powerful mage, as it happened. The sensations involved were…quite intense. So much so that I've found myself craving them. And that disturbs me."

Harrison tilted his head. "Dr. Stone, forgive me, but I am not certain I see—"

"I've been having trouble taking power, even from willing contributors, without risking their injury," Stone said, forging ahead in a rush. "Which, in turn, means I've been avoiding all but the simplest magical techniques. And as you might have guessed about me, that's…unacceptable, if there's any alternative."

Harrison didn't reply right away. Instead, he rose gracefully and went back to the window, where he stood gazing at the panoply of stars outside the window. After a long silence, he said softly, "And you consider me your alternative."

Stone got up too, unable to remain still any longer. "Teach me, Mr. Harrison," he said. "Please. Teach me how to use your power source safely, so I can tap into it instead of taking power from other people. That's why I worked out the way to come here. That's why I've put myself through all this hell trying to find you, when I wasn't even certain I'd gone to the right place."

Once again, Harrison didn't reply.

"Mr. Harrison—?"

"I am not a teacher, Dr. Stone." Harrison didn't turn back toward him, but continued to face outward toward the night sky. "I believe I mentioned that to your apprentice when she found me at the Obsidian."

Stone stared at him, his breath stilling in his throat. "I'm not asking you to teach me magic. I *know* magic. All I need is the key to accessing your power source—this dimension. I know it can be done from Earth—I've done it to my limited extent, and you—well, I've seen what you can do." When Harrison still didn't answer, he continued, a little louder, "You sent me the fundamentals, and I worked them out. Why would you have done that if you hadn't expected me to use them in a practical capacity?"

"Perhaps I wanted to see if you could make any sense of them."

"Well, I *did*. But I haven't been able to work out how to do it without burning myself out. I can't lose my magic for an indefinite period every time I cast a spell. But if I go back to black magic, I'm afraid it's only a matter of time before I kill someone. I did it once, and almost did it again."

Harrison turned. His expression was, as usual, unreadable as his gaze settled back on Stone. He still didn't speak.

Stone took several deep breaths, trying to calm his racing nerves. Could Harrison really be saying he wouldn't teach him? After all he'd gone through to get here? After all the hours he'd spent studying the handful of handwritten pages that were all he had to work with? "Mr. Harrison—please don't make me beg you. I will if necessary, if it will do any good. I'm a wealthy man these days—if it's payment you want—"

"I have no need for your money, Dr. Stone. I have more than I could ever use."

"What, then?" Stone stopped, once again forcing calm into his voice. "What can I offer you? If it's in my power to do it, consider it done." He paused, as a terrifying thought struck him. "You...*can* teach me, can't you? Is there something required that I don't have? Is there a reason my magic doesn't function here?"

Harrison considered. "I don't think so," he said. "I know of no reason why you could not learn, under the right conditions."

Stone took a long drink from his glass, not even pausing to appreciate the fine scotch as it went down. "Look," he said. "Let me just put it all out on the table: I will do whatever you ask of me, if you can teach me how to use your magic without the burnout. But if you can't—or won't—do that, then I ask that you send me home. I'll learn to cope with my issues somehow. But I've had just about enough of being a mundane in this gods-forsaken world of yours."

He wheeled around, stalking back and forth to bleed off some excess energy in lieu of shouting at Harrison. "How did you even *find* this place, anyway? Are you some kind of interdimensional adventurer or something?"

Harrison continued to stand almost preternaturally still, following Stone's manic progress only with his gaze. "You are making an erroneous assumption, Dr. Stone."

"And what's that?"

"That I 'found' this place at all."

"What the hell does that mean? I don't—" He stopped. "Bloody hell. You're not from Earth at all, are you?"

Once again, the brief flash of approval, almost too fast to spot, appeared. "The answer to that is…complex. But no, I am not entirely of Earth."

"Not 'entirely'?"

Harrison turned back to the window again. "You didn't come here to discuss me, Dr. Stone."

"No. I suppose I didn't." Stone drained the rest of his drink. "I still have so many questions, but—well, I suppose I don't really need to know the answers to them right now. If you agree to teach me, then I can find out whatever you're willing to tell me, over time. And if you don't—*can* you send me home?"

"Of course."

A sudden, profound sense of relief settled over Stone at his words. "And…you'd be willing to do that, at least?"

"Sending you home would not be an issue. I can do it tonight, if you wish."

Stone thought about it. It was certainly tempting. *You can go home. You can get your magic back, take power from Jason, be as strong as you ever were. You lose nothing.*

Except, pointed out his other little voice, *that you'll have wasted all this time—gone through all this hell and misery—*

for nothing. Go on, if you want to—take the coward's way out. Be a mouse.

Wait, he told it. *I thought you* wanted *me to give up this mad plan.*

The little voice had no reply to that.

He studied Harrison's tall, straight form. The man was an enigma—and a damned annoying one. He wondered if the two of them could even manage to tolerate each other long enough to get anything done, or if they'd end up locking horns like a pair of stubborn bulls. In his experience, egos the size of his and Harrison's didn't play well together for long.

Still…

"I don't wish," he said firmly. "Not until you've given me a definitive answer about whether you'll teach me. I notice you haven't done that yet. Does that mean you're considering it? Because I suspect you don't give a damn about sparing my feelings or letting me down easily."

"No," Harrison said. "I do not."

"Then…what's your answer?"

Harrison finished his drink and floated the empty glass to a nearby table, then turned back to face Stone again. The silence stretched out for one minute, two, three as he studied him with a steady, unblinking gaze.

Stone, for his part, remained still and silent. He wasn't sure if Harrison was scanning his aura, reading his mind, checking out his arse, or ruminating about the local sports scores, but whatever he was doing, Stone was determined not to be the first one to flinch. He returned the scrutiny, taking the opportunity to get a good look at Harrison.

If the man was using an illusion to maintain his current appearance, it was a damned good one. Seeing through illusions had a lot to do with magical ability, but not every-thing—it helped, certainly, but it was more about a combination of strength of mind and how strongly a person suspected that there *was* an illusion. If you had no reason to think something was an illusion, or if the illusion fit seam-lessly enough with its current surroundings, you could have the strongest mind in the world, or be the most potent mage, and it wouldn't matter.

Stone *did* suspect an illusion—not many people looked like Harrison naturally—but even with his suspicions he couldn't see past it.

When Harrison spoke again, it was as if the long silence had not occurred. "I have reservations about working with you, Dr. Stone."

"Reservations?" Stone blinked. "Why?"

He paced along the window, still gazing out at the stars. "You are essentially asking to enter into an apprenticeship with me—albeit one of a comparatively shorter duration."

Stone hadn't considered it that way. "How long do you think it will take?"

"I cannot answer that, Dr. Stone. Not yet. So you are ask-ing me to enter into an agreement with you for an unspecified period."

"Yes…I suppose I am. Why do you have reservations about that? Is it because of the time?" He hadn't thought about *that,* either. It was entirely reasonable that Harrison would refuse because he was a busy man, and couldn't spare the time required for the task. Something sank inside him; if Harrison turned him down for that reason, what could he say? If someone showed up on his own doorstep and asked him for training, he'd have given the same answer without a second thought.

"No. The time has nothing to do with it."

"What, then?"

Harrison returned to his chair and sat, leaning back but never taking his eyes off Stone. "You are a successful man in every respect. You are one of the most powerful mages on Earth. You are at the top of your mundane career, you've successfully taken an apprentice to the completion of her training, and you possess considerable resources, both economic and social."

Stone frowned. "So do you. What's that got to do with—"

"Tell me this, Dr. Stone," Harrison said, his eerie gaze sharpening to laserlike intensity as he leaned forward. "If I were to agree to teach you, on the condition that you truly apprentice yourself to me, what would your answer be?"

"Truly apprentice myself?"

"In every respect. Could you, in honesty, agree to follow my every rule, do every exercise I order you to do, all without question or protest?"

Stone almost answered instantly, almost said, "Of course I could!" But then he paused. *Could* he? He'd never been in denial about his ego, his issues with authority, his constant need to question, to test boundaries, to rebel against irrationality. He'd managed to do it with William Desmond—barely—but he'd only been fifteen years old then, dazzled by the idea of learning to do magic. And even then, he'd almost blown his apprenticeship by disobeying Desmond's rules. Could he do it now, with over twenty more years' experience under his belt?

"Let's be clear, Mr. Harrison," he said evenly. "Is that an offer? I don't fancy giving an answer to a question like that if it's merely a hypothetical. *Can* you teach me to control this energy?"

Harrison's gaze didn't waver. "All right, then, Dr. Stone—yes. It is an offer. I can teach you. But that is my condition. You must agree to follow my direction without question, for the duration of our training, regardless of whether you see the point of it. If you fail to do that, then I will send you home. Do you accept my terms? If you like, you can consider my offer tonight and give me your answer in the morning."

Stone cast a sharp glance at him. He realized once again that he barely knew this man, and remembered his speculations about whether Harrison was any different from the other cruel, arrogant Talented in this world. If he agreed to the terms, what was he getting himself into? What did Harrison mean by "regardless of whether you see the point of it"?

"All right, Mr. Harrison," he said briskly, almost before he realized he was speaking. "I accept your terms. When can we start?"

Harrison's expression didn't change—the man had the best poker face Stone had ever encountered—but Stone nonetheless got a brief impression of surprise. He nodded once and stood. "Tomorrow, then. We will begin in the morning, and you can move into the tower after your first training session. I'll ask Errin to have your things sent over."

"I haven't any 'things,'" Stone said with a snort. "Travel light, I do—I suppose it makes sense, since I'm supposed to be dead." He wondered if he'd called Harrison's bluff.

"We will see to that. Tomorrow morning. Until then, Dr. Stone."

He was being dismissed, just like that. Annoyance rose, but he quickly squelched it. He suspected he was going to have to do a lot of that in the coming days. He hoped it didn't take too long for Harrison to teach him to access the magic, or likely both of them would end up regretting their agreement.

| CHAPTER TWENTY-SIX

W HEN HARRISON'S DRIVER ARRIVED at dawn in the sleek, black car, Stone was waiting for him.

He carried nothing with him—when he'd arrived back at Errin's house the previous night and told her he'd be moving to the tower the next day, she hadn't asked questions about why. She had, however, told him she'd have Vynna get his clothes ready to send over.

"No, they're all yours," she said when he protested. "Can't very well have you running around in your old prison uniform, after all." She grinned. "I don't know what you two are up to, but I'm sure I'll find out soon enough."

"If we don't kill each other first," Stone muttered. He hadn't slept much the previous night, his mind refusing to stop going over disturbing implications of his agreement with Harrison. Why had he made that kind of open-ended promise? What would Harrison order him to do, dangling the promise of magic over his head in exchange for—what? Would he ask him to kill anyone? Did he have something planned against the Talented? Would he be conscripted into some kind of rebel army going against the mage houses?

He knew there was no point dwelling on it, but that didn't mean he could stop. *Remember,* he told himself more

　　　　　　　　　　　　　　　　R. L. KING

than once, *if it gets too bad you can always just tell him to get stuffed and have him send you home. You won't be any worse off than before.*

But he wasn't going to do that, for no other reason than sheer stubbornness. After everything he'd gone through to get here, he could take anything Trevor Harrison threw at him.

When he arrived at the tower, the driver didn't pull the car through the illusionary wall. Instead, he drove around to the other side. Stone was surprised to see that the land stretched out as far as he could see here; he'd thought the tower perched atop the mountain with no surrounding acreage. As they drew closer, he spotted two slim figures standing atop a large rock, looking out into the hazy morning. One was Harrison; the other he didn't recognize. A hundred yards or so to their right stood a small building.

Harrison turned as Stone got out and the car drove silently off. "Good morning, Dr. Stone."

"I suppose it is. Bit early, but I'm getting used to that."

"You have not reconsidered your agreement to my terms?" He leaped from the rock and landed gracefully next to it. The other figure remained in place, facing away from them.

"No. Did you expect me to?"

Harrison studied him in his unsettling *I may or may not be reading your mind* way. "I had thought it a possibility."

"No such luck, Mr. Harrison. If you can teach me to control this energy, you've got yourself an apprentice."

"As you wish." Harrison inclined his head, then indicated the other figure. "This is Kira Talon. She will be assisting in your training."

Kira Talon jumped down and landed next to Harrison. She was several inches shorter than he was, with a wiry frame, short, choppy dark brown hair, and glittering green eyes. Everything about her was boyish, from her no-nonsense clothes to her briskly attractive, androgynous face. She looked Stone up and down. "Pleasure to meet you." Her voice was like the rest of her: purposeful and direct.

"Indeed," Stone said. Kira Talon—her name marked her as a mundane. He wondered how a mundane was going to assist in teaching him magic, but didn't ask.

"I have been considering your course of training," Harrison said. "The first step is to get you into proper physical condition."

Stone blinked. "Physical condition? What's that got to do with magic?" True, he was hardly in his best shape right now following his recovery, his time on the streets of Drendell, and his stay in the Temolan prison, but he knew plenty of mages—good mages—back on Earth whose only form of exercise was walking to the refrigerator.

Harrison didn't respond, except to continue fixing him with his steady gaze.

"Oh. Right," Stone said, getting it. "Our agreement. So I'm not even allowed to ask about this?"

"By the terms of our agreement, no. You are not. But in order to safely handle the energy you will be manipulating, your body must be in its best possible condition. A strong will is also important—I don't think that will require significant additional attention, though it too will be required for you to get through this training. It won't be easy, Dr. Stone. Not at all. If you expected me to impart some secret to you, to allow you to flip a switch and activate your magical abilities, then you will be disappointed."

That may have been the longest speech Harrison had ever made in Stone's presence. And he had to admit—part of him *had* hoped it would be that simple, that Harrison would give him a brief demonstration to show him what he'd been doing wrong, correct a variable in his calculations, anything to get things on track again. But it couldn't take long to get himself back into shape, right? Some good food to fill him out, a few runs around the area to get his endurance back, a little time in the gym—sure, it would take longer than he hoped, but it wouldn't be difficult. The hardest part would be managing his impatience—but he supposed that was where the willpower came in.

"All right, then," he said. "It's your show. Tell me what you want me to do."

"I have some things I must attend to today," he said. "I will leave you in Kira's capable hands. For purposes of our agreement, consider her direction as you do my own. She will report on your progress."

"Wait—you're leaving?" Stone protested. "I thought you were going to—"

There was that look again. The one that said, *you agreed to this, and you're* already *arguing about it?*

He sighed. "Fine. Fine. I trust we'll talk later?"

"Of course. Good day, Dr. Stone. Kira." Without another word, Harrison strode off across the open field back toward the tower.

At least he didn't fly. Or teleport, Stone thought sourly. He turned back to Kira Talon. "So. Here we are."

"Here we are," she agreed. She looked amused.

"So—what are you, exactly? His personal trainer?"

The amusement grew. "No. I'm his student. Or used to be. Now I'm more of his associate."

"Oh?" he looked her over, surprised. "I'd have thought you weren't a mage, based on your name."

"You can't always tell by names," she said. "The mages get upset when the non-magical use their name styles, but if a mage uses a non-magical name, they don't care. They can't even comprehend why anyone would want to." She appeared to be in her late twenties, definitely too old to be an apprentice. "Anyway, we should get started." She nodded toward the small building. "Go get changed into something comfortable to work in, then come back out here. Be sure to bring a pair of gloves."

"Changed? We're starting now?"

"Is there a better time? I thought you were in a hurry to get moving with your training."

"Right." Wondering what "something comfortable to work in" meant, he headed off to the building. What would he need gloves for? Were they going to be boxing?

It was a small cabin, more like an upscale utility shed or locker room than someplace anyone might live, though it did have a tiny bathroom and an even tinier kitchenette. Hanging neatly on a rack on the opposite side he found a small selection of T-shirts, work shirts, and loose-fitting trousers, all in his size. Beneath was a pair of work boots and some leather gloves. Definitely not boxing gloves, either. *What the hell has he got me doing?*

The day was already looking to be warm, so he quickly swapped his fine outfit from Errin's place for a T-shirt, work pants, and the boots, grabbed the gloves, and hurried back out to where Kira waited for him. "What are we doing?"

"I'm not doing anything," she said. "You're going to build a wall."

He stared at her. "A *what*?" He must have misheard her. She couldn't have said *a wall.*

She pointed toward the other side of the small cabin, where a pile of rocks was neatly stacked. They varied in size, the largest about a foot in diameter. He hadn't noticed before, but someone had already dug a shallow trench extending outward from the cabin, so the wall would stand next to it.

Stone looked at the pile, then at Kira. "You're having me on."

"Not at all. Just go to the pile, grab a rock, carry it over, and place it in the trench. We'll focus on the base layer today."

"What the *hell* has this got to do with learning magic?" He couldn't help it. There was garden-variety irrational, and then there was this.

She shrugged. "Not my place to question. Not yours, either. That's what he said to have you do."

Stone paused, glancing again at the stack. There were a *lot* of rocks there.

Maybe it's a test. He wants to see if you'll follow his directions, no matter how daft they look.

Fine, then. If that's what he wants…

He stalked over to the pile and hefted one of the rocks. It was heavier than it looked, but at least it was smooth so he wouldn't tear up his arms. With some effort he carried it to the trench, which was only a few inches deep, and dropped it in.

"Don't just drop them," Kira called. She'd sat down on another, larger rock. "You need to place them precisely, or the wall won't be straight. And lift with your legs, not your back."

"Right." Stone returned to the pile and grabbed another rock. This time when he reached the trench, he bent and set it next to the first one.

"Better," Kira said. "That's it. Just keep it up until I say stop or you can't go on any longer. Don't hurt yourself—that's not what we're trying to do here."

Easy for you *to say.* Stone cast several nasty glances in her direction as he continued trudging back and forth between the pile and the trench, lugging the rocks and placing them along the track. They seemed to grow heavier as he went, and by the time an hour had passed he was drenched in sweat and every muscle in his body hurt.

"Take a break," Kira called to him. She'd hopped down off her rock perch and now carried a tray with a pitcher of ice water and a couple of glasses.

Stone swiped his hand across his forehead and slogged over, panting. He hadn't seen her leave, but for the last half-hour or so he'd gotten himself into a mindless rhythm, using his meditation techniques to focus on the task. She must have gone then.

He took a glass of water and dropped to the ground, resisting the temptation to chug the whole thing at once and collapse.

Kira sat down next to him. "Are you doing all right? Nothing hurt? I was serious—we're trying to build you up, not injure you."

"Nothing...permanent, I don't think," he said between drinks and panting breaths. "Every muscle in my body hurts, but I suppose that's the point, isn't it?"

"Don't worry—we'll take care of that when you get back to the tower. We'll be here for a couple more hours, and then we'll go back for lunch." She eyed him critically. "You look like you've always been thin, but now you're just skinny. Need to get some muscle on you."

Stone slugged down more of the water, then refilled the glass from the pitcher. "So why has he got you doing this? You said you were his student—is this the way he teaches? My apprentice would have told me to get stuffed if I had her building walls instead of learning magic. And I wouldn't have blamed her."

She chuckled. "Not me—but my situation was different from yours."

"How so, if you don't mind my asking? What did he tell you about me?"

"We can't talk long," she said, glancing toward the trench. "It's not good for you to rest too long—your muscles will stiffen up. Let's walk for a few minutes."

Stone didn't want to drag himself back up yet, but he did it anyway because he knew she was right. If he stayed here too much longer his body would become one with the ground and he'd never get up.

She fell into step next to him. "So...what he told me about you was that you're not from here. That you're from another world." Her glance in his direction suggested she wasn't sure she believed it.

"I am. I didn't think anybody but Harrison knew about that sort of thing, though."

"Not many do. As far as I know, Errin and I are the only ones he's told."

"So the others—the ones in the cities—don't know anything about it?"

"Not that any of us are aware of—and even if they did, they couldn't do anything about it."

"So they don't know how to travel back and forth?"

"Not that we've ever heard. And Trevor pays close attention to that kind of thing."

Stone nodded, wondering if Harrison had ever told Kira that not only was he aware of other worlds, but he routinely traveled between them. Instead of asking, though, he said, "You said our situations were different. How so?"

She didn't answer for a while. "You asked me before why I have a non-magical name."

"Yes…"

"I was born into one of the most prominent magical families in Sholandre. Raised in luxury. Had a perfect childhood with my younger brother, and everybody thought I'd follow in my parents' footsteps with impressive magical power."

Stone frowned, slowing his pace. "But you *do* have magical power, don't you?"

"I do now, yes. But most children manifest it at puberty. I didn't."

"So…magic doesn't always pass down?"

"Not always, but *almost* always. The most powerful magical families in the cities stay that way because the power does pass on fairly reliably. I don't know how much you know about the mages'—I refuse to call them 'the Talented'—society, but the most powerful mages have the most power in other areas, too. Usually that means the power stays with the same people, but sometimes someone turns up with more—or less—and that changes their position. That's how social status is determined in the cities—by how much magical power you have."

"What happened with you, then?"

"I hit puberty with no sign of magic. None. I was as non-magical as those rocks over there." Her voice held no bitterness; she was simply stating a fact.

"And…"

"And…they're very strict about what happens when a child from a magical family turns out to be non-magical. Essentially, they become a non-person. They're removed from their family and shipped off to a special home down in one of the non-magical cities. As far as their families or any official records are aware, they're dead."

Stone stopped. "That's…barbaric. And your parents *allowed* this?"

Kira looked at the ground, and her expression grew hard. "No. They didn't. And they're dead now because of it."

"Bloody hell…"

"I don't want to talk about that part," she said, starting up again. "Come on—you need to get back to work. But yes—I was raised among the non-magical people, and grew up as one of them. That's why my name was changed. My original name, back in Sholandre, was 'Kiriana.' They re-named me 'Kira' when I got sent away. I like it better. It's simpler. More to the point." She nodded toward the trenches. "You work, I'll talk."

Stone resumed toting rocks, with Kira following along the side of the trench. "I'm not sure I understand, though," he said. "If you were raised among the non-magical and manifested no magical abilities—"

"That's just it—I did. Many years later, when I was an adult. That almost never happens. It was quite a surprise, as I'm sure you'd guess."

"Indeed. What happens when that occurs? Did Harrison find you?"

"That's a story for another time, I think. But as for what happens—you have to understand the way the mage houses work. They guard power jealously, and in their society you can't have magical power without pledging yourself to one of the houses. Usually the one you were raised in, though occasionally people switch. It's hard to do, but it happens."

"So what happens if you refuse?"

"You become a criminal. A traitor. They hunt you down and, depending on how powerful you are and what you did before they catch you, you're either forced to swear a magical oath to one of the houses, executed, or exiled to the Wastes."

Stone suddenly remembered what his interrogator in Temolan had said when he'd asked about Harrison. "A traitor," he'd called him. "Is that what happened to Harrison? Did he belong to one of the mage houses and then leave?"

She gave him a rueful smile. "Sorry. One thing you learn fast about Trevor—you don't talk about him to other people. If he tells you anything, you keep it to yourself. He's the most private man I've ever met."

"So you know and aren't telling, or you don't know?"

"Doesn't matter," she said. "Either way means the same thing: you're not getting it from me. Come on—you need to pick up your pace a little. Maybe I should stop talking and let you work." She glanced at her watch. "I'll let you know when it's time to stop, and I'll leave the water here. Don't take too many breaks, though."

Stone didn't have a watch, but by the time Kira, who'd spent the rest of the morning sitting on a rock reading a book, told him it was time to quit, he barely thought he'd manage to drag himself back to the little cabin to shower and change back to his regular clothes. After carrying rocks from the pile to the trench all morning and managing to fill in about half of the first layer, every muscle and most of the bones in his body ached and he felt he could devour one of the fat cow-creatures all by himself. Raw, if necessary.

The driver showed up as if on cue—Stone wondered if Kira had called him—and took them back up to the tower. This time they did pass through the illusionary wall, and before long, after another trip via the magical teleporter, Kira opened the door on a room. "This will be yours for as long as you stay with us. You can let Anzo know if you need anything." She indicated the rolling robot-like thing, which had turned up about the same time they had.

Stone expected another room similar to the one back at Errin's house—comfortable, simply but elegantly furnished—but as he stepped through the door he stopped in surprise.

First, it wasn't a single room, but a suite. He stood in the front room, which resembled a smaller version of Harrison's penthouse quarters with its fine hardwood floor, exquisite leather furnishings, and minimalist artwork. It had the same sweeping, floor-to-ceiling window, but only on a single wall and the view indicated it was on a much lower story, perhaps halfway up the tower. It even included a small bar on the far side of the room. It looked completely modern by Stone's standards; overall, except for the lack of electronic amenities like a television set, it could easily have existed in the Obsidian back on Earth.

"Is this all right?" Kira asked.

"It's brilliant."

"I'll leave you here then, but let me show you a couple more things before you go. If you have any questions after, you can ask Anzo. He's at your disposal while you're here."

He narrowed his eyes at the construct, which seemed to be watching him through its softly glowing blue eyes. He wondered if this was the same one as before—its eyes were a different color, but everything else looked the same. "What is that thing? My own personal robotic valet?"

"I don't know what 'robotic' means," Kira said, tilting her head. "He's a mechano-magical construct. We have quite a few of them around here. This one is assigned to you for now. He can guide you where you need to go, answer your questions, or show you where things are."

She first took him to a spacious bedroom. It included another full-wall window facing a panoramic view of the open space beyond the tower's peak, a king-sized bed, and a walk-in closet stocked not only with the clothes that had been brought from Errin's place but also, Stone was surprised to see, a selection of more Earth-like garments including jeans, black T-shirts, shoes and boots, athletic wear, and a few suits and dress shirts.

"These styles are odd," Kira said, "but I'm told they'll make you feel more at home."

"Absolutely," Stone agreed.

"Come on—one more thing before I leave you alone. You're going to like this." She disappeared through a door.

Stone followed and found himself in a bathroom the size of a small bedroom. In addition to a spacious shower, a soaking tub, and all the other usual amenities, it also included a partitioned area with some kind of odd-looking machine in it. It had a narrow, padded bench, a console with various controls, and the whole thing was surrounded by a skeletal metal canopy.

"What's this?" he asked.

She smiled and indicated it. "Lie down. Relax and put your hands at your sides."

"But what is—"

"Just trust me."

Tilting his head in suspicion, he climbed onto the bench and lay down.

She flipped a couple of switches on the console, made a few adjustments, then pushed a button.

Instantly, the thing began to emit a low, soothing hum, and something in the canopy above Stone's head lit up, bathing him with a mellow, comforting yellow glow. A few seconds later, his whole body began to feel pleasantly warm, as if he were lying in the sun on a temperate summer afternoon. "What—" he began again.

"Relax," she murmured. "It will only take little while longer."

Stone settled back. Whatever this machine was doing to him, it certainly didn't hurt. In fact, he could almost convince himself that all the aches and pains from this morning's exertions were melting away, if that hadn't been an absurd concept.

The humming grew quieter and then stopped, and the yellow glow faded. "There," Kira said. "You can sit up now."

As soon as he sat up, he could do nothing but stare at her in frank amazement. "What…did you *do*?" he whispered.

"I told you we didn't want to hurt you. You can build up a lot faster if you don't have to worry about injuries."

Stone raised his hand and looked at it. "This…is…*amazing.*" He still hadn't raised his voice above a whisper. He hopped off the bench and spun to study the machine. "How did you—"

"How do you feel?" She seemed amused by his reaction.

"I feel…perfect. Brilliant. Nothing hurts. I thought I might have pulled some muscles before, but…I feel like I've just taken a handful of industrial-strength pain pills."

"Oh, it's not masked," she assured him. "That wouldn't be productive. It's gone."

He was still staring at the machine. It didn't look like much; aside from the framework, the bench, and the console, the only other components were two closed compartments at the head and foot of the bench. "Bloody hell, is this some kind of…magical healing machine?"

"Exactly."

"You…you people can build *magical healing machines?*" Stone was aware he sounded like an idiot, but he didn't care. This was revolutionary.

"Well, we don't mass-produce them or anything. There are a few around here, all hand built. And don't think it's a miracle machine, either—it doesn't work on real injuries. It's more of a novelty than anything, to be honest, but it works well on minor injuries like muscle fatigue, sprains, that kind of thing, and it's good at stabilizing someone who's badly hurt until they can get proper attention. For *real* injuries we still need healers."

Stone crouched, examining one end of the machine. "I would very much like to know how this works. Who built it?"

"Trevor and Errin built the prototype and figured out how to make it work, with help from one of our best healers. They use a combination of magic, machines, and some magical metals and crystals from the Wastes. That's all I know about it, and all I want to." She grinned. "Anyway, I need to get going. Anzo can show you everything you need."

Stone tore his gaze from the fascinating machine. "More rocks later?"

"No more rocks today. You've got another session this afternoon. Anzo's got your schedule, don't worry. Trust him—he won't lead you astray."

After she left, Stone regarded Anzo. "So…you're my new personal assistant."

"Is there something I can do for you?" it asked. As before, its voice was pleasant and faintly mechanical, like a living being talking through a speaker.

"Er—right now you can clear out and let me take a proper shower. How long do I have before I have to be somewhere?"

"Your afternoon session is scheduled to begin in two hours."

Stone spent longer than he normally did in the shower, mostly because his mind refused to shut down. He still had so many questions about this place, and he had to remind himself that the questions weren't the important thing. As intrigued as he was by the "mechano-magical constructs" that seemed to be commonplace around here, and as much as he wanted to dig into their design, that wasn't why he was here.

You're not planning on staying, he told himself firmly. *Do what you need to get your mind around this magical style, then have Harrison send you home where you belong.*

He dressed in jeans and black T-shirt, feeling much more at home in the familiar clothes. When he emerged from the bedroom, Anzo was waiting silently by the front door. "All right," he told it. "Take me where I need to go."

"This way, please."

It took him to one of the teleporters—apparently they had been set to recognize him, though he had no idea whether he'd have access only to specific pre-programmed areas or if he could direct them. Instead of going outside, though, the thing let him off on another floor of the tower. Anzo was still there, and took him down a hallway to another set of double doors.

He pushed them open, wondering what would be next. Would Harrison be inside?

Behind the door was a small, elegant dining room. Simply furnished, it contained only a six-person table surrounded by comfortable chairs. Another spectacular view, this one of the town at the foot of the tower's hill, spread out in front of him.

"Good to see you again," said a voice. "I'm glad to see I didn't hurt you."

Stone turned to the figure seated at the end of the table and started in surprise. It wasn't Harrison. "Karol."

Like Stone himself, Karol was looking much better following his stay at the Temolan prison. Dressed now in loose-fitting pants and a snug shirt, he rose and flashed an easy grin at Stone. "You look good for a dead man."

Gone were any vestiges of his "slow-witted" act from the Arena. He reminded Stone a little of Jason now—tall and muscular, with an athlete's grace. "Are you my latest trainer, then?"

"That's right." He looked Stone up and down. "I've got my work cut out for me, it seems. Sit down—you need to eat before we can start, so we can talk while we do that."

Stone didn't sit. "Where's Harrison? I thought *he* was going to be training me. In magic, not in…this."

He shrugged. "I don't know where he is. But he asked me to do this, and he says you've agreed, so here we are. Please sit down—I'm sure you're hungry after this morning."

"Yes, well, lugging rocks around for three hours will do that." Stone dropped into the chair at Karol's right. "I know I agreed to this and I'm not planning on backing out, but this is the oddest way to teach magic I've ever seen."

A door on the other side of the room opened, and another mechanical figure rolled in, pushing a cart. This one looked similar to Anzo, who waited outside the dining room. Efficiently it offloaded several plates, serving platters, and other items from the cart, then rolled off.

"That's not for me to judge—magic isn't my area. I'm just doing what I was asked to do. Please, eat." Karol indicated the table.

Despite his suspicion, Stone didn't need a second invitation. The plates and platters contained a combination of the familiar and the exotic: steak, steaming vegetables, rice, bread, all in abundance. Best of all, it smelled like whoever had prepared it had used actual spices. He filled up his plate and waited for Karol to do the same, then started in. "You produce all of this here?" he asked, pouring a glass of water from a sparkling carafe.

"Most of it. Some of it's imported from the farms outside Drendell and the other cities, and some I'm not sure where it comes from. But eat all you want—good meals are part of building you up."

The food was excellent, simple but exquisitely prepared. For a few minutes Stone concentrated on eating, but then he looked at Karol. "I suppose I should thank you for not snapping my neck like a twig back in Temolan."

The big man chuckled. "You were never in any danger. But you did a good job making it look convincing. It made it much easier to get you out after you were 'dead.'"

"I was told you were placed inside that prison. You aren't a mage, are you?"

"No."

"Bit dangerous, then, isn't it? They could have killed you at any moment."

"They could have, true. But the prisons are where some of our best non-magical prospects are, so we need people on the inside to identify them."

"Prospects? You mean people who are brought back here?"

"Exactly."

"So you're building some kind of hidden utopia."

Karol chuckled again. "Not even close. There's nothing utopian about New Argana. We have as many squabbles and disagreements as any group of people. What we're building here is a refuge—a place where magical and non-magical people can work together without any of the stupid prejudices you find in the rest of the world."

"And Harrison started this whole thing? Errin was telling me he's in charge."

Karol considered, refilling his plate with vegetables. "That's...not quite accurate. He's not in charge, though he could be if he wanted to be, of course. Nobody's going to oppose him. And nobody even bothers trying to tell him what to do."

"Why not? Would they be punished?" Stone remembered once again the way Harrison had killed a squad of survivalists back on Earth without even breaking a sweat, and without any hint of remorse.

"Punished?" He snorted. "No. Where did you get an idea like that?"

"Well, he's clearly got a lot of power—I mean, look at this place."

"He does, no doubt about that. That doesn't mean people—at least people *here*—are afraid of him. But he's not interested in being in charge. All he wants to do is be left alone to work on his projects, do whatever he does, and keep this place protected and concealed from the rest of the world. The town outside the tower is pretty self-governing. As long as nobody reveals our existence to the Talented, he doesn't care what they do."

"I see." Stone wondered how much Harrison had told Karol about other worlds; since Kira had said she and Errin were the only ones here he'd told, Stone decided not to say anything about it either. Instead, he gestured around him.

"So, he built this tower? How does that work? He's just one man. Did he have help?"

"Nobody knows. The tower was here when the settlement started. They tell me it has something to do with magic, but I don't get involved in that. Makes my head hurt."

"How long ago was that?"

"Many years. A long time before I got here five years ago, but there were people who've been here a lot longer who weren't here at the beginning either."

Hmm, Stone thought. So either Harrison was older than he looked, or time worked much differently here. Or both.

"Anyway," Karol said, "finish up and we'll get started. You can go back to your room and change into exercise clothes afterward, and we'll start with some easy warmups while lunch settles down."

Stone sighed. At least it wasn't toting rocks.

After he got changed, Anzo took him to yet another room inside the tower. The place was odd—the hallways were all the same, with the slate-colored carpet and gray walls, and none of the doors were labeled, so it was difficult to navigate without the little rolling construct's help. He wondered if Harrison had designed it that way, to make it hard for anyone who got inside to find their way around. He wasn't even sure how many teleport pads the place had. It definitely reminded him more than a bit of the Obsidian back in Vegas, though. Maybe Harrison had borrowed the hotel's plans when designing the Nexus.

He stopped in the doorway, staring in amazement when Anzo opened it. "Bloody hell…"

It was a gymnasium. Not just something hastily cobbled together from Fifties-era tech, but a modern-day, fully stocked gym. Stone hadn't spent much time in such places, but he recognized various machines, a free-weight area, and a large open floor with different types of apparatus—thick ropes, medicine balls, mats, and similar items—arrayed around it. As with every other room he'd seen so far in the tower, one entire wall was a window looking out over the landscape; another wall was a mirror.

Karol was already there, consulting something on a clipboard on the other side of the room. "Ah," he said, looking up. "There you are. Come on in and let's get started. We've got a lot to do today."

"This is…incredible," Stone said. "I didn't think you had this kind of thing here."

"We have all kinds of things here."

Stone approached, taking a closer look at the machines as he did. To his surprise, he recognized some of the labels on them. *This stuff is from Earth.* Apparently Harrison was importing more things than even most of the residents here might believe.

"Right, then. Let's get on with this."

For the rest of the afternoon, Karol put Stone through a series of grueling exercises—everything from lifting weights to cardio conditioning to calisthenics to techniques that seemed like a combination of yoga and martial arts and left Stone's muscles screaming for relief.

Once, while they took a brief water break, Stone sagged against one of the machines and swiped a towel across his brow. "I think," he said, between breaths, "I've just alienated every muscle in my body."

Karol chuckled. "You probably did. You don't get much exercise normally, do you?"

"I run," he protested.

"Well, that's a start, I guess. Don't worry, though—you'll see improvement fast if you do what we tell you."

"I'm beginning to think that healing machine in my room is a curse, not a blessing." He was already anticipating getting back to use it again. "I won't even be able to claim pulled muscles as an excuse, will I?"

"No. But it's also why you won't have to do this as long."

"That's something, I suppose." Nobody, as yet, had told him how long he *would* have to do this. "Do you have any idea how long this will be going on? I can't stay here forever—I need to get back to…where I come from. I've got obligations."

"That will be up to you," Karol told him. "And Trevor, of course."

Stone tightened his hand on the towel. "I think we'll need to have a discussion, he and I."

| CHAPTER TWENTY-SEVEN

MORE TIME PASSED, and Stone began to suspect he wasn't to get his wish.

Every day began the same way: an alarm awakened him at dawn, after which he paused to check whether his magic had returned before rising from bed. When each day brought the same disappointing revelation that it had not, he set about his routine: breakfast, a morning filled with various unconventional exercises directed by Kira, lunch, afternoons with Karol at the gym, dinner, a welcome session with the magical healing machine, and early bedtime. In between he interspersed several long, refreshing showers, during which he tried his best not to think too hard about what he'd gotten himself into. That way lay madness, or at least failure.

Sometimes he broke up the routine by taking long runs around New Argana, usually outside the town where he could be alone with his thoughts. During the rare times when one of his instructors (*bloody taskmasters,* as he'd begun to think of them) gave him a couple hours' break and he wasn't too exhausted, he went into town to look in the shops, grab a drink at one of the bars, or chat with some of the locals. He deliberately kept such conversations light and mostly content-free after discovering that attempts to ask more probing questions were met with brisk changes of subject.

Kira and Karol weren't much more helpful in that regard—it wasn't that they didn't *answer* his questions, but rather that their answers raised more of his curiosity than they satisfied. Finally, he just gave up and focused on the routine, making a mark on a notepad next to his bed each night before he fell into it. This couldn't go on too much longer, right?

In all that time, Harrison was nowhere to be found. Stone had not seen him since the night they'd made their agreement, which added significantly to his growing stress and frustration. When he asked Kira, Errin, or Karol where he might be found, all of them claimed not to know.

"You have to understand about Trevor," Errin told him when he stopped by her house on one of his runs. "He does what he does, and he doesn't answer to anybody. You get used to it. He'll turn up when he thinks you're ready for him, but right now he's probably off dealing with some other issue that has nothing to do with you." She offered him an encouraging smile, looking him up and down. "Don't worry—it's not that he's ignoring you. He's like this all the time. Just keep doing what you're doing, and he'll show up eventually. It looks like the exercise plan is working, anyway."

"Brilliant," Stone muttered. She was right—he already had more energy and was certain he was growing stronger—but none of that mattered if he couldn't use magic. Harrison might be trying to turn him into a gym rat, but it wasn't going to work.

Around the two-week mark, the routine changed. The sessions with Karol remained mostly the same, but the day after he finally finished the wall Kira had him build (completed, the thing was five levels deep in rock and nearly thirty feet long), she greeted him near a strange apparatus she'd constructed near it.

"What's this?" he asked, eyeing what looked like a metal frame built over a large, deep tub.

"Your assignment for the day." She nodded at it. "You're going to hang up there as long as you can."

"What the hell?" He moved forward and peered into the tub. Water filled it almost to the brim, to a depth of about five feet. Dipping his hand in revealed the water to be ice-cold. "You're having me on, right?"

"Not at all. This is the next stage of your training. Physical endurance combined with willpower. I'll remove the tub in half an hour. If you can remain there that long, you won't get a dunking. Otherwise…"

He glared at her. "Harrison told you do this? Where the hell is he, anyway? I want to talk to him."

"He's not here. Haven't seen him for days. He left word you should start the endurance training as soon as you finished the wall. Unless," she added with a sly sideways glance, "you're ready to give up."

Anger rose, but Stone drove it down. That was what Harrison wanted—for him to give up—and he'd be damned if he'd give the man the satisfaction. "No," he muttered. "I'm not ready to give up. Let's get on with it."

She used magic to levitate him up, and held him there until he'd grasped the bar and indicated he was ready. "I'll be back in half an hour," she said. "Good luck."

The first day, he lasted fifteen minutes, the last few owing more to sheer stubborn willpower than physical strength.

Kira, who'd perhaps been watching him discreetly from a distance, showed up shortly after and sent him to dry off. "We'll try again tomorrow," was all she said.

The next day, he made twenty minutes. "This is rubbish," he told her through chattering teeth when she returned. "It's not training—it's sadism."

"Want to give up? You can, you know. Any time you want."

"I'm *not* giving up. And you can tell Harrison that for me."

She merely smiled in that maddening way of hers and tossed him a towel.

It was a full week before he managed the entire thirty minutes, using a combination of more stubborn willpower, deep meditation techniques, and good old-fashioned anger. By the time Kira turned up that day, his arms shook until he thought they'd never be still again, and hurt so much he was sure they'd fall off before he could get to the sweet relief of the healing machine.

"There," he growled, dropping to the ground after she slid the tub free. "Done, damn you."

"Nice job," was all she said.

It went on like that for the next week, with Kira coming up with increasingly more difficult and frustrating exercises. She had him climbing cliff walls (which he found he was good at), walking tightropes (which he wasn't) and running until he couldn't manage another step—followed by urging him to keep going anyway. Through it all he persisted—grumbling to himself all the while about what he'd say to Harrison when he saw him, but he persisted. Every night he made another tick-mark on his notepad before falling into bed; it had become a rote thing by now, and he'd stopped counting them because doing so made him angrier.

Whatever Harrison was up to, he'd just about had his fill of it.

CHAPTER TWENTY-EIGHT

O N DAY THIRTY, HE FINALLY HAD ENOUGH.

It had been a day like every other: Kira had sent him out on a multi-mile run around New Argana and its surrounding area, and afterward, following the usual substantial lunch, Karol had done his best to reduce him to a lump of quivering muscle with his increasingly brutal workouts. Karol himself wasn't brutal, of course—he remained his usual amiable, cheery self—but by the time Stone had trudged back to his suite and availed himself of the healing machine, his frustration and despair at the futility of all this had reached a higher boiling point than it ever had before.

Savagely, he made another tick mark on his pad, then paused to count them for the first time in a couple of weeks.

Thirty.

He'd been carrying on this charade for *thirty days,* with no sign of Harrison. The man hadn't even made an appearance—not at the Nexus, not at Errin's place, not anywhere in town. For all Stone knew he could be off gallivanting on another dimension while his would-be apprentice killed himself trying to fulfill his pair of taskmasters' increasingly impossible tasks.

Instead of going to bed, he stumped out to the front room and poured himself a substantial shot from one of the bottles at his well-stocked bar. He grabbed the first one he spotted, not caring what it was. He'd been mostly avoiding alcohol except for an occasional nightcap since he'd started his training, but tonight none of that mattered. Nothing mattered. For all he knew, Harrison would keep him at this for the next six months before pronouncing him ready for the next stage.

If he ever planned to do it at all.

Stone didn't stop at the single shot. He tossed it back and poured another, glaring at the starlit view out the window without seeing it. When he finished that one, he poured still another. If Kira or Karol wanted to complain about his inevitable hangover the next day, let them bloody *try*.

"I have had just about *enough* of this!" Stone snapped aloud at his reflection in the glass. "I haven't seen Harrison since we started this whole charade—I'm starting to think he's been having me on this whole time, trying to see how much of this ridiculous treatment I'd put up with before I gave it up. Anzo!" he yelled, slamming the empty glass down. "Where the hell are you?"

"I am here," the construct's pleasant voice responded from the other side of the room. "Is there something you require?"

"Damn bloody *right* there is. I want you to take me to Harrison. Right now. I don't want any excuses, either. Just do it. *Now.*"

"Mr. Harrison is—"

"I don't give a damn if Mr. Harrison is in the middle of an orgy with a manatee, three elephants, and a racehorse! You take me to him right *now!* Got it?"

"Yes, sir. Follow me, please."

Stone blinked. He hadn't expected that to work. Was Harrison actually *here,* then? He half-thought Anzo would tell him it couldn't fulfill the request because the man was off in some other city, or on Earth, or on another dimension entirely. "Er—all right, then." He hurried to catch up, weaving only slightly.

Anzo led him down a familiar hall to a teleport pad. "This way," it said, rolling onto the pad.

Stone joined it. "Where is he?"

The view shimmered, then reformed on another hallway. "He is in the main workroom."

"Wait—he's right here in the building?" Stone looked around, but the décor didn't provide any clue—like all the other halls in this place, this one had the same gray walls and slate carpet. *He's here, and he can't even be arsed to stop by and check whether they've killed me yet with all this exercise rubbish?* Damn, but the man was maddening.

"Yes. This way, please."

Stone supposed it wouldn't do him any good to take out his growing irritation on Anzo. The construct only did what it was programmed to do, after all.

Anzo rolled to the end of the hallway and stopped before yet another set of double doors. "Just through here."

"It's—as simple as that?" Stone regarded the doors suspiciously, wondering whether, if he'd lost his temper a couple of weeks ago, he could have cut this whole thing shorter.

"I do not understand the question," Anzo said. "As simple as what?"

"Never mind. You can leave now. Thank you. Off you go."

Anzo remained for a few more seconds, then its eyes flashed briefly and it rolled off down the hall, back toward the teleporter pad.

Stone raised his hand to knock on the door, but then his anger rose again. Damn it, Harrison wasn't going to have the chance to duck out some hidden exit and avoid him. He wrenched the door open and strode inside the room.

And stopped.

The space inside the door was cavernous. Not in the sense of a large room, but in the sense of an aircraft hangar. The ceiling rose so high Stone couldn't even see it in the faint light; likewise, it was hard to tell how far off the black walls were. This room, unlike most of the others Stone had encountered inside the tower, did not have any windows, floor-to-ceiling or otherwise.

Scattered around the floor were what looked like various projects in different stages of completion: more of the mechano-magical automobiles; consoles with their panels opened and their parts spread over large tarps; half-assembled engines. There were even a few anthropoid constructs, some like Anzo, others even more human-looking. He didn't see any sign of any living beings inside, but music—was that Beethoven's *Moonlight Sonata*?—echoed its haunting strains through the space.

His gaze skated over all of the machines, but the thing that riveted his attention instantly was the massive—what? Vehicle? It was hard to tell from where he stood—crouching in the middle of the floor, held upright by a metal framework. The thing rose at least two stories tall; it had a sleek, black hull similar to a ship, but it didn't have the design of any sailing ship Stone had ever seen on Earth. It also looked unfinished, with large skeletal sections uncovered and open to the outside. Beyond it, a much smaller but similarly-shaped craft stood.

He was about to take a step forward when a spray of sparks erupted out of the side of the larger ship high above, catching his attention. He looked up, and only then did he spot the shadowy figure hovering near the top of the structure. Something looked wrong about its proportions—its head looked too big for its body—but it was too dark up there to be sure. "Harrison? Is that you?" he called over the music.

The sparks stopped, and so did the music. The shadowy figure set something down inside the hull of the ship, then slowly lowered toward the ground. As it did, it pulled something from its head and held it in one hand.

Stone approached warily. "Harrison?"

"Dr. Stone."

It was indeed Harrison. When he touched down near the structure, Stone stared at him in surprise. "Er—"

In the small number of times Stone had been in Harrison's presence, he'd never seen the man dressed in anything but a fine, tailored suit, or at least spotless creased trousers and a crisp formal shirt. He didn't know how much of it was magic and how much was just that Harrison was one of those guys who'd apparently been born in a full set of formalwear, but either way, seeing him now was jarring.

The thing he'd taken off and now held was some kind of welding mask. In place of his usual suit he wore heavy trousers, stout black work boots, and a snug-fitting white tank top. His arms, face, and shirt were smudged with dirt and streaked with oil, a wrench poked out of his back pocket, and his hair was in disarray. Whatever he'd been doing, he looked like he'd been at it for quite some time.

Nevertheless, he still carried himself as if he *were* wearing the tailored suit. His chill gaze settled on Stone as he put the welding mask aside. "Is there something I can do for you?"

Stone's anger rose again, jolting him from the shock of seeing Harrison looking so uncharacteristic. *This* was what he'd been doing, instead of keeping up his end of the agreement? Poking around at some grimy machine? "Yes. There is. I want to talk to you."

"This is not a good time, Dr. Stone. Perhaps we can—"

"It *is* a good time. Listen—I won't take much of your time away from—whatever the hell it is you're doing here—but this is getting ridiculous. I've been patient for a long time, but I want answers."

Harrison regarded him for several seconds with his unsettling, unblinking gaze, then nodded once. "Come, then. I want to finish this tonight, so we will have to speak while I work." Without waiting for an answer, he turned and disappeared through one of the openings in the ship's scaffolding.

Stone hurried to follow him, growing more frustrated as it seemed he was destined to spend his time chasing after the people who had the information he needed.

As he stepped over the scaffolding, a light flared in the open space inside, illuminating a large, intricate-looking machine that might have been an engine near the back end. It too was held in a smaller version of the same framework that supported the ship itself; Harrison floated up to the first level of this scaffolding and pulled the wrench from his pocket.

Stone, currently unable to do any floating of his own, climbed up the framework and stood a few feet away from Harrison. "What is this thing, anyway?"

"It is an airship. Or, rather, it will be when it is finished."

"An airship. Like something out of H. G. Wells?"

"Somewhat." Harrison made an adjustment with the wrench, then held out his hand and another tool sailed into it from a nearby array of them on a table.

"Is this another of your magical-mechanical inventions?"

"It will run on magical power, yes. This one is a joint project, with Errin. She designed the mechanical part of the engine, and I designed the magical part." He made another adjustment, then turned back to Stone. "Why are you here, Dr. Stone?"

As fascinated as he was by the concept of a magic-powered airship, Stone refused to let that sidetrack him. He glared. "I told you—I want answers."

"To what questions?"

Was he serious? His face still revealed nothing; Stone got the sudden urge to grab him and shake him, to force him to display *some* emotion—even if it was only irritation at being interrupted. "You're having me on, right? What questions do you *think*? It's been over a month that you've had your people training me, and I haven't seen even a hint of magic yet. I've been running, lifting weights, building your bloody *wall* for you—and you haven't even turned up to check on how I've been doing. I don't know you very well, Mr. Harrison, and it's occurred to me more than once that you might be playing some sort of sick joke on me. I don't know what you're trying to accomplish, but whatever it is, I've had quite enough of it. Either keep your end of the agreement—teach me how to use your magic so it doesn't burn me out—or send me home." He gripped the scaffolding so hard his knuckles whitened and his hands shook. "Or—have you discovered that you *can't* teach me after all, and you just haven't got 'round to telling me yet?" His voice shook too, with growing anger.

Don't do this, his mental voice warned. *You're going to push him too far.*

I don't give a damn *how far I push him.* He's *pushed* me *too far!*

Harrison watched him without expression, his posture relaxed and attentive. He looked like an anthropologist observing a primitive but fascinating ceremony. When Stone finished, he said softly, "You've been drinking, Dr. Stone."

"Damn bloody *right* I've been drinking! What else have I got to do around here, but work out and drink? Nobody will tell me a damned thing! I keep thinking this is going to be over soon and we're going to get on with it, but it just keeps going on with no end in sight. I can't keep this up forever. I've got places to be. Responsibilities. They probably think I'm dead back home, and I've not even got anything useful to show for it." He took a step forward. "So what's it going to be, Mr. Harrison? Are you planning to keep your end of the bargain?"

Harrison turned away from him and picked up the wrench, then floated a few feet up and made another adjustment to the weird engine. "I was the same way..." he said, barely loud enough for Stone to hear.

"What?" The sudden shift startled him. For the first time, he glanced at the table where Harrison had been picking up tools, and saw not just a half-full glass, but a bottle next to it. He narrowed his eyes and looked up at Harrison. "What are you talking about?"

"When I arrived here. I was like you—impatient. Skeptical. Angry."

"You aren't making sense." Stone paced back and forth along the narrow catwalk. He had a hard time picturing the intense, controlled Harrison ever being visibly angry about anything. "What are you talking about, when you arrived here?"

He lowered back down, put the wrench back in his pocket, and selected a larger one. "I had wondered when—or if—you would come to me." He seated the wrench around the head of a large bolt, gripped it with both hands, and pulled, the muscles in his arms and back straining against it until it broke free. He removed it, examined it, and pulled a small panel free of the structure.

Stone watched him. The suits had hidden it well, but the man was definitely drinking his own Kool-Aid regarding physical fitness. Like Stone himself, he looked like he had next to no body fat; he was still slim but carried more muscle than Stone did. Maybe there was something to this whole magic/fitness thing after all. But his anger rose again at Harrison's words. "What do you mean, you wondered? Did you *expect* me to come to you? Were you waiting to see when I'd finally have enough and call you on this rubbish?"

Harrison's expression chilled. "I'll remind you, Dr. Stone, that you agreed to my terms."

"I did. You're right. But that was with the assumption that you were playing straight with me. So—were you? *Are* you going to teach me magic, or was this all a waste of both our time?"

"By the terms of our agreement, I could send you home tonight." Harrison leaned in closer to the open panel, levitated a screwdriver to his hand from the table, and made another adjustment.

"Yes. You could. If you were just waiting until I reached my wits' end and tracked you down, then okay—this is me at my wits' end. You win, Mr. Harrison. Either show me there's some reason you're waiting so long to teach me, or I'm ready to call it a bad job and go back home. I don't like it, but at least I'll have my life back."

Harrison turned back around, and now there was something challenging in his eyes. "You are giving up, then. I am disappointed, Dr. Stone. I thought you had more…conviction."

Stone's anger, already simmering, boiled at his words. "Conviction? What kind of bloody conviction do you want me to *have*? How long do you want me to wait, with no information? How long am I supposed to follow along with this absurd course your underlings have got me on, without any solid information about *why* I'm doing it? Be honest with me, Harrison—would *you* do it? Would *you* put up with this kind of nonsense, or would you demand some explanation? I said I would do what it took to learn to control this magic—and I *will*. You can push me as hard as you want. I won't break, I promise. But I need *reasons!*"

Harrison had turned away from the panel and continued to watch Stone's outburst, arms crossed, expression once again neutral. "Is that your final decision?"

Don't do this, the little voice said. *You're throwing away everything you've worked for.*

Bugger everything I've worked for. This bastard is playing with me, and I've had my fill of it. "Yes! That's my final decision."

"As you wish." Harrison's gaze shifted to a point somewhere over Stone's shoulder. "Anzo. Escort Dr. Stone back to his suite. He will be leaving us tonight."

Something inside Stone froze, and clenched. So that was it. He'd taken things too far, and now Harrison was calling his bluff.

Good one, Stone, said the drawling, mocking little voice in his head. *Trying to bluff a world-class poker player. Brilliant job, that.*

He didn't move. "No. I'm not leaving."

"Stay, then. It doesn't matter to me either way. But if you'll excuse me, I have work to do." He turned back to the panel.

Stone glared at him, heart pounding, fists clenched.

He was being dismissed. After everything he'd done, everything he'd endured to get here, Harrison was disregarding him as if his presence meant nothing more to him than one of his tools.

Maybe it was the drinks. Maybe it was the frustration. Maybe it was Harrison's insufferable calm. Whatever it was, something snapped inside him.

Growling, he launched himself across the platform, grabbed Harrison's shoulder, and spun him around. "Don't turn your back on me, damn you! You are going to tell me what this is about!"

Harrison barely reacted. His jaw tightened infinitesimally, and his chilly gaze grew even colder. With an offhand gesture, he sent Stone staggering back toward the edge of the platform.

"Go home, Dr. Stone. I was wrong—I cannot teach you. You don't have the will." His voice was as emotionless as ever, but a faint hint of contempt tinged its edges.

Stone barely caught himself as he tumbled over the edge. He gripped one of the supports before he fell and hung there, holding on by one arm. He was stronger now, surprisingly so, a month into his accelerated physical training program. He certainly could have pulled himself back up by muscle power alone—but he didn't need to. His rage made him stronger than he ever could have been under normal circumstances.

"Like *hell* I don't!" he yelled, flinging himself back up and scrambling to his feet. "This isn't about will—it never was. You're nothing more than another of those sadistic bastards back in the cities! The only difference is, at least they're honest about it! Don't talk to me about *will!*"

Harrison sent him reeling again, with no more effort than he might use to brush dust off his clothes. "Show me, then."

"Show you *what*?" He scrambled up once more. He didn't even feel like himself anymore. His body felt light, effortless. All his fatigue and despair had burned off, replaced by a kind of mad energy—a glowing hot core that originated deep inside him and radiated outward. It was the adrenaline, he knew, combined with the rage—but that was fine with him. Whatever it took to get the job done. He lunged at Harrison again.

Suddenly he couldn't move.

He stopped in mid-step, one foot hovering a few inches above the ground, the other braced to launch him forward. "What the *hell*—?" His voice pitched louder, echoing around the cavernous space.

"Show me, Dr. Stone," Harrison said, calm as ever. His gaze was laser-focused, implacable, fixed on Stone's eyes. "Show me you have the will. Show me you're worth my effort."

"Harrison, damn you, let me go *now!*" Stone tried to fling himself free of the paralyzing grip, but no matter how hard he strained, his limbs refused to respond. It felt as if he were encased in a statue.

"You have only to say the word." Harrison turned away from him again, picked up the screwdriver, and returned to his work inside the panel. "Admit defeat, and I will release you and send you home."

"I am not admitting *defeat!*" Stone's heart pounded harder than ever, until he feared it would burst free of his chest like that thing from *Alien.* Maybe if he was lucky it would hit Harrison and wipe that gods-damned calm off his face.

"Then you will remain until I am finished here." Still Harrison didn't turn around.

Stone could barely see straight now. How *dare* this arrogant bastard treat him like this? How dare he claim he could teach Stone magic and then use that promise to string him along, to play with him like a cat with a gullible mouse?

"*Harrison!*" he yelled, and didn't even bother trying to temper how insane he sounded. He didn't *care* how insane he sounded. All he wanted to do at this point was show this man what a bad idea this was.

Harrison ignored him. He put the screwdriver down, levitated another wrench over, and removed a small assembly from inside the panel.

"Harrison! Look at me, damn you!"

No response. Harrison made an adjustment on the assembly, used magic to move it back inside the housing, then bolted it back into place.

Stone, rage growing until he thought he might burst a blood vessel, strained against the iron-hard hold. He tried flinging his whole body forward. He tried rocking back and forth. He tried moving each limb individually, concentrating all his effort on it. All the while his heart continued to pound, and the red haze of anger scattered his thoughts. It wasn't working—but he would *not* admit defeat. No way was he going to give this man the satisfaction of that. He'd bloody *die* here in this awkward, lunging position before he did that.

You don't have the will. Harrison's calm, mocking words echoed in his mind, zooming around like frantic moths caught in a jar. *You don't have the will.*

Like *hell* he didn't. He was all *about* the will. It was the cornerstone of everything he was. And damn it, he was going to make this bastard *see* it if he had to die trying.

He clamped his eyes shut and gritted his teeth. He couldn't clench his fists, but that didn't matter—in his mind, that was exactly what he was doing. In his mind's eye, he pictured Harrison's face, his unruffled expression, his cold, contemptuous gaze.

You don't have the will.

"*I DO!*" he screamed.

In his mind, he drove back the rage, the humiliation, the despair, and shoved them aside. Instead, he reached out as he had done before when he'd been desperate and without any other options. He couldn't feel the power, but he knew it was there, dancing tantalizingly just out of his reach.

It was there, and he was going to claim it.

Even if it killed him.

Inside, the burning core grew until it threatened to burn him out. It stretched outward, filling his arms, his legs, tracing its way along his nerve pathways until he thought his limbs would fly off.

He screamed again, but not in pain. The burning didn't hurt, but rather seemed to swell with a pressure he could no longer contain.

All at once, it was there.

And it demanded release.

Without even fully knowing what he was doing, he reached out, took hold of that surging core. He gathered it together, focused on the force holding him immobile.

With an inarticulate yell that was more a roar of rage than a scream, he released the power.

His world went white for a second, with no idea whether the loud *whoom* that sounded was real or just inside his head. When his vision cleared he was on his knees on the platform, panting as if he'd just run a four-minute mile.

Harrison was gone.

Stone quickly leaped to his feet, heedless of his limbs' protests. *Oh, bloody hell, what happened? Did I vaporize him?* With frantic urgency he hurried to the platform's edge and looked over.

Harrison lay twenty or so feet away, splayed on his back against one of the smaller machines with tools and glittering pieces of the broken bottle and glass scattered around him. As Stone watched in horror, he sat up and slowly stood, gripping the edge of the machine.

Relief washed over Stone, along with two simultaneous thoughts: *Now he's going to kill me,* and *I don't care—he deserved that.* He watched Harrison warily, ready to duck back if it looked as if the man was preparing to retaliate.

Harrison didn't retaliate. He stood a moment, watching Stone. Aside from breathing a little harder than usual, he appeared none the worse for wear.

"I—" Stone began, but stopped, when he got a good look at Harrison's expression.

Was that...*approval?*

"Well done, Dr. Stone," Harrison said.

Stone gaped at him, confused. The surging energy had receded now, but he could still feel it inside him, quiet and patient. Waiting. "What the hell—?"

"Well done," Harrison repeated. "I was certain you could do it. You simply needed the proper...catalyst." He lifted off the ground and touched down on the platform. "Now, we can get started."

CHAPTER TWENTY-NINE

STONE WASN'T SURE HE'D HEARD what he thought he'd heard. "Get…started?"

Harrison raised his hands, righting the fallen table and replacing the scattered tools on it. Then he gathered up the shards of the bottle and glass and dropped them into a nearby receptacle. "Yes. Now I can keep our agreement."

"You…couldn't before? Sorry about the…er—" He gestured toward the receptacle. "But what the hell did I *do*?"

"Magic." Harrison spoke as if it were the most obvious thing in the world.

"Wait—you're saying I—" Tentatively, hardly daring to hope, Stone held up his hand and attempted to shift to magical sight.

His familiar, purple-and-gold aura shimmered around it, but faintly. It felt as if he were having trouble locking it in.

But it *worked*. For the first time in weeks, his magic was *working*. He staggered back, catching himself against the side of the airship. "Bloody hell…" He looked at Harrison, who watched him silently. "But wait. Are you saying that all I needed to do was—what? Come to you? Lose my temper?"

"No." Harrison levitated the panel back into place and screwed it shut. "Although I had wondered how long you would endure my…unique training methods."

"So it was all some kind of *game*?" Stone's anger reared its head again, but now that his magic seemed to be on the way back, it was harder to hold on to it. "Some kind of—what—practical joke, to see how much I'd put up with?"

Harrison's gaze chilled again. "Dr. Stone, I know we have spent little time together, but have I ever seemed the type to indulge in jokes, practical or otherwise?"

A sudden, quick impression of the elegant mage planting a whoopee cushion or leaving a full bucket of water on the top of a half-open door flashed in Stone's mind, and he almost grinned at the absurdity of it all. "Point taken. Well, what, then? *Was* there a point to all that workout rubbish?"

"There was. Two, in fact. Excuse me a moment." He glanced past Stone to Anzo, who still waited silently near the door. "Anzo. Bring a bottle of the Balvenie. And two glasses."

Anzo's eyes flashed acknowledgment, and he rolled off.

Harrison nodded toward the airship. "If you'll forgive me, I do want to finish this tonight. Do you mind if we speak while I work?"

"Er—no. Of course not." Stone was still reeling from Harrison's sudden change of demeanor, from coldly mocking to courteous and almost pleasant. "So—the points?"

"Yes." Harrison returned to the lower level and examined one end of the massive engine. "The workouts were not merely designed to occupy your time. In order for you to effectively manage potent and unfamiliar magical energy, especially at first, it is best if both your body and your will are in optimal condition."

"I suppose that makes sense," Stone admitted. Even previously, when he'd tapped this dimension's power without having any idea what he was doing, it always left him tired and spent—and that wasn't even counting the magical burnouts. "But you could have *told* me about it."

"I could have," Harrison agreed. "But I remind you: *you* came to *me*. You asked for my assistance. Begged, in fact. That did not place me under any obligation to explain my methods."

Stone didn't like it, but once again he had to admit the man had a point. "What about the other thing? You said there were two."

"Yes." Harrison summoned a large wrench from the table and snugged it around an inch-diameter bolthead. Once again, his muscles knotted as he put pressure on it until it broke loose.

"Why do you do that?" Stone asked him.

"Do what?"

He nodded toward the engine. "With the wrench. You've easily got enough power to do all of that with magic, don't you?"

"I do. But I prefer physical effort when working on machines. It is a habit I acquired from my younger days, before I had access to magic."

"Before you had access to magic? You mean when you were a child, or a teenager?"

"No."

Stone watched him work in silence for a while. "Does it work differently here? Do mages not begin their apprenticeships in their late teens?"

Harrison continued with what he was doing. "Apprenticeships are not handled here as they are on Earth. But in any case, my training was…non-standard."

"Non-standard? How old were you when you found out you had magic?"

"Thirty-seven."

Stone stared at him. He didn't even look that old *now,* and there was no way he could exhibit his level of power and control with only a few short years of training. "You're having me on."

"No, Dr. Stone. It is true."

"Well—look, I don't want to pry, but as long as you seem not to mind answering—how long ago was that? You don't look old enough to even *be* thirty-seven yet, let alone have discovered your magic so late."

"I am older than I look."

Stone moved around on the platform so he could see Harrison from the side rather than the back. "So—that's not really what you look like, then? Are you maintaining some kind of illusion?"

"No." Harrison stepped back, swiped his hand across his brow, then attacked another recalcitrant bolt with the wrench. "I use illusions when I go into the cities, but this is my true appearance."

Stone switched to magical sight again. To his delight, his aura appeared clearer, and stronger. Tentatively, he attempted to levitate one of the smaller screwdrivers on Harrison's tool table.

It rose a couple inches, but then the power slipped and he lost control of it. It clattered back to the tray. Harrison glanced over briefly, but didn't seem startled or alarmed.

"Sorry," Stone said, wincing. "Getting ahead of myself, I guess."

"That is understandable, after you have been without your magic for so long. But I suggest taking your progress slowly. As I mentioned before, it does not function as a switch. We will begin in earnest tomorrow."

"Right…" Stone paced back and forth, studying the engine. "I won't ask you how old you are—I suppose it's none of my business. So let's go back to the second point."

"Yes. The second point is the more important of the two. Acclimation."

"Acclimation?" Stone blinked. "You mean—I needed to get used to the place before I could do magic here?"

"Exactly. Magical energy is all around here, far more than it is on Earth. But in order for a practitioner who is not native to this dimension to properly wield its energies, he must be acclimated to them. This takes time, pure and simple. It is not possible to speed the process along."

"So you're saying that if I stayed here long enough, my magic would have come back naturally? Even back in Drendell, or in the Temolan prison?"

"Yes…and no." Harrison removed another panel and reached inside a cavity, using a light spell to illuminate his work. When he pulled back, his hands were slicked with grease. "Given time, you would have regained the *potential* to use magic. But without training, you still wouldn't have gained the ability to wield it effectively. If you had tried, likely the authorities in Temolan would have killed you before you could escape."

"I…see." Stone nodded at the engine. "Anything I can do to help you with that? It feels wrong standing here watching you work."

"Thank you, no. I am almost finished."

"I have returned," a familiar voice called. Stone glanced up to see Anzo standing balanced on his single wheel outside the opening in the hull, holding up a tray containing a bottle and two gleaming glasses.

"I'll get that," Stone said, hurrying over to claim the tray. He carried it back, pushed a few tools aside, and set it on the corner of Harrison's table.

Harrison wiped his hands on a rag, used magic to open the bottle and pour two shots, and nodded toward one while levitating the other to him. When Stone had picked it up, he raised his own glass. "To the return of your magic."

Stone raised his. "A-bloody-men," he said, and took a sip. The scotch was exquisite, even better than what he'd had before. "So—not to seem impatient, but now that my magic's back, how long will it take me to learn to control it? It's fine here, but I do have obligations back home. It will be fairly inconvenient if the world starts thinking I'm dead."

"It will not take long. A few days, perhaps."

"Well, that's good to know, at least." He looked around, taking in the airship, the other machines, and the hangar itself. "This is all—amazing. This is the first time I've traveled to another dimension, at least physically. I have so many questions about how you got here, but—" He sighed. "Probably best if I just do what I came here for and get back home."

"Probably true," Harrison agreed. "Now, however, I do want to finish this tonight. Errin has an innovation she wants to test, but she can't do it until I correct an issue with the magical-mechanical interface. If you'll excuse me—come to my workroom tomorrow morning and we'll begin. Anzo can escort you there."

"Absolutely. Good night, Mr. Harrison. Thank you—and...I apologize for losing my temper before." He chuckled. "And flinging you across the room. I'm sorry for that, too."

"Understandable, given the circumstances. I will see you tomorrow."

Stone finished his scotch, set the glass down, and headed for the opening in the hull where the construct waited. Behind him, the *Moonlight Sonata* started up again.

When he reached the opening, he stopped and turned back. Harrison had returned to his work on the platform, his back to Stone.

Unable to resist, Stone shifted to magical sight again, this time looking not at his own aura, but at Harrison's. Would the man be masking it?

It appeared that he was not. He had one of the strangest auras Stone had ever seen—a shifting, potent combination of a deep black that somehow glowed, and the kind of intense purple you usually only saw in black lights. As Stone watched it, reveling in the simple pleasure of being able to do so again, he noticed to his surprise that it appeared uneasy—almost unsettled. He continued to study it, feeling like a voyeur but unable to tear his gaze from it nonetheless.

There was no question about it—something was amiss with Harrison's aura. Stone had seen similar behavior before in his own, usually when he was troubled about something. He wondered how much Harrison had had to drink before he arrived, then recalled the mental image of the broken shards on the floor. There had been almost no spilled liquid along with them, which meant the bottle had been nearly empty.

To his horror, Harrison turned back around at that moment, as if he'd sensed Stone's scrutiny. His gaze was chilly again, his expression back to its customary cold mask. "Is there something else you need, Dr. Stone?"

"Er—no. I'm sorry. I was just leaving."

He started to turn away, then stopped again. "Mr. Harrison?"

"Yes?"

"Is everything all right?"

Harrison didn't answer.

"I know it's none of my business. But I couldn't resist a look at your aura—just testing out the magic. And it looked a bit—well—off."

Stone was still watching his aura. It flared briefly, then settled back to its normal calm, unruffled state. He didn't miss the way Harrison's hand tightened around his wrench, though, nor the way his gaze shifted away for less than a second before returning to Stone.

"Everything is fine, Dr. Stone," he said in a firm tone.

"Er—okay. All right. Sorry, didn't mean to pry. I'll see you tomorrow, then." Stone held his gaze a moment longer, then stepped through the opening toward where Anzo waited.

As he followed it back to the teleportation pad that would take him to his suite, he pondered Harrison's odd behavior. Something *had* been wrong, he'd stake his magic on it. But did it have anything to do with him, or had he just caught the man during an introspective moment? He couldn't say without knowing Harrison better, and he hardly seemed the type you could pop down to the pub with for a few pints. In fact, he seemed like the type who did most of his drinking alone—something Stone, unfortunately, was more familiar with than he wanted to admit.

He picked up his pace to keep up with Anzo, trying to put the situation out of his mind. He wasn't, nor did he have any desire to be, Harrison's therapist. All he wanted was for the man to show him how to use this magical energy so he could get the hell out of this place and go home. He had enough of his own problems to be getting on with, without looking for more. As fascinating as this new world was—especially this part of it, where magic and technology worked together and nobody was trying to kill him—all he wanted was to get back home to something familiar: his job, his new house, Raider, Verity.

Things were finally starting to happen. In only a few days he'd have his magic back and he could return home where the world made sense.

He wondered if Harrison would show him how to travel back and forth between Earth and Calanar, as he himself did. Would that even be possible, and if so, would he even want to do it?

First things first, he told himself.

He had his magic back, and that was enough for tonight.

CHAPTER THIRTY

STONE COULDN'T SLEEP.

He made a good try at it for a couple hours, tossing and turning in the big, comfortable bed, trying to find a position he could settle into. Even as he did, though, he knew his insomnia had little to do with his physical comfort, and everything to do with the fact that his brain refused to shut off.

He also knew from past experience that he wasn't going to get any sleep in this state, so he might as well give up trying. He slipped out of bed and stood for several moments looking out the window at the panoramic view stretched out before him. This time of night most of the lights in the town's buildings were out, leaving only the twinkling glows of the stars. Pressing his palms against the cool glass, he took several deep breaths in an attempt to calm his racing thoughts.

It didn't help. All he could think of was that his magic was back—even better, *Harrison's* magic was back. He hadn't blown Harrison off that platform with black magic. That wasn't possible: it had been weeks since he'd arrived on this dimension, and even when he'd attempted to draw power back in Drendell it hadn't worked. He had taken the first steps toward what he'd set out to do when he'd come here:

tapped the energy of this dimension to do magic, without burning himself out. He still only had the beginnings of it, but in a few short hours Harrison would show him more. "A few days," he'd said. That was how long it would take before Stone could have his life back. After everything he'd been through, it hardly seemed possible.

But now, he couldn't sleep. Normally back on Earth when sleep eluded him, he'd go to his study and work on a spell or ritual design, grade papers, or read. Sometimes he'd go for a run to clear his head. He couldn't do any of those things here, though—he hadn't seen any sign of a library in the tower, and up until today Harrison's associates had kept him so busy with his fitness and willpower exercises that he wouldn't have had time to do it even if there had been. And as for running—he wasn't sure he knew how to get out of the tower on his own this late—or that he could get back in if he did. Best not to risk it.

Pacing the suite, he even wished it included a television set. He didn't often watch TV, but right now a stiff drink and something mindless to lull him to sleep might be just what he needed.

He could hardly believe his next thought—*who are you, and what have you done with Stone?*—but it occurred to him that perhaps if he couldn't go running, a workout could help calm some of his restless thoughts. Over the past month, as much as he rebelled against the grueling pace Harrison's associates had put him through, he had to admit it had done good things for his body—he felt better than he had in a long time; with a bit of vanity he knew he *looked* better, too. It might even be worthwhile to find the time to keep up some sane version of the regimen once he got back home. If nothing else right now, physical exertion might tire him out enough so he could get two or three hours of rest before facing Harrison in the morning.

He donned workout clothes and called Anzo. As always, the helpful construct responded instantly, taking him to the teleport pad and calibrating it for the floor containing the gym. He wondered if, once Harrison had taught him more, he'd be able to manage the network himself without having to rely on his ever-present magi-mechanical valet.

As he expected, the gym was empty—who else would be daft enough to want to work out at this time of night? He dropped his towel on one of the benches and began a few warmup stretches. As he did, his thoughts turned to Jason Thayer. He hadn't thought about his friend for a while—most of his thoughts about Earth had centered on Verity, Raider, and his work at the University—but he wondered what Jason would think if he were here right now. For as long as Stone had known him, he'd always been a fitness buff, even to the point of buying a secondhand weight set and bench for his apartment back when he barely had enough money to afford his rent. Stone had always given him good-natured teasing about it, but now that he'd tried it, he couldn't deny the benefits. He glanced at himself in the mirrored wall, pleased with what he saw. He'd never have Jason's beefy, muscular physique—but he didn't want it. He'd always be thin, but now he could actually make out real muscle definition in his arms and chest. If he turned a little and the light hit him just right, he even thought he could see an ab or two.

He chuckled self-consciously and turned away from the mirror. *This isn't about vanity, you prat. It's about magic. Just get on with it and stop admiring yourself.*

He spent the next hour going through one of the circuits Karol had designed for him, but by the time he finished, all he felt was tired. A good kind of tired, true, but not at all sleepy. If anything, he felt *more* awake.

Frustrated, he swiped his towel across his brow and let his breath out. It was going to be a long rest of the night, he could see. Might as well settle in and accept it.

Before he headed out for a quick shower, just because he could no more stop doing it than a child could stop worrying at a loose tooth with his tongue, he tried shifting to magical sight again. Now that his magic had returned, he still experienced the fleeting terror that it would depart again just as suddenly.

To his relief, though, his aura sprang instantly around his upraised hand. Once again he thought it might be wishful thinking, but it did seem stronger than before. Perhaps he should try something a bit more strenuous—lifting one of the lighter dumbbells stacked neatly in racks against one wall, perhaps—to see how hard that might be.

As he turned toward them, magical sight still active, he thought he glimpsed movement off to his left.

He tensed, whipping his head around. Was someone else here? Had Karol come in for a late-night workout when he wasn't paying attention, or had Anzo rolled in to deliver some message?

But no—the place seemed as deserted as it had before, silent and shadowy with only a few of the lights turned on.

"Hello?" Stone called. "Is someone there?"

No answer. The only sound was his own breathing.

"Karol? Harrison?"

Nothing.

He'd dropped magical sight when he'd turned his head. Now, he held his breath and shifted over again, feeling a bit stupid. He doubted Harrison's high-tech gym was haunted, or that anyone was lurking around invisibly watching him exercise. He wasn't *that* vain.

There it was again.

This time he saw it more clearly: the shadowy, indistinct form of a figure moving across the floor.

He tensed, trying to focus in more closely on it, afraid to take his gaze off it for fear it would disappear again.

The figure flickered and faded. *What the hell—?*

Stone took a few deep breaths and forced himself to relax. *Nobody's in here. You're tired, you've had too much to drink—you're seeing things. Just go back to your room and try to get some sleep.*

It was good advice. He probably should have listened to it.

Instead, he sat down on a nearby bench facing back into the gym instead of toward the mirror, took a few more centering breaths to calm himself, and shifted his sight once more.

This time he saw more of them. They were all around him—flickering, shadowy, barely there, but definitely moving. One of them appeared to be running on one of the treadmills, while another stood only a few feet away from Stone, flexing its spectral biceps in the mirror.

This time, Stone didn't drop the sight, and he kept his breathing steady and his nerves calm. Instead of focusing on a single one of the figures, he tried to take them in as a group. A favorite phrase of his old university physics professor popped into his head suddenly: *the act of observing disturbs the observed.* Perhaps by devoting too much attention to an individual figure, he'd somehow frighten it off.

But what *were* the observed? What were these odd figures flitting around in what should be a deserted gym on another dimension? *Were* there ghosts, or echoes, or something similar, on Calanar? He realized he had no idea—until earlier this evening, he hadn't had access to magic here. For all he knew, there could have been ghostly entities all over the place, moving on their unseen errands while he remained oblivious to their presence.

He made a mental note to ask Harrison about it tomorrow. If nothing else, he'd want to know about potential intruders if he wasn't aware of them. Picking up his towel again he rose, about to switch magical sight off again, when something else caught his eye.

Wait.

No, that was just too absurd.

Was one of the ghostly figures wearing a—Mickey Mouse T-shirt?

He spotted it for only a second before the figure turned away, but he was sure he'd seen the character's familiar round, black ears and red shorts.

At least he *thought* he was sure.

His head made a warning throb; he recognized the feeling instantly as the leading edge of magical fatigue. His wisest decision would be to stop trying to use magical sight, go take a hot shower, and go back to bed.

He couldn't resist one more look, though. He got up and followed the figure in the Mickey shirt, glancing at it out of the corner of his eye so he didn't startle it into disappearing.

It crossed the gym and stopped at one of the bikes, paused for a long drink from its ghostly water bottle, then climbed on and began spinning. So far, it seemed not to have noticed Stone.

He edged around, still avoiding a direct gaze until he was in position. His head throbbed again; he couldn't keep this up much longer or he'd risk sabotaging his real lesson tomorrow.

Just one quick look…

Moving casually, he sidled to the front of the bike, which faced the window looking out over the moonlit land behind the tower. Then, before the thing could become aware of his presence, he jerked his head sideways and focused on it head-on.

In the couple of seconds before it flickered and faded, he saw it with unmistakable clarity.

The person—it looked like a young woman—wore a gray T-shirt. Mickey, in the classic pose familiar to anyone older than a toddler, regarded him with an ever-present cheery grin. Stone even thought he could make out the word *Disney-land* below it before the figure juddered and faded.

The bike itself hadn't moved, of course, though he was sure he'd seen the woman pedaling.

"Bloody hell…" he murmured.

That was it. Time for bed, whether he could sleep or not. Suddenly, he had no desire to be watched by a fleet of ghosts, no matter where they'd come from—even if they were only in his mind.

CHAPTER THIRTY-ONE

THE NEXT MORNING, Anzo showed up early. "I've come to take you to Mr. Harrison," he announced when Stone opened the door.

He was ready, though he still felt like something soft and heavy was perched atop his head. He'd managed to sleep for a couple hours, but moved like a zombie when he dragged himself out of bed and into the shower shortly after sunrise. One thing he missed most about Earth was the weapons-grade coffee he preferred—the stuff he didn't consider potent enough unless it stripped the coating off its container. He added asking about getting some proper coffee to his collection of mental notes, but right now it occupied a low point on his priority list. "Coming, coming," he grumbled, but already the prospect of finally getting his magic sorted out had begun to perk him up.

This time, the teleportation pad deposited them in a different part of the tower—Stone was getting a bit more adept at noticing subtle variations in the hallways, and he hadn't seen this one before.

Anzo stopped in front of another set of featureless double doors. "Mr. Harrison is waiting for you inside."

This time, Stone did knock. After only a few seconds, the doors swung open to reveal a large, nearly empty room with no windows. It wasn't nearly as big as the hangar last night had been, but its ceiling did rise higher than a standard room. The only furniture consisted of a long table with no chairs at the other end, and a large board, shiny black but with the smooth surface of a whiteboard, behind it. Several objects Stone couldn't identify were spread out along the table, covered with a cloth.

Harrison stood in front of it, dressed once again in more characteristic tailored black trousers and crisp slate-gray shirt. "Good morning, Dr. Stone. I trust you slept well."

"Slept like rubbish, if you want the truth. But that's all right." He took a quick glance at Harrison's aura; it looked as normal as it ever did, with no sign of the disturbance from last night. "If you're ready, I'm ready. Let's get started. But I've got a question for you first, if you don't mind."

"What is that?"

Stone began to pace, heading generally toward Harrison. "Last night when I couldn't sleep, I popped down to the gym for a workout, thinking it might help tire me out. It didn't—at least not the way I hoped—but I saw something while I was there. I'm hoping you can explain it, because I'm still not convinced I wasn't going mad."

Harrison's eyebrow rose. "What did you see?"

"Ghosts. Echoes. At least that's what they looked like. Nearly transparent figures wandering around the gym—in fact, the oddest part was that it seemed they belonged there. One of them was on an exercise bike, and another jogging on a treadmill. And as if that wasn't strange enough, one of them was wearing a Mickey Mouse T-shirt. Unless you're importing fashions from Disneyland, I doubt that's something that evolved around here. So I was hoping you—what?"

Stone stopped when he noticed Harrison was regarding him with far more intensity than he had been a moment ago. "Is something wrong?"

"How did you see these figures?" Harrison asked. "Were you attempting magical sight again?"

"I was. No point in denying it. Sorry if that goes against some rule, but you can hardly blame me."

It didn't appear that Harrison was blaming him for anything, though. He looked thoughtful, though the focus of his gaze didn't waver. "Attempt magical sight now, Dr. Stone," he said.

"Er—right. But if you could—"

"Please. Tell me what you see."

Stone narrowed his eyes, but decided not to protest. Instead, he shifted to his magical senses and looked around the room.

At first, he saw nothing except his own aura and Harrison's. The room appeared as empty as it did to normal sight, save for the table and board at the front. But as he looked around, other faint shapes shimmered into being. They weren't moving, and didn't appear alive; after a few more moments, he realized they were rows of chairs, set up facing the front table with a wide aisle between them. They were even less substantial than the figures he'd seen in the gym, to the point that they faded as soon as he wasn't looking directly at them.

He shifted back, blinking in confusion.

"What did you see?" Harrison asked calmly.

"I—didn't see any of the echoes this time. But I did see *something*. If I didn't know better, I'd say it looked like the room was full of chairs."

"Chairs."

"All lined up in rows, facing the front table there. Sort of like…a seminar room. Come on, Mr. Harrison—tell me I'm not seeing things."

"You are not seeing things, Dr. Stone. Although it surprises me that you were able to see anything at all."

"Why?" Stone narrowed his eyes. "You can see them too, can't you?"

"Of course."

"Can anyone else? Other mages?"

"I have never encountered anyone else who can—or at least if they have, they haven't spoken of it. But that too doesn't surprise me."

"Why not? What's different about us?"

Harrison gave him a challenging look.

"Wait," Stone said, catching on. "This has something to do with the fact that you and I both have ties to Earth?"

"Precisely."

"But…why should that matter?"

"It matters a great deal. Come here, please. Stand behind this table, and I will demonstrate." Harrison moved around the table as well, facing out toward the empty hall.

Suspicious, Stone joined him. "What are you—"

Harrison fixed his gaze out over the room, appearing to scan it from one side to the other. Then he concentrated for a moment, and the area beyond the table shifted.

"Bloody…hell…" Stone whispered.

All across the hall in front of him, rows of gray-padded chairs shimmered into existence. They looked exactly as Stone had seen them with magical sight, except that now they were as solid and substantial as he himself was.

"What…the hell—?" He wheeled on Harrison. "Invisibility?" But even as he said it, he didn't think it was true. He'd walked around the room only a few moments ago. Invisibility could fool the senses, but it couldn't make something insubstantial. It was also one of the hardest spells to maintain—most mages found rendering even themselves invisible to be taxing, let alone a whole room full of furniture.

"No. Nor is it illusion. The chairs are there. If you don't believe me, check for yourself."

Stone walked back around the table and approached the first row of chairs. He gripped one, and when it felt solid, he picked it up. If this was some kind of trick, it was a masterful one. Magical sight revealed nothing unusual—it looked like a normal, mundane conference-room chair. He didn't see any sign of the echoes he'd spotted before; by everything he could see, the physical chairs had taken their place.

He set it back down and stared at Harrison. "All right—I'll bite. You've got me stumped. How are you doing this?"

The chairs faded, leaving the room empty again except for the table and the covered objects upon it. Harrison paced behind the table as he spoke. "Calanar is a small dimension, Dr. Stone. You might even call it a 'pocket dimension,' though by that standard it is quite expansive. However, compared to Earth, as I'm sure you have surmised, it is orders of magnitude more highly magical."

"Yes, I'd worked that bit out."

Harrison picked up a marker and sketched an irregular shape on the board. It showed up bright yellow against the board's black. "This is a rough map of Calanar." Around the shape, near the coastlines, he made five *Xs*—one each on the east and west edges, one at the top, and two at the bottom. "These are the floating cities."

Stone moved forward, watching with interest. "Which one is Temolan?"

Harrison pointed at the lower right-side *X*, then drew another irregular shape around it, stretching out for some distance on either side of it. "This is Drendell, below Temolan."

Next, he drew several lines between all of the cities. When he finished, they formed a bordered star shape, with lines connecting each city to its four counterparts. "You will be familiar with this part," he said.

Stone frowned. "Ley lines?"

"Yes. A network of ley lines connects each of the cities to the others—that is how the residents can travel between them using the teleportation network. The ley lines here are far more potent than they are on Earth, and the mages in the cities have spent a great deal of effort augmenting and learning how to manipulate them."

"That's fascinating," Stone said, and he wasn't lying. He would like very much to have the time to study all of this—but not now. "But what's this got to do with the chairs?"

Once again, Harrison shot him a challenging look. "You are not asking the correct questions, Dr. Stone."

Stone almost protested, but then he got it. "Where are you in all this? Where's this tower?"

Harrison offered him the marker. "It should not be difficult for you to answer that yourself, if you've been paying attention."

Damn, this man must have been taking lessons from William Desmond, his old master. Stone took the marker and studied the map a moment, then remembered Errin's words on the walk they'd taken his first day here. "Ah. Of course." He stepped forward and drew another *X,* this one in the center of the map in the space bounded by the crisscrossed ley lines.

"Very good." Harrison took another marker from the tray and outlined the space enclosed between the intersecting lines at the center of the star in glowing green. "This location was not chosen at random. Errin mentioned that she told you about the war, and about Argana."

"Yes—the sixth mage city that was destroyed in the war."

Harrison's hand tightened on the marker, just a bit. "Yes. Prior to the war there were other cities, many of them, all interconnected by ley lines. But the levels of magical energy used by the various combatants during the war warped many of them, resulting in the vast, nearly unlivable areas in the continent's center and leading to the creation of the floating cities." He put the marker back in the tray.

"So the tower here is where Argana used to be?"

"Not precisely. Argana itself is gone—vaporized during the war. The vast majority of its residents were killed, and those who survived were almost all absorbed into the other mage houses, forced to renounce allegiance to Argana and ally themselves with their new homes. All of this happened many years ago."

"Errin said the war happened before anyone alive was born." Stone tilted his head. "You must be a *lot* older than you look, then."

When Harrison didn't answer that, Stone studied the map again. "So you built the tower in this space between the ley lines? *Did* you build it, or did someone else? Errin called it 'your tower.'"

"The area enclosed by the ley lines," Harrison said, once again ignoring Stone's question, "is something I am certain none of the mages in the coastal cities ever suspected. Because it is all but impossible for any of them to travel in the Wastes—as far as I have ever heard, none of them even try any longer after so many were lost during early attempts— they have no way to discover one of the side effects of their efforts."

"Which is?"

"Put crudely—I can explain it to you in more detail if you wish, but some other time—the ley-line boundaries form a natural pool, where magic accumulates. Think of it as a section of a river where protruding rock formations disrupt the flow. The effect is that this area is even more profoundly magical than the rest of the continent. That is one of the reasons your body acclimated itself to the magic more quickly here than it would have if you had remained in Temolan. The cities' ley-line intersection points are also powerful magical areas, but the energy here is…unique. More potent and stable than anywhere else in Calanar."

Stone shifted to magical sight again, wondering for a moment why he hadn't noticed the ley lines, but then the answer came to him. "So…you're not located at a confluence of ley lines here, but in sort of a—magical pool *between* them?"

"Yes." Harrison nodded approval.

"But that still doesn't explain the tower. It looks a bit like the Obsidian—is that a coincidence, or do you just have a thing for tall black towers?"

"It is not a coincidence. They are the same place."

Stone stopped his pacing and stared at him. "What?"

"The tower here and the Obsidian in Las Vegas are the same place, occupying space in multiple dimensions."

"Now you *are* having me on. That's impossible."

In answer, Harrison indicated the open area. The chairs reappeared, remained for a few seconds, and then disappeared again.

Stone's brain refused to process this new information. For several moments he alternated between gaping at the space where the chairs had been and back at Harrison. "But—you can't—it's not—"

"Normally, you would be correct," Harrison said. "This location presents unique opportunities."

"So…that's why you call it the Nexus? Because it's—what—sharing space in more than one physical location?"

"Yes. The tower itself exists in multiple places simultaneously. As for the interior spaces—"

"Wait," Stone interrupted, remembering the gym. "So you're telling me that the people I saw in the gym last night—"

"Were actually in its counterpart at the Obsidian. It is more difficult to maintain the interior locations in multiple dimensional spaces—it requires more energy, so only a few of them are permanently set up to do so. My suite is one of them. Normally even the gym is confined to its Earth location—I altered parts of it during your stay here, along with your suite, so you would have unrestricted access."

"And…" Stone had to push to get the words out; he felt stunned, as if someone had just punched him in the gut. "You can't do this with people, can you?"

"No. At least at my current level of magical ability, I haven't found it possible for a living being to exist in more than one dimensional space at the same time. But it is quite possible to shift between them."

"Aha!" Stone said in triumph, pointing at him. "So that's how you got out of the Evil's dimension?"

"Yes. I have attuned myself to this location, which permits me to return here from any other location—not simply one that occupies concurrent space with it on another dimension."

Stone didn't think he'd blinked since Harrison had dropped this bombshell. He did now, and swallowed. "This is…bloody *amazing,*" he said. "But what about the airship—the workshop? Surely you don't have an airship in your garage in Las Vegas?"

"At the Obsidian, the workshop is part of the underground parking garage. The airship and other projects exist here, but not there."

"I—I don't know what to say." Stone looked around the room again. It must have been a conference room back in Las Vegas. "Does anyone else know about this? Here or on Earth?"

"Errin knows in general terms, and Kira has accompanied me to Earth for a brief time. Neither of them knows precisely how the tower functions—Kira is a talented mage, but she doesn't have the ability to travel there on her own. And Errin—she is a genius with things mechanical, but lacks the necessary magical concepts to comprehend all the nuances. She is fascinated by the technology I have brought to the tower, though, and has already made significant progress in studying electronics."

"But she doesn't know where you've brought it *from*."

"Not specifically, no. That is something I don't reveal, even to those I trust implicitly. If it should ever fall into the wrong hands, it could prove disastrous."

"But yet you've revealed it to me. And you barely know me."

"You have told me, Dr. Stone, that your objective is to learn my magical methods, at which time you will return to Earth. Is that no longer true?"

"No, no—it's quite true. As I said before—this is all fascinating as hell, and I hope I'll get the chance to discuss it with you at greater length…some other time. After I've had a chance to settle back in to my life at home and assure everyone I'm alive and well." A thought struck him. "When I learn to handle this power—will I be able to come back here on my own?"

Harrison considered. "Potentially," he said at last. "You did manage to find your way here before, so I have no reason to believe you could not do it again. You wouldn't be able to come *here*—not to the Nexus, or anywhere else in New Argana—without my consent. The magical protections are far too formidable. But you could probably do as you did before."

"But would I be in the same situation? Without my magic until I'm acclimated? Or does the acclimation stay effective? I wouldn't fancy turning up in Temolan without magic—those bastards almost killed me last time, and I've no reason to believe I'd be that lucky a second time."

"I don't know the answer to that. It is something that might be worth study—but that might not be necessary."

"Why not?"

Harrison waved off the question. "First things first, Dr. Stone. You must learn to control the power before you can experiment with it. Shall we begin?"

Stone didn't even mind being dismissed this time. Harrison was right—as insistent as they were, the dozens of questions currently multiplying inside his head could all wait until later. The magic was the important thing. "Let's do it. What do I need to do?"

Harrison returned to the board. With a wave of his hand, the map of Calanar disappeared. "You did an admirable job with the notes I sent you. As I said before, I didn't expect you to."

"Well, first I had to get past the fact that you're the only person I've ever met who writes more illegibly than I do," Stone said dryly. "After that, it was all downhill."

"I deliberately sent you only the rudiments," Harrison continued, ignoring Stone's words. "If you could not comprehend those, no chance existed that you could progress further."

"Is that how people learn magic here?" Stone leaned against the table, arms crossed. "That lot back in Temolan hardly seemed like they'd be willing to put in that kind of effort."

"They would not. Most of them rarely expend effort for anything, if they can avoid it."

Stone blinked. Had he actually heard an edge to Harrison's normally calm tones? "You're not fond of them, then?"

"You have seen them, Dr. Stone. What do you think?"

"Honestly, I wasn't sure at first. Remember, I don't know you very well—and there was that matter with those survivalists out in the desert. For a while at first, I wondered if you were somehow connected to the mages in the cities. I was afraid I might find you in Temolan, wearing one of those ridiculous outfits and terrorizing the mundanes." Before Harrison could speak, he raised a hand. "But that didn't last long. You can be a hard-arse, true, but I've never seen you show outright cruelty. And anyone who'd be willing to do what you did with that portal—well, there didn't seem to be much common ground between you and the 'Talented.'" He put contemptuous finger quotes around the words.

"To answer your question—no, that is not how they learn magic. Remember, they are native to this dimension, so the process of acclimation is not necessary. They are also not attempting to access the energy across dimensions. Most of the information I sent you concerned itself with how to do that. The actual magic is secondary, and has little to do with the power source. Each mage's potential is different, and consists of a combination of inherent power level, and learned skill."

Stone tilted his head. "So it's a bit like cars, then: an economy car and a Ferrari both run on the same power source, but the Ferrari can do more with it."

"And the Ferrari begins with more of it," Harrison said. "It is a flawed analogy, but it will do as a start." He turned back to the board and begin dashing off figures. "Where you are fortunate, though, is that I do not need to teach you magic. You already know magic—probably better than I do, since your training was more formalized and structured. What you must learn to use this energy source is how to tap it safely." He stepped back. "Do you remember this?"

Stone studied the figures, trying to make sense of Harrison's rapid scrawl. "Yes. That's the gist of what you sent me in the notebook. The equations describing this dimension's location."

"Yes."

"Was there something wrong with the formulae, or with how I interpreted it? Is that why I was able to reach the energy, but it burned me out when I used it?"

"No. I did make an error, but not in the formulae. I failed to account for acclimation. Remember, I have never dealt with anyone with no connection to Calanar attempting this."

"You mentioned that," Stone said. "If you don't mind my asking—what's your connection to this place? You said before you weren't 'fully of Earth.' You certainly seem a lot closer to Earth people than you do to the others I've met here."

"I am half Calanarian." Harrison didn't turn back from the board. "My mother was a native of this dimension, and my father of Earth."

"Indeed?" Stone asked, surprised. "So someone else found this place? Or did your mum find Earth?"

Harrison seemed to tense for a moment, but then resumed writing on the board. "The lack of acclimation no doubt resulted in the issues you experienced. Because your body was unfamiliar with the energy you were asking it to channel, it overwhelmed your magical pathways. The time you spent here should alleviate that."

"You're not going to tell me, then. That's fine—I shouldn't have asked. So—why wasn't I able to do anything when I got here? Even on Earth, without this acclimation, I could still use the energy, even if it burned me out. Here, I couldn't even do *that*."

Harrison made an adjustment to one of the equations, then wrote another one below it and stepped aside. "Based on this, can you answer your own question?"

Stone once again studied the scrawls. Harrison might claim not to be a teacher, but it was exactly the way he himself would have treated an apprentice. It was always easier to impart information to someone if you made them figure it out themselves than if you told them directly. "Wait…" he said slowly. "I think I see it. The first formula shows how to reach this dimension from Earth. It's a bit like a map. But I still don't quite see—"

"You are close, Dr. Stone. Think of it more as a switchboard than a map."

"Ah!" Stone grinned in triumph. "I see it now. The notebook you sent me showed me the direct connection between my dimension and this one. It was sort of—hard-wired. So when I used the same principle to try reaching Calanar's energy *from* Calanar, it didn't work because my starting point was wrong."

"Well done." Harrison pointed at the second formula. "And this one?"

It looked similar to the first one, with a couple of significant differences. Stone pushed off the table and moved in closer, restless with anticipation. "Yes…yes! You've altered the variables—instead of Earth's dimensional space pointing at Calanar's, this one is Calanar-specific."

"Yes."

Stone could hardly bear to hope. "Bloody hell…that's all it is? That's all I need?"

"Try it." Harrison swept a hand and the cover lifted off the table, revealing a number of items: a large rock, a book, a stack of papers, a couple of heavy dumbbells from the gym, and a basket of various-sized metal spheres. "Begin by levitating the book."

Stone drew a couple of centering breaths, took one more look at the equation, and then, heart pounding, faced the book on the table. He visualized the pattern in his mind, the same way he did as second nature back on Earth when he did magic, but updated it using the new information Harrison had given him.

"Here goes…" he muttered, and released the power.

The book lifted neatly off the table.

Stone sagged back, momentarily overwhelmed. *Yes!* After nearly two months without it, he was doing proper magic again, and it felt *wonderful!* He didn't even care that as soon as he lost concentration, the book crashed back to the table.

He grinned at Harrison, likewise not caring whether he looked as giddy as the most callow of apprentices after his first successful spellcasting.

But then he sobered. Sure, he'd done magic using the Calanarian energy source—once. But he'd done that before, and every other time the single effort had burned him out. Holding his breath, he faced the book again and focused.

Once more, it rose from the table and hovered there.

"Oh, that's brilliant…" he whispered. This time he managed to hold it in place. The power came easily, effortlessly.

"Take it slowly," Harrison said. "Your body is still getting used to the power."

"Will it burn me out again if I use too much?" Now that he had his power back, the thought of losing it again was more than he could handle.

"Unlikely, but I suggest moderation, at least at first. Think of this in the same way as your workouts: you have to build the muscles before putting them under load. The healing machine can't help you in this area."

"Got it. Take it easy for a while. I can do that."

"Judging by your current performance, I don't think it will take you long." Harrison moved to the end of the table. "Try a shield."

It took Stone a moment—using the new power source for anything but 'spray things with a firehose' while simultaneously calling up the pattern for a spell was still a bit like trying to juggle chainsaws—but after a moment his usual shimmering shield flared around him. Maintaining it seemed to take less effort than it had on Earth; he wondered if it was because Calanar was so much more magical, or because this energy source was inherently more efficient than either black or white magic.

Something slammed into the shield. Startled, he barely held it firm as a second missile hit it. Harrison was using magic to fling the metal spheres from the bowl at him at high speed.

Now that he was expecting it, Stone had no trouble keeping the shield at full strength. "Throw the rock," he challenged, pointing at it on the table. The thing looked like it weighed at least twenty pounds—it would either be a good test for him or he'd have to allow time for another session with the healing machine.

Harrison didn't hesitate. The rock lifted from the table and rocketed toward the shield.

And bounced off.

Harrison caught it before it reached the floor, but Stone barely noticed. He was staring in wonder at the spot where it had hit.

That rock might not have demolished his shield back on Earth—at least not the black-magic version. After all, he'd managed to use one to contain the detonation of a small bomb only a couple of months ago. But even that had been at a cost: the psychic feedback had nearly wiped him out. Now, as Harrison sent the rock back to its place on the table, Stone didn't even feel a faint warning pain.

"This is amazing…" he said, shaking his head.

Harrison put him through several more exercises: manipulating the various spheres independently while keeping them afloat; using delicate control to page through the book; lifting the dumbbells and moving them around the room; vaporizing the sheaf of papers with a blast of fire. They kept at it for over two hours, and each time Stone performed the requested action with little effort. He grinned the whole time, feeling like a child who'd just gotten all his favorite toys restored after losing them to a long-term punishment.

"Are you experiencing any fatigue?" Harrison asked at one point.

"A bit," he admitted. "But nowhere near what I'd have on Earth, at this level of sustained magical expenditure." It was true—black and white magic both had their advantages, but both eventually tired him if he used too much without resting. Now, after two hours of near-constant casting, he felt about as tired as he might if he'd walked a few blocks at a brisk pace. It was exhilarating.

"Excellent."

Stone glanced at the board again. "I still can't quite get my mind around the fact that it's so simple. It seems a bit...anticlimactic, to be honest. After all that time you had me carrying rocks and lifting weights, I thought the actual magic would be a bit more difficult."

"I caution you not to overexert yourself," Harrison reminded him. "It might seem easy, but you are still training. That was what I meant when I said it isn't as simple as flipping a switch. Fortunately, since you are already well accustomed to handling magical energy, the adjustment period should be brief. We will leave it here for now, I think—we will have another session tomorrow. Until then, practice these techniques and any others you want to try, but be mindful of fatigue. Give yourself time to rest."

"Absolutely," Stone said. "I feel like I could do this all day."

"Good day, Dr. Stone. I will see you tomorrow."

Stone watched him head for the door. "Mr. Harrison?" he called.

"Yes?"

"Will I be able to do this when I get back to Earth? The same power level I had before? Will it be this easy?"

Harrison considered. "I have not seen your full power level yet, so I can't answer that question. I suspect there will be some attenuation when you return home, but I have no reason to believe it will be significant."

"Brilliant. Thank you. For—well—everything." Stone's voice shook a little, but he did nothing to stop it. He'd almost accepted that his mad plan of coming here and learning Harrison's magic would end in failure and despair—but now, for the first time in weeks, he could see the end. If he progressed as fast as Harrison seemed to think he would, he could be back on Earth by the end of the week.

Back to his life.

Right now, even the prospect of having to explain where the hell he'd been for the last two months didn't daunt him. He'd figure something out.

CHAPTER THIRTY-TWO

STONE TRIED TO HEED HARRISON'S ADVICE for the remainder of the day, but he could no more fail to take his newfound powers out for a test drive than he could have sprouted wings and flown to the moon. His only concession was that he did allow frequent rest breaks, waiting for the tiredness to settle before beginning again.

He tested various magical techniques, taking a notebook with him and keeping notes about his relative ability level compared to what he could do on Earth. What he discovered delighted him: in every case he could measure, it seemed he not only had greater raw power, but his control and endurance had likewise taken a significant jump. Even if the "attenuation" Harrison mentioned lowered his abilities' potency once he got back home, he'd still see a measurable increase.

The best part was, aside from the mild fatigue he expected, the magic didn't tire him as it had before. When he'd been a white mage, he had to be careful to either stick to slow-acting, ritual-based magic, remember to charge up his power objects for extra punch, or accept that some techniques would take their toll on him. As a black mage he'd had access to more immediate punch, but at the cost of having to take power from other people—either using the dull but dependable method with Jason, or the more exhilarating but potentially dangerous method with anyone else. Both the white and black techniques had their advantages and disadvantages, which their respective practitioners learned to deal with because they had no other choice.

This method, though, didn't suffer from either of those problems. The power was there, all the time—Calanar brimmed with magical energy, to the point where the difficult part wasn't gathering enough, but learning to control and channel it so it didn't overwhelm him. He wouldn't have to take it from anyone or generate it himself—as long as he had access to Calanar and his body held up, he'd have the magic.

He discovered one fact quickly: his relative skill levels stayed constant. The spells he was good at on Earth, like levitation and shields, remained comparatively strong here. Those he was weaker with, such as invisibility, likewise remained problematic—when he attempted to see how long he could stay invisible before growing too tired to maintain the spell any longer, he lasted only three minutes. That was an improvement over what he could do on Earth, but not much of one, and he had to rest longer afterward. Although he didn't test it by deliberately injuring himself, he suspected his lackluster healing skills wouldn't benefit much from a Calanarian infusion either.

That was all right, though—he hardly expected everything to improve. Hell, even if he got back to Earth and discovered he was no more powerful than he'd been before, the mere fact that he had a steady, readily-available source for his magic that he didn't have to risk injuring anyone to access was more than he could have hoped for. The rest would sort itself out when he got home.

He wished he didn't have to wait until tomorrow to have another lesson. Would Harrison even have anything new to show him? It seemed he'd gotten what he needed—the ability to access the Calanarian magical source. Now, all he had to do was refine it. Harrison himself had said there probably wasn't anything else he could teach Stone about magic.

As he sat on the sofa in his suite and stared out over the darkened, panoramic view, a sudden wave of homesickness so strong it was almost a physical sensation crested over him. Homesickness was nothing new, of course—before, he'd occasionally caught himself missing the big things about his life on Earth: Verity and Jason, his work, Aubrey, Raider. Now, though, even the smaller bits ached: jamming with The Cardinal Sin, going to the pub with Eddie Monkton and Arthur Ward back in London—hell, he even had an irresistible jones for a big order of chicken tikka from A Passage to India, along with a double-sized cup of strong, hot coffee.

He got up and pressed his hands to the glass, leaning into it until his forehead rested against the cold, smooth surface.

What am I doing here anymore?

It was a fair question. The place was fascinating, to be sure: magical innovation back on Earth was nowhere near as advanced as it was here, and he yearned to study it. How could he find out teleportation existed and not want to learn how it worked? How could he know it was possible to combine magic with technology and not want to delve into how he could do the same? Especially now that his own magic functioned again, his curiosity nearly overwhelmed him. He could spend years studying this stuff.

But not now.

He pushed off the window, coming to a decision.

He had what he needed now—the rest would come later.

Or it wouldn't, if Harrison wouldn't allow him to come back here after returning to Earth.

To his surprise, he found he didn't care either way.

"Anzo?" he called.

The little construct rolled into view. "Is there something you require?"

"Do you know where Mr. Harrison is?"

Anzo's blue eyes flashed in their *seeking information* pattern. "Mr. Harrison's location is not available."

"He's not here?"

"My programming does not permit me to reveal his location to others without permission at this time."

Well, bugger. "What about Errin? Or Kira? Are they here?"

"Kira does not wish to be disturbed. Errin is in the downstairs work area."

Maybe she had a way to contact Harrison. He could wait until tomorrow, of course, but he had to at least try. "Can you take me to Errin?"

"This way."

A few moments later, he stood in front of the same double doors where he'd met Harrison previously. "Thank you, Anzo. I'll take it from here."

Anzo's eyes flashed acknowledgment and he rolled off.

Stone pushed the door open and stepped once more into the cavernous workroom. As before, the first thing he noticed was the music, but this time it wasn't Beethoven. It sounded like some kind of driving instrumental rock piece, but with instruments he didn't recognize and had never heard before.

"Errin?" he called, but his voice didn't reach above the sound.

He ventured further into the space, which was as dimly lit as it had been before. The half-skeletal form of the airship rose in front of him, dominating the area with the scattered other projects arrayed around it. He saw no sign of her yet, but then remembered what Harrison had said about needing to finish something so Errin could work on it. He walked over to the ship and poked his head in through one of the openings. "Errin? Are you in here?"

The driving beat ceased, and a figure stepped around the massive engine. "Alastair! I didn't expect to see you here." She brushed strands of hair off her forehead as she approached. "What can I do for you?"

She was dressed in a style similar to Harrison's when he'd been here, with work pants and heavy boots; instead of a tank top she wore a blue T-shirt under a multi-pocketed black vest, and instead of a wrench poking out of her pocket she had an entire leather tool belt slung low around her waist. She'd pulled her long, dark hair back into a loose ponytail under a cap with a bright miner's lamp strapped around it. She switched it off as she drew next to Stone.

"I'm looking for Mr. Harrison. Anzo says he can't tell me where he is, but I was hoping you could reach him."

"Is something wrong?" She pulled off her leather work gloves and stashed them in one of the toolbelt's pockets.

"No—nothing's wrong. I just wanted to ask him something."

R. L. KING

"Anything I can help you with? I think he's busy going over some things with Kira tonight." She grinned. "Mage stuff. I don't ask."

Stone must have looked skeptical, because shook her head, chuckling. "No, seriously. I just realized how that might have sounded to somebody who doesn't know them very well. Kira isn't much into that kind of thing, and Trevor—well, I don't ask that either. None of my business."

"It's all right," he said. "And I suppose I can wait until the morning." He nodded toward the airship. "Did you sort out your problem with the magical interface?"

"Ah, he told you about that? Yes, it's all good now. Congratulations on getting your magic back, by the way. That must feel good."

"It feels brilliant." He glanced over his shoulder toward the entrance. "I won't bother you, then—I'll talk to Harrison tomorrow."

"You're not bothering me." She tilted her head. "In fact, you can help me, if you're willing."

"Help you? How? Trust me, you don't want me anywhere near delicate machinery. My mechanical skills are legendary in their nonexistence."

"Don't worry. I'm not asking you to fix anything. But I need some magical power, and with Trevor and Kira both busy, I thought I'd have to wait until tomorrow too."

"Er—of course I'll help, if I can." Intrigued, Stone stepped in through the opening. "What do you need? I warn you, I'm still getting used to having magic again, so my power's a bit spotty."

"Not a problem. This is brute-force stuff, not finesse. Come on." She disappeared around the side of the engine.

Stone followed, and found her standing in front of a large open panel. Inside, a series of intricate workings hummed softly. When he shifted to magical sight, he wasn't surprised to see the flickers of arcane residue around it. It didn't look like the aura of a living thing, though it had characteristics in common with one. More like the leftover energy one might encounter in an area where someone had been using significant magic in the recent past. "What do you want me to do?"

"I had to shut it down to work on it, so I need a solid jolt of magic to get it back online again. Normally Trevor does it—once it's running it takes power from the ambient magical energy, but it needs something to get it moving when it's stopped."

"Ah. Sort of like a magical jump-start."

She gave him a sideways glance. "I've never heard that term, but it sounds right. Anyway, thank you for helping out. Come over here, in front of this panel."

When he did, she pointed inside. "See that chamber there, with the metal rod inside it?"

"Yes."

"The cylindrical chamber is made of a highly magic-resistant metal. The rod inside is particularly sensitive to magical energy."

"Ah, I see," Stone said, studying the apparatus. "You generate a magical charge inside the chamber, and then it kick-starts some sort of reaction that directs the energy up to power the rest of the mechanism?"

"Exactly," she said with approval. "Maybe you're not as hopeless as you thought you were."

"Oh, understanding the principle isn't the issue. It's the practical part I'm rubbish at."

"Well, it's a start, anyway. What I want you to do is grip the rod, then channel raw magical energy into it through your hands." She faced him again, looking serious. "Are you sure you're ready for this? Trevor said you'd just started working with your magic today. I don't want to cause any setbacks."

"No, no, it's fine. I've been practicing all day. You're sure this isn't going to explode on me or anything?"

She laughed. "No, no, it's quite safe. This is just a bigger version of the engines that power the ground vehicles around here."

Stone stepped forward and gripped the shining metal rod with both hands. "Say when."

Errin clamped a pair of leads to something at the base of the rod, then backed off holding a small box attached to it with a pair of wires. "Whenever you're ready. Just give it a good jolt. You'll know it worked when the whole thing starts humming."

Stone focused, shifted to magical sight, and released the energy through his hands. This sort of thing was easier than most of his spellcasting, since it didn't require any sort of pattern to transform the power. It crackled around his hands, radiating outward in a brilliant splash of color. First the rod and then the entire machine began vibrating with a low, thrumming hum.

"That's it," Errin called. "You can stop now. That's got it."

Stone let go and took a few steps back. The engine continued humming along, surprisingly quiet for something so large and intricate, but the rumbling coming up through the floor gave the definite impression of power.

Errin gripped his arm. "Thank you. Just what I needed." She held up the box, showing Stone a series of meters. "You were generating some serious punch." She flashed him a conspiratorial grin. "More than Kira, though don't tell her I said that."

Stone returned the grin, feeling irrational pride at her words. "Nowhere close to Harrison, I'd imagine, though," he said, deceptively casually.

"Couldn't tell you. I don't use this with him. Not since the first time, when he blew out all my meters." Her sly grin widened. "You men amuse me. Always trying to outperform each other."

"Erm." Stone cast about for a quick change of subject. "Why are you building an airship, anyway? It hardly seems practical to have something this big to get around such a small area. Wouldn't the smaller one be enough?"

"It's an experiment." Errin moved back in to unhook her meter from the engine assembly and close the panel. "Trevor wants something we can use to get across the Wastes."

"Why?" he asked, surprised. "I thought nobody went into the Wastes because it was sort of a magical fallout zone."

"It is, and they don't. Hence the 'experiment' part."

"Sounds dangerous."

"It's—" She paused, glancing back over Stone's shoulder at something. "Excuse me a minute."

Stone turned to see what she was looking at, and was surprised to see Harrison stepping through one of the holes in the hull.

"Ah, you're done early," Errin said. "Did you need something? Alastair's already helped me get the engine started."

Harrison nodded to Stone but quickly turned his attention back to Errin. "We've had a communication from Drendell. Galen says Rovenna from Temolan may be ready to join us."

"Seriously? What changed her mind?"

"He said she watched as two of her acquaintances incinerated three people in Drendell after they failed to get out of the way quickly enough."

Errin's expression hardened. "Nice to see she's got *some* conscience. Do you believe her?"

"I don't know. This month's Underground in Drendell ends tonight. I'm leaving shortly to meet her there and discuss it."

"Yourself?" Anger turned to concern. "Trevor, that's a bad idea. Send Kira."

"Her aura reading isn't strong. I want to be certain before making a decision."

"I'm sorry," Stone put in; it seemed they'd forgotten his presence. "If you don't mind my asking, what are you talking about? Who is this Rovenna?"

"She is a high-ranking official in Temolan," Harrison said. "An aide to one of the Council members. We have long suspected her to be growing dissatisfied with the way the mages treat the non-magical."

"And you think she might want to—what? Defect?"

"That is what I plan to find out."

"What's the Underground?"

"It's a bit like the Arena," Errin said. "Except instead of using people, they use magical constructs. There are quite a number of mechanically talented people in the cities, and there's an underground culture where they work with sympathetic mages to create the constructs and test them against each other. We attend sometimes, because it's a good place to find people who might benefit from coming here."

"You attend these things?" Stone asked Harrison.

"Frequently, using disguises. I spend a significant amount of time in the non-magical cities, searching for like-minded people."

"What about the mage cities?"

"He never goes there," Errin said, her expression darkening again. She turned back to Harrison. "Anyway—let me go, with Kira."

"No. I will go." Harrison's tone suggested he would entertain no arguments. "You can come if you wish, as well, and ask Karol to accompany us." He glanced at Stone. "Forgive me, Dr. Stone, but I must postpone your training for a day or two. Anzo mentioned you were looking for me—is there something I can do for you?"

Stone's thoughts moved fast. Harrison was here now—he could simply do what he'd come here for, tell the man he felt he could take things on his own from here, and ask him to send him home to Earth. He hoped they could talk more at some later date, but even if that ended up not being possible, at least he'd have his magic and his life back. That was what he wanted, right?

But then he pictured the conflagration raging at Faran's shop back in Drendell—the blasted-out space and the sheet-covered body of Runa, who, while she hadn't exactly been kind to him, had treated him fairly. The woman who was dead, along with her husband, due to some sadistic mage's whim.

Because they'd helped him.

"I want to go with you," he said quickly, before he could think too hard about it and reconsider. Even so, some corner of his mind was aghast: *What the hell are you doing? This isn't your fight. Go home where you belong, you idiot!*

Errin looked surprised, and even Harrison showed a fleeting reaction.

"What?" Errin demanded.

"I want to go along with you to Drendell. My magic's doing well, and I've always been strong with auras. I can help."

"Out of the question," Harrison said.

"It's not safe," Errin agreed. "You're supposed to be dead, remember? If they find out you're not—"

"Safe?" Stone snorted. "These bastards have nearly killed me. They've treated me like garbage, killed people who helped me, tossed me into prison for existing, and tried to torture me into giving up what I know about you lot. I haven't been bloody *safe* since I got here. And now I've got a chance to do something worthwhile. I want to take it. You said you've got disguises." He pointed at Harrison. "If you can disguise *him*, you can damned well disguise me."

Harrison regarded him for several silent moments, expressionless, his unblinking gaze even more unsettling than usual. "Why were you looking for me, Dr. Stone? What did you intend to ask me?"

Stone saw no point in lying. "I was going to ask you to send me home. I've been practicing with my magic all day, and I'm sure I've got the principle down. I thought I could take things from there on my own. I wanted to get back to my life."

"But now you have changed your mind?"

"No—I *still* want to get back home. But I've seen what these bastards can do. If I can help get someone out of their clutches, I want to do it. Especially now that I can fight back against them. Please—let me do this. You've seen me in action. You know what I can do. I won't be a liability."

The silence stretched between them as Harrison's gaze still didn't waver. Finally, he inclined his head. "Very well, Dr. Stone. You can accompany us."

"Trevor—" Errin began.

Harrison raised a cautionary hand. "No, Errin. I understand his reasoning—and I *do* know what he is capable of. Can you have our smaller construct ready to transport in an hour?"

She sighed, clearly aware arguing would be useless. "Yes, I'll be ready. Do Karol and Kira know yet?"

"Kira does—she was with me when I got the communication. I will find Karol. Dr. Stone, I must go now. Meet us at the teleportation pad on the lower level in an hour."

"I'll be there."

When Harrison left, Errin sighed. "He can be so damned stubborn sometimes."

"What's the problem?" Stone followed her as she exited the airship and crossed the workspace to where he'd noticed the series of anthropoid structures in various states of repair when he'd first come here. "He's got all kinds of power, doesn't he? I'd be surprised if they could get near him."

"He does, and it wouldn't be easy," she agreed. "But he's wanted in every one of the mage cities. Sometimes I think he takes dangerous chances just because he gets some kind of rush from it. Like he's taunting them." She shrugged. "I get it—I like a rush too. That's why I build machines like this. But there's daring and there's foolish."

"Do you think he's being foolish?" Stone asked. He watched while she selected one of the constructs, a humanoid collection of gears, wires, and shiny metal surfaces about six feet tall, and began tinkering with something in its abdominal area.

"Honestly, no. Rovenna has been making noises about wanting out for a long time, but she's in a difficult spot due to her position. It's entirely possible this latest incident pushed her over the edge, and it makes sense to want to be there to catch her. I just generally like to plan these things a bit better. Doing it on such short notice disturbs me."

"Do you trust this Galen?"

"I do. He's one of our most reliable agents in Drendell. If everything goes well, we can be in and out in a couple of hours. And if we *can* get Rovenna on our side, it will be a big win for us." She pulled a sheaf of wires from the construct's core and examined it. "Everything worthwhile is worth taking risks."

"True indeed," Stone said. "All right—I'll let you get on with what you're doing."

As he left, he couldn't resist glancing back at Errin, and didn't miss her troubled expression as she continued working on her task.

CHAPTER THIRTY-THREE

HALF-CONVINCED HARRISON and the others would leave without him, Stone arrived early at the downstairs teleport pad. He was waiting with Anzo when Errin and Karol arrived, the humanoid construct rolling along behind them. Both of them looked serious, but not tense. Errin wore a black gear bag over her shoulder, and Karol had a backpack.

"Are you sure you want to do this?" Karol asked Stone. "It's not likely to be dangerous, but we can never be certain."

"I want to do it," Stone said firmly. Even though Harrison had mentioned illusions, he'd changed out of his black T-shirt and jeans and into a Calanar-style outfit. "You lot have helped me more than you know—I want to repay the favor."

Harrison shimmered into place on the pad. "Are you all ready?" he asked them without greeting.

When Karol and Errin nodded, he turned to face Stone. "If all goes well, we will only remain for a short time. Please stay close to us, don't reveal your identity to anyone, and don't display any magical abilities unless necessary."

"Don't worry," Stone assured him. "I have no desire to draw attention to myself."

Harrison pulled a handful of small items from his pocket and offered them around.

Stone took one; it was a simple chain-link bracelet. "Illusion generator?"

"Yes." He turned first to Errin, then to Karol, focusing on them for a couple of seconds each. Errin changed from dark-haired and athletic to a shorter, stockier form with shoulder-length, mouse-brown hair. Karol's broad-shouldered, muscular physique morphed into a portly, dark-skinned, middle-aged man with a receding hairline.

"Won't mages be able to penetrate these?" Stone asked, clasping the bracelet around his wrist.

"Not without a great deal of effort," Harrison said. "They are of a more advanced design than those you saw in Las Vegas." He concentrated on Stone for a moment.

"What do I look like? Anybody got a mirror?"

"Boring," Errin said with a grin. "Just the way we like it."

Harrison shifted last, becoming a thoroughly nondescript young man with short, dark-blond hair, drab gray work shirt, and dark pants.

"Where are we meeting Rovenna?" Karol asked. "Is she coming to the Underground?"

"Yes. Galen will bring her."

"Is that safe?" Stone asked. "If it turns out you can't trust her, won't that compromise the location?"

"The Underground's never held at the same place twice," Errin said. "They move around for just that reason."

"Let's go," Harrison said. "Karol and Errin first with the construct. I will follow with Dr. Stone."

All business now, Errin stepped onto the pad and the machine followed her. As soon as Karol joined her, Harrison focused on them and they shimmered out.

"I meant to ask you if you plan to show me how to work these things," Stone said.

"We will discuss that when we return. This one will not function for you as configured, though—only Kira and I have the key." He motioned for Stone to step on.

He did. "You mean leaving this area? Only you and Kira control that?"

"It is a safety measure. The pads are magically keyed only to certain auras." Harrison stepped onto the pad next to Stone.

Once again it seemed as if nothing had happened, except the view suddenly changed from a featureless hallway to a small room with battered wooden walls and no windows. Stone looked down; the only sign of the teleport pad was a stained circular rug on the floor.

Kira and Karol had already stepped aside with the construct, standing near the room's single door.

Harrison moved off the rug and motioned for Stone to do the same. Then he made a brief gesture and the rug flashed green before settling back to its normal, dull pattern. "Remember this location," Harrison told Stone. "The teleport pad here has been attuned to the auras of everyone in our group. If anything goes wrong, get back here and it will return you to the Nexus. If we are temporarily separated and you need to bring anyone with you, have them grasp your bracelet."

"How far is where we're going from this location?" Stone asked.

"The pad is centrally located to most of the Underground venues in Drendell," Errin told him. "We'll only have to go half a mile or so—and we've got a vehicle."

They followed Harrison, with the construct floating along with them, up a flight of stairs that looked rickety but felt solid. Another door opened into a narrow garage, where an enclosed van that seemed like its best days were well behind it waited. Stone couldn't read the writing on the side.

As he climbed into the back with Errin and helped guide the construct to a sitting position, he couldn't help noticing Harrison seemed even more vigilant than usual. In fact, all three of his companions were watching all around them—not nervous or fearful, but definitely paying attention to their surroundings.

"Are you expecting trouble?" he asked, taking a seat behind Karol, who was driving.

"We always expect trouble," Errin told him. "These things usually go fine, but we can't get complacent. There are a lot more of them than there are of us."

Stone settled back and remained silent, memorizing the route they took. This was a different part of Drendell than he'd spent his time in, so nothing looked familiar. He wondered how big the mundanes' city was, and how much of it was inhabited. Several street lights illuminated their way, though more were barely flickering or non-functional. A light, steady rain fell.

Fortunately—especially since Stone still hadn't learned to read the language—their route didn't involve many turns. Only a few minutes later, they were pulling up in front of a looming, shadowy building that looked like a darkened warehouse. At first it didn't appear anyone was there, but after a moment a man stepped out from behind a pile of boxes and ambled up to the driver's-side window. "Can I help you?"

"We've got a delivery," Karol said. "For Loman."

"Ah, right. They're expecting you. Go on in." He pulled open a roll-up door and stood aside.

"Security seems a bit sparse," Stone commented as they rolled through and the man pulled the door back down behind them.

"That's just what you see," Errin said. "They've got lookouts stationed in several points—mages and non-mages—as well as warning wards."

"This isn't the only way in, either," Karol said. "Most of the Underground locations have at least two ways in and out—a main one and a hidden one." He drove the van to the other side of the warehouse and parked it next to a battered pickup truck. "We walk from here."

They got the construct out, Errin gathered her tools and Karol his backpack, and they headed for a rusting, industrial-looking elevator. Next to it, a pair of men were rearranging a stack of crates using a forklift. Karol trotted over and had a brief conversation with them, and then they returned to their work.

"They're mages," Errin told Stone. "They know us, so it's not a problem."

The rattling, unsteady elevator didn't fill Stone with confidence as they descended, but apparently it was more sturdy than it appeared because soon it opened on a wide passageway. Faraway voices echoed against the concrete walls, followed by a muffled cheer.

Once again, Karol jogged ahead toward a substantial, closed metal door. Stone thought he would knock, but as he approached another man shimmered into existence off to the side. The two spoke, and then the man receded back into whatever illusion hid him.

"They've got this all worked out, don't they?" Stone murmured to Errin as Harrison headed toward the door.

"They have to. You already know what the mages do to people who break the law. They can't be too careful about this."

"How often do they run these things?"

Karol opened the door and held it for the rest of them to go through. "A few times a year, spread out over the five major cities. We don't always go—we weren't planning to go to this one, actually, until this situation with Rovenna turned up."

"Usually we only go when we've got some good prospects to help out, or we've got a new construct to test." She patted the humanoid machine's metal shoulder. "This one's actually not quite ready, but it can fake it long enough for us to talk to Rovenna."

Without the heavy door blocking it, the sound from inside got much louder—a combination of shouts, cheers, and numerous conversations. Stone stopped a moment, taking the place in.

It looked as if it had once been an underground parking garage, though one that had fallen to ruin many years ago. Wooden beams and metal scaffolding reinforced its walls in several places, and while it appeared the support columns were sound, the floor in several places was cracked and buckled as if an earthquake had disrupted it. The main illumination came from a series of large fixtures in the high ceilings, though brighter portable lights had been scattered around the floor. The whole space was roughly rectangular, measuring perhaps a hundred feet on the long side, and a bit less on the short side.

If Stone had to estimate, he'd guess there might be about fifty to seventy people here, both men and women, spread out around the floor and mostly arranged around two make-shift "arenas" delineated by metal barriers. On the far side of the room, several temporary structures that looked like shed-tent hybrids had been set up, along with several spread-out tarps covered in what looked like various machine parts. Off to the left Stone spotted a temporary bar with several more people loitering around it. As he watched, another cheer went up from the left-side arena ring.

"Come on," Errin urged him, coming back to take his arm. Harrison, Karol, and the floating construct had already gotten ahead of them. "We need to get set up."

They hurried over, following Harrison and Karol to one of the structures. A woman with a clipboard gave Karol a sheet of paper as they entered.

The inside was empty except for a tarp spread on the floor, a single small table, and a bright, adjustable work lamp. Harrison directed the construct to the middle of the tarp and set it down. "I will find Galen and see if Rovenna has arrived."

"We'll get this thing ready to go," Errin said. She dropped her bag on the table and began laying out tools. "How much time have we got, Karol?"

Karol consulted the sheet. "We're up in two fights, in the north arena."

"What about me?" Stone asked. "All right if I take a look around?"

"Yes, but stay close," Errin told him. "We need to stay together so we can be ready to go. If Trevor makes contact fast, we might leave directly after our fight." She pointed off to the side, near the bar, where a series of wooden crates were stacked about seven feet high. "The other exit is on the other side over there, behind that stack of boxes. They're all connected, so they can be shoved aside."

"Do you expect to make a quick escape?" Stone asked.

"No, but it never hurts to know where all the exits are."

"If you wouldn't mind," Karol added, "take a look around at the auras, and see if anybody looks suspicious."

"Got it." Stone slipped back out and found a spot to the side of the tent where he could get a good look at the area.

Currently, the left-side arena was between bouts. One man and woman, both dressed in work clothes and vests similar to Errin's, were leading their combatant—a mostly-humanoid, three-legged thing that looked like it had been assembled from scrap metal—back toward their tent as the crowd parted for them. Stone could barely make out the other construct, which was shorter, squatter, and painted bright red, as its three handlers gathered around it in obvious disappointment. Most of the crowd had already begun gravitating toward the other ring, where another pair of constructs circled each other warily.

Stone watched in fascination. This was an area of magic he'd never seen on Earth—as far as he knew, either nobody there had figured out how to combine magic with technology or else they hadn't bothered to try. He knew it was possible to summon a spirit into an inanimate object and animate it that way, but it was difficult and dangerous enough that he'd never heard of anyone doing it on a scale this large. Maybe he could ask Harrison about it once they returned to the Nexus, before heading back home. Probably not something he himself would have much success with, though—his mechanical aptitude had never been high, and he could see from the design of the various constructs that whoever had built them, magic aside, had some serious skills in that area. He wondered where Harrison had learned it—from the sound of it, he'd been tinkering with mundane machines since well before he discovered his magic.

He shifted to magical sight and examined the crowd, almost irrationally happy to be able to perform such a simple act after his long period of forced mundanity. Auras sprang up around the people, surging and flaring with excitement as their owners urged on their favorite fighter. It occurred to him that he hadn't given any thought to wonder if Calanarians' auras would look any different than those from his own dimension, but apparently they didn't. As was usually the case back home, most were a single color—bright blues, reds, oranges, greens, yellows. A couple, both belonging to people whom other traces of magic around them marked as likely mages, had two-tone auras—one green with gold, the other red with blue. He couldn't currently spot Harrison's eerie black-and-purple aura, but that didn't disturb him. He'd probably gone off to meet with Rovenna in private, and in any case, he was probably disguising it.

Stone moved closer to the ring, still pretending to watch the action inside. He couldn't see much past the crowd, but that was all right since it wasn't the crowd he was observing. Without moving his head much to give himself away, he scanned the areas off to either side of the ring, including the other ring.

By now, most of the spectators there had moved to this one, and the losing construct's three handlers were levitating their unmoving bright-red charge back toward their tent. In general, the mood seemed excited, anticipatory, with just a hint of wary nervousness around the edges—completely understandable, considering their clandestine operation was illegal and could potentially get them killed if anyone caught them.

Another cheer went up from the crowd, followed by a loud metallic crash. Stone moved forward a little more, positioning himself behind a pair of shorter spectators so he could get a look at the action.

One of the combatants, a beefy thing shaped like a black trash can with arms and legs, had knocked over its opponent, which was taller, less bulky, and painted blue with gold highlights. The trash can loomed over its opponent, raising arms made of cords and metal conduits.

The other one wasn't done yet, though. As the trash can's fists came down, the blue-and-gold construct rolled neatly sideways and leaped back to its feet, using a powerful leg sweep to knock the trash can's stubbier limbs out from under it. The black construct fell over and landed on its back, flailing its arms and legs as it struggled to roll over.

Stone kept magical sight up as he watched, even more intrigued by what he was seeing. The constructs didn't have auras—only living things had auras—but they did glow with some kind of aura-*like* magical energy emanating from inside their central cores. It was different than what Stone had seen when he'd provided power to Errin's airship engine—that had been raw energy. This stuff felt, for lack of a better word, *processed.* He wondered if this had something to do with the way the constructs could possess a limited form of autonomy, like Anzo back at the Nexus. His curiosity burned again, and he ached to ask Harrison about all of this. *I could stay a bit longer,* he reminded himself. *A few more days won't matter.*

But no—he'd been gone long enough. Assuming time here ran at anything like the same rate as it did back home, he'd already been here close to two months. The fall quarter would be starting soon, if it hadn't already, and he didn't want to think about what would happen if he failed to show up with no explanation or excuse. Hell, they might even go looking for him, and what then? It wasn't as if they could find him anywhere on Earth.

No, he'd need to go home. Perhaps he could come back again after things had settled down, if Harrison would be willing to talk to him. That could all be worked out later. For now, he was supposed to be keeping an eye out for anything suspicious.

He drifted around the outer edge of the crowd, moving in the direction of the other arena, still scanning auras. Now he did spot Harrison in his nondescript illusionary disguise: he stood in a shadowy alcove in a corner past the bar, his aura likewise disguised to make him look mundane. Two other people were with him: a tall, statuesque woman and a small, slim man, both dressed in work clothes. The man wore a light bag slung over one shoulder. Stone wondered if the woman was Rovenna. He didn't approach the group or even acknowledge it, though, allowing his gaze to skate over them and continue his aura scan. He noticed Harrison didn't acknowledge him either.

He was about to head back to the tent and see if he could be of any assistance with getting their construct ready for its fight when another figure caught his eye. Curious, he sidled closer for a better look.

The figure stood at the back of the crowd about ten feet from Stone, and appeared to be watching the battle with interest. By now, the trash-can construct had managed to right itself and was attempting to bowl its lighter opponent down using its greater mass and lower center of gravity. The crowd cheered as the blue-and-gold fighter stepped aside again and the trash can crashed into the railing.

Stone pretended to be interested in the match while watching the slight figure out of the corner of his eye. It wore a dark garment halfway between a tunic and a hooded sweat-shirt, with the hood pulled up over its head. Stone couldn't see its face; in fact, the strange garment made it impossible to tell whether it was male or female. A quick look at its aura revealed a steady, pulsing green, but when he focused closer he noticed an oddness about it—a kind of flickering around the edges that he'd never seen before. Nobody else seemed to be paying any attention to the figure; even those standing close to it didn't appear more nervous than anyone else. As far as Stone could tell, it was as interested in the battle as everyone else.

He used another cheer (the blue-and-gold construct had managed to flip the trash can on its back again) to cover a quick glance back toward Harrison and his companions. The woman was still there, deep in conversation with Harrison, but the slim young man was now gone. It didn't take Stone long to spot his aura, though—he was heading toward a doorway on the opposite side of the room. Stone couldn't read the sign above it, but the image clearly identified it as the restrooms.

The hooded figure moved now, drifting around the outer edge of the right-side ring in the direction of the bar. Stone tensed, careful to keep his aura under control, trying to decide if he should keep the figure in sight or if that would draw too much attention to himself. He remained where he was for the moment but kept watching; the figure passed Harrison's alcove without slowing, moving instead to stand in front of the bar. *He's just getting a drink*. But nonetheless, Stone switched direction and walked back toward the tents. He didn't want to disturb Harrison during his meeting, but at least he could ask Errin and Karol about the strange individual.

"Wondered where you went," Karol greeted as Stone entered. "We're about ready to go here."

Errin crouched on the tarp in front of the construct. She had a panel open on one of its legs and was making an adjustment. "See anything interesting?"

"Everything out there is interesting," Stone admitted. "Harrison's talking to some woman over by the bar—I assume she's who he came here to see. But I did see someone I wanted to ask you about—looked a bit suspicious."

Instantly, both of them focused on him. "Suspicious how?" Errin asked, glancing toward the flap covering the tent's entrance.

"Not sure. He wasn't doing anything odd—just watching one of the fights, and then went over to the bar. But he was dressed strangely, and his aura looked a bit unusual. Want to take a look?"

"You do it, Karol," Errin said. "I need to finish this—we'll be up any minute."

"Right," Karol said. "Let's go."

Stone led him back out as another cheer went up from the crowd. He couldn't see what was going on past all the people, but apparently one or the other of the fighters had finally won the bout.

"He was over here by the bar when I saw him last," Stone said, choosing the opposite direction around the crowd that wouldn't take them past Harrison and the woman. "Or she— I couldn't tell."

"What did they look like?" Karol once again seemed hyper-vigilant, his gaze in constant motion.

"Hard to say. He was wearing an odd hooded thing. But nobody in the crowd acted like he was unusual in any way." He studied the few people in front of the bar, but no longer saw the hooded figure among them. "Damn. He's gone off somewhere."

"Come on. Let's find him fast." Karol slipped between the bar patrons and the crowd around the ring as the latter group began to drift back toward the other ring.

Stone noticed the trash-can construct lying on its back in the middle. One of its arms lay a few feet from it, and its left leg was bent at an angle that would have been crippling for a human fighter. He hurried to catch up with Karol, still scanning the crowd. Where had the hooded figure gone? Had he left already?

"Do you see him?" Karol asked as they rounded the far side of the crowd and headed for the area between the two rings.

"No. I'm wondering if he might have gone. We could ask the door guard—"

Karol paused. "Let's finish looking in here first. If he's gone, he's not our problem. He's probably nothing to worry about, but I want to get back to Errin. We'll be up as soon as they clear out the ring." He set off again, moving fast.

"Right." Stone caught up with him, shifting between magical and normal sight, trying to spot the figure's pulsing green aura among all the other mingling colors.

As they reached the other side of the ring and approached the tent again, they passed the slim young man who'd been with Harrison and the woman before, on his way back from the restroom. He nodded politely to them, adjusting his heavy shoulder bag as he pushed through the crowd. Stone nodded back.

"I don't see him." Karol stopped in front of the tent, looking frustrated. "It's all right, though—if he's not here, he's not here. I'll go tell Trevor about him, just in case—can you go back to Errin and tell her I'll be along in a minute?"

"Of course. Sorry for the false alarm."

"Don't be—we need to be careful. I'll feel much better when we're out of here. Back soon." Karol strode back through the crowd toward Harrison's group.

Stone watched him go for a few seconds, feeling suddenly uneasy. As he turned toward the tents, something nudged at the edges of his thoughts—something wrong—but he couldn't put his finger on what it was. *You're just jumping at shadows,* he admonished himself. *Whoever that guy was, he's gone.*

He pushed past the tent flap. Errin had put the panel back on the construct's leg and was looking impatient. "Where's Karol? They're going to call us any minute."

"He'll be back. He had to go tell Harrison about—"

A sudden, wrenching chill gripped Stone as the elusive reason for his uneasiness locked into place.

An image flashed to his mind's eye: the woman's slim aide, heading back from the restroom.

The man's shoulder bag hadn't been heavy when he'd gone in.

Bloody hell.

He spun toward the door. "Get ready to go!" he called over his shoulder.

"What—" Errin demanded, but that was all Stone heard before he was out and away, running across the crowded space, shoving people out of his way with magic, his gaze locked on the shadowy forms of Harrison and the woman. The slim man with the newly-heavy bag had nearly reached them now, and Karol was only a few steps behind.

"Karol!" Stone yelled, flinging up a magical shield. "The aide! He's a—"

The young aide smiled.

The world went white, and a massive *boom* echoed through the chamber.

| CHAPTER THIRTY-FOUR

S TONE'S WORLD EXPLODED INTO SCREAMS, flashing lights, and disorientation.

He staggered as something slammed hard into his shield, throwing him backward. Something else—an odd wrenching feeling—clawed at him but was gone before he could identify it.

The shield vanished—but it had done its job. Stone scrambled back to his feet, physically uninjured but mind spinning with confusion.

What had happened?

The scene in front of him was something out of a horror movie. Everywhere he looked were fallen bodies, bleeding bodies, struggling figures—and that was only close to where he stood. Beyond him, on the other side of the space, nobody was struggling. Instead, more bodies and parts of bodies were strewn around as if a child had rampaged through a doll factory. Most of the lights had gone out; only those on the opposite side of the room, behind Stone, still functioned. Smoke and dust further obscured vision.

"No!" he yelled, coughing, his voice rising to join other screams to his left, to his right, and behind him. None in front. His mind still reeling with shock, he vaulted over some of the fallen bodies and ran toward where his friends had been. Where was Harrison? Where were Karol and the woman? Where was the traitorous aide?

Something caught his eye. He glanced down and stopped, stunned. Only a few feet ahead of him, Karol's broken body lay splayed, his illusionary disguise gone now. His left arm was gone, his open, unseeing eyes staring up at the ceiling. "No…" Stone moaned. All around him, the screams of pain and panic still echoed.

He spotted movement in front of him. Figures were moving in the smoke now. He plunged ahead, stumbling over more bodies. "Harrison!"

The figures had surrounded another blood-soaked body, lifting it from the ground. It sagged in their grip, unconscious or dead.

Stone skidded to a stop. "Oh gods, no…"

The sagging figure was Harrison, and he too no longer had his disguise.

Already the other people—at least four of them—were dragging him away.

"Stop!" Stone screamed. He flung a bolt of pure magical energy at one of the figures, and roared in triumph as it screamed and dropped. "Let him go, damn you!" He was close enough to see them now: two men, one woman, none that he recognized. All of them wore the high-collared long coats of the Talented, including the one he'd dropped. How had everyone here missed them? How had they gotten in?

He gasped when Harrison's eyes fluttered open and he raised his head. Blood ran down his face from a deep cut in his forehead, and he looked disoriented—but for just a moment his gaze met Stone's and it sharpened.

"Get them…out…" he rasped, barely audible. "I'll…follow…" Then one of his captors hit him with something and he slumped again.

Before Stone could react, all of them vanished.

"No!" he screamed, letting the spell he'd been preparing to throw at them fizzle. "Damn you, *no!*"

All around him, chaos continued to erupt. The big metal door slammed open and more long-coated figures rushed in.

This time, Stone reacted instantly. His heart hammering, he flung up a disregarding spell—easier than invisibility in his current state. A quick final glance at the space where Harrison had been showed more horror: the woman he'd been speaking to lay crumpled against the wall next to the man Stone had dropped. She had a bloody, gaping wound in her chest, and her neck was bent at a sickening angle. If that had been Rovenna, either she'd been accidentally caught in the bomb blast, or she hadn't known about this any more than Harrison had.

There was no sign of the treacherous aide. Either he'd disappeared in the chaos, or the bomb he'd detonated had blown him to unrecognizable bits.

Stone didn't have time to wait. The long-coated interlopers were pushing through the smoke- and dust-filled air, using magic to kill every living being they encountered. He'd have to act fast if they were to have a chance of getting out of here. Where was Errin? Was she hurt?

He ran back to the tent, keeping low and risking invisibility long enough to get him there. Even stunned, staggered by psychic feedback, Stone's body sang with the magic. He called it, and it came to him as if it had been waiting for him all along. If he hadn't been terrified, it would have been an exhilarating feeling. Now, he could only hope his endurance would last long enough to get him and Errin out of here.

She was outside the tent, scanning the crowd. Looking for him? Looking for Harrison? Her expression showed terror, but also resolve. She hadn't lost her head like many of the others around her had.

Stone shimmered back to visibility next to her. "Errin!"

She jumped, wheeling to point a strange-looking gun at him, but then gasped and lowered it when she saw who it was. "Alastair! What's going on? Where's Trevor? Where's Karol?"

"We have to get out of here," he panted. He grabbed her upper arm and tried to drag her toward the hidden exit. "Come on. Leave the robot."

"Wait! Where's—"

"Karol's dead." His voice shook. "They took Harrison. It was the woman's aide—he had some kind of bomb in his satchel. She's dead too. Come on!"

"Took him?" Her gaze darted back toward the other side of the bar. "Where—"

"He's gone. They disappeared. He said to get you out," Stone urged. "That he'd follow. Come *on!*"

She didn't ask any other questions. Gripping her gun, she hurried after Stone.

"Stay low," he said, calling up the disregarding spell over both of them. "If we can—no!"

He pulled to a stop, terror gripping him again. The secret exit, the one hidden by the stack of crates, had swung open, and more long-coated figures were swarming through. "It's some kind of raid! They planned this!" He whirled around, looking for another exit. "Is there another way out?"

One of the figures spotted them. He yelled something and started to run in their direction, but made it only a couple steps before his body spun and a chunk of his head flew off. He collapsed as Errin lowered her gun.

"I don't know!" she said. Her eyes showed cold resolve, and her voice shook only slightly. "I haven't seen—"

"Come!" said another voice behind them. "Hurry!"

Stone whirled, ready with a spell, but let it die uncast.

The hooded figure—the one he and Karol had been looking for—stood crouched behind them, its head swiveling back and forth as it watched the scene.

"Who are you?" Stone demanded.

"Come with me," it urged. Its voice was low and odd—it was impossible to determine if it was male or female. "I know another way out."

"Over here!" yet another voice shouted. "They're here!"

"We have to go!" Errin hissed, grabbing Stone's arm and pointing with the gun. "They're coming!"

Three long-coated figures were heading toward them, their hands wreathed in magical energy. Before Stone could extend his shield around the hooded figure, one of them lashed out. The figure cried out in pain and staggered, almost falling.

Stone roared and threw his own spell at the group. From the other side, one of the mages he'd seen working on one of the fighting constructs cast one at the same time, and both spells flowered around the invaders' shields. One shield flared and dropped, its owner falling.

"Come!" the hooded figure cried, its voice shaking with pain now. It was barely standing, a darker stain appearing against its dark cloak. All around them the screams and yells and smoke and dust persisted as the raiders continued to swarm. "We don't—have long."

Stone glanced at Errin fast. "Should we trust him?"

"No other choice now," she said grimly. Then, to the figure: "Okay. Go."

Immediately, the hooded figure turned and started to head toward the restrooms, but made it only a couple steps before staggering again and dropping to its knees. "I—can't—"

"I've got you." Stone struggled to maintain the shield spell as he bent to scoop up the fallen figure, thankful that his accelerated workouts had built his strength. He barely noticed the slight weight—whoever this person was, they were small and thin under their cloak. "Errin—I can't cast—"

"I've got this. Go!" Errin squeezed off two more shots from her odd-looking gun, dropping another of their pursuers. She pulled something from her multi-pocketed vest and flung it back toward them. Instantly, billowing black smoke rose, quickly filling the area behind them.

"Nice trick," Stone said, shifting the figure to one arm.

"Even better—it interferes with magical sight." She caught up to him and hurried through the doorway. "Men's or women's?"

"Women's," the figure said. Its voice was weak, shaking with pain. "Stall closest to the wall."

"Just hold on," Stone said, feeling the slim body tremble in his grasp. "We'll sort you out when we get out of here." He hoped their rescuer didn't die before they could get him or her to someone with better healing skills than he had. He pulled up another disregarding spell, hoping their pursuers wouldn't get through the smoke before they'd disappeared into the women's bathroom.

Errin shoved the door open and held it for them. "Hurry."

Stone surged through, ignoring three terrified women who'd taken refuge in the small space. "Stall by the wall."

Errin ran ahead and flung open the door. "It just looks like a normal stall!"

"Push...the dispenser...left..." the figure breathed.

Stone relayed that, and a second later Errin whooped in triumph. "Come on in!"

When he reached the stall doorway, he saw she'd swung open a panel in the wall, revealing a passageway. "Go! Go!" He glanced back at the three frightened women. "You lot! Come in here. Close the panel behind you. Wait before you follow us, though. I don't trust anybody right now." Without waiting for an answer, he shoved through the panel into the passageway.

There were no lights, but Errin pulled a flashlight from another pocket in her vest, illuminating a narrow wooden hallway that veered off to the right. The passageway smelled like rotting wood and old food.

"What about the truck?" Stone asked. "Can we get back to it?"

"Don't want to," Errin said, pushing ahead. "They'll be all over it by now. This was planned."

"It was that aide of Rovenna's," Stone said. "He had a bomb in his satchel. Somebody passed it off to him." A sudden thought gripped him, sending a lance of icewater down his back. "Wait!"

"Why?" Errin sounded impatient. "We've got to—"

"He didn't have the bomb when he headed to the bathroom. He must have got it here. What if the others—" He glared at the figure, tightening his hold on it. "How did you know about the secret exit? Are you one of them? Answer me!" He shook the thin body.

The hood fell away, and he gaped in shock.

Whatever he held in his arms was a humanoid female—but she didn't look like any human he'd ever seen. Her pale skin was gray, her shaggy, silvery hair shining with a greenish overlay. Her eyes, crinkled with pain, were solid black.

"Bloody hell…" he whispered. "What *are* you?"

Errin, who'd been some distance ahead, came back and peered around Stone's shoulder. "She's a Traveler," she whispered, looking as shocked as Stone did.

"What's a Traveler?" The figure moaned again, and he adjusted his hold on her. "Can we trust her?"

"Remember I told you about them when you first got here? The nomads who live in the Wastes?"

Stone vaguely recalled something about that. He checked the hallway again in both directions—so far no one seemed to be following them. "What's she doing here?"

"They come into the cities sometimes—the non-magical cities—to trade. They hate the Talented."

"So she couldn't be the one who passed off the bomb to Rovenna's aide?"

"No way—they're virulently anti-technology." She grabbed Stone's arm. "Come on—we've got to get back to the teleporter before they find us. We can't stay here. It's too dangerous on our own, even with your magic."

"What about Harrison?"

"He said he'd follow us?"

"Yes. He was in bad shape when I saw him, though."

She looked grim. "He's hard to kill. They'll never hold him."

Stone remembered how quickly he'd recovered from a point-blank, mortal gunshot wound. "You're sure? We can't just leave him—"

"We have to," she said, looking even more grim. "He knew the risk when he decided to do this. And he doesn't need a teleport pad to get back."

Stone looked down at the pale figure in his arms. Whatever she was, she was going to die if she didn't get medical attention soon. He made a decision, even though he felt as if he was betraying Harrison by leaving him here. "All right. Let's go."

Behind them, back toward the Underground venue, voices sounded.

"Bugger! They've found the panel!" Stone snapped. "Have you got any more of those smoke grenades?"

Errin pulled another from her vest and chucked it down the hallway. "Come on. I don't know where this lets out. We've got to get back to the pad."

Clearly the Traveler wouldn't be any more help in getting them out. She lolled in Stone's arms; he couldn't tell if the gray of her skin was natural or a sign she was gravely injured. He tightened his hold on her and followed Errin, glancing back over his shoulder periodically.

Errin moved fast but with care, keeping her gun and flashlight both pointed forward, scanning the narrow passage ahead of them for threats. Behind her, Stone switched back and forth between magical and normal sight, sure more of the Talented must be lurking invisibly ahead, waiting to ambush them. He kept the shield up around all three of them, pleased at how little it tired him to do so. He could get to like the magic level on this world, if it weren't for so many of its residents who were determined to kill him.

The voices behind them had faded—either the smoke had slowed them sufficiently that they lost the trail, or else they were following more silently.

No one approached, though. Eventually, after several more heart-pounding minutes and three changes of direction, they reached a narrow metal stairway leading upward to a low wooden door. They stopped and exchanged glances.

"Anything could be out there," Stone murmured. "They could be waiting for us." He shifted the Traveler woman, carefully propping her against the wall at the stairway's foot. "Let me take a look—"

"Let me," Errin said. "You don't know your way around town. I need to figure out where the teleporter is from here."

"Wait," he said, realizing something now that they weren't running for their lives. "Should we take it? Shouldn't we stay here and try to figure out where they took Harrison?"

"It will be easier to do that back at the Nexus," she said, already mounting the staircase. "They won't be able to hide it—we've got friends in some pretty high places."

"Are you sure they're not in on this?"

"Not…completely," she admitted. "But we've got no chance of finding him from here. And she needs help," she added, pointing at the Traveler.

Stone reluctantly had to admit she was right. They'd probably taken Harrison to Temolan, and they had no way to get there. "Go," he said. "Let me scan the area first, though."

He joined her at the top of the stairs, cracked the door open a couple inches, and peered out using magical sight. Outside, the earlier light rain had increased to a steady fall; he saw no signs of auras on the darkened street.

He pulled back. "I think it's all right. Just—hurry."

"No problem." She slipped out and jogged into the street, while Stone kept an eye on her from the doorway. In less than two minutes she was back, shaking rainwater from her hair.

"We're in luck. The passage took us closer to where the teleporter is. We're only a couple blocks away, on the other side from where we left."

"So we just walk from here?" He glanced at the Traveler again. "She needs help."

"Let me take a look. Watch the hallway."

"I'll do better than that." Stone pressed his back against the wall and used magical sight to make sure nobody was coming. Then he wove an illusion a few feet back, reveling once again at how easily the magic came to him. "There. Anyone coming this way will see a dead-end wall. Hurry up, though—I can't hold this forever."

"Yeah. Nice job." She crouched next to the Traveler woman, pulling aside her cloak to reveal a bloody, uneven wound on her left side. "Damn, this looks bad. We've got to move. Illona back home can fix this up, but we need to get to her fast." She probed the wound, and the Traveler woman moaned and opened her eyes. "Sorry…" she said gently. "What's your name?"

"J-Jeritha," the woman whispered.

"Okay, Jeritha. Can you do anything to help yourself? We're going to get you help, but we still have to get to our teleporter."

"I will...try..." She took a deep breath and her gaze fuzzed out again.

Stone shifted his attention between her and the illusion, watching her with magical sight. Her odd, jagged green aura smoothed out a little, overlaid with a shaky gold. "She's trying, but I think she's too out of it to manage much. We've got to go." He bent to pick her up, trying to be as gentle as he could. She seemed to be unconscious again, or else in some kind of trance. "Let's go. I'll follow you, but stay close so I can keep us shielded."

One more check out the door revealed no one approaching. Errin exited first, keeping low and ducking behind a parked vehicle. Stone followed, trying to jostle Jeritha as little as possible. He kept the shield up and continued to scan the area with magical sight, but so far luck seemed to be favoring him. The only aura he saw was the faint green one of some small animal that dashed away as soon as it spotted them.

The shield didn't stop the rain, so by the time they reached the ramshackle building that was their destination, all three of them were soaked. Stone pulled Jeritha's hood over her head to protect her from as much of it as possible, but it didn't do much good. She'd already begun to shiver.

They crept around the building, and now the surroundings looked more familiar. Stone still spotted no sign of pursuers as Errin opened the door to the garage where they'd gotten the truck, and stood aside to let him and Jeritha in. The door swung slowly shut behind them. They crossed to the other door and hurried down the deceptively broken-looking staircase.

"Okay," Errin said, opening the door to the room where they'd left the teleporter. "We—"

If Stone hadn't had magical sight up, and hadn't thought to check the space behind them at that moment, he'd have missed it. When he saw the glitch on the staircase, he didn't stop to analyze it or ask questions. Instead, he gathered magic and flung a wide-spectrum concussion blast forward. If he was wrong he'd look like an idiot, but if he wasn't—

Three figures shimmered into existence, flung backward by Stone's spell. They tumbled over each other, shouting and cursing. "Get them!" one yelled as all three struggled to disentangle themselves.

Another raised a glowing hand and threw another spell. The wall next to Stone splintered and exploded, sending chunks slamming into the shield.

"Run!" Errin yelled.

"You first! I'll hold them off!" Stone poured more power into the shield, directing a bolt of magical energy at one of their pursuers, who barely dived out of the way.

The other two pointed glowing hands at him as, behind him, he heard the door open. "Time to go," he muttered, shifting Jeritha in his grip again. He filled the space in front of him with another wide concussion spell, sacrificing power for spread, and then slipped backward through the door and slammed it shut.

"Hurry!" Errin yelled.

"Do you have to prepare it?"

"No, it'll respond to our bracelets." She pointed at Jeritha. "She'll have to grab yours, though."

Stone shook Jeritha, fearful of injuring her. "Jeritha. Wake up." He glanced toward the door again, knowing they'd only have seconds.

The Traveler woman moaned and cracked her eyes open. "Mm…what?" she mumbled.

He shoved his arm next to her hand. "Grab my arm," he ordered. "Touch the bracelet. Quickly!"

Some of his urgency must have gotten through to her, because her hand fluttered and her slim fingers settled around his wrist. Her grip was weaker than a child's.

"There! Go!" he called to Errin.

She leaped onto the tattered rug, and Stone hurried to join her.

The door shattered into pieces. The three mages poured through the opening.

Heat flared around the shield. Stone's last sight before the tiny room shimmered from view was a fireball the size of his head streaking toward their location.

| CHAPTER THIRTY-FIVE

S TONE DROPPED TO HIS KNEES as reality reformed and they reappeared in the Nexus's teleporter room. He lowered Jeritha carefully down and looked around for Errin.

She was already scrambling off the pad and hurrying to a nearby console. "Do what you can for her—I'll call Illona and have Anzo bring a gurney."

Stone took off his jacket, folded it into a pillow, and slipped it under Jeritha's head. "Hurry. I can't do much."

While they waited for help to arrive, he tried using his minimal healing skills to stabilize the unconscious Traveler woman. He concentrated on the ragged wound on her side, fearing she'd already lost too much blood.

The door flew open and a woman swept in, followed by Anzo pulling a mobile version of the magical healing machine in Stone's suite. "I'll take care of her," the woman said, motioning Stone out of the way.

Stone got up and watched as the woman—he remembered seeing her before, but had never met her—carefully levitated Jeritha onto the machine's narrow surface as she delivered crisp orders to Anzo. Without another word to

Errin or Stone, they departed as quickly as they came, Illona already weaving spells as she went.

And then the room was filled with sudden silence, and just as suddenly fatigue settled over Stone as the events of the night caught up with him. He slumped against the railing surrounding the teleporter pad and let his breath out, finally feeling his racing heart begin to slow. "Bloody hell..." he murmured.

"Yeah." Errin looked as tired as Stone felt, her face smudged with dust, her dripping hair in a wild tangle. "Are you all right? That was a lot of magic you were throwing around, so soon after getting it back."

He swiped his arm across his brow. "Tired. I'd love a nice hot shower and a long session with the healing machine—but not yet. We've got things to sort out." He glanced up at her. "Are *you* all right?"

"I'm fine." She clenched her fists and began to pace, her face darkening with anger. "Somebody betrayed us."

"Yes, that's obvious—whoever that aide was."

"Maybe. But I think it went deeper than that."

"Why?"

"Come on—we need to find Kira." Errin headed for the door.

Stone caught up with her. "Why do you think it went deeper?"

"Trevor said Rovenna's decision to join us was sudden. You said she was killed?"

"Yes. I saw her—that bomb blew her to hell. She was at ground zero when it went off."

"That's—hard to believe," Errin said. "Especially since it took out Trevor too."

"Why do you say that? He's powerful, sure, but he's not invulnerable. And he can't anticipate everything."

"No. He can't. But he knew this meet could be dangerous. He'd have had his shields up, and I've seen those hold up to a lot more than a bomb that'd fit in a bag."

"Well…" Stone said, "if he didn't know the aide was the assassin, could he have had him *inside* his shield, along with himself and Rovenna?"

"That's true," Errin admitted. "Did you see the aide's body?"

"No. But I couldn't see very well—it was dark, and there was a lot of smoke and confusion." He frowned as something else occurred to him. "One other thing I thought was odd, though I didn't have time to think anything of it before. When the bomb went off, everything went white for a second. I heard a loud noise, but there was something else, too. A sort of—wrenching sensation. Then my shield went down and I had to focus on putting it back up again."

"And you don't know what this sensation was about?"

"No. I've never felt anything like it before. And I doubt we'll have a chance to go back there and analyze the scene."

Ahead of them, Kira Talon came running around a corner. "What's happened? Anzo said something happened at the Underground." She looked around. "Where are Trevor and Karol?"

"Trevor's not back?" Errin asked, with a disturbed look at Stone.

"No," Kira said. "Why would he be? He'd come with you, wouldn't he? Where's Karol?"

"Karol's dead," Errin said. "And they took Trevor."

Kira's gaze sharpened. "Took him? Who? Took him where?"

"Slow down," Stone said. "We're still processing all this."

"Where is he?" she demanded.

"Come on," Errin said. "Let's go sit down and we'll catch you up."

They adjourned to a nearby conference room, Kira nearly radiating impatience. She didn't sit down as Stone and Kira both dropped into chairs at the table, but instead paced in front of the window, looking out into the darkness. "Tell me everything."

Between the two of them, Stone and Errin filled her in on the night's events. Halfway through their story, she stopped pacing and leaned wearily against the window. "Damn," she said. "The whole thing was a setup, then. Poor Karol…"

Errin looked down at her clenched fists. "Have you heard back from Galen? Have you tried to reach him?"

"He's not answering any communications. Was he at the Underground?"

"I didn't see him." She looked at Stone. "Did you?"

"I don't know what he looks like," he reminded her. "He wasn't the aide, was he?"

"No. He's one of our agents in Temolan. He set this up with Rovenna."

"Could he have betrayed you?"

"I can't believe that," Kira said. "We've worked with him for a long time. He's helped dozens of people get out of Temolan and come here."

"Things change," Stone said. "Could they have threatened his family? Captured him and…I don't know…brainwashed him somehow? Offered him something he couldn't refuse?" He remembered what one of the Talented had told him during his capture: *We don't pay them. We make them offers it would be in their best interest to accept.*

"I don't know," Errin said with a sigh. "It's possible, I guess. We won't know unless we can track him down."

Kira paced again. "What about this Traveler you brought back with you? What do you know about her?"

"She saved our lives," Errin said. "Showed us another exit out of the Underground when the Temolan people had the others blocked. She was badly injured—we couldn't leave her there to die."

"Where is she now?" Suspicion showed on Kira's face as she glanced toward the door.

"At the infirmary. Illona's working on her. Maybe she can tell us something when she wakes up—like what she was doing at the Underground."

"Why wouldn't she be there?" Stone asked. "You said the Travelers hate the Talented."

"Yes, but they rarely come into the cities, they rarely go alone, and they distrust technology as much as they hate the Talented. They think it's every bit as responsible for the war as magic was."

"But you said you lot sometimes deal with them."

"Trevor has some kind of…understanding with a couple of the bands," Errin said. "They'll deal with him, but only in the towns. They won't come here, and they never go to the floating cities."

"So now we've got one of them here," Kira said.

"We can send her home when she's out of danger," Errin said. "For now, you need to check the teleporter and see if it's still online."

"We need to go back to Temolan," Stone said. "Somebody's got to find Harrison."

"Not yet," Errin said. "They'll be on the lookout for us. And besides, Trevor said he'd follow. As soon as he can, he'll come back here. Like I said, he doesn't need a teleport pad."

"But do they know that?" Stone asked. "Do they have any way to stop him from leaving?" He addressed this last question to Kira.

"We've never heard of anything like that," she said, still looking stressed. "Trust me, the mages in the cities aren't very innovative. They've got a lot of old magical devices powering their infrastructure, but these days most of them don't know how to do more than repair them when they break. They've hardly built anything new in living memory."

Stone didn't like it—he wanted to head back and try to track where they'd gone before the trails faded—but Kira and Errin knew Harrison better than he did. If the Talented didn't know how hard he was to kill, they might not take proper precautions with him. And if he could teleport back to the Nexus without a pad, it was likely he'd be back as soon as they left him alone.

"We can't just *sit* here," Kira said, mirroring Stone's thoughts.

"Contact our agents in Temolan," Errin told her. "See if they can figure out where Galen is. If he doesn't know we suspect him, he might not run." Her expression hardened. "I'd like to question him, at least."

"Good idea," Kira said. "Call me if anything changes." She swept out of the room, leaving Stone and Errin once more alone.

"So, what—we just wait?" Stone asked. "How long do we wait before we act? We can't just leave him there if he can't get away."

"I agree." Errin pushed back from the table and stood. "Come on—let's go see if Illona has Jeritha healed yet. I want to talk to her too."

Stone followed her out the door. "You don't suspect her, do you?"

"I don't know what to think. She *did* save our lives, but the Travelers are...strange. It's hard to know what their motivations are. I want to know what she was doing at the Underground."

They took the teleporter to another floor, with Anzo trailing along behind them. Errin pushed open another door, revealing a small, well-stocked infirmary. Stone spotted two more permanent versions of the magical healing machines, along with three other beds.

Jeritha lay on one of the beds, covered with a white sheet. Her eyes were still closed, her complexion the same pale gray as before. Next to her, another of the magical-mechanical constructs similar to Anzo rolled back and forth, occasionally checking a reading on a machine.

Illona, the healer, turned as they entered, looking them both over with a critical eye. "Do you two need to be checked out?"

"No, we're fine—just tired," Errin said. "Long night." She nodded toward Jeritha. "How is she?"

"I got her healed—she's resting now. She'll be fine. It's a good thing you got her here when you did, and that she's a Traveler. Otherwise she might have died." She adjusted a setting on one of the machines. "She's a tough one. Her aura's like nothing I've ever worked with before."

"Can we talk to her?" Stone asked. "We've got some questions."

"I don't think—" Illona began.

"Listen," Errin cut her off. "Somebody's betrayed us, the Talented have Trevor, and we need to know if she knows anything about it. We won't stay long."

"All right." The healer still sounded reluctant. "I'll be nearby." She addressed the little construct. "Let me know if anything changes."

Stone shifted to magical sight and examined Jeritha's aura. It looked stronger than before, but still unlike anything he'd ever seen, either here or on Earth. Its main color was green, but around the edges, in the place where his own had a golden nimbus, hers reached swirling, iridescent tendrils outward. That was what he'd mistaken for jaggedness before—either that, or it had changed since then.

He touched her shoulder. "Jeritha…"

She shifted under his touch and tried to move away from him.

"Jeritha, please wake up. We need to talk to you."

Her eyes fluttered open. They were still the same solid black as before, eerie and unsettling and alien. "What…?" she whispered. Her expression grew fearful and she tried to sit up.

Errin gently pushed her back down. "It's all right," she said. "You're safe. Your injuries have been healed."

Her hand moved under the sheet, touching her side. "Where are we?" she asked, more strength in her voice.

"We're from the Nexus," Errin told her. "That's where we are now. Do you know it?"

She nodded and closed her eyes again.

"Jeritha," Stone said, keeping his tone soft. "You saved our lives, and we're grateful for that. Thank you. We wouldn't have gotten out of there if it weren't for you."

"Did you know something was going to happen?" Errin asked. "Why were you at the Underground in the first place? I've never seen any of your people there."

"We were...meeting someone there," she said. "To trade." Once again she tried to sit up; Stone helped her, propping a pillow behind her. "The auras were...strange. I knew something would happen, but I didn't know what."

"Why did you help us?" Stone asked. "How did you know who we were?"

She swallowed. The little construct next to her bed offered her a glass of water; she cast it a quick look of distaste before taking the glass without touching the construct, then drank the water gratefully before continuing. "I recognized your aura," she said, nodding at Errin. "I have seen it before. You were with the one you call Harrison."

Errin's gaze sharpened. "They took him. You didn't know about the bomb, did you?"

"No. I thought the man with them might be planning something, but I couldn't tell what it was until it was too late."

"All right." Errin sighed. "You can stay here until you're feeling well enough to leave—we need to get in touch with your people to let them know you're safe. Can you tell us how to do that?"

She closed her eyes. "I have…already contacted them. They know I am safe. They know you have assisted me. They are grateful."

Stone exchanged glances with Errin, but she only shrugged.

"Well," Errin said, "I guess we should—"

The door opened, and Kira strode in. She looked grim.

"What's wrong?" Stone asked.

"What *isn't* wrong?" She motioned for him and Errin to move away from Jeritha's bed, and then lowered her voice so the Traveler woman couldn't hear. "I've just had a communication from our top contact in Temolan. They *have* taken Trevor. They've got him in some kind of magic-nullification device some of their people have been working on."

"So he can't get away?" Errin demanded.

"No." Kira clenched her fist. "He says they've got a couple of mad alchemists, and they've got Trevor drugged up with something nasty. They're trying to get our location out of him."

"Wait," Stone said, glancing back to Jeritha, who'd closed her eyes again. "You said mad alchemists?"

"Yes. I don't know their names, but he says they're a bonded pair, as cruel as they are brilliant."

"I remember them." Stone shuddered, recalling the way the two Arena fighters had behaved when dosed on some of the couple's sadistic concoctions. "Bloody hell."

"Can our contact do anything about it?" Errin asked. "In his position, he's got to be able to—"

"His hands are tied," Kira said. "If he reveals himself, you know what they'll do to him. He's working on some plans, but he says it will take time. He has to be careful."

"Trevor doesn't *have* time." Errin slammed her fist into the wall. "You know what they'll do to him—and they won't be able to kill him. Once they figure that out—"

"Wait," Stone said. "How do you know any of this is true? You've already had one agent go rogue on you. How do you know this one hasn't too? And how does he know all of this?"

Kira and Errin exchanged glances, almost as if trying to decide how much they should tell him. Finally, Kira let her breath out. "Our top agent in Temolan is Olystriar, on the High Council. If he was going to betray us, he's had countless opportunities in the past."

"Well, then—what are we waiting for? We need to go back there and break Harrison out."

"I'll gather some gear," Errin said, already heading for the door.

"Wait." Kira held up a hand.

"What?"

"I didn't tell you the other bad part."

"There's another one?" Stone asked.

"Yes. We can't *get* back. The teleporter in Drendell's been destroyed."

| CHAPTER THIRTY-SIX

STONE FROZE. "What do you mean, destroyed?"

"It's offline. I can't contact it," Kira said.

"Damn!" Errin smacked the wall again in frustration. "The group following us must have destroyed it, either on purpose or accidentally when they threw that fireball."

Wait—you only had one teleporter?" Stone demanded.

"Only one in Drendell," Kira said. "It's dangerous to have too many, and up until now it's been well hidden. We have one in each of the surface towns."

"Well, then—can't we go to one of the other towns and get to Drendell from there?"

"We need to go to Temolan. We don't have teleporters there. I told you before—Trevor won't voluntarily set foot in any of the floating cities. Anybody who wants to meet with him in person has to come to one of the surface towns."

"And getting from any of the cities to any of the others is hard," Errin added. "You need all sorts of permits and authorization papers. It's bad enough moving from one of the surface cities to another, on the train. Getting to the floating cities is worse. You need papers that will fool their gatekeepers."

Stone paced. "And Harrison's the only one who can travel between them without using a teleporter."

Kira nodded soberly. "It's never been a problem before. Most of the people here don't *want* to ever go back, and we've been using the teleporters for years without anyone finding them."

"So, what do we do? We've got to get back there somehow. If they've got him, we can't leave him there and hope he can get out on his own."

"We're not going to," Errin said grimly. "Let me see what I can do."

"Can you build another teleporter?"

"Yes—maybe—but the problem is, we need to have a functional pad at the destination. If we could get to Drendell, we wouldn't *need* to build it."

"You can't build one that will send someone there without a terminal pad?"

"That's a lot harder. I might be able to, with Kira's help. It won't be fast, though."

"Damn," Kira said. "I can help, but I don't have Trevor's mechanical skills, or his knowledge about how magic and technology work together. And like you said, even if we *can* work something out, it will take too long."

"I've got his notes," Errin said. "It's at least worth taking a look. Between the two of us, maybe we can—"

"Too bad that airship of yours isn't functional yet," Stone said. "We could fly there."

"That won't work." Errin shook her head. "We've got a smaller one that's functional now, but flying across the Wastes is suicide. There's no way to know what's out there."

She turned back to Kira. "Come on—let me hunt up those notes, and we can get started on—"

"Wait," said another voice.

All three of them turned, to see Jeritha sitting further up in bed. Her complexion was still gray, but she looked more alert than she had before.

"What is it?" Errin asked. "Did you need something?"

"I might be able to help you," she said. "I'm sorry to listen, but I heard what you said about the teleporter."

"You can get us to Temolan?" Kira asked, astonished. "Can you teleport?"

"I can't teleport you there," she said. "But did you say you had a ship that could fly?"

The three crowded back around her bed. "We do," Errin said. "Something Trevor was working on. It's small and fast—just an experiment, really. A toy. But like I said, there's no way we can fly through the Wastes. We'd crash and burn before we made it halfway there. Too many unpredictable magical fields, pockets of active war magic—"

"I can help," Jeritha repeated. "I can navigate through the Wastes."

They all gaped at her. "You can?" Kira asked. "How?"

"Are you sure?" Errin gripped the edge of the bed and leaned in closer to the Traveler woman.

"I live there," she reminded them. "With my band. We navigate the dangerous areas every day. I can see the magic, and help you steer free of it." Her expression was sober. "It won't be without danger. I cannot guarantee safety. But I am confident I can do this."

Errin, Kira, and Stone exchanged glances. "What do you mean, you can 'see the magic'?" Stone asked Jeritha. "Are you talking about magical sight? Auras?"

"Yes…but more than that. I know those with the Talent can see magical energy around living beings. But we—the Travelers—can do more. Magic is all around us. We see it all the time."

Kira was staring at her as if this were new information. "That's…"

"That is how we navigate in the Wastes," she said. "I should not be telling you this, but you saved my life and I want to repay my debt. If you will take me with you in your flying ship, I can guide you where you wish to go."

CHAPTER THIRTY-SEVEN

"I DON'T LIKE IT," Kira said.

She, Errin, and Stone were back in the conference room now, after excusing themselves from Jeritha to discuss their next steps.

"I don't either," Errin said. "Not a bit. But we don't have any other choice. We can't leave him there. They've been after him for years—I don't even want to think about what those sadistic monsters are doing to him."

"But can we trust Jeritha?" Kira sat at one end of the table, her fists clenched. "The Travelers don't like us any more than they like the Talented."

"That's not true," Errin said. "I've talked to Trevor about it. They don't hate us—they hate technology. They're afraid we'll all stumble around and start another war, and this time it will wipe them all out along with us."

"What's the difference?" Kira demanded. "Either way, she wants us to put ourselves completely at her mercy." She shuddered. "If anything went wrong—if she betrayed us— we'd never make it out of there alive."

Stone was pacing. "Let's think a moment," he said. "Are there *any* other ways we can do this? You said it would be difficult to get there if we took a teleporter to another city. How difficult?"

"Nearly impossible," Kira said. "We have agents in the other cities, but nobody who could get us the kind of documentation we'd need to get into Sholandre or one of the other floating cities. That kind of identification is magic-based—it's not something that can be forged by non-mages, or even most mages. And without it, we can't get near the teleporters."

When Stone started to say something, she held up her hand. "That's the easy part. Even if we *did* manage to get to one of the other floating cities, travel between them is heavily regulated. Even most of the mages can't get permission to do it—and even those who do are almost all restricted to bounded public areas." She sighed. "The mage houses aren't at war anymore, but that doesn't mean they trust each other. They're always sending agents into other cities to gather intelligence—mostly to make sure nobody is violating the treaties preventing the creation of any more war spells or weapons."

"So it's a cold war," Stone said. When both Kira and Errin looked at him questioningly, he waved it off. "Never mind. The point is, it sounds like that angle is more trouble than we have time for. But even if we can make it to Drendell, how will we get to Temolan if we don't have this special magical authorization you mentioned?"

"Olystriar can help us with that. That's why it's so important that we don't compromise his cover—Temolan is the only city where we have a Council member on our side. He can do a lot of good from his position, but if he's caught—" Kira shuddered again.

"He can get us the credentials we need to get to Temolan," Errin said. "After that, I assume we'll mostly be on our own," she added with a glance toward Kira.

"He can tell us where they're holding Trevor," she said. "He might be able to help us get in, but he said not to count on it." Her fists clenched again. "He said he was willing to blow his cover if it means getting Trevor out of there, but naturally he'd rather not."

"We may have to bring him in if he's in too much danger." Errin got up and stared out the window. "Losing such a high-level contact would be a blow, but I don't want his death on my conscience."

"So it sounds like we either trust Jeritha or we're out of luck," Stone said.

"Unfortunately it seems so," Kira said.

"Well, then—let's get on with it. Is there any point in waiting? If Jeritha's healed up—"

"There's one other problem," Errin said.

"What?"

"The airship. I told you—it's small. We built it mostly as an experiment, to work out some of the problems we'd need to solve before building the larger one. We've used it a couple times as a transport to fly injured people back from the distant farms and ranches."

"How small?" Stone asked. "How many does it carry?"

"Three. And even that will be tight."

He let his breath out. "And there are four of us. Five, coming back."

"If we get Trevor out of there, he can get back on his own if necessary," Kira said. "But that still leaves four. Jeritha has to come so she can navigate. So which of you two are coming with us?"

"Hang on," Stone protested. "Why do you assume it's you who's going?"

"I'm the logical choice," Kira said. "They'll need magic."

"I've got magic. And plenty of it now."

Errin raised her hands. "Hold on, you two. This isn't productive."

"We'll both go, then." Kira said stubbornly. "I know the way the Talented work better than either of you, but having two mages—"

"—will mean nothing if the ship develops a mechanical problem halfway across the Wastes," Errin pointed out. "Remember, we've never tested it on a trip this long before. You'll need me if something goes wrong. Also," she added before Kira could cut her off, "I've been working with Trevor on several anti-magic devices of our own. We might need them to get past some of Temolan's magical defenses."

"I'm not staying behind," Kira said. She glared at Stone. "I'm sorry, Alastair—no offense intended, but this isn't even your world. Trevor's my teacher. He saved my life. I'm not going to trust—"

"You're right," Stone cut her off, glaring right back. "This *isn't* my world. And I can't get *back* to my world until we get Harrison back. You can't send me home, can you? If you can, I'll leave you lot to it and be on my way. But you can't, can you?"

Kira didn't answer.

"*Can* you?"

"No," she snapped. "I can't."

"Kira…" Errin began, carefully.

"What is it?"

"There's something else you're not thinking about."

"And what's that?"

Errin spoke in a firm but diplomatic tone. "With Trevor gone, you're the only one who's attuned to the teleporters out of here. If you leave too and something goes wrong, no one here will be able to leave."

"We'll recalibrate them," Kira insisted.

"We can do that…but it takes time. We need to get going. And…" she added, even more carefully, "you're not going to want to hear this, but I've seen Alastair in action. He's stronger magically than you are, and he's got more experience. I know you want to go—I get that—but we've only got one shot at this. We need to take our best chance at success."

Kira flung herself out of her chair and stalked to the window.

Stone checked her aura. She wasn't even trying to hide her agitation. He remained silent, sensing anything he said at that moment would touch off a growing powderkeg.

"Kira…" Errin ventured.

The young mage pounded the window once with her fist, whirled, and let out a loud sigh. "You're right. I know you are. But I don't have to like it. Staying here—sitting around waiting for news while somebody else gets things done— that's not who I am."

"I don't think that's who any of us are," Stone said softly. "Believe me, I wish we could all go. But—"

"Yeah. Okay." She returned to the table and threw herself back in the chair. "You'd better get ready to go. I'll get in touch with Olystriar and let him know you're coming. When should he expect you?"

Errin stood. "I need to do a quick check of the ship. Assuming we can fly at full speed and don't run into any problems, it will take around three hours to get to Drendell. We can't land there, though—we'll have to set down outside town and hike in."

"What if something finds the ship?" Stone asked.

"They won't. Nobody ever goes outside the towns, and even if they do, it's got built-in magical protections to keep the curious away."

"Let's get on with it, then."

"Meet me at the workroom in half an hour." She departed at a jog.

Alone now with the still-agitated Kira, Stone felt suddenly uncomfortable. "I'd—better get going too," he said, heading for the door.

"Alastair."

He stopped and turned back. Kira stood behind the table, regarding him with a serious, contemplative look. "Yes?"

"Get him out. Bring him home."

"We'll do our best. You know that."

"I do. But—be careful, too. If they've advanced enough that they've got something that can take Trevor down, you need to watch out for yourselves. I don't know what they're up to, but I don't like it."

He held her gaze for a few more seconds, then nodded. "We'll be back soon."

| CHAPTER THIRTY-EIGHT

WHEN STONE SHOWED UP WITH ANZO at the downstairs workroom-hangar, he found Errin already there. "Everything look all right?" he called.

She was pacing around the sleek, small craft with a clipboard in one hand and some kind of meter in the other. As Stone drew up to her, she stuck the meter in one of her pockets and wrote something on the clipboard. "Looks fine. Trevor and I keep this thing in top condition, even when it's not in use. I just hope it has the range to get where it needs to go—and that Jeritha really can navigate us there."

Stone studied the ship. It was about the size of a small plane, with stubby wings and an aerodynamic body painted shiny black. "How does it fly?" he asked. "Those wings don't look big enough to keep it aloft."

"They don't need to—they just add a bit of stability when it's in the air. The engine's a smaller version of that one," she added, nodding toward the larger, unfinished airship. "Almost all of the propulsion and lift comes from magic."

"So it's not just like a rocket engine?"

She tilted her head. "If you mean is it powered by simple engine propulsion, no. The magic provides the power, but there's also a levitation spell woven into its structure. Once we reach cruising height, the engine pushes us forward."

"That's…fascinating. We don't have anything like that where I'm from."

"Trevor says the magic there isn't strong enough to power something like this."

"Probably true," Stone agreed, but the temptation to remain here and study this new branch of magical application still gripped him hard. Perhaps someday…

But not now. Now, he needed to focus. He tried not to think about what Harrison must be enduring at the hands of the Talented; if he truly was difficult—or even impossible—to kill, the insane alchemists might be the least of his concerns. "Anything I can do to help?"

"I need to finish going over this checklist. If you can load those into the cargo area, that will help." She pointed toward a small stack of boxes and bags piled near the ship.

"On it. Where's Jeritha?"

"She's coming. Illona just called and said she's bringing her down."

"Have you got a plan for when we get there?"

"We'll talk about it on the way. We've got a long flight, and it's going to be close quarters."

Stone had barely finished loading the gear when Illona arrived with Jeritha behind her. The Traveler woman looked better now: her solid-black eyes had a shine that hadn't been there before, and she walked slowly but without limping. She was clad in a simple white shirt and loose sand-colored pants; a dark gray hooded cloak with the hood thrown back revealed her silvery-green hair and pale-gray complexion. It must be natural, Stone decided, wondering if it had been a result of the war magic everyone was so terrified of.

"You're sure you can do this?" Errin asked her. "No shame in admitting it if you can't—I'd rather come up with another solution than crash-land in the middle of the Wastes—or worse."

"I'm sure," she said, with quiet dignity. "As I said—what you call the Wastes are my home. I can warn you of danger with enough time to avoid it." She offered a faint smile. "Do not worry. You have saved my life, and as I said, I will repay my debt to you. My people are grateful for what you have done, so they have agreed to aid me in this."

"Aid you?" Stone asked. "How can they do that?"

"I cannot say," she said. "But I assure you, we will not be alone." She glanced toward the airship, and a brief look of mixed fear and revulsion crossed her delicate features. "Is it time?"

"Just about." Errin ticked off the last box on her checklist and put the clipboard aside. "Kira called—she's been in contact with Olystriar's people. Once we land we'll need to get to the location they've provided, and they'll have more information for us then. He says he's still trying to find out exactly where they're holding Trevor."

"You trust them, then?" Stone asked.

"I do—but that doesn't mean we aren't going to take precautions." Errin opened ship's small door, revealing three seats: two in front and a third centered behind them. "Jeritha, you'll sit up front with me so you can get a clear view. Let's go."

Stone climbed in to the rear seat after the two women had settled themselves. As Errin had indicated previously, the cockpit area was cramped; no way could they have fit a fourth person in, at least without someone sitting in someone else's lap. As it was, Stone had to draw his long legs up in an uncomfortable tuck. It would be a long trip. "How far is it from here to Drendell?"

"It will take us a bit more than three hours, if everything goes well. We've clocked this craft at significantly faster than we'll be going today, but never for that far. Also, it's better to be careful and give Jeritha plenty of time to spot any problems up ahead."

"Do we have a route set?" Stone asked. "Some kind of flight plan?"

"No—we're going to play it by ear. Remember, no one's ever flown into the Wastes before. The Travelers don't use technology, and the Talented, even if they had something like this, are terrified of the wild magic out there."

She flipped a few switches and made some adjustments on the console in front of her. "Everybody strap in. We're ready to go."

Stone belted himself into his seat, leaning forward to watch the takeoff.

It certainly wasn't like anything he'd ever experienced before. Errin turned the little craft so it pointed toward a large open area, then pulled back on a lever. The ship rose a few feet from the floor and began floating slowly forward. As it did so, she pressed a button and pulled another lever; something rumbled to life in the back and settled into a mellow, purring thrum.

"So far so good…" Errin murmured.

They picked up a bit of speed as they went, appearing to head straight for a solid black wall. Stone was familiar enough with the Nexus's illusionary protections that he didn't flinch as they approached it. Oddly, neither did Jeritha. He wondered if her superior skills with magical sight worked on illusions too.

As soon as they passed through the illusionary wall, Errin pulled back her lever again and the ship rose once more. Stone peered out through the front window, watching the land recede beneath them until all he could see was a network of green patchwork below. He thought about asking how large New Argana was, but decided not to in case Errin didn't want to reveal such information with Jeritha present. Instead, he continued watching as they picked up speed again.

"We'll be crossing the ward soon," Errin said.

"Yes, I can see it up ahead," Jeritha said. Her expression was hard to read; she seemed tense and not altogether happy to be where she was, but her aura was—at least as far as Stone could tell—calm. "Please slow down as much as possible once you've passed through, so I can take a look."

"Looks like you've got a ward around the ship, too," Stone said, still watching with magical sight.

"We do, but it's not much of one," Errin said. "Remember, this ship was only meant to fly inside New Argana. It won't hold off much of anything, so we're counting on Jeritha."

Stone continued to watch, maintaining a tense grip on the arms of his seat, until the little craft passed through the shimmering ward that concealed and protected New Argana from the outside world. The sensation as they crossed it was like nothing he'd ever felt before. Usually, when a magically active person was attuned to a ward, they either felt nothing at all or else a faint buzzing sensation. If the person wasn't attuned, a number of things could happen, depending on how powerful and nasty the caster was: they could be prevented from crossing over at all, they could be immobilized or rendered unconscious, or, in the worst cases, they could be instantly killed or even vaporized.

In this case, though, Stone got a feeling of immense power—not a buzzing, exactly, but more like a subsonic hum, such as one might experience when standing in a room full of heavy-duty electronics. The feeling lasted longer than he'd expected, too, persisting for nearly ten seconds. This ward was definitely a big deal.

He glanced at Jeritha. She had her eyes closed and appeared uncomfortable, but not in any kind of pain. When they made it through, she relaxed, opened her eyes, and let her breath out.

"How did Jeritha get out if she's not attuned?" Stone asked. "And what will those wards do to anyone who isn't?"

"We don't prevent people from getting out," Errin told him. "It's getting *in* that's the difficult part. It would be hard to even get near them, since we've got significant illusions preventing anyone from finding us. But if they manage it, the wards are deadly."

"I see." So Harrison didn't play around here anymore than he did on Earth.

He glanced forward, tensing in shock. As soon as they'd passed through the ward, the entire view through the front window had shifted. Instead of lush green farms, ranchland, and rolling hills, a craggy, rock-strewn landscape lay spread out before them. Stone spotted green patches, but most of what he could see looked barren, scrubby, and inhospitable.

"Bloody hell." He indicated the view. "All that was caused by magic?"

"It isn't all like that," Jeritha said. "There are more livable areas—some of them are quite beautiful, in fact. But they're dangerous to get to unless you know how." She held up a hand. "Please—let me concentrate. I can do this, but we'll all need to work together."

Stone leaned forward in his seat again, noticing Errin's tight grip on the craft's steering yoke.

What followed for the next three hours was a tense, white-knuckled journey across terrain Stone could only describe as a magical hellscape. The little craft flew smoothly and silently, its arcane-powered engine easily handling the task of keeping them aloft, but all three of them were forced to remain constantly on guard to shifting conditions.

Jeritha and Errin bore the brunt of it, the Traveler remaining closely tuned to the astral energies and calling out course corrections frequently enough so Stone lost any doubts he might have had about the area's unpredictable dangers, and Errin struggling to keep up with them despite flying blind.

To the non-magical eye, the land streaking by below looked primarily wild and green, with craggy, far-off mountain ranges, hazy, low-lying cloudy or foggy patches, and the occasional meandering river or tranquil lake. But even Stone, who didn't have anything close to Jeritha's sensitivity, saw another story when he shifted to magical sight. The magic was alive out here, colorful and dangerous in the manner of creatures back on Earth that lured prey using their bright hues. He knew Errin wasn't seeing the way patches of spiked crystalline structures blazed with unnatural light, or how magical energy arced and danced between them. She didn't see the miasmic green glow lingering over a lake that otherwise looked pristine and inviting, the jagged red streaks stretching out like banners behind a massive herd of creatures that resembled spiny buffalo, or the enormous, sparkling energy cloud crawling across an area covering several square miles.

Even without such capability, though, Errin retained a scientist's curiosity about what passed below them. "I wish we could get some photographs of this," she commented at one point after they'd steered clear of what was clearly the ruins of a city, already mostly reclaimed by rocks and underbrush. Before they'd flown out of range, she'd pointed out several dark mounds that might have been the remains of broken machines the size of buildings.

"I'm not sure they'd register properly," Jeritha said. "The magic here protects itself from discovery. It—turn north, quickly!"

Errin wrenched the yoke in that direction, and after that she concentrated on flying and didn't ask any other questions.

Stone, meanwhile, with less to do, focused on examining the ground below, using both magical and normal sight. He agreed with Errin—he'd definitely like the opportunity to explore this area more thoroughly. But one look at Jeritha's tense expression convinced him that perhaps sometimes limiting one's curiosity was a good thing. Right now, he'd settle for getting through this nightmarish environment and landing near Drendell in one piece. "How much further is it?" he asked, after the little craft's dashboard clock showed three hours had already passed.

"It isn't far now," Jeritha said, without taking her eyes off the view out the front window. "A few more minutes, and we should be—"

"What's that?" Errin demanded, pointing.

Stone twisted in his seat to look out the side window. At first he didn't see it, but then his gaze locked onto a dark, winged creature wheeling in the sky some distance away. "Bloody hell—is that a bird?"

Jeritha couldn't take her attention from the forward view for long, but she cast a quick glance to the side and tensed. "It's a *wyvora.*"

"What's that?" Errin asked. "Do we need to worry about it?"

That seemed a pertinent question, as the winged creature was moving closer to them, perhaps curious about this new species of flying thing invading its space.

"It isn't a bird," Jeritha said, with yet another glance sideways. "*Wyvora* are large flying reptiles."

"You people have *dragons*?" Stone asked, gripping his chair arms.

As the thing drew even closer, though, he could see it didn't look much like an Earthman's idea of a dragon. Black as the night sky, it had leathery wings, spindly, clawed fore- and hind legs, a thin body, and a long, narrow head featuring a mouth bristling with teeth. Its eyes burned with a red light. If Stone had to say anything about it—aside from the fact that it looked dangerous due to its sheer size—it would be that it looked unhealthy. *Like everything else out here,* he reminded himself. That didn't mean it couldn't kill them, though.

"Can it take out the ship?" he asked Errin.

"I don't know. Does it cast spells?"

"No," Jeritha said. "They normally hunt prey on the ground. They don't come near our bands or settlements."

"How do we deal with it?"

Again, a reasonable question. The *wyvora* opened its mouth and emitted a high, squawking screech audible even through the airship's hull, then streaked toward them.

"Turn a little west," Jeritha said urgently. "It's the magic we have to worry about, not the *wyvora*."

"I'd say it would be wise to worry about both," Stone muttered, already gathering energy for a spell if need be. "You focus on the magic. I'll deal with this thing if it gets too close. Are there any weapons on this ship, Errin?"

"No." She, too, kept her focus on the way forward, but couldn't help snatching nervous glimpses toward the approaching monster. It was close enough now that they could all clearly see its leathery black hide, burning eyes, and rows of jagged teeth.

It might have been playing an elaborate game of chicken with them, but Stone wasn't inclined to wait around and find out. He gathered magical energy and formed it into a ball of fire outside the ship, then flung it straight at the *wyvora's* gaping open mouth.

The thing's screech grew louder, echoing through the ship's tiny cabin. It beat its wings with frantic urgency, wheeling away with smoke trailing from its mouth.

"Take us down," Jeritha's words came fast. "We're getting close. Bear a little to the right."

Errin banked the ship right, pushing the yoke forward to lower the nose and begin their descent. Due to its design it could lose altitude faster than a standard plane, which made for a harrowing ride.

Stone, in the back, held tight to his seat arms and kept his eyes on the *wyvora*. It had slowed and now circled a hundred feet or so away. Its glowing red gaze was fixed on the ship, but so far it hadn't approached again. It circled back and forth, never taking its focus from its would-be prey.

"There's a place we can land just ahead," Jeritha said. "See—you can already see the lights from Drendell."

Stone risked a quick look. She was right: up ahead, a wide nest of lights twinkled from the ground. He wanted to be relieved, but couldn't yet—not while that winged monster still had them in its sights. At least if it came after them once they'd landed, he could deal more effectively with it, and Jeritha's navigator duties would no longer constrain her.

"Hold on," Errin snapped, and touched a control on the dash. The airship slowed to almost a full stop, hovering fifty feet or so above the ground, and then began a slower, elevator-like drop straight down. "Is that thing still out there?"

Stone checked again, using magical sight to supplement his mundane vision. "Damn!"

The *wyvora* was approaching them again, still higher in the air but closer. It moved more cautiously this time, but seemed to have recovered from Stone's last fireball. "I'll get it."

"Let me," Jeritha said. She twisted in her seat and fixed her attention on the beast, her face wreathed in a look of calm concentration.

The *wyvora* screeched again, but this time it almost sounded like a question instead of a challenge. As the ship landed with a *thump* on the rocky ground, it beat its massive wings a few times, indecisive, and then streaked off into the night.

| CHAPTER THIRTY-NINE

OR A FEW MOMENTS, the tiny cabin was silent as its three occupants waited for their jangling nerves to calm. "Well…" Errin said at last, unhooking her seat restraint, "that was…quite a bit more eventful than I'd hoped."

"But at least we're in one piece," Stone said. "And the ship is still functional. It *is* still functional, right?"

"As far as I know. We can stay here and I can check it out, but it will take time. Time I'd rather not take right now," she added with a glance toward the distant city.

"No," Stone agreed. "We need to get Harrison out of there before they find out we're looking for him and move him someplace we can't reach."

"Exactly my thought." Errin set a few controls on the dashboard, then pushed herself free of the seat. "Once we have him back, between the two of us we can fix any minor problems, magical or mechanical."

"Will the illusions and whatnot keep the ship safe?" Stone asked. He followed her out, glancing around at the dark, rocky terrain surrounding them. "It looks a bit…exposed out here."

"Like I said before—nobody comes out this far. The illusions and wards will keep any scavenging animals away. And if we do this right, we won't be gone long."

"Some of my people aren't far from here," Jeritha said. "They won't come near your ship, though."

"I guess it's as safe as we're likely to be," Stone said, though he wished he felt as confident as he sounded.

Errin already had the cargo bay open and was going through the boxes and bags, arranging gear in a backpack. "Just give me a few minutes to get this together and we can go."

"What all have you got in there?" Stone watched with interest as she continued stuffing small mechanical and electronic devices into the pack.

"Some things I've been working on with Trevor. Some of them are weapons—you saw one in action back at the Underground. A few are more experimental." She held up a metal box about the size of a large paperback book. "This is an illusion generator, for example—it creates a small area of invisibility, but only for a couple of minutes. And this one," she added, pulling out something that resembled a small box with a metal screen over one end, "creates a magic nullification field. It's really tricky, though—we've never been able to get it to work for longer than a second or two before it fails."

"Magic nullification field?" Stone switched to magical sight and examined the little thing, which appeared inert at the moment. "How does that work?"

"It disrupts the flow of magical energy in a specific way around an individual person. It would take me a long time to explain it—the basic idea is that magic is a form of energy, just like any other type. Any kind of energy can be manipulated, but the problem is you have to be able to access it before you can do it. Trevor and I have been working on it for a while now, to give non-magical people a weapon against the mages. I wouldn't trust it with our lives, though—not without a lot more testing."

"Wait a minute..." Stone said as she slipped it through a loop inside her pack.

"What?"

He sharpened his gaze as his mind returned to the scene from a few hours ago. "Could the mages—the Talented—have that technology?"

Errin stiffened. "Why do you ask?"

"Do you think that's what they did to Harrison? Maybe that bomb they set off wasn't just a bomb. What if it incorporated some kind of magic damping effect? If they could take down his magic even for a few seconds—especially if they injured and disoriented him with the bomb—then that would give them enough time to knock him out. And after that..." He shuddered, thinking again about the alchemist couple.

Errin considered her answer carefully, but her aura betrayed her tension. "I wouldn't have thought so—like I said before, the Talented aren't innovators as a rule. They don't need to be. Anything they want to do, they can do with magic."

"Not as a rule," Stone agreed. "But is it possible?"

"Of course it's possible. And if they *did* have people capable of that, you can be sure they'd be working for the authorities—voluntarily or otherwise." She let her breath out. "Damn. We need to get going." She reached into another of the boxes, withdrew a long, hooded gray cloak, and offered it to Jeritha, who'd been watching them in silence. "Here—you should put this on. It's not safe for you to be seen. Let's go."

After giving the ship one last check to verify the wards and illusion generators were functioning, they set off toward the distant glow of Drendell. Stone didn't know what time it was now, but from the look of the sky they had perhaps another hour or two before dawn.

They walked for several minutes in silence, each alone with his or her own thoughts. They moved with care, watching their footing; the rocky, dry terrain was riddled with treacherous holes and dropped off frequently, and they didn't want to give themselves away by using lights. Stone and Errin stumbled several times, but Jeritha traversed the hazards almost as if they weren't there. Stone wondered how much more she was seeing than he was, even with magical sight.

Before long, their surroundings gave way from rock and scrubby dead grass to the blasted-out ruins of buildings. Out here at the leading edge of where Drendell used to stand, the ruins were little more than foundations, with the occasional part of a crumbling wall, but Stone spotted the rising forms of half-intact structures ahead. He still saw no sign of human habitation.

"What do we do when we get into town?" he muttered. "Are we meeting someone at a specific place? Contacting them?"

"We'll make contact at a designated location," Errin said. "It's one we use sometimes for meetings. We'll need to check it carefully first, though."

"Do you trust this person we're talking to? It's not—the man himself, is it?" he added, avoiding the use of Olystriar's name even though it was unlikely anyone was listening to them out here.

"No. It's one of his agents. He's as suspicious as we are, since he has every bit as much to lose if we betray him."

"What about Galen?"

"When Kira contacted our agent, she told him to keep a lookout for him, and to take him into custody if he turned up. We should be able to handle him, though—he's not a mage." She shook her head. "I can't imagine what would cause him to betray us."

"We don't know he did yet, remember. Perhaps he—" Stone stopped.

"What?"

"Shh. I thought I heard something."

All of them stopped moving. Stone switched on magical sight, scanning the area around him.

"There," Jeritha whispered, pointing ahead of them.

Stone followed her line of sight to a squat, crumbling building. "I don't see—"

Something—several somethings—leapt over a low wall and streaked toward them.

"Bloody hell!" Stone backpedaled as he recognized the forms: a pack of the mutant wolf-creatures that had nearly killed him after the Temolan Guard had dumped him outside Drendell. He counted at least five of them, and though he couldn't get a good look in the pre-dawn dimness, his magical sight gave him the impression of unwellness.

Each one looked subtly different: some larger, some smaller, all of them skinny and mangy with malevolent glowing eyes and open, drooling mouths. One had a vestigial head like the one he'd seen before, and another had several non-functional limbs hanging off its patchy sides.

Next to him, Jeritha and Errin were already in action. Errin pulled something from one of her vest pockets and aimed it at one of the creatures, but didn't fire yet.

Jeritha raised her hands and focused intently on a large, shaggy form at the other end of the pack. After a moment it shook its head violently as if a cloud of insects had materialized around it, then growled and darted off.

The others kept coming. Stone pulled up a shield around himself and the others, directing a wide-angle concussion spell at the three in front. It hit two of the creatures, sending them tumbling backward with yelps of confusion.

The other one propelled itself above the spell with a mighty leap, only to slam into the shield. Stone got a brief impression of unhinged malevolence in the thing's eyes, before a blast sounded from his right and the creature fell back, the top of its head missing.

One of the remaining creatures, either more intelligent or more cautious, held back. It fixed its attention on Stone, its glowing red eyes meeting his, and then let loose with a keening howl.

Stone's body went rigid, and he couldn't move.

No, no! In horror, he remembered what had happened when he'd first encountered these things—how his body had seized up. At the time he'd thought it was either fear or simple injury and exhaustion, but this was the same thing now. His heart pounded in panic as the thing's skinny hindquarters bunched in preparation to leap—

He couldn't see what was happening to his left, he recognized Jeritha's voice as she barked a sharp command. The creature instantly calmed, and the hold on Stone broke.

Panting, he backed off as the wolf-thing cast a final glare at him, then one at Jeritha, and then slunk off back toward its hiding spot.

"Come," Jeritha said with some urgency. "We need to get away from here before they bring more of their pack."

Stone and Errin didn't have to be told twice. They picked up their pace and hurried forward; as the sun began to rise they could already see the taller structures that made up the edge of the city proper only a short distance ahead.

"What the hell *are* those things?" Stone demanded, glancing back over his shoulder with magical sight, half-convinced the whole diseased pack of them would be bearing down on his group. So far, his experiences with Calanar's wildlife had not been positive. "A couple of them nearly killed me when I got dumped outside town a while back."

"It's the magic," Jeritha said. "The war magic. It affected the animals even more than the people. A lot of them died, but many were—changed."

"Still?" Stone asked. "It's been a long time since the war, right? Are there still this many mutant animals running around? They don't breed that way, do they?" The thought of any of those horrific things managing to put up with each other long enough to mate made him shudder.

"It's magic," the Traveler said again. "It corrupts them. We avoid them when we can—they aren't usually brave enough to attack our bands, but if they do, we deal with them. They deserve pity, honestly." Her delicate features twisted in disgust. "It wasn't their fault, what happened to them. They're doing the best they can with what they've been left with."

"All the same, I'd be happier if they'd stay the hell away from us," Stone muttered. "Sorry, but I have a hard time feeling sorry for something that's trying to rip my throat out."

They picked up their pace after that, keeping close watch for any other potential attackers. Stone didn't allow his tense vigilance to drop until they reached the outskirts of Drendell proper, and even then he kept magical sight up as much as was practical. Oddly, he noticed the opposite from Jeritha: she'd seemed relatively calm even in the face of the mutant wolves, but as they approached Drendell she slowed her pace.

"Are you all right?" he asked her.

"I...don't like cities," she said. "Too many people, too...claustrophobic."

"Were you here alone before? When you were meeting someone at the Underground?"

"No. My companion and I were looking for someone there, but we were separated when the bomb exploded."

"And now you don't know if he's alive?"

"I do. He is alive—he managed to escape by concealing himself until the others left. He won't help us, though."

They exited the ruins at the end of a potholed, weed-choked street. Ahead, a cross street was deserted except for a couple of rusting, derelict vehicles parked across from each other.

"Why won't he help us?" Stone asked.

"He doesn't trust us, right?" Errin asked.

Jeritha didn't answer.

Errin motioned for them to duck into an alleyway and faced Jeritha. "Listen," she said, gently gripping the other woman's arm. "You don't have to do this. You guided us here safely through the Wastes—that's more than we could have expected. We'll need you to guide us back if we make it out of here, but there's no reason you have to come with us for the rest. This isn't your battle."

Jeritha's strange, black-eyed gaze came up, and her expression was resolved. "No. I have promised to help, and I will. Let's go."

They kept moving. Stone used a disregarding spell to keep the curious from paying much attention to them, though he needn't have—as the sun came up and the early-morning workers began taking to the streets, no one gave them a second look. Nonetheless, Stone's reaction to seeing people surprised him. *You don't have to hide anymore,* he reminded himself. *You can deal with whatever they throw at you now.*

They reached the address Errin had without incident. It was a two-story building halfway up a narrow side street lined with nondescript apartments and rooming houses. Their destination was on the second floor, a single-room apartment in the rear.

"Now, we wait," Errin said, opening the door. "Our contact should be reaching out to us soon."

Stone insisted on scanning the place with magical sight before entering. When he was satisfied, he dropped into a chair. "Do you lot keep safe houses in all the cities?"

Errin tossed her pack on the apartment's single bed, pulled something out of it, and placed a small device on the windowsill before pulling the shade down. "We have several places like this, yes. Quite a few of the people who sympathize with us choose to stay in the towns rather than coming to New Argana—they help us move around without being seen."

"Why don't they come?" Stone asked. "I can't imagine why anyone without magic would want to stay in hellholes like this, at the mercy of the mages, if they had an alternative."

"They have a lot of reasons." She repeated her performance with the other window, placing another device and lowering the shade before switching on a lamp. "Some have extended families here that they don't want to leave. Some feel they can do more good by remaining behind and helping others find their way to us, or to the wider resistance movement."

"There's a wider movement not connected with you?"

"Oh, yes. Absolutely. A lot of people in the cities don't even believe we exist."

"Good point," Stone admitted. "When I was here looking for Harrison, the only people who'd heard of him thought he was some kind of rumor, or ghost—or that he'd died years ago. It's possible they were lying to me, but I don't think so."

"It's difficult," Errin said. She was digging in her pack again, laying out various items on the bed. "New Argana isn't large yet—we don't have the infrastructure to bring in thousands of people. Also, if we draw too much attention from the Talented, they might decide it's worth their while to join forces and try to take us down."

"Could they do that?"

"I don't know. Trevor's powerful, but he's only one man. We have other mages, of course, and our magical-mechanical technology gives us an edge, but…"

"But what?"

She looked sober. "I've heard too many stories of what happened during the war—how powerful those weapons were. If they decided we were enough of a threat to revisit some of that research…who knows what they might be able to do. Already, we've heard rumors that some of the younger Talented believe the stories about what happened during the war are exaggerations."

Jeritha shuddered. "You have just explained why our people refuse to deal with those from the cities, and why most of them won't even deal with your group. The danger is too great."

Stone could certainly understand where the Traveler woman was coming from. "So you keep everything as quiet as possible and work under everyone's radar."

"I don't know what 'radar' is," Errin said. "But if you mean we stay underground and spend most of our time helping indirectly, then yes. There might come a time when we're strong enough that we can try something more overt, but not yet. And that's why it's so important to get Trevor back—aside from the fact that he's our friend, of course. I didn't think it was possible for them to take him down, but obviously I was wrong. If I was wrong about that, I might be wrong about whether they can get him to talk."

"And if he tells them about New Argana…about the Nexus…" Unable to sit still any longer, Stone got up and began pacing.

"Exactly. I know some of them suspect something is out there, but I'm sure they don't know exactly what it is. They don't know about the Nexus. If they did…well, you met some of them. You know what they'd be likely to do."

"That might make them willing to put up with each other long enough to do something about it." Stone remembered the incident at Burning Man, where the top-tier Evil—a group who normally couldn't stand being in the same room together—put aside their differences long enough to hatch a plan to build a massive portal to their home dimension. If the Evil could do it, the Talented could certainly manage it as well.

"Exactly. If they knew where we were and decided we were a big enough threat—well, they've got treaties that forbid using war magic against each other, but we're *already* out in the Wastes where nobody goes, so they could easily rationalize using it against us."

Stone nodded soberly. Human nature, apparently, was as alive and well on Calanar as it was on Earth. "I hate sitting here on our hands waiting to hear from someone."

"So do I. But we don't have a choice. Until we have more information, it would be foolish to move."

It was close to an hour later before the phone rang, startling all three of the apartment's occupants. Errin leaped from her chair at the kitchen table, where she'd been fiddling with one of her devices, and snatched it up. She said nothing, but listened for close to a minute. "Yes. Three. Two women, one man," she said at last. Another pause. "Got it." She hung up.

"What's the plan?" Stone asked. He'd stopped his incessant pacing to watch her.

"I've got an address to meet them. There's a vehicle behind this building—we'll take that." She began gathering the gear she'd removed from the backpack and stowing it back inside.

"Do they know where Harrison is?"

"They won't say anything on the phone. Let's go."

Jeritha rose from the bed; Errin had urged her to rest while she could. "Are you sure you trust these people?"

Errin retrieved her devices from the two windowsills and put them in her pockets. "As much as we can. We'll be careful. Come on."

They found the vehicle, a blocky sedan covered half in gray primer and half in rust, parked where Errin had said it would be. She got behind the wheel and removed the keys from under the sun visor. Stone took shotgun, and Jeritha ducked low in the back seat.

When Errin fired the car up, it shuddered and rattled, loud popping backfires erupting from its battered exhaust pipe. Stone doubted the thing would make it more than a mile—until they drove off. Despite all the noise and shaking, the car rode as if on a cushion of air. "Nice," he said. "Magic?"

"Actually, no." Errin grinned, turning a corner. "The car might look like it's ready for the scrap-heap, and they've added a few 'extras' to make it sound like it too, but under the hood it's beautiful. Tires, too."

"Well, that's encouraging, at least." He kept magical sight up as they drove, watching the auras as they passed more people on their way to work. To his surprise, he soon recognized their surroundings. Some of the buildings and shops they passed were the same ones where he'd made his deliveries for Faran's butcher shop. His hand tightened on the armrest as they passed the burned-out hulk of the shop itself. Apparently nobody had bothered to rebuild it yet; blackened beams stuck up from its ruined foundation, and the light morning rain pattered over piles of rubble.

"Are you all right?" Errin asked, glancing over at him.

He pointed. "The Talented murdered the people who owned that shop. For helping me." His voice came out cold and strained.

She gripped the steering wheel harder. "I'm sorry."

"So am I. I almost want a couple of those entitled bastards to try having a go at me now—let them see what happens when the prey fights back."

"I know," she said gently, reaching across to give his arm a brief squeeze. "I get it. But we need to wait, even if you do see any of them. We can't blow our cover."

"Don't worry—I can control myself, unlike them. But once we get Harrison out, if any of them try anything, they'll find out what a mistake that was."

They drove a few more blocks, passing a few other vehicles and more pedestrians, then turned on a narrow side street. Errin slowed the car. "Do either of you two see anyone?"

Stone switched to magical sight and scanned the area, including the roofs of nearby buildings. "No. If they're here, they're hiding well."

"I see no one," Jeritha confirmed, peering over the back seat.

"Good." Errin made a quick right into a narrow garage, then jumped out and pulled its door shut behind them. She retrieved her pack, placed one of her devices on the car's bumper, and motioned toward the door at the other end.

The door was locked, with a mechanical pushbutton panel above it. Errin tapped in the code and pushed it open.

Beyond was a short hallway with another door at the end. That one, also locked, opened onto a small abandoned shop, its display window and the smaller one over its door boarded up with plywood.

Stone held up a light spell, illuminating an old wooden counter, a floor covered in trash and debris, and several broken chairs. Whatever the shop had been before, all its fixtures had been removed, either on purpose or by scavengers.

"Nice place," he said. "When does this person get here?"

"I am already here," said a disembodied voice.

| CHAPTER FORTY

STONE, ERRIN, AND JERITHA all spun toward the counter, the mages gathering magic and Errin swinging her gun around.

"Stop," the voice urged. "I am a friend."

A figure shimmered into being behind the counter: a tall, dark-haired man with a neatly-trimmed beard. Despite his obvious magic, he was clad not in the Talented's standard high-collared long coat, but a simple shirt, jacket, and trousers, such as any middle-class citizen of Drendell might wear.

Stone didn't relax, and neither did Jeritha. Between them, though, Errin lowered the gun. "Who sent you?" she asked.

"Our mutual friend, who has a fondness for fine wine," the man said. "Have you brought any today?"

"The vines won't be ready for another month," Errin replied. The last of the tension drained from her shoulders. "What has our friend discovered?"

The man didn't answer right away; his gaze moved over Stone and finally settled on Jeritha. "A Traveler?"

"We trust her," Errin said. "She saved our lives during the raid at the Underground, and helped us come here. You can speak in her presence."

He considered a moment, then looked at Stone. "And this man?"

"You needn't worry about him. He's an old friend of the man we're looking for. We trust him completely as well."

The man seemed to take Errin's word for it, nodding once. "All right, then. We must speak quickly—I cannot be out of communication for long, or dangerous people may become suspicious."

"Tell us the plan. Will our friend be able to help us?"

He motioned for them to come closer to him; when they did, he raised his hand and an almost transparent bubble flowered around them. "It will not be easy to get to the man you seek. They're taking great care with him."

"Is he in Temolan?"

"Yes. They're holding him beneath the surface, in a specially-prepared magic-null field."

"I didn't know they had such a thing," Errin said, her jaw tightening.

"It is experimental. One of the Council members has assembled a small team of highly intelligent and unethical researchers to work on her special projects."

"Are those two mad alchemists part of this team?" Stone asked.

The man looked surprised that he was aware of them. "Yes. Millia and Vestereth. They are brilliant, particularly when working together, but they have little in the way of morals."

"So they've got him drugged," Errin said. She looked as angry as Stone felt, but kept it under tight control.

"Yes. Aside from their intention to keep him docile and prevent him from using his magic, they have been trying different formulations on him in an attempt to induce him to reveal information about his organization and where he originates."

Damn. "Do you know if they've gotten anything out of him yet?" Stone asked.

"I am not certain—I'm not privy to their sessions, nor is our friend. However, our friend has heard a rumor that they are fascinated by his unusual resilience, and are trying to determine its cause."

"Bloody hell…" Stone murmured. "So in addition to torturing him for information, they're experimenting on him?"

"So it would seem," the man said. "It has not been long, of course, so I doubt they have had time to do too much yet. But from what I know of them…"

"What about the others?" Errin asked. "The rest of this team?"

"There are five in all, including Millia and Vestereth. Some of the finest—and most dangerous—minds in Temolan. From what our friend has heard, all of them have been redirected to this project by their patron."

"And who is that?" Errin asked. "Which of the Council members? Or is there more than one?"

"Only one as far as our friend is aware. She has always been…unconventional in her methods."

"I know who you're talking about." Errin let her breath out. "Of course, it's got to be her. So the rest of the Council doesn't know about it?"

"Oh, no doubt they do, if our friend is aware. They not entirely approve, but they turn a blind eye because they recognize the potential usefulness of her research if the political climate should change at some future date."

"You mean they'll be all too happy to make use of her unethical experiments if the situation between the mage houses goes south at some point," Stone said.

"Just so, yes."

"So what can we do?" Errin asked. "How do we get the man we're looking for out? Do you know exactly where he is?"

"Not at present, but I know where he will be this evening."

"They're moving him?"

"Yes. It was not possible to keep the raid at the Underground a secret from the other Council members, and rumors are already circulating about who they have captured. That is how our friend heard about it. They insist on being apprised of the situation, so those who have captured him have arranged to move him to a more neutral location."

"And what do they plan to do there?" Stone asked.

"That I do not know. If previous experience serves, they will set up some sort of display to impress the others with how far their research has progressed." He glanced around, looking suddenly fearful. "I must go now—I've already stayed too long." From his pocket he pulled an envelope, which he handed to Errin. "This contains directions for how to get to another location. Give me an hour to have your identification prepared, then go there and you'll find it, disguises, and directions for how to get to Temolan."

"Got it," Errin said, pocketing the envelope. She gripped his arm. "Thank you. For everything. I know how much you're risking."

The man studied their faces, looking serious. "You will need to be very careful, especially with a Traveler and a non-Talented. I've arranged for you to meet someone once you arrive in Temolan, but getting to him will involve some risk."

"We'll manage," Stone said. "Thank you."

"Good luck to you," the man said. "Remember, give me an hour before you go to that address." He stepped back, the bubble faded, and then after a moment so did he.

Stone let his breath out. "I feel like I'm in some kind of bloody spy film. I keep expecting a squad of assassins to show up any second."

"The Talented don't play around," Errin said. "Most of them don't have a lot of ambition, but we represent a significant threat to their way of life. They're far too arrogant to sit still for that."

"So now we wait," Stone said, resuming his pacing.

"Yes. That's the hardest part."

The hour crawled by. Jeritha returned to the bed for more rest and Errin sat at the table tinkering with her devices, but Stone couldn't sit still. He stalked the small confines of the apartment, glancing at the clock every couple of minutes and pausing frequently at the windows to peer out through the cracks in the blinds using magical sight, convinced a group of Talented agents had surrounded them and were preparing to attack.

No such thing happened, though, and eventually Errin stood and gathered her tools into her pack. "Let's go. This address isn't far."

Jeritha rose gracefully and pulled her cloak back on. "I don't sense anyone nearby," she said. "We should be safe."

Stone wasn't so sure, but she seemed to have a greater sensitivity for such things than he did, so he followed the others out.

Now, at midmorning, more people were out and going about their day's activities. Nobody paid the old car any attention as they drove to the new address, another apartment building down yet another narrow side street. This time they had to park out front. Stone put a disregarding spell on the car, and Jeritha checked out the interior before they went in.

Inside, they found a large box and a smaller one in the corner of the front room, hidden under an illusion. After Stone dispelled it, Errin opened the larger box to reveal three paper-wrapped parcels. She opened the first one and held up a long, high-collared black coat trimmed in electric blue. Her lip curled in disgust. "I know it's necessary, but it's going to be hard to wear one of these ridiculous outfits and keep a straight face." She handed the coat to Stone. "I think this one's yours."

"I completely agree about wearing that," Stone said. He took the coat and looked it over. It included several small pins on the lapels, similar to the ones he'd seen before. This was the first time he'd seen them up close, though: each one sported what looked like a magical sigil. "What's with the blue, anyway? Every one of these bastards I've seen has either worn a blue coat or another color with blue highlights."

"It's Temolan's color," Errin said. "All the mage houses have a color and a symbol associated with them. The houses require their affiliated mages to wear the symbol—it's part of their identification. The color's more of a fashion choice, but most of them do it out of pride."

"Ah, to show which team they cheer for," Stone said, shaking his head. "I should have expected that lot to be a bunch of pathetic conformists." He slipped the coat on; at first it seemed a little too snug, but he tensed as the thing shifted on its own and settled around him as if it were a live thing trying to get comfortable. When it stopped moving, it now fit like it had been tailored for him.

"Nice trick," he admitted grudgingly. "I'll have to work on a spell like that back home." He spread his arms. "So, how stupid do I look in this thing?"

Errin tilted her head. "It suits you, actually. No insult intended." She removed another coat, brown with dark blue trim, and offered it to Jeritha. Like Stone's, it conformed perfectly to her body when she put it on.

"No coat for you?" Stone asked Errin.

"I won't be able to pass as a Talented, so my role will be as your servant." She sighed, looking resigned as she pulled a rough-looking set of clothes from the box. "I hope you're good at playing an arrogant bastard, because you'll need to keep me safe if anyone else gets out of line. You'll also have to treat me like I'm not worth your time, so they don't get suspicious."

Stone closed his eyes. "I can do arrogant with the best of them—but cruelty will be difficult."

"Remember our mission. We'll do what we have to do." She went back to digging in the large box. Also inside the box were the remainder of Stone's and Jeritha's outfits: rich-looking shirts and boots, with trousers for Stone and a long skirt for Jeritha. Like the other Talented's clothing Stone had seen, these appeared to have been enchanted to repel dirt and keep them crisp and bright.

"Keep an illusion over those until we're ready to leave," Errin said. "They'll draw too much attention in Drendell."

"What's in the smaller box?" Stone asked.

She opened it and spread the items on the table. There were two signet rings, a sheaf of papers, three stiff cards, and two small leather bags, each of which contained a quantity of shiny gold and silver pyramid-shaped objects.

"Is that money?" Stone picked up one of the gold ones. It had writing stamped into all of its sides, including one of the sigils displayed on his jacket's pins.

"Yes." Errin handed each of them a ring and a card, and pocketed the other card. "These are identification for the Talented—the ring and the card together. Both of them are magical."

Stone shifted to magical sight and examined them. Both glowed with faint magic, and when he slipped the ring on his finger, it radiated warmth for a moment and then settled in to match his aura. The card made the same change. "Nice one. Seems a bit…insecure, though. So all someone would have to do is steal some of these and they imprint on their wearer?"

"No, not exactly. From what I understand, the issuing authority has to prepare them to do that. The blanks won't work on their own. That's why our friend is so important."

"No image?"

She chuckled. "No point. When people can make themselves look like whatever they want—especially when they don't like their true form getting around—an ID photo would be useless. Besides, you can't fake an aura, right?"

"It's quite difficult, at least where I come from." He unfolded the sheaf of papers, which were covered in the same flowing, elaborate print he'd identified as the Talented's written language. "Is it going to be a problem that I can't read any of this?"

"Shouldn't be. If all goes well, we won't be there long. I can read some of it. Can you, Jeritha?"

"A bit. Not much."

"We'll be fine. I'll read the signs, and you do whatever you need to do so nobody uses me for target practice."

"How are we going to get to Temolan?" Stone asked. "I don't know how to operate the teleport pads, and I assume Jeritha doesn't either."

"If our IDs hold up, it won't be a problem. We'll have to pass through a checkpoint, but the pads operate automatically. The ones from the surface cities only go to one location in the public area. Ah! I forgot." She fished in one of her vest pockets and withdrew three small objects. "These are something else Trevor and I came up with a while back. Alastair, can you attune them to us?"

Stone took them and studied them. They appeared to be gold drops with clips on them. "Earrings?"

"Right. They're communication devices, designed to only work between those they're attuned to. They have a very short range, but we shouldn't be apart anyway."

Stone shifted to magical sight and instantly spotted the magic swirling around the little devices. Attuning them to himself and his friends was similar to what he'd done with the illusion generators he'd built before. He clipped one on his ear and gave the others back.

"Is it working?" Errin's voice sounded in Stone's ear, crisp and clear even though she'd barely moved her lips.

"Very nice. I'm definitely going to need to spend some time with you lot after we get this all sorted out."

"I hope you'll have the chance," she said at normal volume, her expression sobering. "We should go. I want to get to Temolan and meet our contact soon, so we'll have time to prepare for tonight."

Stone glanced out the window again, shifting back to magical sight and wishing he could shake the feeling that someone was out there watching them.

CHAPTER FORTY-ONE

"**A**RE YOU TWO READY FOR THIS?" Errin asked.

They sat in their battered vehicle, parked a block down from a trim, two-story building in the heart of Drendell—the location of the teleportation pad that would take them to Temolan.

"I just want to get on with it at this point," Stone said. Like the others, he now wore his disguise, and had wreathed all three of them in a disregarding spell. He glanced at Jeritha, whose illusion spell hid her gray complexion and silvery-green hair; she was now pale and green-eyed, with a dark-auburn bob.

"I hate to do this to you—a lot of it is going to be on you and your magic, and that makes me nervous so soon after you've got it back. But we don't have a lot of choice. I hope our contact in Temolan can help us more when we reach him."

"We'll be fine," Stone said. "Let's do it before I lose my nerve."

It was mid-day so they had no hope of waiting for the street to be empty, but they did take careful looks around—physical, technological, and magical—to make as sure as possible no Talented were nearby. Stone and Jeritha used a tricky combination of magic to hide their exit from the vehicle and keep them invisible until they ducked into a side street, then dropped the spell so they could stride from that direction toward the building.

As disgusted as it made him to do so, Stone called up his mental images of the Talented he'd interacted with and did his best to channel their attitude of entitled arrogance. He drew himself to his full height and walked with purpose, keeping Errin in sight at all times. Jeritha walked on the other side of Errin, maintaining the same demeanor even though Stone knew she hated it as much as he did.

The building was in much better repair than the others near it, and it wasn't hard to sense the magical traces in and around it. Stone and the others swept through the door, trying to look like they knew where they were going.

Inside, a large open atrium was flanked on either side by glass-walled office cubicles. On the left side, a sweeping staircase led to the second floor. The walls were painted the same pleasant cream Stone had seen in some of the Temolan buildings, while the floor was blue stone with silver accents. Artwork—probably the Talented's answer to the sort of inoffensive modern art employed on the walls of every office building in Earth's corporate sector—hung at intervals, and several small, bright chandeliers floated languidly high above them with no visible tethers to the building. Everything in here was as immaculately clean as the mages' outfits.

The lower floor wasn't crowded; Stone spotted perhaps fifteen people in all. Most went about their business without paying any attention to those coming and going, while three—two Talented and one whose rougher outfit marked him as non-magical—waited in two separate lines near the middle of the open floor. Ahead, past a silver railing, Stone spotted a large teleport pad flanked by a man and a woman in identical blue coats. As they hung back and watched, another long-coated woman entered, strode past them, and took her place at the end of the Talented's line. The two attendants directed each of the Talented in turn to the teleporter pad, and only when they'd all disappeared did they wave the non-magical man up. They examined his identification much more closely than they had the others', their faces wreathed in distaste. Stone noticed they didn't touch his papers, but levitated them in front of them.

"Bloody bastards…" he muttered.

"Stay calm," Errin murmured back, watching as the non-mage stepped onto the platform and disappeared. "We should go while no one else is here. Make it look good."

Stone took a moment to calm his aura, then set his expression to the kind of cold unapproachability he used when he wasn't in the mood to interact with anyone back on Earth. He gave Errin a gentle magical shove and was pleased when she stumbled forward as if he'd pushed her much harder, then strode up to the pad.

The two uniformed Talented flicked an annoyed gaze at Errin, then focused on Stone. "Identification, please," the man said. He sounded bored.

Stone handed over his card, then held out his hand with the signet ring as he'd seen the previous Talented do. The scan seemed to take forever, but after only a couple of seconds the man nodded once. "You're cleared. Who is…*this*?"

"She's my servant. I had some errands in Drendell."

"Do you have her identification?"

"You heard the man," Stone snapped to Errin. "Show him your identification."

"Yes, sir," she said meekly, and pulled it from her pocket.

This time, the man didn't take the papers, but levitated them as he had with the other non-magical man. He glanced over them, then at the bag she carried. "What is in that bag? Let me see."

"The bag is mine," Stone said, injecting as much imperiousness into his tone as he could manage and meeting the man's gaze directly. "I didn't feel the need to carry it when she can."

The man considered and nodded with a sly smile. "Of course not. It's all the Dim are good for, after all—manual labor. Have a pleasant day."

"And you as well," Stone said. He didn't do it through gritted teeth, which was a victory.

Meanwhile, Jeritha had no trouble getting past the female attendant. Stone shoved Errin forward again and the three of them stepped on to the platform.

The Talented's teleportation pads weren't as smooth as the ones at the Nexus; Stone felt an electric jolt similar to the half-remembered sensation when the Guard had originally taken him to the surface. A moment later, they stood in a large, open area with soaring ceilings, more floating lights, and long-coated people bustling back and forth.

"Grand Central Station," Stone muttered as they stepped off the pad, hoping the earring device would deliver his words to his friends. On either side, several more pads disgorged more people, all of whom immediately strode away. Stone noticed that the few unaccompanied people dressed in work clothes headed in a different direction than the others.

"This is the central public area of Temolan," Errin told him as they joined the throng. "No one who isn't sworn to the Temolan mage house is allowed outside this district without special permission—mages or non-mages. The exception is the workers, whose identification gives them access to the specific other parts of town where they need to be. If they're caught outside those areas, they're subject to exile or execution."

Stone didn't doubt that. "Where are we going? Do they have cabs or anything here, or has someone arranged transportation?"

"Most people don't use personal transportation in the public area—the hovertrain goes around the perimeter of the city, and there are more configurable teleportation pads once you get out of the public sector."

"So we walk, then? Do you know where we're headed?"

"Yes. Our contact left me a map. Let's get out of sight and then we can get our bearings. I've never been to Temolan before. I'm assuming you haven't either, Jeritha?"

"No," she said, obviously fighting hard to keep her nervous disgust from showing as she looked around at the tall, cream-colored buildings. The soaring structures were beautiful—whoever had designed them had obviously put as much of a premium on aesthetics as on function—but also gave an uncomfortable feeling of looming over the crowds below, as if preparing to pounce on anyone unworthy of being in their presence. Even the rows of delicate trees planted along the spotless streets seemed somehow sinister in their perfect alignment.

"Is our contact meeting us in the public area?" Stone asked. He wondered if the Talented who lived in the city experienced the looming feeling too, or if it was a byproduct of knowing one didn't belong here and wasn't welcome.

"Yes. They have buildings with accommodations for visitors from other cities—we're meeting him at one of those. Our identification *should* get us out of the public area, but I don't want to test it until we've made contact with him."

They chose a secluded corner of a small sidewalk café, sitting at an outdoor table. Stone went inside and got drinks (reluctantly heeding Errin's suggestion to bring her only a simple glass of water) and then refreshed the disregarding spell as he sat back down. At least the money hadn't been a problem—he'd watched the customers in front of him and handed over one of the silver-colored pyramids in payment, receiving a few copper ones in change.

Between the three of them, they managed to identify their current location on the map, and from there to determine where they needed to end up. Fortunately the public area was not large—only a few blocks around the outer edge of the city—so they wouldn't have to walk far.

"How many people are in one of these cities?" Stone asked. "What's the mage population like in comparison to the non-mages?"

"Nobody's done an exact count," Errin said. "But the mages number a fraction of the non-magical people. Our best estimate is that each of the floating cities has thirty to fifty thousand people, with around ten times that for the surface cities."

Stone wondered how many Travelers there might be, but didn't want to ask where they might be overheard. "So if the non-magical people ever got themselves sorted and made an effort—"

"Not likely any time soon." Errin took a quick glance around before lowering her gaze again like a good servant. "Most of the non-magical people are, if not content with their situation, too scared to do anything about it. And sadly, a lot of them *do* live up to the name 'Dim.' They want nothing more than to do their work, raise their families, and stay as far away from any conflict with the mages as they can." Another quick glance. "Best if we don't talk about that here, though. We should get going. I don't like being out in the open like this."

They left the restaurant and headed up the street. Stone kept the disregarding spell up and forced himself not to look at every person they passed; instead, he kept his purposeful gaze straight ahead as if intent on some important business. He was glad Jeritha was small and slight, which gave him a valid excuse to slow his normally brisk pace. Nobody paid any attention to them, not even the uniformed guard standing at a corner halfway to their destination. Stone tensed a little as they walked by, but the man seemed to be looking at something across the street and ignored them.

"Just around this corner," Errin said through Stone's earring. "Second floor of the third building down."

The area wasn't crowded, but it wasn't deserted, either. People walked leisurely up and down the street, and occasionally someone or a small group would enter or leave one of the buildings.

"Is this safe?" Stone asked. "Will anyone overhear us?"

"We'll have to be careful, but it's part of the treaty between the mage houses that the residence areas of the public sectors are to be kept surveillance-free. That's in addition to the fact that almost every building in the cities is warded."

She shrugged. "I wouldn't trust the 'surveillance-free' part, to be honest, but unless they suspect us they've got no reason to focus their effort on bugging random rooms."

Stone hoped she was right, but as they entered the building she'd pointed out, his heart beat faster. He focused on keeping his aura under control so no one would suspect his tension.

They took the stairs, avoiding the floating magical elevator platform. The second-floor hall was empty, but Stone took a look around with magical sight to verify nobody was lurking invisibly. "You can't see into the rooms, can you?" he asked Jeritha.

"No. As Errin said, everything is warded."

"All right—let's do this before somebody shows up."

They hurried to the door at the end of the hall and Errin knocked.

There was no answer.

Stone exchanged glances with Errin. "Aren't they supposed to be here?"

"Yes." Now she looked tense too. "He should have been waiting for us."

"Something's wrong," Jeritha said.

"Should we wait for—" Stone began.

"No." Her gaze darted back and forth. "We need to go."

Errin tried the door. It pushed open easily. "Not locked. That's a bad sign."

"They're coming!" Jeritha whispered, even more urgent now. "Go inside!" She gave Errin a little shove in that direction.

Stone didn't wait to ask questions. He hurried inside behind them, closing and locking the door.

They both saw the unconscious body at the same time. It lay on the other side of the room, bloody and flayed—a portly figure in a shredded long coat.

"Oh, no!" Errin said. "He's—"

The figure moaned.

"He's alive!" Stone started to hurry over, but Jeritha grabbed his arm.

"No!" she hissed. "It's an illusion! They're—"

The prone form faded from view as two long-coated figures shimmered into existence, one rising from behind a chair, the other slipping in through an open doorway. Both raised their hands, energy crackling around them.

Stone, Errin, and Jeritha acted instantly and as one. Jeritha popped up a glimmering shield around them while Stone let loose with a blast of magical energy at one of the attackers. The man's attack danced and sparked around the shield, but didn't get through. An instant later he screamed, staggering back and slamming into the wall, his body juddering.

Errin, meanwhile, fired three rounds from her gun, catching the second figure in the center of the chest, the throat, and the face in quick succession before he managed to erect his own shield.

"Bloody hell!" Stone swept his gaze around the room, looking for more attackers. "Jeritha, if you hadn't spotted—"

"More are coming," Jeritha interrupted. "We have to go. Now!"

Errin didn't hesitate. "Go—out the window!"

Jeritha was already there, off to the side. She poked her head around only enough to peer out. "I don't see anyone else out there," she said. "Come on!"

Someone tried the door.

"Go!" Errin hissed again.

"Stay close!" Stone said, hurrying over. "Jeritha, can you keep us invisible?"

"Yes."

"Do it."

Once the window was open, he quickly cast a levitation spell around all of them. His heart pounded harder as he glanced back over his shoulder toward the door, then focused on the task at hand and sent them out one at time: Jeritha first, Errin next, and finally himself. As he cleared the window and used magic to close it behind them, he barely spotted the door slamming open and three more figures swarming into the room.

"Where?" he whispered. He couldn't see his friends now, though he could still feel them gripped in his spell.

"Up," Errin said. "Across the street, to the roof."

Once again, Stone didn't stop for questions. He lifted them high and then sent them floating across to the opposite building, then lowered them carefully behind the roof line so they wouldn't be visible to anyone looking out the other window. To his relief, his newly augmented magic seemed to be holding up—the jackhammer thudding of his heart had nothing to do with exhaustion from casting. "What now? Was that supposed to be our contact in the room?"

Jeritha let her breath out and dropped the invisibility spell, and Stone got his answer from Errin's grim expression.

"That was him," she said. "I'm sure he's dead. I don't know how they found out, but—"

"Do you think they know we're coming?" Stone asked, re-casting the disregarding spell. "If they had us under observation as we entered—"

"I don't know. But we need to get out of here."

"Do you know where we can hide? Can you reach—" he dropped his voice even further. "—our high-level contact?"

"No. It would be suicide—for us *and* for him—to contact him while we're still inside the city."

"Well, what, then? We don't know where—our friend—is, do we?"

"We know where he'll be. That was in the information we got earlier. But he won't be there for several hours. We need to find someplace to lie low between now and then. But without any contacts in the city—" She let her breath out. "We can't stay up here long. Someone will spot us."

Stone scanned the area for anyone approaching them, but saw nothing. "There's no one else you can reach? You don't have any other contacts in Temolan?"

"Not that we can trust."

"Do you know how to reach the one who helped us earlier?"

"No. That was on purpose. And it's worse than you think—I've got a location for where they'll be taking our friend, but it's deep inside the private sector of the city. I don't have any idea how to get there." She let her breath out and her shoulders slumped. "Well, we'd better get down from here and find some place to hide, and change our illusionary disguises."

"Damn." Stone made another quick scan, trying not to dwell on what kind of deep hole they'd dug themselves into. It was possible that the Temolan authorities had merely found out about their contact in the room, killed him, and lay in wait for anyone who came to find him. If that was the case, then changing their illusionary disguises and finding a bolt-hole somewhere might be enough to conceal them for the rest of the day until they could go after Harrison. But if the Talented knew who they were and why they were here, they could be walking into a trap. Assuming, of course, that they could even *find* Harrison's location without anyone to show them the way. If only they could—

"Wait!" He held up a hand as Jeritha and Errin rose and prepared to move.

"What?" Errin's posture and expression both suggested she had no desire to remain here any longer.

"Do you know how to contact people in Temolan? Do they use telephones, the post, or—I don't know—magical owls?"

She tilted her head, casting him a look of pure confusion. "What?"

"How do people contact each other here? Is it like in Drendell? Do they use telephones? Is there a directory?"

"No telephones—they wouldn't use something that mundane. They have magical communication orbs."

"Can we get to one? Are there public ones?"

"I think so—but we'd need to be careful."

"Can I or Jeritha make it work?"

"I don't think it's difficult if you have magic. But—"

"Come on, then."

"Alastair, what—"

"I think I know someone we can contact. But we need to get away from here first."

| CHAPTER FORTY-TWO

"**Y**OU NEED TO TELL ME what's going on," Errin said. Somehow—Stone wasn't sure how no one had spotted them, but apparently his disregarding spell and Jeritha's magic had done the trick—they'd managed to get off the roof, slip down several side streets, and duck into an out-of-the-way alley several blocks from the room where they'd found their contact's body. Across the street, they'd identified a bar with a communication orb in the back. They watched it now from their vantage point, the disregarding spell at full strength on all three of them.

Stone hadn't revealed anything about his plan to Errin and Jeritha—partly because he wanted to get the hell away from where they might be under surveillance as quickly as possible, and partly because he wanted to go over it to make sure he hadn't missed any potential flaws. It would be dangerous, but they had few options at this point.

"I know someone in Temolan," he said. "At least I hope I do, assuming she's still here."

"Who?" Errin asked, surprised. "How can you—"

"I met her in Drendell. She's a healer. She worked at the hospital where they took me after I was injured, and she saved my life."

"But if she's in Drendell—"

"She's not—at least I don't think she is. She got recalled to Temolan. I don't think they had anything specific on her, though—the person I talked to after she left seemed to think they just got tired of her 'wasting her talent' healing lowly mundanes."

Errin narrowed her eyes. "What makes you think she'll help us?"

"If they had a problem with her talking to me, they shouldn't be watching her anymore. I'm dead, remember? And since I've been in disguise ever since then, I doubt they know I'm back. Plus, they also don't know I have magic." When Errin still looked skeptical, he added, "We don't have a lot of choices, do we? We've got to do something before tonight. You two stay here and keep a lookout—I'll go in the shop and see if I can contact her. If she says no, I'll just hang up and we can find another plan."

"She might not only say no," Errin pointed out. "She might betray us. Alert the authorities that we're here."

"You don't know her. She doesn't have this lot's issues with non-magical people. She wants to help. That was why she was in Drendell in the first place."

Errin looked away, then back at Stone with a sigh. "You're right—we don't have many other options. Okay, let's do it." She hunted in one of her pockets and withdrew a spherical object the size of a large marble. "Put this in your pocket, against your leg. If we see anything suspicious, I'll trigger it and it will buzz. Get out fast if that happens, then circle back around and meet us in that shop." She pointed down the street at another small café.

"Got it. I'll be back soon."

With a new disguise in place to make him look like a balding, middle-aged man, he hurried across the street and slipped into the bar.

Bars, apparently, didn't change much based on whether you were a mage snob or a working-class mundane. Dimly lit and intimate, this one had a row of padded stools along the bar itself and a small number of tables on the other side. Behind the bar, a mirror dominated the wall with several shelves of liquor arranged in front. The only indications mages ran the bar were smaller versions of the floating lights, the preternatural newness and cleanliness of the fixtures, and the way the bartender served his customers by floating glasses to them instead of carrying them. Soft, instrumental music played, though Stone couldn't see any speakers.

This time of day there weren't many customers: Stone spotted only two, both men, one at the bar and one at one of the tables. Both glanced briefly up when he entered but then returned to their drinks. He walked to the bar and waited to be noticed.

The bartender finished serving the other customer and approached him. "What can I get you?"

Stone had questioned both Errin and Jeritha about local drinks, and ordered one Errin had assured him would be innocuous and wouldn't raise any flags. He used his American accent, even though he wasn't sure how his translation spell dealt with accents. As always, no point taking chances.

Drink in hand (he gave the man one of the silver pyramids and got several more bronze ones in change), he headed to the back. Next to a hallway leading to the restrooms, he found a small wooden cubicle a little larger than an Earth phone booth. Its swinging door featured a half-height window through which he could keep an eye on the front of the bar.

He pushed inside, finding a milky, bowling-ball sized glass orb on a carved wooden pedestal. Hoping both that the information Errin had given him was accurate and that Tanissa was still in Temolan, he took a centering breath, placed his hands on either side of the orb, and sent a small magical pulse into it.

Immediately the milky glass went clear, and the orb hummed under his hands. It seemed to be waiting for something.

"Er—I'm trying to reach Tanissa," he said. Would it be enough? He didn't know the rest of her name. How many Tanissas were there in Temolan? He had no idea if it would work, but he concentrated on sending a mental image of her. Once again, his lack of what seemed here to be basic knowledge troubled him. Back on Earth he was one of the foremost experts on magic, but here he felt like an apprentice. Not even an apprentice—a child, perhaps, who'd grown up in a magical family but hadn't been taught any of the specifics yet.

The thing hummed for a few more seconds, and once again he got the feeling it wanted something from him. "Er—Tanissa," he repeated. "I don't know her address, but she's just returned to Temolan recently, I heard."

More humming, and then the feeling changed from questioning to satisfaction. The globe went milky again, but this time a pleasant blue instead of white. Several seconds passed, and then a familiar face appeared.

Tanissa looked suddenly wary when her gaze settled on Stone's disguised form. "Yes…?"

"Tanissa. How…are you?" Either she wasn't using an illusion or else she'd been using the same one in Drendell, because she appeared just as he remembered her from the hospital. She looked tired.

"Do I know you?" she asked, narrowing her eyes. "I don't know you. I think you've reached the wrong person."

She reached out, and instinctively Stone knew she was about to break the connection. "No!" he said, soft but urgent, leaning forward. "Tanissa. You do know me. I'm—disguised. With an illusion."

She frowned, looked around her as if checking to make sure she was alone, then she too leaned closer to her orb. "Who are you?"

Here goes… He tensed, his heart beating faster again. "I don't want to say my name on this thing, in case anyone's listening. You might remember me from your time in Drendell. You saved my life a while back. Remember we spoke about someone I was looking for? Someone you didn't believe existed?" He took another look to ensure nobody was watching, then turned his back on the bar and dropped his illusion for a couple of seconds.

Her eyes went wide as he shifted back to his disguise. "No…" she whispered. "It can't—how can it be? You're—"

"I'm alive, and I'm in Temolan. And I need your help."

"My—help?" She looked around herself again. "How…how did you—"

"Look," he said, "a lot has changed since we spoke last. Some for the better, and some—not so much. Remember the man we spoke of? The one you said was a myth?"

"Yes, but—"

Something buzzed against Stone's leg. It took him only a second to realize what it was—Errin was signaling him. Someone was coming. "Tanissa—listen. I can't talk now. I've got to go. But that man is alive. I've met him here. That's how I got my magic back. And he needs our help."

Another look around: so far the door remained closed, the bartender and the two customers still going about their own business. He spoke more quickly and urgently. "Tanissa—please. Our contact in town has been killed, and we don't know anyone else here. We need your help. *He* needs your help. I know you don't want to be in Temolan. If you help us, we can get you out of here. Somewhere it's safe." He regretted those words almost as soon as he'd uttered them—he had no idea if Errin and Harrison would go along with bringing a stranger into New Argana, and there wasn't even space for her in the airship—but for now, convincing her to help was paramount. He'd figure out the details later, even if he had to arrange something for her on his own. "We need to meet you. Will you do that? Will you trust me?"

Silence. Tanissa's gaze shifted away, not meeting his. Even without the ability to read auras over the connection, he could sense her fear fueling her indecision. He didn't blame her—she'd barely escaped getting killed or exiled before, just for talking to him back in Drendell. This would ask a lot more of her. And if she wouldn't help, then—

"Yes. All right," she said breathlessly, as if trying to push the words out before she changed her mind. "But you'll have to come to me." She gave him an address, and brief directions. "It's a bakery. My friend owns it. She's away but I can get in. Meet me there in an hour. Knock three times. Can you do that?"

"Yes. Yes, Tanissa. We'll be there. Thank you." His leg buzzed again, more urgently. "Must go now. Thank you. We'll see you there." He broke the connection and turned toward the front of the bar.

Two long-coated figures had entered. They didn't appear to have noticed him, but went straight to the bartender.

Stone didn't wait. He summoned an invisibility spell, paired it with an illusion to make it look as if he hadn't opened the door to the communication booth, then slipped quickly and quietly out.

He almost hurried down the hallway toward the restrooms, sure there must be a back door—but then it occurred to him that if these two *were* looking for someone, they'd have staked one of their number out there to watch for escapees. His alternative would be dangerous in one way, but possibly safer because they'd never expect it. In any case, he didn't have long to decide: he could only hold the invisibility spell for another minute or so.

Before he could think about what a rash chance he was taking, he strode back into the bar. Giving the two figures—a man and a woman—a wide berth, he slipped past them and headed for the door. He was about to use another illusion to hide opening the door when it opened from the other side to admit a pair of women, deep in conversation. Stone held his breath until they passed, then slipped out the closing door into the street.

A quick look around with magical sight didn't reveal any obvious watchers. Already feeling the invisibility spell beginning to slip, he hurried across the street and hid behind the boxes where Errin and Jeritha had waited. They weren't there now.

He watched the bar's door from his hiding place. Five minutes later, it opened again and the man and woman exited. With one last perfunctory glance around, they strode off down the street in the opposite direction from the café where Errin had told him to meet them.

He sagged against the wall, letting his breath out. That had been close—assuming those people had been looking for him at all. He had no way to know if it was true. Best to assume it was, though. The quicker they could get away from here and find a place to hide, the better. He only hoped Tanissa's friend's bakery wasn't being watched too.

He gave it a couple more minutes to make sure, checked for watchers again, then strode off down the street as if taking a leisurely stroll.

Errin and Jeritha were at the busy café, seated in the back. They glanced up as he drew closer, trying to look nonchalant but he could see the relief in Errin's aura. Jeritha had a muffin on a small plate, while Errin once again had only a glass of water. He noticed most of the tables were occupied, but the two near Errin and Jeritha were empty. The shop had no other non-magical customers.

"Thank the gods," Jeritha said. "We thought they'd gotten you."

"They might have if you two hadn't warned me. Thanks for that." He dropped into the chair opposite them.

"I don't know if they were looking for you," Errin said. "But they looked like they had more in mind than getting a drink. I figured it was better not to take chances."

"Absolutely." Stone perused the hovering magical menu on the table as if he could read it.

"Did you find the person you were looking for? Will she help?"

"Yes. She's scared, but I don't think she'll betray us. We have to get to her, though. Do you still have the map?"

Together, with Errin pretending to be dull-witted but actually contributing most of the assistance over their earring communicators, they located the address Tanissa had given them.

"That will be tricky," Errin said. "It's fairly far into the private section. The good news is, if our IDs pass the checkpoint to get us in, there should be a lot less surveillance once we're there. They watch more out here because it's where most of the outsiders stay."

"And they're probably arrogant enough to think nobody can fool their detection methods, right?"

"That too."

"We should go, then. She wants to meet us in an hour. Is that reasonable from here?"

"It will be close. We can't use the teleporters, since neither of you two knows how to calibrate them. We'd better go."

The checkpoint was several blocks' walk from the café. By the time they reached it, only half of their allotted hour remained. Stone studied the small building up ahead, noticing the lack of a wall or other overt barrier preventing anyone from getting through by walking around it. Magical sight revealed the truth, though: shimmering magic extended from the street to form a dome enclosing the inner part of the city. "That's quite a ward they've got there."

"It is impressive," Jeritha agreed, though she didn't sound like she thought that was a good thing.

"How do we get through it? Is the checkpoint manned?"

"That's where our identification comes in," Errin said. "If you two were on your own you could just walk through at any point, or take the teleporter—the signet rings allow passage through the ward for residents. Non-residents and all non-magical people have to pass through the checkpoint."

"They *are* a paranoid lot, aren't they?" Stone watched two obvious mundanes disappear inside the building.

"As I told you before, the cities don't trust each other at all. They're constantly afraid of espionage—of somebody from another city finding out what they're up to. And they know about the resistance movement. They don't respect it much, but they're aware of it. Come on—I'll feel a lot better when we're on the other side."

Inside the small building, they found a setup similar to the one back at the original teleporter, in miniature. Instead of a soaring, two-story building with an atrium, stairway, and glass offices on either side, this one had only a single story. A series of high windows let in the midday light, and a cream-colored partition lined with graceful, moving abstract art blocked the view of the area beyond. Several openings in the partition revealed uniformed mages checking identification, and once again the line for unaccompanied non-magical people was longer than the others.

Stone strode to an empty line, with Jeritha and Errin close behind him. "Damned nuisance," he muttered to the waiting mage. "If I didn't have to take my servant with me, I wouldn't have to put up with this."

"I know, and I'm sorry," the man said. He shot a contemptuous glance toward Errin, then focused back on Stone. "Do you have her papers?"

"Right here." He handed them over, using the same impatient but resigned demeanor he used when he had to go to the DMV back on Earth. "Haven't had to do this in a while—it won't take long, right? I'm already late for a meeting."

"No, no, assuming her papers are in order it will be fine." The man examined the documents and studied Errin with magical sight.

"The bag is mine," Stone said quickly, before the mage asked. He took slow deep breaths, focusing on keeping his aura under control. It was all right that Errin looked nervous—that was probably expected—but he couldn't afford to. Fortunately, channeling his contempt for this society as a whole helped. "I had her carry it, because—" He shrugged, as if to say *why the hell not?*

"Of course, of course. We just have to be a bit more careful today—got a notice that some…undesirables might be trying to get into the city, so we need to be on the lookout for them."

Stone only tensed for a second, then relaxed and spoke in a bored drawl. "I hope you catch them. It's pathetic when this kind of thing happens. They should crack down on it."

"Oh, I agree completely." He handed the papers back. "Have a pleasant day. Again, I'm sorry to delay your progress."

"It's not *your* fault," Stone said with a scathing glance toward Errin, who shrank back under his scrutiny as if expecting him to strike her. He stowed the papers in his coat. "Come on," he snapped to her. "I won't slow down for you, so keep up."

They didn't speak to each other until they'd exited the building and headed off down a side street that pointed them in the right direction toward the bakery. "I'd rather not repeat *that*," Errin said. She looked annoyed.

"Nor I," Stone agreed. "Being forced to treat you like that—" He shook his head in disgust. "You're brighter than the whole bloody lot of them."

"Probably," she agreed with an amused smile. "It's all right—I just have to keep reminding myself why we're here." She glanced at Jeritha, who hadn't spoken in a while. "Are you all right?"

The Traveler nodded. "That was close. I didn't want to say anything, but just as we got through the checkpoint, I saw the two from the bar coming in."

"Damn," Stone muttered. He checked back the way they'd come, but the street was clear. "You said you could see magic all the time—does that mean you can spot anyone trying to follow us invisibly?"

"Yes. And I've been doing that. But if we'd gotten there only a few minutes later—"

"Let's not think about that," Errin said, checking her watch. "Time's ticking, and we've got quite a distance to walk yet."

Stone pulled out the map and studied it, fixing the route in his mind so they wouldn't have to consult it again. "Let's go."

The inner section of Temolan was even more beautiful than its outer counterpart. The buildings were all tall by necessity—even at the level of magic on Calanar, it wasn't practical for a floating city to sprawl like Drendell did—and each one, though they all shared an overall consistency of design, possessed its own individual style differentiated by slight variations in paint color, unique carvings, and the delicate, multicolored magical vines crawling up their sides. The general style seemed to be that businesses—restaurants, shops, bars, and similar places—were on the bottom floors, with the upper ones reserved for residences.

Most of the streets ringing the city weren't straight, but instead meandered in easy curves with shorter, straighter streets radiating out from the center. The overall effect was peaceful, mellow, and pleasant, especially against the brilliant, jewel-like blue sky, a few shades darker than Earth's. Most of the other people on the streets ambled by in no particular hurry; occasionally a sleek, hovering ground craft would float past on one of the streets.

"I could get to like this place," Stone said. "If it wasn't populated by conceited bigots, I mean."

"Careful," Errin said. "Don't look like a tourist. You and Jeritha are supposed to live here, remember."

"Sorry, sorry." He picked up his pace.

The other thing he noticed right away when checking with magical sight: magic was *everywhere* here, even more than it had been in the outer sector. Every building had multiple shimmering wards around it, and faint traces of magic hovered over the streets, the trees, the people. He saw no sign of anything as prosaic as a trash receptacle, even though the streets and buildings were so preternaturally clean and unweathered it almost looked as if they weren't real—like a life-sized architect's rendering of the city of tomorrow. He wondered if the abundance of magic would actually help disguise them: with so much ambient arcane energy, he imagined most of the Talented had become adept at filtering it out and noticing only what they needed to pay attention to. Sure, he and his friends would have to remain on their guard, but perhaps not as much as he'd feared before.

By the time they reached the address Tanissa had given them (after only two minor wrong turns), it was five minutes past the allotted time. Stone couldn't read the elegant, looping script on the front of the pleasant first-floor shop with a large display window, but the hovering magical image of a delicious-looking loaf of bread and selection of muffins in front of it was enough to verify they were in the right place. He couldn't see the shop's interior through the window.

"Do you see anything?" he asked Jeritha over their link.

"No—I've been watching, but I think we're safe for the moment."

Taking advantage of that before it changed, Stone hurried over to the bakery's door and tried it. It was locked, as expected, so he knocked three times.

Instantly, as if whoever waited inside had been anticipating their arrival, it swung open. The three of them slipped inside and it closed behind them.

Stone's first impression of Tanissa was that she looked even more tired than she had during their brief communication on the orb. Not as if she hadn't slept, but as if whatever she'd experienced since returning to Temolan had worn down her spirit. She still had the same short bob and sturdy figure he remembered, but the intelligent, kindly spark in her eyes was conspicuously absent. Instead of the white coat she'd worn at the clinic, she wore a blue blouse, dark trousers, and a short jacket with a few pins. No high-collared coat, Stone noticed.

She tilted her head, studying the three newcomers with wary care. "Stone…?" she ventured.

"It's me, yes." Stone dropped the illusion for a moment so she could see. "It's good to see you, Tanissa. I was concerned when I heard you'd been called back here."

"How did you know that?" She looked around constantly, as if expecting someone to burst in on them.

"I went back to the clinic to ask for your help, but Byra said they'd come for you. Are you all right?"

She let her breath out. "Define 'all right'. Did they hurt me? No. It's probably my family's doing—they're influential enough to pull strings, so everyone treats me as mildly eccentric instead of actively dangerous. They can't imagine why anyone would want to waste their time in Drendell healing the Dim when they could live in splendor here." Her voice dripped with bitterness. "So here I am."

"I'm damned glad you are. We're in trouble, and we need your help if you're willing."

For the first time she seemed to notice Errin and Jeritha, and her eyes narrowed in suspicion. "Who are these people?"

"I won't tell you their names—probably safer. But they're working with me. I trust them completely."

She studied them for several moments, obviously using magical sight. "So what do you want me to do?" she asked. "What kind of trouble are you in? And how do you have *magic*?"

"Long story. I always had magic—something just happened to…short-circuit it for a while. It's back now, though. And as for the trouble we're in—do you remember the man I was looking for? The one you said was a legend or a ghost?"

"Yes…"

"Well, he might be a legend, but he's not a ghost—not yet, anyway. That might change. Have you heard of the Underground?"

Her wariness intensified. "I've heard rumors."

"We were there. *He* was there. The Talented raided it, and they took him. They're holding him prisoner now, and we need to get him out."

"Wait a moment." Tanissa paced, her aura radiating stress. "You're saying this man who's rumored to be one of the most powerful mages on the planet got *captured?*"

"Someone he trusted betrayed him. Apparently this comes from the top levels of the Talented's power structure. Anyway, yes, it's true."

"So…what do you want *me* to do? I'm not a fighter. I'm a healer. I wouldn't know how to—"

"We know where they'll be taking him tonight. But our contact—the person who was going to give us a place to lie low until then—was killed, and we're not entirely sure how to get where we're going."

"So…you need a place to stay? You're not asking me to go with you?"

"No. I wouldn't ask that of you—I certainly wouldn't turn it down if you offered, but I understand that's too much to expect. If you could let us stay somewhere until tonight and help us figure out where we need to go, that's all I'm asking."

Still, she looked skeptical. Fearful. She glanced at the door again.

He gripped her shoulders gently. "Tanissa—please. I know you hate it here. I know you care about helping non-magical people. This is a way you can make a difference."

Her shoulders trembled under his hands. She looked at her feet for several seconds as Stone and the others remained silent. Then her gaze came up, decisive now. "All right. I'll help you. But—"

"But what?"

"You said if you were successful, I could come with you. Away from here. Did you mean that?"

Stone exchanged glances with Errin, who looked surprised but recovered quickly.

"Yes," he said firmly. "It might take a bit of time—the way we got here was a bit…unconventional, and we don't have room for another person. But—"

"We'll find a way," Errin said. "I promise—we'll make this work." To Stone, she added, "I might be able to make a few modifications. It won't be comfortable, but we'll get there."

"I don't care about comfort," Tanissa said. "If it means I can get out of this gods-forsaken hellhole to someplace where people aren't insane, I'll do whatever I need to do."

"All right, then," Stone said. "Thank you, Tanissa."

"Don't thank me yet. I'm still nervous about this. They haven't bothered me much now that I'm back here, but I know I'm still under suspicion. We'll have to be careful. I can't take you back to my place—I'm sure they'll be watching it. Probably the best thing is to stay here until tonight. It won't be the most comfortable place, but at least there are good things to eat."

CHAPTER FORTY-THREE

STONE KNEW HE SHOULD SLEEP—he hadn't gotten more than a brief rest since the previous night at the Underground—but his mind stubbornly refused to calm down and allow it. Finally he gave it up, left the bakery's back room, where Jeritha and Errin were dozing on a couple of sofas, and drifted out to the front of the shop.

Tanissa sat at one of the tiny tables, picking at the remains of a small, yellow-frosted cake. She didn't appear to notice Stone, or at least didn't acknowledge him. Her expression as she looked out the shop's front window was pensive.

"Are you all right?" he asked gently.

"I don't know. Just…thinking." She indicated the cake. "Want one? My friend really is a wonderful baker."

"Thank you, no." He'd already had a muffin and a glass of cold tea earlier; he hadn't had much of an appetite even before that. "Don't let me stop you, though."

She chuckled. "I've always had a sweet tooth, ever since I was a little girl." She tore off another chunk of the cake. "Especially when I'm stressed about something. Probably why I don't match the Talented ideal of what the ruling class should look like."

It occurred to Stone, though he hadn't actively noticed it until now, that none of the Talented he'd seen had been unattractive, overweight, or disfigured. "*Do* they look like that? Or do you just refuse to use an illusion to pretend?" He indicated the seat across from her with a questioning raised eyebrow.

She waved him toward it. "It's probably true. Very few people here use their real appearance, unless they're making some kind of point with it. My mother used to drop not-so-subtle hints all the time that she wished I'd use some magic to make myself more attractive. I didn't care, though—it doesn't matter much to me."

"No shame in honesty. You look fine. A good sight less plastic than most of the people around here."

She popped another piece of the cake in her mouth, chewed, and swallowed while watching him with an odd, searching look. "You are an unusual man, Stone. I knew that when I met you, but now—you seem different than before."

"Different? How? I'm still me."

"You, but…more so. More confident. Like you've gotten closer to where you want to be."

"Well, I can't say I'm complaining about having my magic back. At least now I don't have to put up with anything those elitist bastards care to throw at me."

She nodded and looked away. "You do seem more confident, though. *I* have magic, and look at me. Stuck somewhere I don't want to be. I'd much rather be back in Drendell helping in the clinics, but that's not what my betters think I'm suited for." Her voice dripped with contempt, but then her expression changed. "This place—the one you mentioned, where you said I could go if I helped you. What's it like?"

"It's…quite nice. Not large, but it's growing, slowly."

"Your friend—she's not a mage, is she?"

"No."

"But you treat her with respect."

"Of course I do. She's brilliant. And what difference does it make whether she's a mage?"

"It doesn't. That's what I mean. So that's the way it is, wherever this is?"

"Yes. They've got mages and people without a hint of magic, and no one cares. Everyone has their own talents."

She gave a wistful smile. "You aren't lying to me, are you, Stone—or should I call you Alastair now? Because I don't think I could handle letting myself believe there's a place like that and finding out it's all some kind of dream."

"It's not a dream. It's real—I told you, I've been there. They have their problems like anyone else, but respect for each other isn't one of them. I think you'd like it there." He almost told her about the mechano-magical healing technology, but stopped himself. Those weren't his secrets to reveal.

"It does sound like I would." She finished her cake and pushed the plate aside. "But before we can go there, you need to find your other friend."

"Yes, and that won't be easy, I won't lie to you. He's being held by some of the top people in Temolan, and I'm sure they'll try hard to prevent us from getting him out of there."

"You could all die trying to do that," she said, looking down again.

"We could, yes."

"And then where would I be? Sitting here, or back at home, waiting for you, maybe never knowing what happened?" She swallowed and shook her head. "I don't like that.

I'm tired of waiting, and going along with what these people tell me I need to do. If you're serious that there really is someplace where they don't care if you're a mage or not, I want to go there. So…" She took a deep breath, and seemed to be considering something deeply, but when she spoke again her tone was firm. "I want to help. I want to come along and help you rescue your friend."

That was not what Stone had expected. "Tanissa—"

"Please. There's nothing for me in Temolan—in this society. I can help. If they've hurt your friend, I can heal him. And you said you didn't know how to get around. I can help with that too."

She reached across the table and gripped Stone's arm. "Please. Don't leave me here."

"I—" He hesitated, but she was right. It would be a lot easier if they had someone along who knew where she was going. "I'll have to ask the others, but…yes. You've got my vote." He stood and glanced out the window; it was already getting dark. "We'll have to leave soon."

"Stone?"

"Yes?"

"Thank you."

He blinked. "For what? It's you who are helping *us.*"

"For remembering me. For giving me the chance to get away from this. For giving me hope that there's something else out there."

He gave her a grim smile. "There is—but first we have to survive tonight."

CHAPTER FORTY-FOUR

"YOU'RE SURE YOU WANT TO DO THIS?" Stone asked Tanissa. "Last chance to back out."

"I can't remember the last time I was more sure of anything," she said softly in the darkness next to him.

The location where the Talented had taken Harrison had surprised both Errin and Stone. Even Tanissa had been startled when they showed her the address.

Stone had expected he'd be in some heavily fortified building in the middle of the most secure part of town, surrounded by people and nearly impossible to get near. Errin had been certain they were in one of the official buildings—perhaps somewhere in the underground prison where they'd held Stone. Privately, Stone wondered how the four of them would ever manage to breach that kind of security on their own. They couldn't rescue Harrison if they couldn't even *get* to him.

But when they'd told Tanissa where he was, she'd frowned. "Are you sure you got that address right?"

Errin consulted it again, then showed it to her. "Quite sure. Why?" She had been skeptical about allowing Tanissa to come along—she'd taken Stone aside and asked him pointed questions about how much he trusted her—but finally relented when she explained *why* she wanted to accompany them.

Tanissa studied it. "This area is residential. It's not anywhere near the official part of town."

"They've got him inside someone's *house?*" Stone asked.

"Or under it," Errin said.

"It's similar to where the bakery is," Tanissa said. "Businesses on the ground floors, and high-rise living space above it. It's not even a particularly rich part of town. Just…normal everyday people."

They were looking at it now from a narrow alley across the street, concealed under twin disregarding spells from Stone and Jeritha. Tanissa had been correct: the picturesque street was lined with tall buildings. Unlike where they'd come from, though, the businesses on the ground floor weren't brightly colored bars, shops, and restaurants, but what looked like office space. That part didn't surprise Stone: a society like this had to run on a lot of bureaucracy. Even mages needed accountants and lawyers. The good part was that, this time of night, the streets were nearly deserted. It would have been quite a bit harder to remain hidden with throngs of people meandering up and down in search of a place to get drunk.

Stone wished they could have gotten something from their dead contact. The man they'd met in the abandoned shop had assumed they'd be talking to him soon, so he'd given them only minimal information. He might not have even *known* anything else, in keeping with the cell-based nature of the resistance movement. Stone supposed that was even more important in the floating cities, where a misstep could mean disaster for a lot of people.

"So, what do we do?" he whispered to Errin. "We can't just go in guns blazing if we don't know where he is. Why would they have him here?"

"I have a speculation," Tanissa said. "You said this isn't something official, right? It doesn't have the blessing of the Council as a whole?"

"That's our understanding," Errin said.

"Then they've got to do it somewhere they won't risk getting caught by the wrong people. I'd be surprised if all the higher-ups—and especially the Council members—don't all have secret locations the others don't know about—and probably a few they all *do* know about, but won't officially admit to." She gave a bitter, rueful smile. "I don't think you know how much you could be underestimating the level these people don't trust each other. It's part of why I hate it so much—all the intrigue and political backstabbing and dishonesty. But they thrive on it."

"We need to find out if they're watching the area," Errin said. "They've probably got people on guard. Is the building warded? Jeritha, can you see anything?"

"I do see wards," she said. "I don't see anyone out here, though. I've been looking. But with so many buildings nearby, they could be watching from anywhere."

"Can you conceal us long enough for us to get inside? If they spot us and tip the people down there off, they could escape before we can get to them."

"I can do it, but getting through the wards won't be easy. It will take time."

"I can handle the ward," Errin said. She pulled a small device from one of her pockets.

"The magic nullifier?" Stone asked. "That will work on wards?"

"Yes, but like I said, it only functions for a few seconds, so we'll need to be fast and careful. It will take a minute or two to recharge after."

"We'll have to hurry after that, then. Once that ward goes down, they'll know something's up."

"Wait!" Jeritha hissed. "Someone's coming!"

The four of them moved farther back in the alley, Stone and Jeritha reinforcing the disregarding spell.

A few seconds passed. A few more. A minute. Still no sign of anyone. "Are you—" Stone whispered.

"*Shh!*"

A pair of figures appeared, walking slowly past the alley. Stone recognized the blue uniform of the Guard and tensed. Had someone found out they were here? He took deep breaths to calm his aura and prepared a spell. If the two mages came after them, they'd have to take them down fast.

But they didn't. Stone sensed his companions' tension as everyone focused their attention on the alley mouth, not even daring to breathe.

The Guardsmen stopped at the end of the alley, peered down it for a moment, then continued on, resuming their conversation.

Stone held his breath for several more seconds, then crept forward to the alley's end. He watched as the Guards' shadowy forms receded, then turned left down another street. "We need to go," he whispered, returning to his friends. "If they're patrolling, they'll be back."

They darted across the street, hidden by Jeritha's invisibility spell, and stopped in front of the door. "Cover me,"

Errin ordered, and once again pulled out her little device. "And let's hope the wards here aren't tougher than the ones back home."

Apparently they weren't. She pointed the device at the door and pressed a button. The little thing hummed for a moment, followed by a *bzzt* like a shorting electrical circuit. Stone, watching with magical sight, saw the shimmering ward fizzle and drop.

"Go," Errin urged. "Fast."

With the ward down, Stone had no trouble popping the lock, and less than thirty seconds later all three of them were through with the door shut behind them.

They looked around, taking in their surroundings. As Tanissa had suspected, they stood in what looked like office space, with pale walls, more of the shifting artwork, and dim, floating lights hovering above. Along one wall, a large aquarium showcased a series of brightly colored, glowing fish.

"Where are they?" Stone demanded. "Check the doors." He cast his gaze around, looking with both magical and mundane sight, but saw only two other doors exiting the office, one opposite the aquarium and the other on the left side of the back wall. He expected them to open any second and more Guardsmen to pour through.

Errin started to head toward one of them when Jeritha held up a hand. "Wait."

"What?"

She pointed toward the rear wall, at the opposite end from the door Stone had spotted. "There."

"I don't see anything," Stone said. "Just that painting that looks like it was done by someone's eight-year-old—"

"It's an illusion. Let me see if I can take it down. Watch the other doors."

By now, the ward Errin had disrupted was back up; they had no way to know if it was tuned to alert anyone to interference. Stone watched one door while Errin and Tanissa watched the other, all of them growing increasingly tense with each passing moment. Even if nobody came up here to confront them, they could even now be moving Harrison to another location if they—

"Got it!" Jeritha announced, stepping back.

Stone hurried toward her, immediately spotting the substantial new door that had replaced the horrible artwork previously covering the wall. "Good job," he said, impressed. He'd never seen anyone take down a powerful illusion that fast before. "Not a lot of guards—not sure if that's a good or a bad sign."

"They might be relying on the wards and the illusion," Tanissa said. "It could make people suspicious to see too many strangers loitering around an area like this."

"I hope you're right," Stone said. "Let's go before someone turns up or they do a runner with Harrison."

Once again, he used magic to pop the lock. "Let me go first," he said. "I've got the strongest shield." When nobody objected, he summoned it and shoved the door open, pressing through. The others hurried to follow.

Beyond the door was a hallway with another door at the end. Two men—conspicuously not attired in the military blue uniforms of the city's Guard—stood on either side of it, looking startled when it opened. They recovered quickly, though, each raising his hands and glaring at the newcomers.

Jeritha pushed past Stone, fixing her gaze on the left-side guard. He struggled for a moment, then stared at his own hands in confusion as if he had no idea why he was here and what he'd planned to do with them.

Stone slammed the other one into the wall with a concussion blast just as he loosed his own attack, a small, brightly-glowing fireball. It streaked down the hall, fizzling out when the man lost consciousness, its dying heat washing over Stone and the others.

"Come on," Errin urged, pushing forward. Stone hastened to follow, extending his shield over her as he took a magical grip on the new door to fling it open.

They burst through, fanning out so they could all hurry through.

Errin gasped.

"Oh, bloody hell…" Stone whispered.

| CHAPTER FORTY-FIVE

S TONE TOOK IN THE ROOM with a fast sweep of his gaze. It stretched perhaps twenty feet side to side and twice that in front of them. They stood at the top of a tiered seating area divided into three levels with an aisle between them; each tier included wide padded benches. Several well-dressed, long-coated individuals, both men and women, occupied the benches, twisting around in shock as the door burst open. Two more guards stood at the bottom of the tiers, on either side.

At the room's front, the floating overhead lights revealed a glass wall, shimmering with magic, dividing the seating area from the open space beyond. Past that was what had evoked both Stone's exclamation and Errin's gasp.

In the center of the open area stood a transparent cubicle perhaps eight feet square. Harrison hung in the cubicle, suspended by glowing manacles around his wrists and attached near the top of either side. Tubes ran from both his arms, snaking through ports in the sides to a pair of IV bottles suspended on either side of the cubicle. He was clad only in ragged pants and appeared to be unconscious; his body was slicked with blood from numerous cuts and gashes.

The sight was so shocking that at first Stone almost didn't notice the other occupants of the lab area: a tall, severe-looking woman with dark hair and a shorter blond man, both wearing what looked like blue lab coats in place of the normal Talented garb. The woman stood next to a bench covered with bottles and apparatus, and the man near the cubicle, holding a clipboard.

"Stop them, damn you!" the woman yelled.

Errin was already moving. She'd stowed the anti-magic device in one of her pockets and had a different one now. She snapped off a shot at one of the guards, who screamed and dropped without getting off a spell.

The other guard, on the other side, yelled something and flung a fireball at her, but Jeritha already had a shield up. The flaming missile fizzled against it and died.

Stone answered it with a roar, aiming a twin-beamed bolt of pure magical energy at the guard's center mass. The man's shield stopped some of it, but the rest got through, staggering him back against the wall.

The people in the seats weren't reacting nearly as quickly—they seemed to be in the grip of shock that anyone could manage to breach their secret sanctum. Stone swept his gaze over them, taking them in quickly: five in all, three women, two men. One of the men, white-blond and dark-skinned, he identified as Olystriar; one of the women was Chanandra, another of the Council members who'd been present at the Arena. He didn't recognize the others.

"We have to hurry," he snapped. "I'm sure they'll have more guards in here soon." Without waiting for an answer, he pointed his hands at the glass wall and unleashed another blast of energy, expecting it to shatter.

It didn't shatter. The blast rattled it and it shimmered more brightly than before, but it held fast.

"Go on!" Chanandra shouted triumphantly. "Waste your efforts. You're fools for coming here!"

Errin snapped off another round from her gun at the Councilwoman. It breached her shield, but her aim was off and it only tore a furrow along Chanadra's arm.

The woman backpedaled and ducked behind one of the benches, casting as she went. A whirling vortex of air settled around Errin—or tried to. Once again, Jeritha's shield held it off, extending outward until the vortex dissipated.

Stone wanted nothing more than to take down that barrier so they could get to Harrison, but they had to deal with the people on this side first. He had no idea how many of the dignitaries were skilled in combat, but their lofty positions certainly indicated extensive magical power. Best to assume they were dangerous.

Two of them, a young man with long hair and an older woman, looked terrified, trying to escape by dashing back up the tiers toward the back door. Stone was about to plug them with another spell when Errin tossed something in their direction. It hit the door in front of them and exploded in a billow of smoke that flowed around them, clinging to them. Shrieks of fear sounded from the middle of the cloud as it gathered closer around them, making them look like oversized, humanoid clumps of dark-gray dryer lint.

"It's attracted to magic!" Errin called to Stone with a grin as he shot her a questioning glance. "Stay away from them."

That wasn't a problem. Olystriar glared at Stone and threw a showy blast at him, shattering one of the benches. It looked good—anyone who didn't know better would have thought the chaos of the fight had thrown his aim off, but Stone was close enough that there was no way he could have missed. Except on purpose, of course.

Stone yelped, diving sideways, doing his best to sell it to the rest of the group. Then he answered with his own spell, slamming a blazing—but illusionary—fireball into Olystriar's chest. The man caught on fast: he screamed and clutched himself, slumping down as if unconscious. The illusionary fire continued to "burn" for a few seconds before fizzling out.

One more dignitary remained, a tall red-haired man who looked terrified at how quickly Stone had taken Olystriar down. Stone's contempt rose: as was the case with many classic bullies back on Earth, the arrogance of these self-proclaimed "Talented" deserted them when they didn't have the upper hand. "Can't take being on the other side, can you?" he yelled, blasting the red-haired man back into the far wall. This time, the spell wasn't illusionary.

Jeritha, meanwhile, was dealing with one of the guards at the front of the room. The Traveler woman wasn't throwing showy magic and she didn't look angry or even stressed; in fact, her entire demeanor appeared peaceful and unruffled as she pointed her hand at the man.

He stopped in the act of preparing a spell, looking suddenly bewildered, as if he had no idea where he was. Stone didn't have time for more than a quick glance, but he saw the man blink a couple times, then lower himself to one of the benches and stare straight ahead. He looked like a moviegoer taking in a film.

"Hurry," Jeritha called. Despite her apparent calm, her face was lined with tension. This wasn't as easy on her as she was trying to make it seem.

The other guard at the front of the room grabbed something from her pocket and threw it at Jeritha. Before any of Stone's group could react, it wrapped itself around the Traveler and constricted, locking her arms to her body, and she fell over backward against one of the benches.

"No!" The voice came from the back, where Tanissa had been standing, so far not involving herself in the fight. Now, though, her eyes flashed with anger. She gestured at the guard.

The woman's eyes bulged, panic blooming across her face as her hands flew to her neck. She tripped and went down, her shield dropping.

"Damn you, you won't win!" Chalandra's face was red, her dark eyes smoldering with rage. Before Stone could stop her—before it registered that Jeritha had been holding a shield on Errin and was no longer doing so—she lashed out and flung a handful of glowing, magical knives.

Stone had no time to consider or to aim. In desperation he threw a shield in front of Errin.

Most of the glowing knives hit it and fizzled into nothingness—but not all of them. Errin shrieked in pain as two of the missiles slipped around the edge of Stone's shield and tore into her—one into her leg and one across her abdomen. Blood flowered and she dropped.

"No!" Stone screamed. He stepped back, whirled on Chanandra, and raised his hands to prepare a killing spell.

But as he did, he got a glance past the Councilwoman, through the glass partition dividing the tiered seating from the laboratory area. A chill ran down his spine.

Harrison was awake.

He still looked like he should be dead. He still hung suspended from the chains in the transparent cubicle. The tubes still snaked from his arms, delivering gods knew what vile concoctions into his body.

But his eyes were open, and never in his life had Stone seen such cold, unmitigated rage.

| CHAPTER FORTY-SIX

I T HAPPENED FAST AFTER THAT, which was why Stone was able to see it before Chanandra or any of the others could attack him. One moment Harrison hung there in the cubicle, eyes blazing, teeth gritted, cords standing out on his neck—and the next second Stone felt the power growing in the room.

"Down!" he screamed, not caring if their opponents heard too. He flung himself sideways next to Errin, pulling up a shield he hoped would cover the others as well.

The room erupted with the booming sound of something heavy shattering, and then the air was full of missiles. It only lasted a couple of seconds, but as Stone huddled under his shield, covering Errin with his body as well as his magic, it seemed as if the whole building might come crashing down around them.

That didn't happen, though. Shield still raised, Stone poked his head up.

"Bloody…hell…"

The room had been transformed. The transparent barrier between the seating area and the lab was gone; the only sign that it had ever been there was the jagged edges along the walls and the shimmering layer of shards coating the benches, the floor, the fallen combatants.

Inside the lab, the cubicle had shattered too. Harrison was on his knees on the floor, the manacles still locked around his wrists but the other ends of the chains lay loose on the ground like a pair of snakes. His back, slashed and bleeding, rose and fell with his fast breathing, and the two IV lines still stuck out of his arms. The bottles at their other ends lay shattered on the floor.

Stone, shocked into immobility, watched as Chanandra, perhaps realizing now that whatever plans she'd had weren't going to progress as she'd hoped, tried to sprint up the tiered steps toward the back door, where the two human-shaped lint balls had finally fallen. She moved fast—too fast—and faded from view as she ran.

Damn you, no! You're not *getting away!* Stone switched to magical sight and readied a spell—

Chanandra shimmered back into view, her high, keening shriek rising to the ceiling as her body came apart.

Later, when he'd had more time to process the situation, Stone would describe the scene as what might have happened if the Councilwoman had swallowed a bomb and it detonated inside her. One moment she became visible, arms and legs pumping, eyes bulging in desperation as she tried to reach the door, and the next she erupted into a red haze of blood and flying limbs. Her severed, wide-eyed head hit the wall behind a terrified Tanissa with a ripe *thunk* and rolled back down the steps, coming to a stop just ahead of the blasted-out partition.

Stone leaped up. "Tanissa! Help Errin!" he yelled.

"Stop them!" Jeritha called, struggling against the magical bonds that still held her. "They're escaping!"

For a second Stone wasn't sure what she meant, but then he looked back into the lab. Harrison lay face-down and un-moving on the floor now, the effort of blowing out the partitions and killing Chanandra evidently exhausting the last of his will-driven strength. But now Vestereth, the male half of the mad alchemist couple, crouched next to him. Before Stone could stop him, he jammed something into Harrison's back, then leaped up and followed his wife toward a door in the back part of the lab—a door that hadn't been there before. The door was already closing behind Millia, who had already passed through it. She held it partially open, waiting for her partner to catch up.

Suddenly, the door slammed shut with a deafening *bang*. Millia screamed as the edge severed her fingers, and Vester-eth's cry of panic answered hers. He clawed at the door, trying to wrench it open, but something held it fast.

Stone's first thought was that Harrison had somehow roused himself again, but a quick glance revealed him still unconscious on the floor, a pool of blood spreading beneath him and shards of shattered glass shimmering against his black hair. Who, then—?

But it didn't matter. Stone's eyes narrowed as he focused back on Vestereth. He remembered the two combatants in the Arena, driven to homicidal madness by the horrific brews this man and his wife had concocted. He remembered the couple's hungering, excited expressions as they watched the two men kill each other—the expressions of scientists observ-ing rats in a maze, not human beings watching brutal murders.

As he raised his hands, Vestereth's gaze met his own, panicked and pleading.

Stone smiled and let his illusionary disguise drop for just a few seconds—long enough for the man to see his true form.

Vestereth's eyes went even wider and more terrified—the eyes of a man who'd just seen the ghost of someone he'd killed.

"Should have picked a different line of work," Stone called, unleashing power fueled by every bit of the rage he'd been forced to stifle while in these people's custody.

Vestereth screamed as flames rose around him, catching his clothes, his hair, cooking his skin. He gave up trying to wrench the door open and took off across the lab toward the ruined partition, licks of flame trailing in his wake. He made it only halfway before dropping first to his knees and then to his hands, twitching and shrieking a few feet away from the fallen Harrison. The smell of burned flesh filled the air. A strange-looking hypodermic needle clattered to the floor next to him and rolled away. Stone watched with dispassionate attention as the man's screams quieted and ceased.

Sudden silence filled the room. Stone spun back toward the others, convinced something else must have happened, but saw nothing except the fallen forms of friend and foe alike. The two lint-balls lay unmoving on the floor near the door, and the guards were all dead. A slick of blood and gore from the exploded Chanandra covered most of the seating area, including Tanissa, who knelt next to Errin, Jeritha, shaking herself free of the magical bonds, and Olystriar, rising from his feigned unconsciousness.

"Is everyone all right?" Stone demanded. "Tanissa? Is Errin—"

"She'll be all right," Tanissa puffed. And indeed, Errin was already stirring.

"You have to go," another voice called.

Stone turned to see Olystriar rising, pulling himself up by the edge of one of the blasted benches. Something snapped into place. "The door—did you—"

"Yes. Not fast enough, I fear." The Councilman kept glancing toward the door at the top of the tiered steps as if expecting someone to knock it down. "You have to go. Now. All of you. I can get you back to Drendell, but—"

Jeritha got up, helping Tanissa pull Errin to her feet.

"We can't go yet," Stone protested. "Errin's hurt. And Harrison—" He turned back toward the lab, hoping Harrison had somehow pulled yet another miracle out of his hat, but no such luck. He hadn't moved. Stone didn't know if he was even alive.

"You don't have *time*," Olystriar urged. His voice shook, but held firm. "Millia will summon help, if the others haven't already found the guards. You need to go now, before we're overrun. I can send them on false trails, but only if you're gone before they arrive."

Stone exchanged glances with Errin, who nodded reluctantly. She looked pale, but at least she was on her feet.

"All right, then," he said. "Show us." He hurried back to the lab and hefted Harrison in a fireman's carry, grateful his accelerated physical training program had augmented his strength enough to do it. If he had to use magic to lift him later he could, but for now this would do. On a whim, he snatched the spent hypo Vestereth had dropped and stuffed it in his pocket.

"This way." Olystriar headed for the same door Millia had left through. It opened easily now.

Stone followed with Harrison, trying not to look at the grotesque little pile of bloody, severed fingers on the floor nearby. Behind him, Jeritha and Tanissa helped Errin.

Beyond the door was a hallway, with a teleport pad at the end. "What is this—some kind of secret lab?" Stone asked bitterly.

"I didn't know about it," Olystriar said. "Not until today. I think Millia and Vestereth set it up to show off some of their handiwork. Give me a moment, please—I need to adjust these settings."

Stone lowered Harrison to a seated position against the wall, looking him over as the Councilman worked. Good—he was still breathing, at least. If he could recover from a point-blank gunshot wound to the chest, he could recover from this. They'd just need to get him back to the Nexus.

Errin, looking pale but better, knelt next to them. "How is he?"

"Bad. But you know him—he'll pull through."

"I know. But I hate seeing him like that."

"How are *you?*"

She touched her bloodstained shirt. "Still hurts some, but I'll be fine, thanks to Tanissa."

Stone was about to ask the healer if she could take a look at Harrison when Olystriar spoke again.

"All right, I've got it. You can all go in one group. This will send you near the edge of Drendell. I urge you—don't remain long. If you have a way to get out of the city, use it. The Council will not take kindly to this, and as soon as Millia gets the word out, the town will be overrun with the Guard.

She's vengeful, and she has a lot of influence. You won't be able to hide anywhere."

"We'll go," Errin said. "Out into the Wastes—they won't follow us there." She touched Olystriar's arm. "Thank you. For everything. Please—don't blow your cover for us. We'll be in touch."

"Go. Now." Olystriar cast another tense glance at the door. "Hurry."

Stone lifted Harrison again and joined Errin, Jeritha, and Tanissa on the pad. When they were all settled, he nodded to the Councilman.

An instant later, the electrical-jolt sensation of the Talented's teleporters took them, and Olystriar faded from view.

CHAPTER FORTY-SEVEN

IT WAS DARK WHERE THEY REAPPEARED. The air smelled like old wood and dusty oil, overlaid with a faint coppery tang from Harrison's bloody wounds and their gore-spattered clothes. Stone shifted to magical sight, looking for auras, but saw none. "Jeritha, do you see anyone?"

"No. I think we're alone."

"Does anyone know where we are?" Stone raised a hand and summoned a light spell around it; the glow illuminated what looked like the interior of a warehouse. The teleport pad was hidden behind a stack of wooden crates.

Nobody replied, except to shake their heads.

"We need to get out of here and back to the ship. We—oh, bloody hell."

"What?" Jeritha asked.

"We can't go to the ship. We might be able to fit Tanissa in if she sits on someone's lap, but Harrison's in no shape to send himself back. We can't get both of them in."

"Let me take a look at him," Tanissa said. "Maybe I can help."

Stone lowered Harrison down and laid him on the floor. "We don't have much time. We still need to find a vehicle. Not a chance we're walking."

"I'll find us one," Errin said. She pulled her coat closed to cover her bloody shirt.

"No. You're still recovering, and it's not safe out there. You heard Olystriar. The Guard will be—"

"I'll go with her," Jeritha said. "You stay with your friend."

Stone didn't like it—it wasn't a good idea to separate with so many threats nearby, but they didn't have a choice. At least Errin's odds looked better with Jeritha's powerful magic backing her up. "Do you still have your gadgets?"

Errin slung the bag around so he could see it. "Good to go. We'll find something."

"We need something that can traverse the Wastes," Jeritha reminded her. "The terrain is difficult, and we might need to take an alternate route."

"On it." Errin gripped Stone's shoulder and glanced at Harrison. "Take care of him—see if you can wake him up. If he can go back on his own, we'll be in better shape."

After they departed, Stone stationed himself against the wall where he could keep an eye on both entrances: a roll-up door that was currently closed, and a normal-sized one through which Errin and Jeritha had departed. He kept the light spell going so Tanissa could see what she was doing.

The healer knelt next to Harrison, passing her hands over him as she concentrated. He lay as still as ever; Stone didn't think he'd moved since they'd arrived. After a few moments, she rocked back on her heels and let her breath out.

"What is it?" Stone demanded. "Can you help him?"

"I don't know."

"What do you mean?"

"He is—I've never seen anyone like him before. His body doesn't react as I would expect."

"How so?"

She gestured at him. "His physical injuries aren't life-threatening, though they should be. Already I can sense his body healing. Based on what I've seen, I think if I just left him on his own, he'd heal without my help. I can speed it along—I already have—but—"

"But what?" Stone cast another glance at the doors, shifting to magical sight. He felt suddenly vulnerable, and realized he'd begun to rely on Jeritha's strange Traveler ability to see magic more deeply than he ever could. Where were they? Had they been captured? He didn't know how long they'd been away, since he had no watch.

"But—I'm sensing problems with not just his body, but his mind. I think they've…done something to him."

Stone tensed, studying Harrison. He slipped his hand into his pocket and withdrew the strange hypo Vestereth had dropped. "Can you tell anything from this?"

She examined it, her gaze shifting as if looking at something Stone couldn't see.

She remained like that for quite some time. While she worked, Stone alternated between casting nervous glances toward the two doors and watching Harrison. He still hadn't moved; at least he wasn't bleeding any longer, but Stone had no way to know if he had internal injuries, or if Millia and Vestereth had poisoned him. He tried to console himself by remembering how Harrison had looked after he'd been shot. Both he and Verity had been certain he'd die, even after they'd done their best to heal him—but not only hadn't he died, he'd recovered enough to move under his own power less than an hour later.

"Come on, Harrison…" he murmured. "We could really do with some of that amazing healing ability of yours right about now…"

Tanissa raised her head, coming out of her trance with a loud exhalation.

"What is it?" Stone demanded. "Do you know what it is?"

"No. Not exactly. I think I was right, though—whatever it is, it's affecting his mind." She'd already pulled the IV tubes free of Harrison's arms, and pointed at one of them on the floor next to him. "They probably used those to keep him docile—some kind of tranquilizer, or something similar." She shuddered, looking down at him with fear in her eyes. "Did you see what he did? The way he blew out the barrier? And…killed Chanandra…?"

"I did. He's dangerous. We know that. *They* knew it too. He's also very hard to kill. If they knew *that,* I'm not surprised they treated him like some kind of dangerous animal." Suddenly, his mind returned to a movie he'd seen many years ago—something about bringing dinosaurs back to life in the modern day. In one scene, they'd had one of the velociraptors in a specially-designed metal transport cage, and everyone around it had *still* been terrified of it even though it was securely confined. The Talented had probably treated Harrison like that—and with good reason, it appeared. Stone wondered if the man was as resilient about recovering from mind-altering substances as he was from physical damage. He hoped so, because if Harrison freaked out and attacked them because he was out of his mind, Stone didn't think any of them could deal with him.

He was spared further thought by the sound of the door opening. He leaped up, readying a spell, but let it drop when Errin's familiar figure slipped in.

"Did you find a vehicle?" he called.

"Yes. Help me with the garage door. There's a chain-lock on it."

Stone hurried outside with her. Parked in front of the roll-up door was a mid-sized thing that looked like a cross between a Jeep and a delivery van, with an enclosed rear section. Jeritha sat in the passenger seat and looked relieved when Stone and Errin appeared.

The garage door was locked with a chain and a stout padlock. Errin leaped back into the cab while Stone popped the padlock, pulled the chain free, and rolled the heavy door up. As soon as the vehicle was through, he lowered the door again and jogged back in through the smaller door.

"Where did you find this?" he asked as Errin and Jeritha jumped out. "Is anyone going to miss it anytime soon?"

"Not if we get out of here fast," Errin said. "We found it in another garage down the street. It's some kind of delivery truck." She opened the hood, climbed up on the bumper, and peered down into the oily-smelling engine compartment with a small flashlight. "If you can disguise it with an illusion, that will be even better. It shouldn't take more than a few minutes to get out of town."

Stone examined the truck. It wasn't as robust-looking as he'd have hoped, but it couldn't be helped—he supposed the residents of the surface cities didn't need off-road-capable vehicles since they'd never dare to brave the Wastes. Still, the roads in town were bad enough that a vehicle would need to be sturdy to handle potholes and rough terrain. "Do you know where we are? How far is it until we're out of town?"

"Not far," Errin said. "It won't take long, especially this early. But we need to get going. You heard Olystriar—they're probably already looking for us."

"Stone?"

It was Tanissa, calling from the other side of the room. She sounded suddenly strained.

"What is it?"

"We have a problem."

Stone, Errin, and Jeritha turned back toward where they'd left the healer with Harrison.

"What's the—" Stone began, then froze.

Harrison was gone.

CHAPTER FORTY-EIGHT

"BUGGER! WHERE'S HARRISON?" Stone ran back toward Tanissa, with Errin and Jeritha close behind.

Silently, Tanissa pointed. She looked even more fearful than before.

Stone held up a light spell to illuminate the end of a row of crates, but he didn't need that to see what had happened. The smear of blood on the warehouse's concrete floor was all it took.

Harrison was at the end of the row, half-lying, half-sitting, pressed against the wall. As the light hit him, he flinched back, eyeing them warily. He still looked barely conscious, and something about his wandering gaze suggested he wasn't entirely present mentally.

"I'm sorry…" Tanissa whispered. "I was just sitting with him when he—"

"Let me…" Errin stepped forward, moving slowly as if approaching a skittish animal. She crouched and spoke in a calm, gentle voice. "Trevor. It's me. Errin. Are you there?"

"Stay away…" he muttered. "Stay back…" His gaze flicked between Errin and the others standing behind her; his tone was ragged but even.

As Stone watched, not daring to speak, he remembered his experience at Burning Man a few years ago, when Trin Blackburn had dosed him with some kind of psychoactive drug designed to enhance fear. Was this the same kind of thing? But Harrison, while he did look fearful, didn't appear to be mad with terror. Stone shifted to magical sight, noting his eerie black-and-violet aura roiled and sparked with flashes of red. Something was definitely affecting him.

"Trevor…" Errin reached a hand toward him. "Come on. We need to get out of here. We're in danger if we stay. We can take care of you when we get away. Will you come with us?"

He looked at her as if he didn't recognize her. He took several deep breaths and pressed himself farther back into the wall. Blood stained his face and ran down his chest; his eyes were unblinking, trading his normal unsettling, unwavering gaze for one of focused confusion. "No…" he rasped. "I won't let you—"

And then, suddenly, he locked in on her and something in his eyes changed. He swallowed again. "Alexandra…?"

"Who's Alexandra?" Stone whispered behind Errin.

"I don't know." She spoke without turning away from Harrison. Then, to him: "Trevor, I don't know who that is. Please—you've got to come with us. We're not safe here."

But he didn't appear to have heard her. He tried to struggle up, but couldn't manage it and fell back against the wall. "Alexandra…please…don't go…" His focus shifted to the others behind Errin, and his expression hardened. "You…Get away from her." The most disturbing part of the whole thing was that his voice was as calm, steady, and unemotional as ever. He *sounded* perfectly sane. Only his eyes gave him away.

Errin cast a quick, desperate look back over her shoulder. "I don't know what to do," she whispered. "He's never been like this. I don't know what he wants. And we've got to *go*. Tanissa—Jeritha—can you knock him out or something?"

Tanissa shook her head. "I'm—sorry—" Terror crossed her pale face and she took a step back. Clearly she didn't want to get anywhere near Harrison, let alone try something potentially threatening around him.

Stone thought about the velociraptor in the movie again. It was an even more apt comparison now, if Harrison wasn't in his right mind. He could destroy all of them—hell, he could probably destroy the whole city block—if whatever dark visions clawing at his mind roused him sufficiently to do it.

"Let me try," he murmured to Errin. "Go get the truck ready. Tanissa, go with her. Jeritha—can you stay here with me?"

"I can stay." Unlike Tanissa, the Traveler woman didn't look frightened of Harrison. She watched him closely, but remained calm next to Stone.

"Are you sure…?" Errin began.

"Go." He had an idea—he didn't know if it would work, but right now they didn't have a lot of choice.

Harrison, unmoving, watched Errin and the relieved Tanissa hurry off toward the truck, then settled his gaze back on Stone and Jeritha.

Stone eyed Harrison, wondering if his next words would get him killed. But if they wanted to get out of here before Millia and the rest of the Talented discovered their location, they'd have to move fast. He took a deep breath. "Support me if you can…" he whispered to Jeritha.

Then Stone faced Harrison and hardened his expression. "Harrison!" he snapped. "Pull yourself together."

Harrison blinked, brief surprise passing across his face, but now he was focused fully on Stone.

"You heard me!" Stone said, taking a step forward so he loomed over Harrison. "Your friends are in danger. Errin is in danger. Alexandra isn't here. Are you going to sit there and let them die because you can't get your sorry arse off the ground, or are you going to *fight*?" He infused his tone with contempt, despite the fact that inwardly he was shaking.

Harrison closed his eyes, writhing back and forth as if in pain, and put a hand to his head. "I—"

"Listen!" Stone forced himself to continue in the sharp, authoritative tone. "Remember back at the Nexus, when you told me to show you I was worth your time? Now it's time for *you* to show me you're worth *mine.* Come on, Harrison! You're better than this! Where's all that willpower I've been hearing so much about? Do *you* have the will?"

Harrison's breath came faster. His arms shook and his jaw tightened.

Next to Stone, Jeritha tensed.

Stone wondered again if he'd just gotten them all killed, but still he pressed on. "Damn you, Harrison, *show* us! *Fight!* Are you going to let your friends die after they risked their lives to save you? *Do you have the will?*"

Harrison's fists clenched. He slumped forward until he rested on them, his back heaving, his whole body trembling. "No…no…" he muttered. "I…will…*not!*"

He went rigid and collapsed to the oily, dusty floor.

Stone ran over to him and rolled him over. "Harrison?"

He was still pale, still bleeding, still trembling. But now his gaze, locked on Stone, was clear and steady. He gripped Stone's wrist, so hard it hurt. "Thank you…" he whispered, and passed out again.

Stone let his breath out, finally allowing himself to release the full-body clench he hadn't realized he'd been holding. "Go on," he told Jeritha. "You'll need to navigate. I'll get him in the back."

She complied without question, casting one final glance back over her shoulder at him before swinging into the truck's cab.

Stone used magic to levitate Harrison, directing his body as fast as he could across to the back end of the truck, which was open. A few empty burlap bags lay in the compartment; Stone vaulted into the back, slammed the door, and stuck a couple of folded ones under Harrison's head. "Go!" he yelled as he moved forward and dropped into one of the two back seats.

Errin gunned the engine and the truck surged forward. Jeritha had already rolled the door up; it thundered back down with a loud *clang* after they passed through. Outside, it was still dark, the streets still quiet.

"Is he all right?" Errin demanded without looking back.

"He will be," Stone said. "Don't count on him for much help for a while, though."

"I hope we won't need any. If we can get out before they figure out where we are, we can get back to the ship. Jeritha, which way?"

The Traveler woman concentrated a moment, then pointed. "It isn't far. We can—"

Something slammed into the side of the truck, so hard it rocked on its wheels.

CHAPTER FORTY-NINE

S TONE HAD TO BRACE HIMSELF to keep from being thrown into the door. He looked wildly around, trying to spot the threat. "What the hell was that?"

"I don't know." Errin's voice was grim. She gunned the engine again, the truck's tires jouncing and juddering over the heavily potholed street. "We can't take too many more of those hits, though."

Stone rolled down the window, pulling up a shield around himself. He wished he could shield the whole truck, but that was nearly impossible to do quickly when they were moving. He poked his head out, looking behind them. "Jeritha—do you see anything?"

"I don't—*there!*" she cried, pointing forward.

Stone pulled back inside in time to see a sleek, floating vehicle dart out from a side street. Another bolt of magical energy streaked toward them.

Errin jerked the wheel sideways, barely keeping the bolt from hitting them dead-on. Instead, it hit on the passenger side, hard enough to punch the door in. Tanissa yelped and shifted over closer to Stone.

"If they hit the tires or the engine we're dead," Errin snapped.

"Keep driving," Stone ordered. He focused on the floating vehicle in front of them, stuck his hand through the open window, and flung a concussion beam at it. Bright light flared around the craft and it veered to one side. "Shields—damn!"

Errin, driving one-handed, dug in her vest pocket and thrust something back toward Stone. "Here—use magic to throw this at them."

"What is it?" He took the little thing—it looked like some kind of knobby grenade. "Anti-magic smoke won't—"

"It's a grenade. Quick!" She jerked the wheel again, briefly tilting the unwieldy truck onto two wheels as it careened around a corner. "It's not far now—they won't follow us into the Wastes. Do it!"

Stone didn't ask more questions. He gripped the grenade in a telekinetic hold, raised his arm again, and used magic to throw it toward the other vehicle with all the strength he could muster.

This time, the floating craft didn't get out of the way. The grenade hit it high up and exploded in a fiery blast. Stone roared in triumph as their shield flared bright again and then winked out—but the roar turned to one of frustration as the vehicle kept coming. "Their shield's down!" he yelled. "Do something before they get it back up!"

The vehicle was behind them now—their quick turn had taken them past it. Stone couldn't see it, since the back end of the truck blocked his view. "Do what you can," he called, then scrambled up and into the rear compartment. All the jouncing had rolled Harrison over; he now lay on his side, pressed against the left wall, and still appeared to be unconscious. Stone ignored him, reached the back window, and peered out.

The sleek white craft was still coming, but farther back now. Were they using more caution now that their shield was down, or had Errin managed to pull away from them? Surely it could move faster, since it didn't have to deal with the potholes—

Another fiery ball streaked toward them, so fast Stone didn't have time to react to it. He flinched back, trying to form a shield, but he knew he was too late. "Brace yourselves!" he yelled, tensing in anticipation of the impact.

It didn't come. Instead, the ball—huge and bright and menacing—hit something and exploded in a dazzling flare of light. "What the hell—?"

"I can't do that again," Jeritha said from the front, her voice strained. "Do something!"

Stone didn't need a second invitation. He fixed his gaze on the little craft—now that the shield was down, he could see two shadowy figures inside—and threw a tight concussion beam at its front window just as the passenger raised its hands again.

The two arcane bolts hit at the same time. Stone's punched through the front window of their floating pursuer. The craft jerked and lurched off to the side, where it slammed into a non-functional streetlight and stopped moving.

The other bolt hit the back doors of the truck's rear compartment, lifting the back end off the ground and blowing the doors wide open.

Tanissa screamed.

The truck fishtailed back and forth as Errin struggled to get it under control.

Harrison's body rolled to the center, then tumbled toward the opening.

"Almost there!" Errin yelled as Stone grabbed Harrison in a telekinetic grip and pulled him back inside the truck. Shocked, he spotted two more floating vehicles entering the road behind them.

"Incoming!" he yelled, holding on to Harrison and trying to use magic to get the doors closed again. "Two more! If this thing has any more power, now's the time!"

Harrison stirred in Stone's grip. "What—?" he began, blinking.

"Stay down," Stone ordered. "We're trying to get to the Wastes, but they're after us."

Harrison didn't stay down. He still looked bad, but not as bad as before. He wrenched himself free of Stone and struggled to a kneeling position, taking quick stock of what was going on behind them. Still breathing hard, he narrowed his eyes and pointed his hand backward.

The front end of the nearest pursuing vehicle lifted, then the whole thing flipped over and crashed to the ground, where it exploded. The other one veered to the side, avoiding the fireball by a narrow margin. Another blast of magical energy streaked from it, headed toward the open back end of the truck.

Stone, braced against the side, barely got a shield up in time. Most of it dissipated, but enough got through to fling both him and Harrison backward.

Harrison wasn't done yet, though. He dragged himself back up, crawled toward the opening again, and this time pointed both hands at the sole remaining vehicle chasing them. It had closed some of the distance while he and Stone had dealt with the incoming attack.

"Throw something at them," he ordered Stone. "Distract them."

Stone summoned a showy fireball and sent it rocketing toward the vehicle as once again Errin jerked the truck to one side. The fireball wouldn't get through their shields and Stone knew it, but they couldn't ignore it.

As he expected, the pursuing vehicle also veered to the side. The fireball hit its shield at the right front, then flared and fizzled on the dark street behind it.

It did its job as a distraction, though. Stone watched in shocked amazement as Harrison made a sharp gesture and one of the streetlights wrenched free of the ground with a metallic shriek. Another gesture and the thing streaked like an oversized javelin toward the pursuing craft.

They'd been so busy avoiding the fireball that they didn't have time to react to the incoming missile. It slammed through their shields and impaled the vehicle through the front window with enough momentum that it continued through and pierced the back end as well. The vehicle rocked, tilted, and crashed into a derelict car parked on the side of the street.

"Go! Go!" Stone yelled to Errin. He couldn't see any other pursuers, but if the others were in communication, he knew it wouldn't be long now. "Are we close?"

"Entering the Wastes now," Jeritha called back. "Let me concentrate."

Stone let his breath out and climbed back into his seat in the back. "You all right, Harrison?"

"I will be." His voice still sounded exhausted and raspy, but stronger than before. Since there wasn't another available seat, he crouched in the back, focusing his attention forward.

Stone did the same thing, peering through the front window. The sun was coming up now, but he still couldn't see much beyond what the truck's feeble headlights illuminated. As they left the road and set off into the Wastes, the ride he'd thought bumpy before got worse. He had no idea how long their tires would last, but hoped it would be long enough. "How far to the ship? Are we heading the right way?"

"Couple of miles," Errin said. "And yes, we are. We—"

"Wait!" Jeritha's cut in, suddenly urgent.

"What?"

"We can't go that way! There's a manastorm coming!"

| CHAPTER FIFTY

"WAIT, WHAT?" Stone demanded. "A manastorm? Where?"

"It's heading for where we left the ship." Jeritha appeared to be concentrating, as if listening to something the rest of them couldn't hear. "They think if it keeps moving in the same direction, it will pass over the ship in less than half an hour."

"Ship?" Harrison asked.

"We flew here in the little airship," Errin told him. "Jeritha navigated us through the Wastes. The teleporter in Drendell was destroyed, so we had no other choice."

"What's that mean?" Stone asked. "Will the storm affect the ship?"

"I don't know," Jeritha said. "Since it runs on magic, it's possible. But there isn't enough time for us to get there and take off. Predicting manastorm paths isn't a precise art. I wouldn't risk it."

"What do we do, then?" Stone asked. "We can't go back to Drendell. They know we're here now, and they'll probably be waiting for us, even if they aren't brave enough to chase us out here."

"Head north," Jeritha said. "My band is a few miles away. We can take shelter with them until the storm passes, then return to the ship."

"I don't like it," Errin said. "This truck won't hold up to this kind of terrain for long." She let out a loud sigh. "We don't have much choice, though. You're right—we can't go back." She swung the wheel around and veered onto a rutted, barely visible track. "This is going to be slow, so I hope nobody suddenly gets brave enough to follow us."

Everyone focused forward as Errin picked a careful path. Stone shifted to magical sight, checking all around them for any sign of disturbance in the ambient magic, even though he knew Jeritha would have a much better chance of seeing it than he did.

"Tell me what I've missed," Harrison said. He'd settled to a seated position in the enclosed rear compartment, his shoulders slumped with exhaustion. He still looked even more pale than usual, the blood drying on his face and upper body giving him a sinister aspect.

Errin had to concentrate on driving, so Stone filled him in on everything that had happened since the attack at the Underground.

"Rovenna is dead, then?" he asked.

"Yes. And I'm sorry to have to tell you, but Karol is as well."

Harrison closed his eyes for just a moment; when he opened them, the smoldering, carefully controlled rage was back. "They will suffer for that," he said, his tone still even and calm.

"What did they do to you?" Stone asked. "How were they able to catch you by surprise at the Underground? I was under the impression that's not easy to do."

"Normally it isn't. They did something to my magic. I am not certain what it was. The last thing I remember at the Underground was my shield failing, and then an explosive detonating nearby."

"So they *do* have magic-damping capability," Errin said. "That's not good news. Especially if it's strong enough to take *you* out." She shot a quick glance over her shoulder before turning her attention back to the terrain. "Do you remember anything about what they did to you?"

"Very little. They wanted to know where I came from, of course. And they seemed interested in testing my resilience."

"They tortured you, in other words," Stone said.

"Yes. They used both chemical and physical methods." Harrison spoke as dispassionately as if he were discussing the weather. "How long was I in their custody?"

"A little over a day," Errin said. "Did you tell them anything? Do you remember?"

"I am not certain. There were periods where I don't remember anything—whether it was because I lost consciousness or because their methods were effective, I can't say."

"Even if they found out anything, though, getting near us won't be easy. So there's that, at least."

Harrison seemed to notice Tanissa, who'd been sitting quietly behind Errin, for the first time. "Forgive me," he said to her. "I don't believe we have met."

"This is Tanissa," Stone said. "I met her when I first arrived in Drendell—she saved my life. And she helped us quite a lot in Temolan while we were looking for you. She's a healer, and she wants to come to New Argana."

Harrison inclined his head. "It is a pleasure, Tanissa. Thank you for assisting us. I regret we couldn't meet under more favorable circumstances."

"I'm...happy to see you're looking better," she said.

Stone didn't miss the way she was looking at him—like a nervous animal, trying to hide her fear. He patted her arm. "Everything's going to be fine. I think New Argana will suit you nicely. But first we need to—"

"Turn more north," Jeritha cut in, leaning forward to grip the dashboard. "The band is moving. The manastorm is progressing faster than expected."

"We can't go much faster than this," Errin said. "The wheels will fall off."

"Let me try something," Harrison said. He took a couple of deep breaths, closed his eyes, and after a moment the truck lifted off the ground and hovered there.

"Bloody hell," Stone said, impressed in spite of himself. Even with the insane levels of magic here, he didn't think Harrison would be capable of such a thing in his present condition.

"You will need to provide the propulsion and steering, Dr. Stone," Harrison said. His voice sounded tight and tense; obviously this wasn't as easy for him as it might have been on a good day.

"Got it. Errin, Jeritha, you tell me which direction."

Jeritha pointed. "Keep going that way for now."

Tanissa was looking at all of them as if she'd fallen in with a nest of madmen. She didn't say anything, though, and instead turned her attention back to the view out the front window.

As they progressed—couldn't really say *drove* anymore, Stone thought with grim amusement—the landscape slowly began to change. Instead of jutting rocks and scrubby brush, he spotted a carpet of multicolored grass, covered with what looked like a thin slick of iridescent oil. Here and there, spiky, crystalline rocks poked out of the ground, glowing faintly in the dawn light. They glowed even more brightly in magical sight, with bits of energy arcing between them. The effect was eerily beautiful—sometimes clusters of smaller crystals, sometimes larger, solitary ones jutting higher, as tall as a person. Occasionally, an arcing energy bolt would jump from one of the larger crystals to another one a few feet away, combining with the weird aurora effect in the sky to create a dazzling lightshow. Stone wondered what Jeritha must be seeing.

"Is this safe?" he asked. Fortunately, propelling the truck forward didn't take nearly the level of magical expenditure Harrison was no doubt putting out to keep it aloft, especially as long as they headed in the same direction.

"It is as long as we keep moving," Jeritha said.

"What if we don't?" Tanissa asked. She gripped her seat arms so tightly her knuckles whitened; she definitely looked as if she was beginning to regret her decision to accompany them.

"The magic level here is variable," Jeritha told her. "It's not necessarily dangerous, but depending on the fluctuations, it could be. I'm feeling some fairly strong surges in the ambient magical level, but mostly behind us."

"Just keep going," Errin muttered. "Trevor, are you all right?"

"Yes. Let me concentrate."

Stone glanced over at him. He was even more pale now under the streaks of blood. His eyes were closed, and his hands, gripping the backs of the two seats in front of him, shook. How much longer could he maintain this pace without a rest? Stone had no idea how far they'd already gone, and how far they'd need to go before—

Something slammed down onto the top of the truck.

CHAPTER FIFTY-ONE

"WHAT THE HELL WAS THAT?" Stone yelled, spinning around as the floating truck veered wildly and tilted to the right.

Whatever it was, it had been heavy: the roof now sported a deep dent that had barely missed Harrison's head.

"What is it?" Errin demanded, looking around. Nothing was visible through the front window.

Another missile hit the truck, this time on the left side. Once again it tilted, slamming Errin, Tanissa, and Harrison into the wall while Stone and Jeritha on the other side gripped their seats and tried to stay in position.

Harrison kept his concentration enough that they didn't crash, but barely. The truck dropped back to the ground and landed squarely on its four wheels, but a loud *crack* sounded from somewhere in the vicinity of the rear axle.

Stone gripped Jeritha's shoulder. "What's out there?"

She had her eyes closed, leaning forward into the dashboard. "It's the *wyvora*."

A chill ripped through Stone. "Those dragon things?"

"At least one. I can't tell if there are more." Even she looked nervous now as she continued to peer out.

"Why are they here? How far are we from your band?"

"Still a couple of miles. And I don't know. They're attracted to unusual magic."

"You mean like us levitating the truck?"

She looked troubled. "This area is highly magical. That shouldn't have been enough to—" She stopped as something else hit the truck, this time on top of the cab. The windshield shattered, littering the cabin with glittering chunks of glass, and another dent appeared above their heads.

"What do we do?" Errin yelled. "Can we fight them?"

"We will have to," Harrison said. Already he'd scrambled up and was heading for the rear of the truck.

"We can't stay in here," Jeritha said. "They're dropping rocks on us. It's one of their tactics, to soften up their prey before they swoop in for the kill."

"Shouldn't we stay under cover?" Tanissa asked. She was even paler than Harrison, wide-eyed with terror.

"It's easier for them to hit a larger target." Jeritha shoved the door open and jumped down, scanning the skies.

Stone joined her, looking up just in time to see another rock the size of a motorcycle rocketing toward the truck. Harrison leaped free just as it hit and crushed the rear compartment. One of the massive, leathery-winged creatures they'd dealt with on their flight over banked away with an eerie, ululating shriek.

"There's another one!" Errin called, pointing.

Stone spun again, following her gesture. Another of the creatures, black and skeletal, glided overhead, clutching yet another rock in its front claws. As it passed over them, it shrieked and dropped its payload.

Jeritha raised her fist to the sky, summoning a shield. The rock hit the shield and bounced off, barely missing Tanissa.

"We can't hold them off forever," Stone said, looking around for a place to hide—a cave or outcropping, perhaps. But aside from the sharply pointed, crystalline mineral structures poking out of nearby rises, he spotted nothing. Even the truck couldn't serve as much of a shelter anymore, with its back end crushed in.

Harrison stood unprotected not far from the truck, his gaze tracking one of the creatures. When it passed over him, he pointed his hand upward and summoned a blast of blue fire.

The creature dodged—they were remarkably agile for things so large—but the blast still hit its rear legs, flowering back along its tail. The *wyvora*'s shriek of defiance turned to one of agony, and it streaked away, smoke trailing behind it.

Energized by Harrison's success, Stone turned in place to keep the other beast in sight. So far, only two had materialized—were more lurking beyond their sight? Would the shrieks from these two call others? They had to deal with them fast. Even if Jeritha's band showed up to help, he didn't think they could handle several more of the things all at once.

Then, to his horror, the creature Harrison had hit twisted in midair, its scream changing again, and headed back in their direction. It flight was more unsteady now, but as it swooped down closer, Stone's whole body chilled when he got a look at its face.

The thing looked as if it was fighting against something. It shook its head in anger, screeching short, sharp cries, and flailed at its muzzle with a front claw.

"What's wrong with it?" Stone demanded. "It looks like it's sick or something. Harrison, did you do that?"

"There's something wrong with the magic!" Jerissa called. "Something's stirring them up!"

"How can that be?" Errin asked. She had her gun out, but the tiny thing that worked so well against humanoid enemies looked woefully inadequate against the winged terrors circling them. "There can't be—"

"Behind us!" Suddenly, Jeritha's nervous expression turned to one of horror. "They're invisible! They—"

Stone dashed around behind the fallen truck, focusing his attention back the way they'd come and shifting to magical sight. At first he didn't see it against the dazzling backdrop of the crystal structures and the dancing magical aurora, but then he spotted the edges of an invisible floating vehicle about a hundred feet behind them. "There!" he shouted, pointing. "They're following us! It's—"

The vehicle shimmered briefly into existence as a massive fireball erupted from it and sped toward Stone and his friends. Then it faded again.

Jeritha and Harrison summoned shields at the same time. The fiery missile, as large as a beach ball, slammed into Jeritha's first and took it down, staggering her backward. It hit Harrison's and dissipated in a spray of flame, so close to them that Stone could feel its heat from several feet back.

"I thought they wouldn't follow us into the Wastes!" Stone yelled, trying to get a bead on the people in the vehicle while still keeping an eye on the two *wyvora* circling overhead. Another rock plummeted down and hit the ground only a few feet from Tanissa, who dived for cover next to one of the larger crystalline structures.

"They must be desperate," Errin called. She'd hidden herself behind the ruined truck, keeping it between herself and the invisible vehicle since she couldn't see it. She pulled one of her magic-damping smoke grenades from her pocket and heaved it in that direction, releasing a billowing cloud of inky black smoke between them and their pursuers.

"Did they summon those things?" Stone asked Jeritha. One of the *wyvora* was still circling; the other had disappeared, probably heading off to find another rock. "Was that the strange fluctuation you felt?"

"It could have been." She looked grim. "It's hard to tell at the level of magic here, but it would take significant magic to overcome it."

"War-level magic?" Errin demanded. "Would they chance that just to go after *us*?"

"That could have been war-level magic," Jeritha said. Her voice shook with anger. "Idiots! Why would they risk such a thing?"

Harrison still stood in the open. He pointed his hand and sent another sheet of blue fire in the direction of the invisible vehicle. The potent attack flared around it and it shimmered back into being: a small, boxy thing painted bright white. This time it didn't fade out again. Four figures tumbled from it and ran toward cover, flinging spells at Harrison's group as they ran.

Harrison caught one of them before he made it. The man screamed as his body erupted in flame, and he fell.

"They want me," Harrison said. He was still breathing hard and didn't look much better than he had before, but he stood straight and confident in the open, constantly scanning. "Flattering, I suppose."

"We'll be flattered after we deal with them," Stone said. One of the *wyvora* streaked downward, front claws extended, burning gaze fixed on the terrified Tanissa. Stone loosed a massive lightning bolt at it, hitting it in the center of its chest. It screamed and banked, heading back skyward.

The three remaining Talented didn't remain idle. With unnatural suddenness, the cloud of black smoke, which had been spreading into a wall extending in both directions, dissipated. All three of the attackers immediately launched coordinated attacks from three different hiding places: the battered truck lifted off the ground and fell down toward Errin, while twin blasts of magical energy flew toward Harrison and Jeritha.

Harrison, Jeritha, and Stone acted instantly, as if they'd trained together for years. Stone sent a concussion beam at the truck, knocking it away from Errin's hiding spot; it crashed to the ground a few feet beyond her. Jeritha summoned a shield to block the incoming attacks. Harrison made a savage gesture and brought up a section of the rocky ground, sending several missiles hurtling toward two of the Talented ahead of another sheet of blue fire.

Neither got out of the way in time. One of the rocks smashed into the first woman's head, throwing her back into one of the crystal formations, where the blue fire incinerated her. The other tried a shield—it blocked the rock, but the magical attack ripped through it as if it weren't there. He screamed and dropped; a moment later, one of the *wyvora* swooped down, grabbed him in its grasping front claws, and streaked away, trumpeting a shriek of triumph.

Stone had a half-second to be relieved before more shrieks from the distance sent a chill down his back. He glanced around and froze when he spotted two more of the dragonlike creatures in the distance. "More of them are coming!" he yelled. "What's calling them?"

"It's their vehicle!" Jeritha called. "Something inside is doing it! And we've got to get out of here! The manastorm is moving again! It's coming this way!" Her voice, so calm before, now carried the edges of panic.

Apparently the last remaining Talented had heard her too. He popped to visibility behind the vehicle, summoning a glimmering shield around both it and himself.

"How long have we got?" Stone demanded.

"Minutes. Maybe not that long."

"Bloody hell!" Even if they *did* deal with the *wyvora,* the war magic that was calling them, and the remaining Talented pursuer, they no longer had a vehicle. How were they going to get away from a fast-moving magical storm?

First problems first. "Harrison! Let's take out that shield!"

At Harrison's curt nod, Stone gathered magical energy. Even now, in the midst of their dire situation, he couldn't help but revel at how *easy* it was. The magic came to him readily, singing through his body with an indescribable feeling. It wasn't like the kind of rush he got from taking black magic power from others—but he didn't *need* that rush anymore. As long as he could do this, he'd never be tempted again. He was certain of it.

If I live through this. He released the energy at the same time Harrison did, sending it directly at the vehicle. It was just like Jason had told him once, when trying to explain to him how to fight: punch *through* your opponent, not *at* him.

The two massive magical blasts hit the shimmering shield at the same time. It flared bright, then brighter, then vanished. Off to the side, the remaining Talented pursuer let out a loud shriek of pain, staggering from his hiding place and clutching his head. Harrison vaporized him in a gout of searing blue flame.

Stone immediately switched his focus. They'd taken out the last of the Talented. The vehicle was unprotected now. If they could destroy it, then maybe they could—

"Stone! *Look out!*" Tanissa screamed.

Stone had only a second to register the shadow that had appeared above him, blotting out the weird, shifting aurora-light. Before he could react, something huge and black clamped around him, lifting him off the ground.

"No!" Errin yelled.

Stone couldn't see, but he didn't have to. He knew what had happened: one of the *wyvora* had swooped silently down while he'd been focused on the vehicle and snatched him in its claws. He struggled in the thing's grip as a fetid, rotten-meat stench engulfed him. Where were the others? Why weren't they shooting at it? He tried to twist in its grip and yelped as one of its claws dug into his shoulder. He had to summon the magic, but his mind wouldn't settle on the pattern, lock in the necessary formula. It had only been a couple of days since he'd gotten his magic back; apparently the new paradigm wasn't as second-nature as he'd thought yet. But if he didn't do something soon, he would—

What happened next happened fast. He felt the *wyvora* jerk in a spasm, its claws first tightening around him until he screamed, then releasing him.

He was falling.

Only half-conscious now, disoriented, bleeding from a deep wound in his shoulder, he tried to twist his body, to cast a spell, to—

Pain.

More than pain.

White-hot agony, so sharp and sudden and profound that his mind refused to process it. His whole existence shrank to a bright cocoon, and he barely heard the terrified yells of his friends as grayness rose around him.

What had happened? Had he hit the ground? He must have—he'd been falling. How high up had he been? Why hadn't anyone caught him? Where was the *wyvora*? Thoughts, jumbled and fragmented, dashed around his head, whirling until they didn't even make sense anymore. He tried to struggle up.

Something wrenched, bringing with it new flowers of agony. Stone's eyes flew open, and what he saw almost made what was left of his rational mind flee from him.

He was on his back, looking up into the dancing, multi-colored aurora effect of the sky. But as beautiful as it was, he barely noticed it.

What he *did* notice—what he couldn't miss because it filled every corner of his sight, his mind, his existence—was the sharply pointed, blood-soaked crystalline spike poking up through his chest, and the way his arms, legs, and head dangled, unsupported.

No no no no no

His thoughts weren't even that coherent, though—nothing like *bloody hell, I've been impaled,* or even *I'm going to die.* He was beyond that kind of rational language. All he had left was pain, and horror, and the creeping, inexorable feeling of his life-force draining away as he knew there was nothing he could do about it.

Once again he thought he heard his friends screaming something, but their voices blended together and didn't form recognizable words. Were they coming to help him? Had the *wyvora* gotten them?

He didn't know.

He didn't care.

His fading attention, laser-focused now, was riveted on the bloody spike poking from his chest. He couldn't breathe. He tried to cough, but that only brought more pain, and more blood.

Why couldn't he just *die* and get it over with?

And then something else happened.

He couldn't explain it. He didn't try.

It wasn't as if the pain disappeared. It was still there, constant and sharp and bright, lancing through him every time he made even the slightest move.

But now there was something else, too.

As somewhere off in the distance the sound of his friends' cries changed, another feeling settled over him, gathering around him. He couldn't describe it, because he'd never experienced anything like it before. The closest he could get was that it felt like it *belonged* with him. It pressed in around him, humming with the frequency of some fundamental, primal engine. His arms and legs tingled, and he no longer felt as if they dangled helplessly as the spike held him impaled. His whole body felt electric, as if he had been plugged into the pulsing power source of the universe.

Somehow, he managed to open his eyes, to raise his head just enough to see. He only managed it for the briefest of moments—perhaps a second or two—but in that short space of time everything *changed.*

The spike poking through his body wasn't streaked with blood anymore.

Instead, everywhere the bright red of the blood had been was now a luminous, unearthly silver, dancing and arcing around the crystal. More silvery light limned the thing's edges, flowing out to surround his body like a ghostly aura. Around it, the sky's aurora grew brighter until the colors flamed with such unearthly intensity that it was impossible to look at them any longer with a mortal gaze.

Stone clamped his eyes shut, but still the silver and the wild colors refused to recede. They mixed with the pain and formed something new, something extraordinary. Something—

Screams again.

Him? Someone else?

He still didn't know.

The dazzling aurora vanished as something heavy and black rose above him, and the ground shook with a freight-train rumble.

An earthquake rumble.

An end of the world rumble.

And then, nothing.

CHAPTER FIFTY-TWO

VOICES.

Muddy and indistinct at first, slowly resolving themselves into coherent words.

"—waking up—"

"—all right? You—"

"—call him—"

He opened his eyes, with no idea what he'd see. Nothing? Darkness? A white room?

A pale, familiar face hovered over him.

Tanissa. Smiling. "Hello," she said softly. "How do you feel?"

That was an important question, but for a moment he couldn't remember why. When he did finally remember, he jerked upward, his hand flying to his chest, expecting to feel something sharp and pointed sticking through it, or at least a horrific, bloody crater.

Instead, he felt a blanket, and unbroken skin.

What?

How can that—

Tanissa gently pushed him back down. "You're all right. Just lie back. You've been through a lot."

Another figure approached the bed. Stone blinked, and the figure resolved itself into Illona, the healer at the Nexus. She had one of the little rolling constructs with her. Tanissa stepped aside, and she and the construct took a few readings.

"I'm glad to see you're awake," she said. And then the two of them departed, leaving him once more alone with Tanissa.

"I—" Stone swallowed, and sat up more slowly. This time, Tanissa let him do it, propping him with pillows. His thoughts churned; he wondered if they had him dosed up on so many tranquilizers and painkillers that they could drop a truck on him and he wouldn't feel it. Had they used an illusion to make his chest appear unmarred, thinking the true reality would have been too much for him to bear without preparation? He touched the center of it again, then looked at Tanissa in confusion. "Where—?"

"Shh," she said. She was still smiling. "You're all right. You're at the infirmary at the Nexus."

"We—made it? But how—?" Nothing made sense. His last memory had left them all in a dire situation: his body impaled on the spiked crystal, the *wyvora* closing in, the fast-moving manastorm approaching, Jeritha's band and their own airship too far away to help—how had they escaped all of that?

The door opened, admitting Errin. She grinned when she spotted him. "Alastair! Illona just called and said you were awake. How do you feel?"

He shifted his gaze between her and Tanissa, searching for the answer he wanted to give them. Finally he settled for: "Confused."

"I can understand that." She pulled up a chair and sat next to the bed. "The last few hours have been pretty confusing for all of us."

Stone looked past her. "Where are the others? Harrison? Jeritha? Are they—Did they—?"

"They're fine," she assured him. "Jeritha's back with her band. She and Tanissa helped heal you." She patted Tanissa's arm. "Tanissa's quite a healer. She'll be a great addition here. Illona's already excited to be working with her."

Stone swallowed, his mind still reeling with confusion. "But—"

"Shh…" Tanissa said gently. "It's been a long day for you. You'll be fine, but you should rest."

She was probably right, but Stone was having none of it. "I want to know what happened," he said, sitting up more. He couldn't quite describe how he felt—tired, a little weak, but certainly not anywhere near as bad as he should have felt after everything that had happened. Even the wound where the *wyvora* had pierced his shoulder was gone, without even a scar to mark where it had been. "How did we get back here? Why aren't I dead?"

"You have Tanissa to thank for that," Errin said.

"Wait…" he said, still trying to make sense of everything that had occurred. "How can that…be? Is there something wrong with my memory? That thing dropped me—I landed on one of those spikes. I was…" He touched his chest again, like a child poking at a loose tooth to verify it was still there.

"You were," Tanissa said gently. "I don't know how you survived either, honestly. You should have died. You're a fighter—I'll say that for you."

"But—the manastorm. Those dragon things. How did—"

Errin gripped his shoulder. "I can see you're not going to settle down until you get the whole story. What happened was that we were luckier than we had a right to be. All of us. The manastorm was coming, and Jeritha was nearly panicking about what would happen if we didn't get away from it. But we didn't have *time* to get away from it. Our truck wasn't running, and Trevor blew up the other one. That stopped the *wyvora*—apparently Jeritha was right about something inside it stirring them up, because as soon as he destroyed it, they took off."

"But—what about the storm?" Vaguely, Stone remembered a bizarre sensation washing over him—something electric and primal and pulsing—but he thought it must have been a side effect of the spike piercing his body. "Did it hit?"

"Trevor used some fancy magic to bring up a section of the ground and make a shelter over us all. So yes, it did hit, but we were protected. He barely made it in time—we were sure it had hit you, but you must have gotten lucky. It tore one of the *wyvora* to shreds before it could get away. The shelter was Jeritha's idea—she said it's a Traveler trick. They sometimes hide in caves or underground shelters to weather the storms when they can't run from them. When they don't have anything else, they use magic to create their own."

Stone let his breath out. "I still don't understand how I'm alive," he said. "How did that spike not—"

"Like I said—Tanissa's a talented healer. She must have gotten to you fast enough—even so, it was close. If we hadn't gotten you back here in time, you probably *would* have died."

That was another question. "How *did* we get back? Did the storm destroy the airship?"

"Unfortunately yes, it did." Errin sounded regretful, almost as if she'd lost one of her own children. "It's a shame—it will take quite some time to build another one. But at least I learned a few things to incorporate into the new design."

"So then how did we get back without it?"

"Trevor. We had to wait a little while for him to recover enough to do it, but he teleported us all back. All but Jeritha—as I said, her band turned up and she decided to stay with them. They were grateful we saved her, and she said to tell you it was a pleasure to work with you, Alastair."

Stone mulled all that over. "Harrison teleported us all back here?"

"With a bit of help from the Travelers, yes."

"Where is he now? Is he all right?"

"He said he'd see you later today," Errin said. "He had a few things to attend to with Kira, and Illona insisted he take some time to rest and recover. I'm sure you can tell how well *that* went over."

Stone barely heard the last of her words; his mind wandered again as another thought occurred to him. Tentatively, almost as if he were afraid to try it, he raised a hand and focused on a glass of water sitting on the table next to his bed. With care he formed the pattern in his mind, then breathed a sigh of relief as the glass rose neatly a few inches and hovered there. At Errin's questioning look, he offered a faint smile. "Just…checking."

She chuckled. "You mages are all alike. Anyway," she added, standing, "we should go and let you rest. If you're feeling up to it, I'll see you later today."

Stone almost protested that he felt fine, but instead merely nodded. "Thank you both…for everything."

"Thank *you*," Tanissa said. She indicated the room. "I'd never have believed all this was possible...and I'm here because of you."

The two of them moved off, Tanissa to the other side of the room where Illona was working on something at a lab bench with her mechanical "nurse," and Errin leaving the room with a wave of farewell.

Stone, now alone, took a long drink from the water glass, then sat up the rest of the way and examined his chest.

The only indication that the crystal spike had pierced him was a tiny scar in the center, about the size of an Earth dime. That was odd—if his memory wasn't playing tricks with him, the thing had been several times larger at its base. It should have destroyed his heart, his lungs—had he somehow drawn sufficient favor from the Universe that it had missed anything vital? That hardly seemed likely.

At least it hadn't obliterated the magical tattoo on his left side—even though he didn't need it any longer to help him channel his black-magic energy, it had taken a lot of talent and effort to produce and he'd grown to like it.

He closed his eyes, his mind refusing to settle. He was safe now. Against nearly insurmountable odds, they'd managed to navigate through terrain that should have been suicidal, rescue Harrison from the Talented's custody, and survive a deadly manastorm, war magic, and winged monsters straight out of a nightmare. Hell, he'd survived an injury that should have killed him instantly, with next to no ill effects.

So, why did he feel so...strange?

Curious, he shifted to magical sight, wondering if his inexplicable feeling of psychic discomfort might be reflected in his aura.

What he saw made him stiffen and drop his hand back to the bed.

He'd expected red flashes, areas where the normally smooth edges of the aura roiled and surged, or even the muddy, muted colors indicating some kind of ill health. None of those would have surprised him, given what he'd experienced.

What he *didn't* expect to see was a third color.

He blinked and sharpened his focus, sure he had to be mistaken. This kind of thing didn't *happen.*

But there it was, so stark and vivid he couldn't have confused it for something else.

The brilliant purple shone as bright as ever closest to his body, with the narrower band of blazing gold surrounding it. Those were normal and expected—he saw them every day when he used magical sight.

But now a third band, silvery and jagged, snugged up against the golden nimbus. It was even narrower than the gold, but still wide and distinct enough to be clearly visible.

What the hell was going on?

Mages with tri-colored auras existed, though they were exceedingly rare. It almost always indicated someone with either significant power or who was unusual in some way. Stone had only ever met one in his life, back home in England many years ago. Two colors were rare, but not nearly as much so—even some strong-willed mundanes could have them. All of the most potent mages Stone knew had them:

Madame Huan, Stefan Kolinsky, William Desmond, Harrison.

But what didn't happen—what, as far as Stone knew, *never* happened—was for someone, mage or mundane, to *change* his or her aura. An aura was like a fingerprint: you were born with it, and it remained constant throughout your life. Skilled mages could conceal or disguise them, but to change one permanently? That was—

Stone let his breath out as a pair of disparate memories came back to him. The first was recent: the electric, silvery energy streaking the spike that had pierced his chest, arcing around it like otherworldly lightning, along with the profoundly disturbing feeling of some kind of current passing through his body. Had that somehow caused the change?

He wasn't sure, though, because of the other memory. This one was older, and he'd almost forgotten it: a conversation between himself and Madame Huan, when he'd been terrified he'd lost his magic following a desperate use of Harrison's technique to destroy the Evil's gateway at Burning Man. She'd examined him for signs of magic, and though at the time she'd found none, he remembered what she'd told him with surprise:

"It's as if there's something…extra there. Your normal aura is that lovely shade of violet with bits of gold overlaying it. But now there's a new color, right at the edge. A sort of…silver. It nearly blends with the gold, which is why it's so hard to see."

He hadn't been able to see it himself—at the time, with his magic not functioning, he couldn't see *any* of his aura, and when it came back, he'd tried but it had been too faint to spot. He'd written it off as some artifact of pushing himself too far—something that had faded as he returned to normal—and hadn't thought about it since.

But now it was back, and there was no mistaking it. Was it the same thing? Was it connected somehow with using Harrison's magic? Had the piercing spike done something to him? Were the two somehow related?

He had no idea. He didn't even know how he could find out. Illona and Tanissa hadn't said anything about it, and they certainly must have examined his aura while they healed him. He wished he could ask Jeritha about it—the Traveler's apparent sensitivity to the astral world might provide a clue—but she was gone now, and he'd probably never see her again.

He bowed his head and rubbed his face with his hands. Whatever it was, he'd either deal with it or he wouldn't—but regardless of which, he knew one thing with certainty.

It was time for him to go home.

CHAPTER FIFTY-THREE

STONE DIDN'T EXPECT ANZO to take him directly to Harrison's suite when he asked, but to his surprise the little construct didn't offer any objections.

A few hours had passed since he'd awakened in the infirmary, and it still amazed him how quickly and thoroughly he'd recovered. New Argana's healers were bloody good at their jobs, that was certain. Stone regretted he couldn't arrange for Verity to spend some time with Illona and Tanissa—the three women might benefit from working together.

Anzo had turned up a while back, escorting him to his own suite so he could shower, shave, and change clothes. He felt a lot more at home now in black T-shirt and jeans than he had in the Talented's high-collared long coat, even if the thing *had* adapted perfectly to his frame. He made a mental note to work on that spell when he got home—especially now that he'd filled out a bit through the chest and shoulders, he'd either need to learn it or spend some serious time with his tailor.

Home. It seemed so long ago now; in a strange sort of way, he'd begun to feel at home here on Calanar. Not so much that he'd want to stay, of course, but enough that he no longer felt completely out of place here. Especially in New Argana. It had crept up on him, this feeling, and he couldn't put his finger on when exactly it had solidified.

Now he stood in front of the familiar wooden double doors, wondering how Harrison would respond to what he had to say. "I'll take it from here, Anzo," he said. "You can go."

"Yes, sir." The little wheeled robot rolled off, back toward the teleport pad. He would miss it, Stone decided. Having his own personal mechano-magical valet and tour guide had helped him acclimate to this place faster than he'd expected. Amused, he tried to anticipate Harrison's response if he inquired about acquiring one to take back to Earth. Maybe he could teach it to do laundry and tidy up the sitting room. It would probably terrify Raider, though.

He chuckled at the thought, but quickly turned serious as he knocked. He didn't think Harrison would appreciate his feline-related speculations.

The door swung silently open on the starkly elegant suite. It was already dark outside, the inky, star-studded sky dominating the view from this high in the tower.

Harrison stood near the window, drink in hand. He turned as Stone entered.

"Dr. Stone. I am pleased to see you looking so well."

"Thank you. I could say the same for you."

It was true—almost *too* true. Harrison showed literally no signs of his recent ordeal. No healing wounds or scars, no unhealthy pallor, no slump to his usual military-straight posture. Clad in razor-creased black trousers and a white shirt with the cuffs turned up, every hair in place and wearing an expression of focused calm, he looked as relaxed and elegant as he ever did.

"What can I do for you?" he asked. "Forgive me for not visiting you in the infirmary, but several matters required my immediate attention."

"About what happened in Temolan, I assume."

"Yes. Your rescue mission has caused significant turmoil among the upper echelons of the Council—particularly following Chanandra's and Vestereth's deaths and numerous other injuries among high-level Temolan officials."

"What about Olystriar? Did he manage to fool them so they don't suspect him?"

"Yes. Olystriar is highly intelligent, and has decades of experience dealing with untrustworthy people. As far as the rest of the Council is aware, he is secluded in his private residence, recuperating from his unfortunate injuries."

"What about the others—the people from the other cities?"

"As you might expect, information has leaked regarding the events at the Underground and at Millia and Vestereth's demonstration. Millia is nowhere to be found—some suspect she may have defected to Sholandre following Vestereth's death and the failure to recapture me. Part of what required my attention was to speak with some of our agents in both cities, directing them to begin spreading misinformation. Kira has taken over that task. With her greater experience in the culture, she is more adept at it than I." He nodded toward the bar. "Would you care for something to drink?"

"Thank you, that would be brilliant." Stone waited while Harrison used magic to pour him a shot and levitate it to him, then approached the window. "What about the war magic? Is anyone in trouble for that?"

"Regrettably, no. Everyone involved is dead now, and the manastorm—which passed considerably closer to Drendell than any in recent memory—obliterated any evidence, even if anyone cared to venture out to investigate."

"That's too bad. I'd imagine that would stir up quite the hornets' nest if it had come to light."

"Indeed. But not necessarily to anyone's advantage."

"How so?"

Harrison sipped his drink and turned back to the window. "As distasteful as I find the cities, each of them serves as a check on the others, precisely *because* none, on its own, dares to risk using war magic. If anyone found out one of them did…"

"…it could start the war all over again." Stone nodded soberly. "I see where you're going." He paced again, taking in the view. Off in the far distance, he thought he could see a faint hint of the colorful aurora patterns from the Wastes. "Did you ever figure out what that agent of yours was up to? What was his name—Galen, right?"

"Galen has been dealt with." Harrison's chilly, unemotional tone sent a shiver up Stone's back. Definitely not a man he wanted to ever get on the wrong side of.

When he didn't reply to that, Harrison said, "Is there something I can do for you? Surely you didn't come here to discuss the Calanarian political situation."

Stone thought such a discussion might prove interesting—but not now. "Yes. I came to see you because…I'm ready to go home. I've got what I need to use magic back on Earth, right? There's nothing else I need to learn?"

"No. You have everything you need at this point—including quite a trial by fire to ensure you can function effectively under significant pressure. All that remains is practice."

"So—you'll send me home, then?"

"Whenever you wish, Dr. Stone. I can do it now if you like."

Stone returned his attention to the view and didn't answer.

"Is there something else?"

"Well…yes. I'm ready to go. I want to get back to my life. I've already been gone for over two months, and it's going to take some fast talking to explain where I've been all this time. But—" He hesitated, and wondered why. He didn't think what he had to say next would come as any surprise to the unusually perceptive Harrison. "Well, I'm not certain I want to *stay* away."

Harrison's eyebrow rose. "You wish to return?"

"I don't know. I might. I'd like to learn more about this world—about how magic works here, about the Travelers, and the cities…It's fascinating. I teach Occult Studies back home, but part of my early research was in cultural anthropology. To have an entirely new society to study…it's…" He shrugged. "Intriguing. And," he added quickly, "there's also the matter of all this 'mechano-magical' stuff you lot are working on. I've never seen anything like that back on Earth. I want to learn how it works. Even learn to build it myself, someday."

"A substantial portion of it wouldn't function properly on Earth. The ambient magic is not strong enough in most areas to support it. Perhaps it might be possible somewhere with a significant confluence of ley lines…"

Stone thought about Caventhorne, at the intersection of five of them, and already his mind was working. "Maybe," he said, cutting off the thought. There'd be time for that later. "So—could I come back sometime? Would I be welcome?"

"You are always welcome, Dr. Stone. But there are factors you must consider."

"What factors?"

"The passage of time, most importantly."

"What do you mean?" Stone set his glass down and perched on the end of the black leather sofa facing the window.

Now it was Harrison's turn to pace. "It is a common issue when dealing with interdimensional travel. Time runs differently here than it does on Earth. Considerably faster, as it happens."

"Faster?" Stone blinked. "You're saying time passes faster here than it does there? So even though I've been away for more than two months by Calanar's standards, it's—"

"Only a day or two by Earth's. Yes."

Stone stared at him. "Wait a moment. I'm sorry—having a bit of trouble getting my mind around this. You travel back and forth between these two dimensions…and I'm guessing others too, right?"

Harrison inclined his head.

"How do you manage the timelines? Do you go to Earth for a week and come back to find that six months or a year has passed here?"

"No."

"No? But then, how—"

Harrison appeared to consider something. Silence hung in the air for several seconds, and then he reached a decision. "Come with me, Dr. Stone. I want to show you something."

Intrigued, Stone followed him as he strode toward the back of the suite. He ascended a short, three-step rise and continued down a hallway lined with several closed doors. As he approached the rearmost of these, it swung open on a small, featureless room with another teleport pad in its center.

"Where does this go?" Stone asked.

Harrison didn't answer; instead, he mounted the pad and motioned for Stone to do likewise.

As always with the Nexus's teleportation devices, Stone felt no jarring or buzzing sensation. He expected them to re-appear in another hallway, but instead, they stood in a room he was sure he'd never seen before—not here or anywhere.

"Bloody hell…" he whispered, turning in place. "Where are we?"

"This is the topmost point of the Nexus tower," Harrison said. His even, emotionless voice sounded odd in here, as if it were echoing from different parts of the room.

Stone had no trouble believing it. Every wall in the room was made of glass. There were eight sections, all angled in-ward and meeting to form a point at the top, perhaps twenty feet overhead. The spotless purity of the glass made it almost invisible, producing the disorienting sensation of standing on a small, unprotected platform at the top of a skyscraper.

Up this high, some of the Wastes' dazzlingly beautiful, multicolored aurora effect danced among the stars, creating one of the most awe-inspiring and unsettling panoramic views Stone had ever seen. If he didn't look down, he could easily believe they were floating in space.

He tore his gaze from the sight and did look down, seeing no sign of a teleport pad. Instead, glowing lines, circles, sigils, and even a few things that vaguely resembled the designs on a circuit board covered every inch of the shiny black floor. In every space on the floor except where Stone and Harrison stood, the designs pulsed with strong, clear white light. Stone tried to make sense of the designs, but found he could not. He'd never seen anything like them in all his studies.

"This is…extraordinary," he said. "You say this is the top of the tower? But I thought your suite was at the top. The view here is—too different to be only a single floor up."

Harrison offered an approving nod. "It would be difficult to explain this place, Dr. Stone. If we had significant time—several months, at minimum—I could probably do it. For now, suffice it to say that this is…the nexus of the Nexus. Even more than the tower itself, the concentrated magical energy here creates a place that exists outside the normal concepts of dimensional space and time."

Stone gaped at him. He couldn't help it. "Are you telling me what you've got here is *time travel?*"

"No. Not as you understand it. It isn't possible to use it to visit the past or the future. I don't know if magical study will ever manage that. But what it *is* possible to do, with the proper calculations, is to fix the moment of an entity's arrivals and departures, and then recreate them at a later date."

"I—don't follow." He felt as if he should, but the concept skirted the edges of his comprehension, skittering away when he tried to pin it down.

"Simply put, in this space one can travel between dimensions, returning to their point of departure—from either side—regardless of the time spent."

"Wait a minute…" Stone's brain threatened to seize as what Harrison was trying to explain fell into place. "Are you saying you can go somewhere else, and—return at the moment you left?"

"Yes." Once again, Harrison nodded approval.

"So…" Stone continued, scanning the otherworldly beauty of the stars surrounding them, "…you could leave here, go to Earth and spend as long as you like, but months or years wouldn't have passed you by here when you returned."

"Yes."

"I…" Stone shook his head, speechless at the implications. Another thought struck him. "But…you couldn't do that for me, right? Because you—the Nexus—had no idea I was coming, so it doesn't have a—what—chrono-dimensional matrix to work from?"

"Perhaps it would not require months after all," Harrison said. "You appear to have an affinity for this sort of thing, Dr. Stone. I am impressed. But yes—you are exactly correct. It matters little since, as I said, only two or three days have passed for you on Earth. But if you should return by means of the Nexus…"

"Then everyone I've met here won't be dead when I come back," Stone finished. "Or," he added, with a sharp look at Harrison, "*almost* everyone."

Harrison didn't answer, but he didn't attempt to deny it, either.

"Can you show me how to do it? Is it something I could do on my own, or would I need your help to manage it?"

"I can show you, in a limited sense, but it will take time." Harrison studied the view, then indicated the sigils and designs on the floor. "Manipulating the Nexus requires a greater degree of understanding than simply accessing this dimension's energy."

Stone didn't answer right away. He wanted to. The temptation to say, "Let's do it now—I'll stay until I get it!" nearly overwhelmed him. To have access to that kind of knowledge—hell, it had the potential to open up not only this dimension, but others as well. If he had a place he could return to where whatever time he spent on his travels was meaningless, how much could he discover about the universe? The mere thought of it made him light-headed. Harrison had just opened the door to the kind of opportunities most mages worth the title would gnaw their own arms off for a chance to have even brief access to. Stefan Kolinsky, for example—Stone had no doubt his black mage associate would give up vast portions of his sizeable magical holdings for even a day's shot at unlocking a fraction of these secrets.

How could he say anything but yes? Not just yes, but the kind of unqualified, unmitigated affirmative one should properly shout from the rooftops?

And yet—

"No," he said, and while the single word was firm, it wasn't without regret. "Not—not now, anyway. If the offer's still open later on, I might take you up on it. But right now…" he shook his head with a sigh. "Now…it's been a long couple of months, and I've got responsibilities back on Earth. People who are depending on me. I know it won't matter if what you're telling me is true, but it would matter to *me.*" He turned back to face Harrison. "Does that make sense to you?"

"It does." Harrison didn't appear disappointed, or disapproving—in fact, his impassive mask was back. "Some other time, then. I don't know when I will return to Earth, but the offer remains open at any point you wish to pursue it."

Stone took a last look around, wondering if he'd ever see this place again. Wondering if he'd have turned down this opportunity ten years ago, or even five. Harrison wasn't a man you could take for granted, or assume everything would be the same the next time you saw him. This might have been his one shot, and he was letting it go. "Thank you, Mr. Harrison. It's been a pleasure, as always, and I'm in your debt for everything you've done for me."

"As am I to you, Dr. Stone. I am grateful you chose to assist my associates in retrieving me."

"You'd have gotten out on your own eventually, and we both know it. I don't think anyone can hold you for long, can they?"

"Likely you are correct. But the experience would have been much more unpleasant."

Stone offered his hand. "Anyway, thanks. For everything."

Harrison shook it; his grip was firm, strong, but not crushing. "Are you ready to leave now?"

"I am." He'd thought about going back to see the others for one last time—at least Errin, Tanissa, and Kira. Now, though, long goodbyes seemed more than he could handle. "Please—just tell everyone thanks, and it was good to know them. Perhaps we'll all meet again."

"Perhaps we will." Harrison indicated the center of the floor. When Stone took his place there, he said, "You will return to the Obsidian. Speak with Mr. Nakamura—he can arrange a flight for you."

"Got it. Goodbye for now, Mr. Harrison." Stone squared his shoulders, stood straight, and fixed his gaze on a point in front of him, taking one last look at the swirling beauty of the stars and the wild magical lightshow outside the glass aerie. He didn't look at Harrison on purpose, perhaps fearful he'd have a last-second change of mind.

As the breathtaking night sky shimmered and faded around him, his last thought before he disappeared was that he'd forgotten to ask about the new silver band in his aura.

| CHAPTER FIFTY-FOUR

H E DIDN'T CALL BEFORE he stopped by Verity's apartment.

His arrival in Las Vegas had been uneventful; as Harrison had predicted, he'd appeared in a bare, feature-less space at the Obsidian that looked like an unused storeroom. From there, he'd had no trouble locating the ele-vator and taking it downstairs, where he called Nakamura on the house phone and relayed Harrison's message. Less than an hour later he was on the Obsidian's private jet on his way back to San Francisco, and an hour after that he was back at his townhouse, walking through it in a daze as a delighted Raider wound around his ankles and threatened to trip him on the stairs.

"Yes, it's good to see you too," he murmured, picking up the cat before retrieving his wallet and keys from the dresser in the bedroom. "We'll talk later. Right now, I've got things to do."

He paused at home only long enough for another shower and a change back into his own clothes. They felt odd, some-how unfamiliar even compared to similar ones he'd worn in New Argana; it took him a few moments to realize that his T-shirt fit more snugly in the chest and a little less so in the waist than it used to. He hadn't gained a lot of muscle in his month of intensive training, but it was definitely enough to notice. It hadn't been something he'd had time to pay much attention to before. He made a mental note to get to work on that custom-clothing spell after life had settled down—and to see about adding some time at Stanford's health club to his schedule.

Now, he hesitated at the foot of the stairs leading up to Verity's second-floor apartment. He knew she was home, because her little black SUV was parked in its customary space. He glanced at his watch again: a bit after nine pm. Definitely not too late to visit—Verity was as much a night owl as he was, so this would still be early for her. The little *31* caught his eye again, and once more he marveled at how Harrison had been correct: it was the end of July, which meant it had only been three days since he'd stepped through the doorway in his attic and stepped out into another dimension.

Three days.

Even though he'd never known Harrison to joke—or even to display more than a wry and restrained sense of humor at all—Stone had been halfway convinced he'd either misheard or misunderstood what the other mage had told him. It simply wasn't possible by everything he knew.

Time to change what you know, then, his little voice, which had been mostly silent for the past few days, suggested. *You're a scientist—you do it all the time.*

Never quite like this, though.

He glanced up the stairs. A faint light shone through the blinds covering the kitchen window, further reinforcing his belief that Verity must be home. Perhaps he should have called first—what if she had a guest? What if Kyla, her Harpy girlfriend from San Francisco, was here?

So what if she is, you prat? Just tell Verity you're back and be on your way.

He had no idea what had caused his sudden indecision, but it annoyed him. Before he had time to reconsider it, he strode up the stairs and knocked softly on the door.

The light behind the blinds brightened and a few seconds later the door opened.

For a moment, the two of them merely stared at each other—her in surprise, him in relief. She wore black sweat-pants, an old Stanford T-shirt, and those little half-socks women wore when they didn't want you to think they were wearing any under their shoes.

"Hello, Verity," he said softly.

"Doc…?" she whispered. She did nothing to hide her wide-eyed confusion. "My God—you're…back? Already?"

"May I come in?"

"Oh!" She stepped quickly aside. "I'm sorry. Just—a little surprised, is all. Come in!"

She led him inside, into her tiny living room. The TV was on, playing some mindless action movie, but it appeared she'd been sitting on the sofa reading a book. "Would you like something to drink?"

"No. Thank you. I'm fine. I just wanted to see you. It's not too late, is it?"

"No, of course it isn't." She swallowed, looking him up and down, almost as if inspecting him for hidden injuries. Then, as if she'd reached the limits of her restraint, she strode forward and flung her arms around him. "I'm so glad to see you," she muttered, her face buried in his shoulder. "But—did something go wrong? Did it not work? It's only been—"

"Three days. I know." He held her close, only now realizing how much he had missed doing it. "It didn't go wrong, Verity. It worked."

Her chin tilted up and she met his gaze. "It...did? In such a short time? Then, you found Mr. Harrison?"

"I found him, yes."

"And he showed you how to do his magic? It doesn't burn you out anymore?"

In answer, he pulled back, surprised at how reluctant he was to break the contact, and gestured at her sofa. It rose smoothly from the floor and floated there, three feet up.

She gaped at it. "Holy shit...And that's not—you haven't—"

"I haven't taken power from anyone since before I left. And I never need to again." He lowered the sofa back into its former spot. "I never *want* to again."

Her gaze shifted between the sofa and Stone. "That's...amazing. I—I don't know what to say."

"Just say you're happy for me," he said with a gentle smile.

"I am. I absolutely am. That's *wonderful.* I want to hear all about it." She embraced him again, this time with more restraint. After a moment, though, she looked up at him again. "Doc...?"

"Yes?"

She took a step back, still gripping his arms, and studied him. "Something's... different." Her eyes widened as her gaze settled on his chest. "Have you...buffed up?"

"A bit, yes," he said, amused. "Side effect of the magical training."

Her eyes narrowed. "In three *days*?" Tentatively, giving him a chance to step back if he objected, she reached out and put her palm on his chest.

"It's a long story. And come on—I don't look *that* different. I'm not Jason or anything."

"No…you don't look that different." She stepped back, taking him in, and then offered a wicked grin. "I like it. But you've *got* to explain to me how you did that in three days."

"I will. But…not just now, all right? We've plenty of time for that. I'm not going anywhere anytime soon."

"So…" she said, moving back over to the sofa and patting the seat next to her, "—you don't have to go back? No more training?"

He thought about the phenomenal, unearthly beauty of the blazing starscape in Harrison's glass-walled sanctum, about all the things he could learn about the universe if only he made the choice to devote himself to them. About how, if he applied himself, he could potentially have access to power no other mage on Earth could claim.

It was all there, spread out before him like some kind of cosmic buffet of knowledge. All he'd have to do would be to reach out and take it.

He could have it all—and he wanted it.

Someday, he wanted it.

He settled himself next to Verity. "No more training," he said softly, pulling her close as she drew her legs up under her and snuggled into the crook of his arm. "I've had my fill of other worlds for now. Time to focus on this one for a while."

Alastair Stone will return in

Book 15 of the Alastair Stone Chronicles

Coming in Fall 2018

If you enjoyed this book, please consider leaving a review at Amazon, Goodreads, or your favorite book retailer. Reviews mean a lot to independent authors, and help us stay visible so we can keep bringing you more stories. Thanks!

If you'd like to get more information about upcoming Stone Chronicles books, contests, and other goodies, you can join the Inner Circle mailing list at **alastairstonechronicles.com**. You'll get two free e-novellas, *Turn to Stone* and *Shadows and Stone!*

ABOUT THE AUTHOR

R. L. King is an award-winning author and game freelancer for Catalyst Game Labs, publisher of the popular roleplaying game *Shadowrun*. She has contributed fiction and game material to numerous sourcebooks, as well as one full-length adventure, "On the Run," included as part of the 2012 Origins-Award-winning "Runners' Toolkit." Her first novel in the *Shadowrun* universe, *Borrowed Time*, was published in Spring 2015, and her second will be published in 2019.

When not doing her best to make life difficult for her characters, King enjoys hanging out with her very understanding spouse and her small herd of cats, watching way too much *Doctor Who*, and attending conventions when she can. She is an Active member of the Horror Writers' Association and the Science Fiction and Fantasy Writers of America, and a member of the International Association of Media Tie-In Writers. You can find her at *rlkingwriting.com* and *magespacepress.com*, on Facebook at www.facebook.com/AlastairStoneChronicles, and on Twitter at *@Dragonwriter11*.

11539307R00362

Printed in Germany
by Amazon Distribution
GmbH, Leipzig